the Edge, it keeps you interested and coming back for more . . . great characters, great writing . . . a must-read series." —*Night Owl Reviews*

"A vastly unique and complex world . . . I got hooked and found myself reading this book nonstop until I flipped that last page . . . If you're a fan of urban fantasy romance, then be sure to check out the Edge series." —*Under the Covers Book Blog*

"Ilona Andrews writes such fascinating worlds and characters . . . The villains are super evil and creepy, the dialogue is quick and witty, and the world is very well done."
—*Smexy Books Romance Reviews*

"Incredible storytelling and awesome adventures . . . The world-building in this entire series is absolutely incredible . . . had me smiling page after page . . . another must-read."
—*The Book Pushers*

"Fast paced, plot driven . . . interesting twists along the way . . . plenty of romantic sparks . . . This is an enjoyable addition to the Edge series." —*Monsters and Critics*

BAYOU MOON

"A thoroughly entertaining blend of humor, action, misdirection, and romance." —*Locus*

"Solidifies the subgenre of . . . . fantasy superbly . . . If you like urban fantasy with . . . . *Bayou Moon* will leave you breathless."

"Megatalent Andrews re . . . . magic, blood feuds, and . . . . moment."

continued . . .

"Even better than the first book! . . . With a great setting, a super action-packed plot, and fabulous characters, *Bayou Moon* is a thrill to read, and I highly recommend it!"   —*Night Owl Reviews*

ON THE EDGE

"A fascinating world combined with pulse-pounding action and white-hot romance makes *On the Edge* a winner!"
                —Jeaniene Frost, *New York Times* bestselling author
                                            of *Once Burned*

"[An] engaging urban fantasy series opener . . . Andrews has created a complex plot and convincing characters that will keep the pages turning."   —*Publishers Weekly*

"A great, fun romance, an offbeat mix of old-fashioned rural magics, contemporary life (complete with Wal-Mart and comic book shops), and magical sword-wielding warriors."   —*Locus*

"The character development is flawless, the plot inventive, and the pace defies readers to put the book down . . . This one is a winner and shows there is still plenty of room for surprises in a genre riddled with tired replays."   —*Monsters and Critics*

Praise for the Kate Daniels novels

MAGIC SLAYS

"Simply amazing. The Kate Daniels series honestly gets better with each new release . . . The world-building continues to evolve and the love between Kate and Curran . . . continues to heat up."
                            —*Night Owl Reviews* (top pick)

MAGIC BLEEDS

"Ilona Andrews is one of the few authors whose books just keep getting better. A series can sometimes stagnate . . . Ilona, though, has no such trouble."   —*Romance Reviews Today*

STEEL'S
EDGE

ILONA ANDREWS

ACE BOOKS, NEW YORK

THE BERKLEY PUBLISHING GROUP
Published by the Penguin Group
Penguin Group (USA) Inc.
375 Hudson Street, New York, New York 10014, USA
Penguin Group (Canada), 90 Eglinton Avenue East, Suite 700, Toronto, Ontario M4P 2Y3, Canada
(a division of Pearson Penguin Canada Inc.) • Penguin Books Ltd., 80 Strand, London WC2R 0RL,
England • Penguin Group Ireland, 25 St. Stephen's Green, Dublin 2, Ireland (a division of Penguin
Books Ltd.) • Penguin Group (Australia), 250 Camberwell Road, Camberwell, Victoria 3124, Australia
(a division of Pearson Australia Group Pty. Ltd.) • Penguin Books India Pvt. Ltd., 11 Community
Centre, Panchsheel Park, New Delhi—110 017, India • Penguin Group (NZ), 67 Apollo Drive,
Rosedale, Auckland 0632, New Zealand (a division of Pearson New Zealand Ltd.) • Penguin Books
(South Africa) (Pty.) Ltd., 24 Sturdee Avenue, Rosebank, Johannesburg 2196, South Africa

Penguin Books Ltd., Registered Offices: 80 Strand, London WC2R 0RL, England

This is a work of fiction. Names, characters, places, and incidents either are the product of the authors'
imaginations or are used fictitiously, and any resemblance to actual persons, living or dead, business
establishments, events, or locales is entirely coincidental. The publisher does not have any control over
and does not assume any responsibility for author or third-party websites or their content.

STEEL'S EDGE

An Ace Book / published by arrangement with Ilona Andrews, Inc.

PUBLISHING HISTORY
Ace mass-market edition / December 2012

ISBN: 978-1-937007-82-9

ACE
Ace Books are published by The Berkley Publishing Group,
a division of Penguin Group (USA) Inc.,
375 Hudson Street, New York, New York 10014.
ACE and the "A" design are trademarks of Penguin Group (USA) Inc.

PRINTED IN THE UNITED STATES OF AMERICA

10 9 8 7 6 5 4 3 2 1

ALWAYS LEARNING   **PEARSON**

To the readers, who stuck with us

Acknowledgments

Steel's Edge marks the end of a series for us. While the stories of the Edge aren't quite over, this particular arc is concluded. We worked very hard to make this book a standout, and we would like to thank all of the wonderful people who helped to make this series a success.

As always, we would like to thank Anne Sowards, our editor, and Nancy Yost, our agent, for sticking with us. We're neither the easiest writers nor the easiest clients, and we appreciate your patience and willingness to work with us despite the craziness life throws our way.

We're grateful to all of the awesome staff at Ace: the production editor Michelle Kasper and assistant production editor Jamie Snider, editorial assistant Kat Sherbo, the artist Victoria Vebell and cover designer Annette Fiore DeFex, interior designer Kristin del Rosario, and publicist Rosanne Romanello.

Special thanks to Sarah E. Younger of the Nancy Yost Literary Agency for fielding many phone calls and resolving minor emergencies.

Because of the nature of this book, we had to seek advice from medical experts, and we're deeply grateful to S.F., Sarah Carden, and especially Michelle Kraut. Any errors of a medical nature are our fault and not theirs.

Finally we'd like to thank our many friends and you, the readers, for believing in the world of the Edge.

PROLOGUE

"MY lady?"

Charlotte looked up from her cup of tea at Laisa. The young girl held an envelope of thick, heavy paper.

"This came for you."

A sudden pain pierced Charlotte's chest, as if something vital had broken inside her. She felt cold and jittery. It was bad news. If it were good news, she would've gotten a scryer call. She felt the urge to squeeze and crumple her blond hair in her fingers. She hadn't done that since she was a child.

"Thank you," she made herself say.

The maid lingered, concern stamped on her face. "Can I get you anything, my lady?"

Charlotte shook her head.

Laisa studied her for a long moment, reluctantly crossed the balcony to the door, and went inside.

The envelope lay in front of Charlotte. She forced herself to raise her cup of tea to her lips. The rim of the cup shuddered. Her fingers were shaking.

She focused on that rim, calling on years of practicing control over her emotions. Calm and collected, that was the mantra of the healer. *An effective healer is neither callous, nor tenderhearted,* her memory whispered in her mind. *She doesn't permit herself to succumb to passion or despair, and she never allows her craft to be compromised by her emotions.*

She had lived by this creed for twenty years. It never failed her.

Calm above all things.

Calm.

Charlotte took a deep breath, counting each rise and fall of her chest. One, two, three, four . . . ten. The cup in her hands was motionless. Charlotte drank from it, set it down, and tore the envelope open. Her fingertips had gone numb. The ornate seal of the Adrianglian Academy of Physicians marked the top of the paper. *We regret to inform you . . .*

Charlotte forced herself to read it, every last word, then stared past the white stone rail of the balcony at the garden below. Down there, a sand-colored brick path ran to the distant trees. Short silvery grass trailed the path on both sides, flanked by a row of low emerald hedges, beyond which flowers bloomed: roses in a dozen shades, their heavy blossoms perfect; constellation shrubs with bunches of star-shaped flowers in crimson, pink, and white; yellow knight spears, their delicate flowerets shaped like tiny bells . . .

She would not be blooming. She would not bear fruit. The last door had slammed in her face. Charlotte hugged herself. She was barren.

The word pressed on her, like a crushing physical weight, a heavy anchor around her neck. She would never feel a life grow inside her. She would never pass on her gift or see the shadow of her features in her baby's face. The treatments and magic of the best healers in Adrianglia had failed. The irony was so thick, she laughed, a bitter brittle sound.

In the country of Adrianglia, two things mattered most: one's name and one's magic. Her family was neither old nor wealthy, and her name was ordinary. Her magic was anything but. At four years old she had healed an injured kitten, and her life took a sharp turn in an unexpected direction.

Medical talents were rare and highly prized by the realm, so rare that when she was seven, Adrianglia came for her. Her parents explained the situation: she would leave them to study at the Ganer College of Medicinal Arts. Adrianglia would house her, teach her, nurture her magic, and in return upon completion of her education, Charlotte would give the realm ten years of civil service. At the end of that decade, she would be granted a noble title, making her one of the coveted elite, and a small estate. Her parents, in turn, would receive a lump sum of money to soothe their grief at losing a child. Even at that age, she realized she had been sold. Three months later, she left for the College and never returned.

At ten she was a child wonder; at fourteen, a rising star; and at seventeen, when her service officially began, Charlotte was the best the College had to offer. They called her the Healer and guarded her like a treasure. In anticipation of assuming her title, she had received instruction from the best tutors. Lady Augustine, whose bloodline stretched back through centuries all the way to the Old Continent, had personally overseen her education, ensuring that Charlotte entered Adrianglian society as if she had always belonged within it. Her poise was flawless, her taste refined, her behavior exemplary. By the time she emerged from the College, now Charlotte de Ney, Baroness of Ney and the owner of a small estate, she had healed thousands.

But she could never heal herself.

Neither could anyone else. After eighteen months of treatments, experts, and magic, she held the final verdict in her hand. She was barren.

Barren. Like a desert. Like a wasteland.

Why her? Why couldn't she have a baby? She'd healed countless children, pulling them from the brink of death and returning them to their parents, but the little nursery she had set up next to their bedroom would remain empty. Hadn't she earned this little bit of happiness? What had she done that was so horrible that she couldn't have a baby?

A sob broke from her. Charlotte caught herself and rose. No hysterics. Elvei would have to be told. He would be crushed. Children meant so much to her husband.

She took the stairs down to the path leading to the northern patio. The old house sprawled in the garden like a lazy white beast, a seemingly random three-story-high collection of rooms, patios, balconies, and stone stairways. The northern patio was on the opposite side of the manor, and she required a few minutes to compose herself. Her husband would need her support. Poor Elvei.

She had just been settling into her new life when Elvei

Leremine came to her with a proposal. She was twenty-eight at the time, barely a year out of the College, and lonely. The life of a Healer didn't leave much time for romantic pursuits. The idea of being married and sharing her life with another human being suddenly seemed so appealing. Baron Leremine was considerate, gracious, and attractive. He wanted a family, and so did she. When a year had passed with no children, she underwent an examination, taking the first step on the grueling eighteen-month journey.

She wanted a baby. She would surround her child with love and warmth, and her son or daughter would never have to worry about being ripped out of her arms because even if her talent passed to her baby, she would go to the College with them. Charlotte stopped for a moment and squeezed her eyes shut. There would be no baby.

A week ago, the months of treatments, tests, and waiting had caught up with her. She felt alone, desperate, and terrified of the future, just as she had when she was seven years old and walking through the massive stone gates of the Ganer College for the first time. And so she sought out the same person who had comforted her then, the woman who became her mother after her natural parents surrendered her. She had gone back to Ganer College to speak with Lady Augustine.

They had walked through the gardens together, just like she was doing now, drifting along the curved stone paths, the College's forbidding stone walls behind them. Lady Augustine hadn't changed much. Dark-haired, graceful, her face classically beautiful, she didn't walk, she glided. Her demeanor was still regal, her features were elegant, and her magic, which could soothe the most violent psychotic in a breath, still as potent as ever.

"Do you think this is a punishment?" Charlotte had asked.

The Lady arched her eyebrows. "Punishment? For what?"

Charlotte clenched her jaw.

"You can tell me anything," Lady Augustine murmured. "I won't betray your confidence, sweetheart. You know this."

"I carry something dark in me. Something vicious. Sometimes I feel an edge of it, looking through my eyes from inside me."

"You feel the urge?" the older woman said.

Charlotte nodded. The urge was a constant specter hanging over every healer. They could knit together devastating wounds and purge diseases, but they could also harm. Using the destructive side of their magic was forbidden. "Do no harm" was the opening statement of the healer's oath. It was the first words of the first lesson she had received, and over the years she had heard it said countless times. Harming was seductive. Those who tried it became addicted and lost themselves to it.

"Is it growing stronger?" Lady Augustine asked.

Charlotte nodded.

"Pardon you for being human."

What? Charlotte glanced at the older woman.

A mournful smile curved Lady Augustine's lips. "My dear, do you think you're the first to have these thoughts? Our talents provide us with the means both to heal and to harm. It's in our nature to do both, yet we're asked to shut half of ourselves off and heal for years and years. This creates an imbalance. Do you think I haven't imagined what I could do if I unleashed my power? I could walk into a roomful of diplomats and plunge the country into war. I could incite riots. I could drive people to murder."

Charlotte stared at her. Of all people, her adoptive mother was the last person she would imagine having those thoughts.

"What you feel is normal. It's not a cause for punishment. You're under a lot of stress, and your body and mind are on the defensive. You put yourself under so much pressure, and that makes you vulnerable. You want to lash out, but Charlotte, you must keep your magic under control."

"What if I stumble?" Charlotte asked.

"There is no such thing as stumbling. You are a healer or you're an abomination."

Charlotte winced.

"I have faith in you. You know what the consequences are."

She knew. Every healer knew about the consequences.

Those who harmed turned into plaguebringers, slaves to their own magic, existing only to deliver death and disease. Centuries ago on the Old Continent, an attempt was made to use the plaguebringers as a weapon during a war. Two of the healers had walked out onto the battlefield and let themselves go. Neither army survived, and the plague they unleashed raged for months and smothered entire kingdoms.

Lady Augustine sighed. "The realm takes us from our families so young because they seek to indoctrinate us. Even with this careful upbringing, they ask for only ten years of service because what we do wears us out. We give so much of ourselves. We're the last hope of so many people, and we're exposed to horrible things: wounds of violence, dying children, families torn by grief. It's a heavy burden to bear, and it has an effect on you, on me, on all of us. To feel the destructive urges is natural, Charlotte. But acting on them will make you a murderer. Perhaps not right away. Perhaps you can even control it for a time, but in the end, the magic will consume you, and you will walk through the land spreading death. There are no exceptions to this rule. Do not become an abomination, Charlotte."

"I won't." She would contain the darkness. She had to— she simply had no choice.

They walked in silence for a few moments.

"Let us imagine the worst," Lady Augustine said. "You're infertile."

Charlotte's heart had skipped a beat. "Yes."

"It doesn't mean you have to be childless. There are hundreds of children waiting to be loved. You can't give birth, Charlotte. That's only a small part of being a parent. You can still be a mother and know all the joys and tortures of raising a child. We get too hung up on bloodlines and family names and our own stupid notions of aristocracy. If someone dropped a basket with a baby on your doorstep, would you really hesitate to pick it up because the baby wasn't of your blood? It's a baby, a tiny life just waiting to be nurtured. Think on it."

"I don't have to. I would take the baby," Charlotte said. She would take it and love it. Whether she carried it to term didn't matter.

"Of course you would. You are my daughter in every-thing but blood, and I know you. I think you'll make an excellent mother."

Tears warmed the back of her eyes. Charlotte kept them in check. "Thank you."

"What does your husband think of all of this?"

"Children are very important to him. His inheritance depends on producing an heir."

The older woman rolled her eyes. "Conditional succes-sion? Oh, the joys of having a noble bloodline and a little bit of money. Is this some new development? I don't recall this being a condition of your marital contract."

Charlotte sighed. "It wasn't."

"Did he mention at any point before your wedding that he required an heir?"

Charlotte shook her head.

Lady Augustine's face iced over. "I do not appreciate being lied to. When did you find out?"

"When we realized there was a problem with conception."

"This was a conversation the two of you should've had before either of you signed your name to the contract. Not only that, but it should've been formally disclosed." She looked into the distance, the way she did when she was try-ing to recall things. "How could I have been so wrong? He seemed like such a solid match, a temperate man. Unlikely to cause any problems."

A temperate man? "What does that mean?"

"Charlotte, you need someone steady, someone depend-able, who will treat you with consideration. You've done over a decade's worth of healing, and your magic is starved and tired of doing the same thing over and over. It doesn't take much to upset this apple cart. That's why I remained here." Lady Augustine indicated the garden with an elegant sweep of her hand. "Serenity, beauty, and a low likelihood of psychological or physical trauma. That's why after a bloody war, some veterans become monks."

So what, she was somehow too fragile to live her life outside of College walls? Charlotte gritted her teeth. "Perhaps Elvei didn't know about the conditions for succession."

"Oh no, he knew. We grow up knowing, Charlotte. He deliberately hid it because I would've never given my consent to your wedding."

Charlotte raised her head. "If he made that a requirement of the marriage contract, I wouldn't have married him. I didn't want to enter into a contract to produce a baby. I wanted a marriage, and I think he did, too."

"He wanted children with a healing talent," the older woman said.

Charlotte stopped.

"I'm sorry, sweetheart," Lady Augustine said. "I shouldn't have said that. It was coarse of me. I'm so furious, and it's clouding my judgment. It's my fault. This was exactly the sort of thing I was trying to avoid, and I've failed you. I'm so, so sorry."

"I'm not a child," Charlotte said. "I'm almost thirty, and I'm responsible for my marriage."

"You're educated, but Ganer College hasn't prepared you for the realities of the world outside these walls. It doesn't matter how old you are, you don't have the experience of interacting with people outside a controlled environment. You've never been betrayed, hurt, or tricked. You've never suffered humiliation. I look into people's souls every day, and what I see there fills me with joy, but also with dread. I wanted so much to spare you."

She was talking as if the end of her marriage was a foregone conclusion. "My marriage isn't over, and Elvei isn't some sort of callous villain. So he didn't tell me about his succession. It's a rather regrettable oversight, but we will deal with it. I understand that love doesn't happen overnight, but I think he cares for me, and I care for him, deeply. We've lived together for almost three years. We wake up in the same bed. He told me he loved me when I began the fertility treatments."

Lady Augustine studied her. "Perhaps you're right, and he simply loves you. If he truly cares for you, he'll deal with it."

They took another step. The mix of worry and anxiety roiled inside Charlotte. Heat rose behind her eyes, and she clamped her hand over her mouth.

Lady Augustine opened her arms.

Charlotte's last defenses snapped. She stepped into the welcoming embrace and cried.

"My sweetheart, my precious one. It will be all right," Lady Augustine soothed, holding her. "It will be all right. Let it all out."

But it wasn't all right, and now Charlotte had to tell Elvei about it.

What they said about coming to love a person you live with was true: she had come to love him. He was always kind to her, and she could use some of that kindness now. She felt weak and helpless. So helpless.

The path brought her to the northern patio. Her husband sat in a chair, drinking his morning tea and peering over papers. Of average height and muscular build, Elvei was handsome in that particular aristocratic blueblood way: precise features, carved with a perfection that seemed a touch distant, square jaw, narrow nose, blue eyes, brown hair with a hint of red. When she woke up next to him, with the morning light playing on his face, she often thought he was beautiful.

Charlotte came up the steps. Elvei rose and held out a chair for her. She sat and passed him the letter.

He read it, impassive, his pleasant face calm. She had expected more of a reaction.

"This is unfortunate," Elvei said.

That's it? Unfortunate? Her instincts told her something was seriously wrong with that placid expression on his face.

"I truly care for you," Elvei said. "Very deeply." He reached over the table and took her hand in his. "Being married to you is effortless, Charlotte. I have nothing but admiration for what you do and who you are."

"I'm sorry," she said. The logical part of her knew she had nothing to do with her infertility. She didn't cause it, and she had done everything in her power to fix it. She wanted a baby as much as Elvei. But she felt guilty all the same.

"Please don't be." He leaned back. "It's not your fault or mine. It's just an accident of fate."

He was so calm, almost cavalier about it. It would've been better if he cursed or threw something. He sat still in his chair, but every word he said was a small step back, increasing the distance between them. "We can adopt," she said, hopeful.

"I'm sure you could."

Alarm blared in her head. "You said 'you.' Not 'we.'"

He pushed a piece of paper across the table to her. "I thought that things might turn out this way, so I took the liberty of preparing this."

She glanced at the paper. "Annulment?" Her composure shattered. He might as well have stabbed her. "After two and a half years, you want to annul our marriage? Are you out of your mind?"

Elvei grimaced. "We've been over this before: I have three years from the beginning of marriage to produce an heir. My brother is engaged, Charlotte. I told you about that two months ago. He'll have three years to produce a child. If I divorce you and remarry, I'll have six months before becoming ineligible to inherit. You can't make a baby in six months. I need an annulment, so my three years can restart, or Kalin will get there before me. He still might, all things considered, as marriage takes time . . ."

This wasn't happening. "So you're just going to pretend that everything we shared in these years doesn't exist and discard me? Like trash?"

He sighed. "I told you, I have a great deal of admiration for you. But the purpose of this marriage was to have a family."

"We are a family. You and I."

"That's not the kind of family I require. I can't lose the manor, Charlotte."

She was cold and hot at the same time, all hurt and anger iced over by shock. "Is it money? You do realize that I can make us as much money as we need."

He sighed. "You're so flawless most of the time that occasionally I forget you're not a blueblood by birth. No, of course, it's not the money. Whoever owns the manor rules the family. It's my inheritance; I was born first, I studied most of my life to take care of our family interests, and I won't let it slip away."

"It's just a bloody house!" Her voice snapped.

Elvei's composure melted, the polite veneer sliding off him. His voice rose. "It's my childhood home. My family goes back sixteen generations. Do you expect me to just let my idiot brother get it while you and I pretend to play house here, in this decrepit ruin? No, thanks. I have higher ambitions in life."

The words burned. "Is that what we were doing?" she asked quietly. "When you and I made love in our bedroom, we were playing house?"

"Don't be melodramatic. We both enjoyed it, but now we're done."

The outrage swelled in her, mixing with hurt. Last night he'd kissed her before they fell asleep next to each other. This was the man she woke up to every morning? "Elvei, you realize, you're telling me that I have no value to you except as a broodmare?"

"Don't make me the villain in this." Elvei leaned back. "I've gone with you to all the tests and treatments. I listened patiently while you got excited over this specialist and that, I sat in the waiting rooms, and I gave it as much time as I could. There are no more treatments left. I just want to have a child, like any normal healthy adult."

Every time she thought she had reached the limit of hurt, he twisted the knife a little more, digging deeper and deeper inside her, cutting at a raw wound.

"So I'm abnormal?"

He spread his arms. "Can you conceive? No. You are defective, Charlotte."

Defective. He actually called her defective. The pain inside her began to smolder with rage. "I'm curious, what's the next word you'll reach for? How cruel will you be, Elvei?"

"You cost me two and a half years."

Two and a half years of disappointment, of painful procedures and shattered hopes, of feeling like she was crippled, but no, it was all about him. She would never have a child of her own, but he only saw himself as the injured party. She should've seen this in him. She should've known. How could she have been so stupid? "You're a terrible human being."

He surged to his feet and leaned over the table. "Had I married someone else, I would've inherited by now. I tried to end this with as much civility as possible, but you've decided to cause a scene. I need an heir, Charlotte, and you can't give me one. What's so complicated about this? I'm done letting you waste my time."

"You told me you loved me." She still remembered how his face had looked when he said it.

"You needed encouragement to begin the therapy. Dear gods, Charlotte, are you really that naive or are you just stupid?"

The words slapped her. The darkness inside her shivered, stretching, getting ready to escape. She clenched herself around it, trying to hold it back.

"Let me spell it out: I married you because of your healing, which you could pass on to our children, and your poise. You are attractive and educated, and I knew that you would never embarrass me in public. Other than that, there wasn't much to recommend you."

The air turned thick and scalding like boiling glue. She couldn't breathe.

"You've been a blueblood for less than three years. My family came to this continent on the Second Fleet, and they were already titled."

The darkness writhed inside her, begging to be released.

"My father is an earl; my mother was a baroness prior to their union. Your father is a cook and your mother is a waitress. In what world could you possibly think that you were in any way equal to me? I granted you a favor. I flattered you by my proposal, Charlotte, and you fell short. Accept it with dignity. I believe an apology is in order."

He'd pushed the blade so far into the wound that he reached the darkness she hid deep inside. Her defenses burst. The darkness slithered out, coating her skin from the inside out. "You're right. You will sit down now and apologize to me." Menace suffused her voice.

He stared at her. "You're hardly in a position to give me orders."

Her magic slid out of her and wrapped over her arms, curving around her body in rivulets of black backlit with deep, intense red. She had never seen it red before. The pale gold of healing, yes, hundreds of times. But this dark, furious black and red? No. *So this is what the magic of an abomination looks like.*

"I can blight your entire family, you moron. I am the Healer. Pick a plague, and your sixteen generations will end right now."

Elvei's mouth gaped. "You wouldn't."

The magic lashed out from her like a striking serpent and bit him. Elvei jerked, his face puzzled. She felt her magic sting him, cutting at the lining of his throat, and a rush of unexpected pleasure flooded her. Oh gods. Fear shot through Charlotte. She jerked the dark current back, pulling her power into herself. She'd let it have just a merest taste, a tiny bite, but it wanted more, and she had to strain to keep it contained.

Elvei coughed, harder and harder, clamping his hand over his mouth. Blood dripped from between his fingers, staining his skin with bright, hot scarlet.

He started to rise but froze halfway.

She realized she hated him, and hurting him made her happy. Power coursed through her, grim but exhilarating. Her magic begged for more.

No. She couldn't let it.

"Sit."

He dropped into the chair.

"You'll have your annulment," she said. "However, you have lived here all this time, and since you don't wish to be treated as my husband, I will treat you as my boarder. You'll reimburse me for rent, food, clothing, gifts, and the services of my staff. You came into this sham marriage with nothing, and you will leave with nothing."

It was a small price to pay, but she couldn't just let him walk away free and clear. Her anger wouldn't let her. She had to have a nominal compensation. If she didn't, her magic would exact its own price.

"I don't have that kind of money," he said.

"I'm not interested in your financial troubles," she said. "I financially supported you all these years, and you don't get to take advantage of me. I'll have my lawyer draft an invoice, and you will pay it in full, or I will force you to make a much more public apology."

All blood left his face. "You'll have your money."

"Send it to the Dawn Mother charity." The money would go to heal children. Some good would come from this nightmare.

Her magic begged to have another tiny nip of him. Charlotte clenched her power in her fist and kept it contained. "Apologize to me for being a heartless bastard."

"I apologize," he said, his voice wooden.

Charlotte concentrated. Magic coated her arm, the radiant golden hue of healing. "Give me your hand."

He stretched his hand over the table. His fingers trembled. She locked her fingers on his wrist, fighting revulsion. They had awakened in the same bed this morning. She'd lain there, thinking that he was handsome and that she would've liked to have his children, while he must've been going over the conditions of annulment in his head. The document had been drafted by a lawyer, which took time. Elvei must've begun the preparations for this moment days ago. Her mind struggled to accept that he could be that cold.

She forced the thoughts away and concentrated on repairing the lacerations in the lining of his throat that she'd made. A moment, and his internal wounds closed. She released him and wiped her hand on the tablecloth.

"You may go. Your things will be sent to you when the charity informs me that your payment has been received."

He jumped to his feet and ran out. She sat there, alone, on the patio of a house that no longer felt like home and wondered what she would do next. The dark current of power coiled and twisted around her. She felt its hunger, beckoning her. It wanted to be fed.

Finally, all the endless lessons and instructions made sense. Her teachers had said that using the healing gift to harm was addicting, but they neglected to mention why. Hurting her ex-husband had brought her pleasure. She wanted to do it again.

Do not become an abomination, Charlotte.

There were no exceptions to the rule. The dark magic would resurface, and the joy it brought would consume her. She'd follow its dark lure into the unthinking abyss where only the next moment of pain-induced euphoria would matter. She was a ticking bomb. She had to contain her powers at any cost.

Charlotte slumped against the chair. She had few options. She could go back to Ganer College and hide away from the world. No, returning to the College where everyone knew her and about her marriage was out of the question. Their pity would drive her over the edge.

She could remain in the manor and live in seclusion and hope that isolation would reduce the temptation to use the dark side of her magic, but she didn't want to be Charlotte de Ney either. Lady de Ney was a stupid, naive girl who was blinded by a handsome face and the promise of a happy tomorrow. She had thought that after the years of training and service, she deserved to be loved for who she was, as if love was some sort of a right. If she stayed here, she would have to face her neighbors and friends, and explain why her marriage had been annulled. No, that wouldn't be a good idea either, especially since Elvei would be moving in the same circles, hunting for a new wife.

At the memory of Elvei, the magic surged inside her. Charlotte hugged herself. Injuring him felt so good. She could imagine making him sick. Maybe just a little bit. Nothing drastic. She knew where he'd lived before their marriage. He still owned that house and would likely return there. And if he married, she might make his happy blushing bride just a little less vivacious. The thought of it would gnaw at her until it consumed her, then she would do it. It was wrong and evil. She knew it, but she was so worn down and her emotional wounds were too raw. She wasn't sure how long she could hold out. She had to disappear someplace away from bluebloods, Adrianglia, and Elvei.

Her memory served up a half-forgotten incident from many years ago when she had been called to heal a group of soldiers. She recalled feeling a strong magic boundary, an invisible wall that seemed to sever their world, and watching the soldiers come through it, one by one, their faces twisted by pain. She spoke to one of them while sealing his wounds. He told her they belonged to the Mirror, a secret counterespionage agency. They had been traveling outside their world, the man had said, in a place where magic was weak. He called it the Edge. The man had been delirious, and she would've dismissed him if she hadn't sensed the invisible wall rising like a barrier of pressurized magic.

In this Edge, a place of weak magic, the pull of the darkness might be weaker too, so even if it managed to get the upper hand, she would do less harm.

The real question was, could she find it?

ÉLÉONORE Drayton leaned back in her rocking chair and sipped the iced tea from a tall glass shaped like the center of a daffodil. The spring sun warmed the porch. Éléonore smiled, cozy in all of the layers of her torn clothes. She had been feeling every single one of her 109 years lately, and the heat felt so nice.

Beyond the lawn, a road ran into the distance, and on the other side, the Edge woods rose, dense, nourished by magic. The air smelled of fresh leaves and spring flowers.

Next to her, Melanie Dove, herself no spring chicken, raised her glass to the light and squinted at it. The sun caught a thin gold thread spiraling inside the glass walls. "Nice glasses. They from the Weird?"

"Mhhm. Keeps the tea cold with magic." The glasses worked even here, in the Edge, where the magic wasn't as strong. It didn't keep the ice from melting indefinitely as the note with it promised, but it lasted a good five to six hours, and, really, who couldn't drink a glass of tea in five hours?

"The grandkids got it for you?"

Éléonore nodded. The glasses came by a special courier, straight from Adrianglia in a box with Earl Camarine's seal on it, the latest in the stream of presents. Rose, the oldest of her grandchildren, had picked them out and written a nice note.

"When are you going to move there?"

Éléonore raised her eyebrows. "Trying to get rid of me?"

"Please." The other witch shook her gray head. "Your granddaughter married a loaded blueblood noble, your grandsons have been after you for months to move, but you sit here like a chicken on a compost heap. In your place, I'd be gone."

"They have their own lives, I have mine. What am I going to do there? The boys are in school all day. George is thirteen, Jack's eleven, and Rose has her own marriage to worry about. I don't even have a place of my own there. Here I have two houses."

"Earl Camarine will buy you a house. He lives in a castle, woman."

"I've never taken anyone's charity, and I'm not about to start now."

"Well, in your place, I would go."

"Well, you're not in my place, are you?"

Éléonore smiled into her tea. They had been friends for fifty years, and for the entire half century, Melanie had been telling anyone and everyone what they should have done with their lives. Age only made her more blunt, and she hadn't been all that subtle to begin with.

Truth was, she missed them. Rose, George, and Jack, she missed her grandbabies so badly, her chest ached sometimes at the memories. But she didn't belong in the Weird, Éléonore reflected. She'd gone to visit and would likely go again, but it didn't feel like home. The magic was stronger, and she'd probably live longer, but here in the Edge, in a space between the Weird with all its magic and the Broken with none of it, was her true place. She was a Drayton and an Edger, through and through. She understood this small town; she knew all of her neighbors, their kids, and their grandkids. And she had power, too. A certain respect. When she threatened to curse someone, people stood up and listened. In the Weird, she'd just be a stone around Rose's neck.

It is inevitable, she reassured herself. Children leave the nest. Everything is as it should be.

A truck rumbled past the yard, Sandra Wicks at the wheel, her bleached-blond hair a teased mess.

"Hussy," Melanie said under her breath.

"Yep."

Sandra waved at them through the window. Both witches smiled and waved back.

"So did you hear about her 'friend' near Macon?" Éléonore asked.

"Mhm. The moment her husband leaves, she hightails it through the boundary into the Broken. It's a wonder her magic still works, as much time as she spends there. Someone ought to clue Michael in."

"Stay out of it," Éléonore told her. "It's none of your business."

Melanie grimaced. "When I was her age . . ."

"When you were her age, they thought wearing a camisole instead of a corset was risqué."

Melanie pursed her lips. "I'll have you know, I wore a slip."

"Well, aren't you a rebel."

"It was made of rayon, too."

A woman stumbled around the bend of the road. She walked unsteadily, swaying as she put one foot in front of the other, her blond hair rolled up on her head, her face smudged with dirt.

"Who the hell is that?" Melanie set her glass down.

Between the two of them, they knew the entire population of East Laporte, and Éléonore was dead sure she'd never seen this woman before. Woolen clothes, Weird cut. Anybody from the Broken would be in jeans or khakis, shoes with heels or sneakers. She wore boots, and she was walking funny.

The woman swayed and fell down on the side of road. Éléonore rose.

"Don't," Melanie hissed. "You don't know what she is."

"Half-dead, that's what she is."

"I have a bad feeling about this."

"You have a bad feeling about everything."

Éléonore stepped off her porch and hurried down the road.

"You'll be the death of me," Melanie muttered, and followed her. The woman slowly turned and sat up. She was tall, but thin, not naturally either. Starved, Éléonore realized. Not a teenager, a woman, around thirty or so. Still a girl by Éléonore's standards.

"Are you all right, dear?" Éléonore called.

The woman looked at her. Yes, definitely from the Weird and from means, too: the face was pretty and unlined, no doubt well taken care of at some point, but now haggard, sharpened by the lack of food, and stained with dirt.

"I've been shot," she said, her voice quiet.

Mon Dieu. "Where?"

"Right thigh. It's a flesh wound. Please." The woman looked at her, and Éléonore read desperation in her gray eyes. "I just want some water."

"Éléonore, don't you dare take her into your house."

Rose was many miles away, and this girl in the dirt didn't

look anything like her, but somehow there were shadows of her granddaughter in the stranger's face. Éléonore grasped the girl's hands. "Try to get up."

"This will end in tears," Melanie grabbed the girl's other arm. "Come on. Lean on me."

The woman pushed herself upright and gasped, a small, painful sound. For a tall girl, she weighed near nothing. They got her up the steps, one tiny step at a time, inside, and onto the spare bed. Éléonore pulled her woolen trousers aside. A small red bullet wound gaped in her thigh.

"Melanie, get the first-aid kit."

"I am, I am." The witch went into the kitchen

"Is the bullet out?" Éléonore asked.

The girl nodded.

"How did you get shot?"

"There was a boy . . ." Her voice was weak. "With a broken arm. I tried to heal the break, and his father shot me." Surprise and outrage vibrated in her voice.

Healing magic was really rare, almost unheard of. Éléonore frowned. What in the world was she doing here in the Edge?

Melanie popped in the doorway with a first-aid kit. "If you can heal, why don't you fix the hole in your leg?"

"Can't heal myself," the girl told her.

"I think you're lying," Melanie said, passing the kit over.

The girl raised her hand. Her fingers brushed Melanie's age-stained arm. A faint stream of golden sparks flared from her fingers, sinking into Melanie's skin. The dark liver spots melted.

Éléonore gasped. Melanie stood frozen.

The girl smiled, a sad, sagging curving of lips. "Can I please have some water?"

Her leg was still bleeding.

"Get her some water, Melanie."

"What am I, a servant?" Melanie went into the kitchen.

Éléonore unscrewed a bottle of rubbing alcohol, poured some on the gauze from the kit, and pressed it to the wound. The girl jerked.

"You're from the Weird, aren't you? What are you doing here in the Edge?"

"I had to leave," the girl said. "I had a horse and money. Somebody stole it. I tried to earn more, but nobody will let me heal them. I tried to help this man's child, and he shot me. He shot me! What kind of insane place is this?"

"That's the Edge for you." Éléonore squeezed some Neosporin from a tube onto the wound. "We don't take kindly to outsiders."

Melanie reappeared with a cup. The girl drank in big, thirsty swallows. "Thank you."

"Who shot you?" Melanie asked. "What did he look like?"

"Tall man, red hair . . ."

"Face like a weasel?" Melanie asked.

"More like a stoat," the girl offered, her voice weak.

"Marvin," Éléonore and Melanie said in one voice.

"He's our resident paranoid nut," Éléonore continued. "The man can't sit still in church because he's scanning the ceiling for black helicopters."

"What's a helicopter?" the girl asked.

"It's a big metal contraption with a propeller on top. The police in the Broken use them to fly around."

"What's the Broken?"

"Oh, boy." Melanie sighed.

"The place you came from is called the Weird," Éléonore said. "You passed through the boundary to get here, a magic barrier, right?"

"Yes."

"Well, now you're in the Edge, between the worlds. On the other side of the Edge, there is another magic barrier, and past it there is another place, just like the Weird, except that world has no magic."

"That's why it's called the Broken," Melanie said. "If you go there, it strips the magic off of you."

"What do you mean, it has no magic?" the woman asked.

Éléonore continued working on the wound. The bullet had entered the thickness of the girl's outer thigh and exited two inches later. Barely more than a graze. Marvin couldn't hit a herd of elephants if they were coming straight at him. "What's your name?"

"Charlotte."

"You sleep now, Charlotte. Don't worry. You're safe. You can stay here until you feel better. Nobody will shoot you here, and we'll have plenty of times to talk about the Broken and helicopters."

"Thank you," Charlotte whispered.

"You're welcome, dear."

The girl closed her eyes. Her breathing evened out. Éléonore finished dressing the wound.

"Found yourself another bird with a broken wing," Melanie said. "And you wonder where George gets it."

"Look at her. How can I turn her away?"

Her friend shook her head. "Oh, Éléonore. I hope you know what you're doing."

IT was the evening of the next day. Éléonore sat on the porch of her house, drinking iced tea from the Weird glass and watching the Edge swallows glide back and forth, snacking on mosquitoes.

The screen door swung open behind her. Charlotte stepped out onto the porch, wrapped in the blanket. Her hair was a mess, and her face was still pale, but her eyes were clear.

"Feeling better?" Éléonore asked.

"Yes."

"Come sit by me."

The girl lowered herself in the chair carefully. That wound must've still hurt.

"How's that leg?"

"It's just a graze," the girl said. "I'm sorry I went all to pieces. It was shock and dehydration more than anything."

"Here." Éléonore pushed the platter of cookies toward her. "You look like it's been a while since you ate."

Charlotte took a cookie. "Thank you for helping me. I don't know how to repay you."

"Don't mention it," Éléonore said. "Where are you from? In the Weird, I mean. What country?"

Charlotte paused for a second. "Adrianglia."

"My granddaughter married a man from Adrianglia," Éléonore told her. "Earl Camarine."

"The Marshall of the Southern Provinces," Charlotte said.

Maybe she knew Rose. "Exactly. Do you know him?"

"I've never met him," Charlotte said. "I do know the family by reputation."

She looked at the woods. Exhaustion showed on her face in a weary, slack mouth and dark circles under the sad eyes. There was clearly a "past" there, Éléonore reflected. The girl didn't seem like an escaped criminal. More like she was a victim, running from something, alone but determined. She'd seen that precise look on her granddaughter's face when Rose ran out of money or the boys came up with some unexpected emergency. It was a "Life kicked me again, but I'll make it work" look.

"So where are you headed?" Éléonore asked.

"Nowhere in particular," Charlotte said.

"Well, you're in no shape to go anywhere."

Charlotte opened her mouth.

"No shape," Éléonore said. "My granddaughter left a house behind. I meant to rent it out but never found anyone trustworthy enough not to destroy the place. It's full of cob-webs now, but if you're not scared of soapy water and a broom, you should be able to put it back together. You can stay there for a while. And if you want to practice healing, we can do that, too. You just need a proper introduction to people. Things are done a certain way here."

Charlotte was looking at her, her eyes wide, looking stunned. "Why? You don't even know me. I could be a crim-inal."

Éléonore sipped her tea. "When Earl Camarine first

showed up in the Edge, I wasn't happy with his arrival. My granddaughter is special, Charlotte. All grandmothers think their grandchildren are special, but Rose truly is. She is kind, smart, and determined. She practiced for years and taught herself to flash white, just like the best of the bluebloods. And she is beautiful. Her mother died, and her father . . ."

Éléonore grimaced.

"I didn't make good choices during my life. I didn't marry wisely, and I've managed to raise a son who ran out on his own children. John left Rose and her two brothers without a dollar to their name. At eighteen, Rose was a mother to two toddlers. She was stuck here in the Edge, working a dreadful job in the Broken and trying to raise her brothers. I wanted so many wonderful things for her, and instead I watched her wither slowly, and there wasn't a thing I could do about it. And then Declan Camarine came, and he promised her everything: that he would love her, and care for her, and take care of George and Jack. I warned her it was too good to be true, but she went with him anyway. Turned out that I was wrong. She lives like a princess now. Her husband loves her. They are talking about children, when the boys get older."

A brief flash of pain reflected on Charlotte's face. So that was it. She was running from a broken marriage or a dead child. You poor girl.

Éléonore smiled. "My granddaughter is happy, Charlotte. She has everything I ever wanted for her. When she first left, I worried about her fitting in with the bluebloods, but her mother-in-law stepped right in and took her under her wing. I'm no duchess, but now I have an opportunity to do the same. I want to pay Providence back for the blessings of our family. We Draytons are many things: pirates, witches, rogues . . . but nobody ever accused us of being ungrateful. A family has to have standards. Even in the Edge. You're welcome to stay as long as you need."

ONE

THREE YEARS LATER

RICHARD Mar ran through the woods. The wound in his side wept dark blood, almost black. A bad sign. His liver was likely lacerated. Congratulations, he told himself. You've finally managed to get yourself killed and by an amateur, no less. Your family would be so proud if they knew.

In his defense, it hadn't occurred to him that a man would conceive, conspire, and execute a plan that involved having his own sister raped by a scumbag just to lay a trap for him. Despite everything Richard had seen, that depth of human depravity had eluded him thus far. He'd thanked Jackal Tuline for correcting that oversight by separating his head from his body. Unfortunately Tuline had six accomplices, and while overall they demonstrated a remarkable lack of proper training, one of them had managed to run him through.

Tree trunks flashed by him, the huge Adrianglian pines straight like masts. His breath came in ragged, painful gasps. Hot pain chewed on his side, biting at the wound with every step.

A distant howl rolled through the forest. The slavers had hounds, and he was leaving a bloody trail. He was in quite a jam, and he saw no way out of it.

The trees swayed around him, turning fuzzy, then coming back into focus. His vision was failing. Richard shook himself and pushed forward. He had to get to the boundary. Beyond the boundary lay the Edge. With the Weird's woods stretching for many miles in every direction, the Edge was his only chance. Not that the Edgers would help him out of the goodness of their hearts. He had been born in the Edge and knew better than most that in the space between the worlds, it was every man for himself. But the Edgers, a paranoid and suspicious lot, owned guns and had itchy trigger fingers. They would see a group of armed slavers ride through their land and shoot at them as a matter of principle.

Dizziness seized him, tossing him against a tree trunk. Richard grabbed the fragrant bark to steady himself, his fingers sticking to the sap, and willed the trees to stop spinning. *Come on, get a grip. This is no way to die.* At least he could go out in a flash of glory instead of bleeding out under some pine.

The forest melted into a gray, rain-drenched swamp. Richard smelled the pungent aroma of the Mire's herbs mixing with the stench of stagnant water. He'd know this scent anywhere—he'd grown up cloaked in it. *He ran across the sluice of muddy soil to the clearing buttressed by the cypresses. Wide holes gaped in the ground like dark mouths. He checked the first one and saw the body of a child, a pale, thin form, floating facedown in two feet of brown water . . .*

Richard shook his head, flinging the memory away. The woods reappeared. He was hallucinating. Splendid. He pushed from the trunk and kept moving.

In the distance, another dog howl rolled, more to the west. They must've broken into two groups. They were a cowardly lot, but they had a lot of practice chasing runaway slaves and were distressingly good at it.

The brush ended abruptly. He saw the ravine, but too late. The carpet of needles shifted under his feet, the edge of the hill collapsed, and Richard rolled down the slope and crashed into a tree. His ribs crunched, and the pain clawed at his side.

The swamp mud squelched under his feet. A man rushed him, weaving between the holes, sword in hand, mouth gaping wide in a scream, his wet hair plastered to his skull by the rain. Richard slashed. The body fell apart before him. Another slaver charged from the left. A second sweep of

Richard's sword, and the slaver's head rolled off his shoulders and tumbled into the nearest hole. Red blood gushed from the stump of the neck and splashed onto the sludge . . .

Reality slammed into Richard in a rush of agony. He gritted his teeth, rolled to all fours, clumsy like a baby learning how to walk, and forced himself upright. A familiar dull pressure pushed at his skin and insides. He took a step forward, and the wall of magic ground against his senses. The boundary. He couldn't see it or smell it, but it pushed on him, as if an invisible hand pressed against his insides. He'd reached the Edge. Finally.

A big furry body sailed over the edge of the ravine. Richard spun about, unsheathing his sword. The sun caught the long, slender blade. The wolfripper dog landed on the slope and sprinted forward, 170 pounds of muscle sheathed in short, dense black fur. Richard leaned forward, closing his left hand on the small ultrasonic emitter in the sword's pommel. A gift from his brother. Kaldar had bought or probably stolen the gadget on one of his excursions to the Broken, and it worked in the Weird. The slavers' dogs hated it, and Richard used it often. He'd never been much for killing dogs. They only did what their masters told them to do.

Three people cleared the top of the ravine. Two men, one thin to the point of being scrawny, the other wearing leathers and holding a dog leash, and a woman, tall, muscular, and with hard eyes. The slaver scouts. *Hello there.*

The dog was almost to him, running fast on massive paws, rugged, big-boned, bred to kill a pack of wolves and get home in one piece. Fifty feet. Thirty.

Richard squeezed the emitter. The sound, too high for human ears, lanced at the dog's sensitive eardrums.

The beast halted.

"Get 'im!" the slaver with the leash yelled. "Get! Get!"

The wolfripper bared big teeth.

Richard squeezed the emitter again, holding the switch for a few painful seconds.

The dog whined and trotted over to the side, circling behind him.

The scrawny slaver on the right of the dog handler swore and pulled a gun from his waistband. Slavers were opportunistic thugs—most of them had barely enough magic to be born in the Weird or the Edge but not enough to succeed at life. They evened the odds with cruelty and Broken contraband weapons, counting on the element of surprise.

The slaver pointed the gun at Richard. He was young, blond, and the way he held the weapon, sideways, made Richard's head hurt.

"We need him alive, you moron," the dog handler said.

"Dude, fuck that." The black barrel stared in Richard's face. "I'll take him out right now."

"Is he an apprentice?" Richard asked, bracing himself.

"What?" The woman stared at him.

"Is he a scumbag in training?" Richard glanced at the gunman. "At least have the decency to hold the gun properly, you fool. If you don't know how, pass it to someone who does. I'm not going to suffer being shot at by anything less than a full-fledged lowlife."

The shooter sputtered. "Screw you."

The gun barked, the sound booming through the woods.

Richard flashed, panning his magic in a defensive screen. Translucent white magic pulsed, forming a half sphere in front of him for a second, just long enough to knock the bullet aside. Even at full health, he couldn't maintain the shield for longer than a moment, but with the right timing, it was enough. He used to flash blue, but being in the Weird had improved his magical strength.

The slaver spat another curse and fired, squeezing the trigger in a rapid rhythm. Boom, boom, boom.

Richard flashed, matching the cadence of shots a moment before they rang out. The white screen pulsed, deflecting the projectiles.

Boom, boom, boom.

A sharp yelp cut through the shots. The gun clicked. The man was out of ammunition.

Richard turned. The dog had fallen. The idiot had shot

their own dog. That's what happened when the destructive potential of a man's weapons exceeded his intelligence.

"What the hell did you do that for?" The dog handler stared at the dog panting in pain on the grass. "You're taking the heat for this one. There's no way the fine's coming out of my pocket."

"Damn it." The gunman shoved the gun back into his belt.

"Could've told you that," the woman said. She was the tallest of the three and had the rawboned build of an experienced fighter. "Bullets aren't going to hurt a blueblood."

He wasn't a blueblood. Far from it. Richard pondered the three slavers. "So far you've shot your own dog and wasted twelve bullets. Any other attempts to dazzle me with your superior fighting skills?"

"We have to go down there and get him," the woman said.

The two slavers looked at him. Neither moved.

"No," the dog handler said.

"It's a bad idea," the thug with the gun added.

"Oh, you whiny bitches." The woman shook her head. "Look at him, he's fifteen years older than you and barely standing. He'll probably bleed out before I get down there."

Richard let himself sway. It wasn't exactly difficult in his current condition. He needed all three of them within striking distance because the trees were threatening to melt again.

"I'm going down there," the woman said. "And just so you know, whatever bonus I get, I'm not sharing."

She started down the slope. The thug with the gun spat to the side and followed her. The dog handler looked at Richard for a long moment and descended after them.

The woman pulled a lean, long sword from her sheath. The dog handler brandished an axe with a short handle. The third slaver pulled out a baton.

Richard fought to stay upright. A drop of blood dripped down from the saturated fabric of his doublet and fell onto the pine needles. Another . . .

The woman struck. She was tall and fast, with sure footing and a good reach. In the split second between reading the intent in her eyes and her body processing it, Richard released his magic. It stretched in a thin lethal line over his blade, coating its edge. He stepped forward, avoiding her lunge, and cut in a savage overhand stroke across her arm. The flash-coated sword sliced through human sinew and bone like sharp scissors through tissue paper. The severed limb fell to the ground.

Before she managed to produce a scream, Richard buried his blade in the chest of the dog handler, piercing the heart, freed it with a tug, turned, and struck backward, sliding his blade along his side into the third slaver's groin.

The woman finally screamed. He beheaded her with one sharp stroke, spun, and finished the scrawny slaver with a single vicious cut to the throat.

Three bodies fell to the ground.

Richard's head swam. His legs gave out. He dropped to one knee, thrusting the sword into the ground and holding on to it like a crutch. What should've taken three cuts had required five. "Simply embarrassing," he whispered. Two red drops splashed onto the green leaves—his blood. The brush around him was stained with it—some of it his, some of it from the slavers.

The dog whined next to him. Richard focused and saw two brown eyes looking at him with a silent canine plea.

"I'm sorry, boy. I can't help you."

Richard forced himself up and staggered forward, to the boundary.

The magic enveloped him, crushing, squeezing, as if the air itself had grown heavy and viscous. His body screamed in protest, feeling a part of its magic being stripped away. The Edge was his limit. He'd tried to enter the Broken once and nearly died. The very magic that made him good with his sword kept him anchored. It felt like he was dying now, but he would survive. He just had to keep going. One foot in front of the other.

A step.

Another step.

The magic licked his skin with a serrated tongue, and the pressure vanished. He was through.

The forest swayed around him, the trees sliding to the side. Richard stumbled forward. Cold slid along his skin. His leg muscles trembled, struggling to support his weight. Cotton clogged his ears, followed by a deep, overpowering nausea. He crashed, half-blind, through the brush.

The swamp clearing stretched before him. The slavers lay dead, delivered by his blade to the afterlife. He dashed from hole to hole. Dead children looked back at him with opaque eyes.

"Sophie! Sophie!"

"Here!" His niece's voice sounded so weak.

"Where are you?" Holes filled with children slumped in the muddy water. He checked each one, sprinting back and forth in panic. A corpse. Another corpse. She was here, somewhere. He had to find her.

The world turned black. He ripped through the darkness by sheer will and saw the edge of a dirt road running through the woods, little more than two tire tracks with a strip of grass growing between them. He wasn't sure if it was real or a remnant of some memory.

The blackness smothered him.

Richard clenched his teeth and crawled toward the road. This was not the end. He wouldn't be dying now. He had things to do.

The rain-drenched clearing with its cypresses swam into his view.

"Help me!" Sophie called.

He stumbled over the bodies of slavers, tracking her voice.

"Help me!"

I'm trying, he wanted to tell her. *I'm trying, sweetheart. Hold on. Wait for me.*

The darkness stomped on the back of his head. The world vanished.

* * *

CHARLOTTE surveyed the groceries laid out on the island of her kitchen. Almost done. Only the big log of ground beef was left. She sliced it with a knife into five equal portions—each one would be enough for a dinner for one with leftovers for lunch—and began wrapping them in plastic.

The first time she'd hired an Edger to bring her groceries from the Broken, the woman had delivered a big pack of ground beef. Charlotte had frozen the whole thing as it was, in the wrapper. Unfortunately, it turned out that once you defrosted the beef in the microwave, it wasn't safe to refreeze it again. She ended up throwing half of the meat out. Lesson learned.

Cooking was just one of the things she had to learn in the Edge. At Ganer College, staff prepared her meals, and at her estate, she had employed a cook. Charlotte sighed at the memory. She'd never truly appreciated Colin until she had to fend for herself in the kitchen. Éléonore had given her a cookbook, and if Charlotte followed the recipes exactly, the result was passable, occasionally even tasty. Decades spent learning to mix medicines ensured that she had good technique and paid attention, but if she didn't have the exact ingredients on hand, trying to substitute things ended in complete disaster. A few weeks ago she watched Éléonore make banana bread. It was all "a handful of flour" and "a dash of cinnamon" and "add mashed bananas until it looks right." Charlotte had dutifully written everything down, and when she'd tried to re-create the recipe, she ended up with a salty loaf-shaped rock.

She'd learned other lessons as well. Being humble. Living a simpler life. The dark magic inside her had long fallen dormant, and that was just the way she liked it.

Bright sunlight spilled through the open window, drawing warm rectangles on the kitchen floor. The day was beautiful. The air smelled of spring and honeysuckle. When she finished, she would go outside and read on her porch swing. And have a nice glass of iced tea. Mmm, tea would hit the spot.

"Charlotte? Are you in there?" A familiar voice called from the front porch. Éléonore.

"Maybe." Charlotte smiled, wrapping the last chunk of ground beef in plastic.

Éléonore swept into the kitchen. She looked to be around sixty, but she'd let it slip last year that a 112th birthday wasn't such a bad thing for a woman to endure. Her clothes were an artful mess of tattered and shredded layers, all perfectly clean and smelling faintly of lavender. Her hair was teased into a fluffy gray mess and liberally decorated with charms, twigs, and dry herbs. In the middle of her hair nest sat a small cuckoo clock.

Éléonore worried her. In the three years Charlotte had known her, the older woman's physical condition had steadily slid downhill. Her bones were getting thinner, and she was losing muscle. She'd slipped on an iced-over path four months ago and broken her hip. Charlotte healed it, but her talent had its limits. She could only heal up to the existing potential of the body. In children, that potential was high, and she could even regenerate severed digits. But Éléonore's body was tired. Her bones were brittle, and coaxing them into regrowth proved difficult.

Old age was the one disease for which there was no cure. In the Edge, as in the Weird, people fueled their life spans with magic, but eventually even magic gave out.

The cuckoo clock sagged.

"It's about to fall," Charlotte said.

Éléonore sighed and pulled the clock out of her hair. "It just doesn't want to stay in there, does it?"

"Have you tried pins?"

"I've tried everything." Éléonore surveyed the island filled with meat and vegetables, all in perfectly sized portions, wrapped in plastic or placed into the Ziploc bags. "You obsess, my dear."

Charlotte laughed. "I like having an organized freezer."

Éléonore opened the freezer and blinked.

"What?" Charlotte leaned back, trying to figure out what the hedge witch was looking at. Her freezer wasn't really gapeworthy. It had four wire shelves, each with a neat label written in permanent marker on a piece of white tape: beef, pork and chicken, seafood, and vegetables.

Éléonore tapped the nearest label with her finger. "There is no hope for you." She sank and landed on a stool. "Charlotte, do you ever make a mess just for the fun of it?"

Charlotte shook her head, hiding a smile. "I like structure. It keeps me grounded."

"If you were any more grounded, you'd sprout roots."

Charlotte laughed. It was true.

"You and Rose would get along," Éléonore said. "She was the same way. Everything had to be just so."

Rose was a constant presence in most of their conversations. Charlotte hid a smile. Being a substitute Rose didn't bother her at all. She long ago realized that for Éléonore there was no higher praise, and she took it as a compliment.

"I've come for a favor," Éléonore announced. "Because I'm selfish that way."

Charlotte raised her eyebrows. "What may I do for you, your witchiness?"

"How are you with handling teenage acne?" Éléonore asked.

"Acne is a side effect of the body's normal processes." Charlotte began stacking her bags into the freezer in neat little towers. "I can treat it, and it will disappear for a while, but eventually it will come back."

"How long is a while?"

Charlotte skewed her mouth. "Six to eight weeks, give or take."

Éléonore raised her hand. "Sold. A friend of mine, Sunny Rooney, has two granddaughters. Nice girls. Daisy is twenty-three and Tulip is sixteen. The parents have been out of the picture for a while—their mother died a while back, and their dad passed away six months ago. Daisy has a decent job in the Broken, so Tulip lives with her. She'll be starting a new school in the Broken this fall, except her face is all messed up, and Daisy says it's causing her a lot of stress. They tried creams and washes, but it won't go away. They're in the front yard now, hoping you might take a look. I'll take care of their bill. I know you just worked on Glen's stomach problems two days ago, and I do hate to ask, but you're their last hope."

She'd heard that one before. Charlotte sat the last bag into the freezer, washed her hands, and wiped them on the towel. "Let's see what we have."

THE two girls stood at the edge of the lawn. Short and about sixty pounds overweight, Daisy had a round face, big brown eyes, and a nervous smile. Tulip was her polar opposite. Thin almost to the point of being underdeveloped for her age, she stood half-hiding behind her sister. Her skinny jeans sagged on her. Her tank top, designed to be formfitting, shifted with the wind. She had caked makeup on her face, and the thick pale paste made her skin appear bloodless. If not for the same chocolate hair and big eyes, Charlotte would've never guessed they were related.

Neither of the young women made any effort to approach. A ring of small plain stones, each sitting a few feet apart from each other, circled the house, and both Daisy and Tulip kept well away from it. The stones didn't affect Éléonore—she had put them there in the first place.

"You left them outside of the ward stones?" Charlotte murmured.

"It's your house," Éléonore murmured back.

Charlotte walked down the path and picked up the nearest stone. Magic nipped at her. A small rock the size of her fist, the ward stone was rooted to the ground. Together, the stones formed a magic barrier that guarded the house better than any fence. The Edge wasn't the safest of places. The Weird had sheriffs, the Broken had cops, but in the Edge, wards and guns were people's only defense.

"Come on in," Charlotte invited.

The women hurried to the house, and she dropped the rock back in its place.

"Hi!" Daisy offered her a hand, and Charlotte shook it. "It's so nice to meet you. Say hi, Tulip."

Tulip promptly hid behind her sister.

"It's okay," Charlotte told her. "I need you to wash your face. The bathroom is straight through there."

"Come, I'll take you," Éléonore offered.

She smiled, and Tulip followed her up the porch steps and right into the house.

"Thank you so much for seeing us," Daisy said.

"No problem," Charlotte said.

"God, this is awkward. I'm sorry." Daisy shifted from foot to foot. "It's just that we tried all the creams and prescriptions, and they're saying laser treatment is the only option. I'm a CPA. I make okay money but not that kind of money, you know?" She laughed nervously.

And that's what always got her, Charlotte reflected. That uncomfortable pleading look in the eyes. People looked at you like you were the answer to all their prayers. She wanted to help—she always wanted to help—but there were limits to what magic could do.

Daisy offered an awkward smile. "Mrs. Drayton said you might be tired. Thank you for seeing us anyway."

"Not a problem." Charlotte smiled. "Why don't we go into the kitchen?"

In the kitchen, they sat at the island, and she poured two glasses of iced tea. Daisy perched on the edge of her chair, looking like she wanted to bolt.

"This used to be Rose's house," Daisy said. "My best friend's sister went to high school with her. I saw her flash at the Graduation Fair. It was crazy. Pure white. Nobody from the Edge ever flashes white. Do you flash?"

In the Edge, most people had a magic talent. Some were useful, some not, but every magic user could flash with practice and proper training. Flash was a pure stream of magic. It looked like a ribbon of light, or sometimes, a whip of lightning. The brighter and paler the flash, the stronger the magic. The strongest flash, pure white, could cut through a body like a cleaver through a stick of warm butter. It was a lethal weapon, and Charlotte had seen the wounds it left, in great detail.

"I don't flash," Charlotte said. She'd never learned to do it because there was no need. "That's not my talent."

Daisy sighed. "Of course. I'm sorry. I shouldn't have mentioned Rose."

"I don't mind at all," Charlotte said. "Éléonore talks about her and the boys all the time."

Daisy fidgeted in her seat. "So how do you know Mrs. Drayton? You're friends, I take it?"

Éléonore was more than a friend. The older woman was her chosen family. "When I first came to the Edge, I came out more to the west, near Ricket. I'd walked away from my horse for a minute to relieve myself, and someone stole it and all of my money. "

"That's the Edge for you." Daisy sighed.

"The plan was to find work, but nobody would let me heal them. I walked from settlement to settlement, trying to find a place to fit in, and when I came to East Laporte, I was starving. No money, no place to stay, my clothes were torn up and filthy. I was at the end of my rope. Éléonore found me on the side of the road and took me in. She made me welcome and got me my first clients. She'd go with me to all of my appointments and chat people up while I worked. I owe her everything."

There was more to it than simple gratitude. Éléonore missed her grandchildren terribly. The older woman had such a strong urge, almost a need, to take care of someone, Charlotte reflected, just as she herself felt the same urge to cure an illness or fix a broken limb. They were kindred spirits.

Éléonore emerged from the bathroom, leading Tulip by the hand. The girl's face was a sea of hard red bumps buried under the skin. Cystic acne. The precursors to scarring were already there.

"Sit," Charlotte invited.

Tulip obediently sat on the stool. Éléonore put a small mirror on the island. "Just in case."

"Look at your sister for me, okay?" Charlotte slid her

fingertips over the hard bumps on Tulip's left cheek. Magic coated her hand, a steady stream of glowing golden sparks.

"It's pretty," Tulip whispered.

"Thank you."

"Will it hurt?"

"No, it won't hurt at all. Now look straight ahead for me. Just like that."

The sparks penetrated the skin, finding the tiny infected hair follicles. The magic pulled on Charlotte. It was a curious feeling, as if some of her vitality were being sucked away, converted into the healing current. Not painful, but alarming and uncomfortable unless you were used to it. Charlotte closed her eyes. For a moment all she saw was darkness, then her magic made the connection and the cross section of Tulip's skin appeared before her. She saw the pores, the hair shafts, the ruptured follicle walls spilling infected fluids into the dermis, contaminating the nearby follicles, and the severely inflamed sebaceous glands.

Charlotte pushed slightly, testing the flesh. Her magic saturated the tissues of the cheek completely. She opened her eyes. The inner workings of Tulip's face remained before her, almost as if she were looking through two different sets of eyes at the same time, choosing what she wanted to focus on next.

Charlotte numbed the nerve endings reaching into Tulip's skin. "Look straight ahead for me."

The flesh of Tulip's cheek contracted. The pus spilled out of a dozen tiny lesions.

Tulip blinked, surprised. "It didn't hurt."

Charlotte tore open an alcohol wipe, plucked it out, and swiped it across the cheek. "See? I told you."

She concentrated on restoring the injured tissue, purging the infection. The bumps on Tulip's face shivered and began to melt, dissolving into healthy, pink skin.

Daisy gasped.

The last of the acne vanished. Charlotte let the current of her magic die, picked up the mirror, and held it up to Tulip.

"Oh my God!" The girl touched her clear left cheek. "Oh my God, it's gone!"

This was why she did it, Charlotte reflected, brushing Tulip's hair from her face. The spontaneous simple relief when the disease was gone. It made everything worth it.

"It's not gone forever," Charlotte warned. "It will probably be back in six to eight weeks. Let's do the right cheek now. We don't want you to be lopsided—"

A vehicle screeched to a stop in front of the house.

"Who in the world could that be?" Éléonore rose of her chair.

"Let's see." Charlotte strode to the screen door and out onto the porch.

At the edge of the lawn, Kenny Jo Ogletree jumped out of a beat-up Chevy truck. Sixteen, broad-shouldered but still lanky, Kenny had been one of her first patients. He'd climbed a pine to chainsaw a branch off so it wouldn't crash on his mother's house, and fell. Two broken legs and bruised ribs from the chain saw's dropping on top of him. Could've been worse.

Kenny's face was pale. She looked into his eyes and saw fear.

"What's wrong?" Charlotte called out.

He ran to the truck back and dropped the tailgate. "I found him on the side of Corker's road."

A man lay in the truck bed. His skin was alabaster white against the dark leather of his clothes. Blood pooled around him in a viscous puddle.

Charlotte dashed down the path, past the ward stone, and into the truck. Her magic swirled from her hands, into the body, and back into her hands. The interior of the body flashed before her. Anterior abdominal stab wound, laceration to the right hepatic lobe, severe loss of blood, hemorrhagic shock. He was dying.

Charlotte leaned over the body, pouring her magic out. It wound about her, binding her and the dying man in a glowing whirlwind of sparks. Her reserves began to drain, as if the magic funneled her very life force out. She directed the current deep into the liver. It flowed through the portal vein branching like a red coral inside the fragile organ tissues. The golden sparks lit the blood vessels from within. She began regenerating the walls, sinking bursts of magic into the liver lobe to mend the damage.

His temperature and blood pressure dropped again.

She pushed more magic into the injured tissues, trying to pull the body out of shock. It fought her, but she anchored it to life with her magic and refused to let go. He would stay with her. He wasn't going anywhere. Death wanted him, but Charlotte had claimed him, and he was hers. She couldn't create new life, but she could fight for the existing one with everything she had. Death would just have to do without.

His heart fluttered like an injured bird. He was in danger of cardiac arrest. She wrapped her magic around his heart, cradling it with one loop of the current while feverishly mending the tears in his flesh with the other. Each heartbeat resonated through her.

Pulse.

Stay with me.

Pulse.

Stay with me, stranger.

The lesions in the liver closed. The blood pressure stabilized. Finally. Charlotte knitted together the injured muscle and accelerated blood production.

I have you. You won't die today.

The man's breathing steadied. She encouraged circulation and held him, watching the internal temperature creep up. She was burning through what meager fat reserves he had to generate blood cells. There wasn't much—he was practically all muscle and skin.

The internal temperature approached normal levels. The heart pulsed, strong and steady.

She held on to him for a little while longer just to make sure he was past the danger point. He had a powerful, healthy body. He would recover.

Charlotte disengaged, slowly, a little at a time, and sat back. Her head swam. Blood stained her hands. Her nose itched, and she rubbed the back of her wrist against it, dazed and disconnected from reality.

The man lay next to her, his pulse even. She gulped the air. She was out of breath as if she had run some sort of crazy sprint. The familiar post-healing fatigue anchored her in place. Her muscles ached. The weariness would let go in a minute. During her time at the College, a difficult emergency healing like this was usually followed by a daylong bed rest for the healer, but she was no longer healing someone every day. She wasn't near her limit.

She'd beaten Death again. The relief flooded her. That's one life that didn't have to end. One man who would survive to see his family. She had made it happen, and seeing his chest rise in an even rhythm made her deeply happy.

His hair was very dark, a glossy, almost bluish black. It fanned around his head, framing his face. He was no longer pale. He probably never was as pale as she perceived. Years of practice attuned her senses to react to specific signs of distress in her patients, and sometimes her magic distorted her vision to produce the diagnosis faster. The man's skin had a pronounced bronze tint, both from a naturally darker tone and sun exposure. His face was precisely sculpted, with a square jaw, a strong chin, and a nose that must've been perfectly shaped at some point but now was too wide at the bridge, the result of an old injury, most likely. Short, dark stubble dusted his jawline. His mouth was neither too wide nor too narrow, his lips soft, his forehead high. His body was in superb shape, but the gathering of faint laugh lines at the corners of his eyes betrayed his age. He was at least as old as she, probably a few years older, mid to late thirties. His skin and clothes were stained with mud and blood, his hair was a mess, and yet there was something undeniably elegant about him.

What a handsome man.

The man's eyelashes trembled. Charlotte leaned over, alarm pulsing through her. Her magic sparked. He should've been out. His body needed every resource to heal.

The man opened his eyes. He looked at her, their faces

mere inches apart. His eyes were dark and intelligent, and that intelligence changed his entire face, catapulting him from handsome to irresistible. "Sophie," he said.

He was delirious. "It's over now," she told him. "Rest."

His eyes focused on her. "Beautiful," he whispered.

She blinked.

"I know that voice." Éléonore climbed into the truck. "Richard! *Mon dieu, que s'est-il passé?*"

Richard tried to rise. His pulse sped up to dangerous levels.

"No!" Charlotte struggled to hold him down. He strained under her. He was strong like a horse. Her magic still spiraled around him, wrapping him in a cocoon of sparks, straining to heal the damage as he moved. Without knowing it, he was leaning on her healing power like a crutch. "I have to put him under. He can't move, or he'll rip everything open."

"Who did this to you?" Éléonore asked. "Richard?"

Richard pushed against Charlotte, lifting her deadweight. She felt the newly mended tissue tearing. His hold on her magic faltered. She felt him slip.

Richard's eyes closed, and he crashed back into the truck bed. Charlotte leaned over him. Out cold.

Éléonore turned to the boy. "Kenny, help us get him into the house."

Kenny grunted. Magic snapped, accreting around him. He reached over, picked Richard up like a toddler, and carried him inside. Charlotte dropped the ward stone back in place, and the four of them followed him.

"Where to?"

"Guest bedroom on the right." Charlotte pushed the door open.

Kenny deposited Richard on the spare bed and turned around. "I've got to get to mom's house."

"Thank you, sweetheart." Éléonore said. "Say hello to your mother for me."

Kenny nodded and went out.

Charlotte knelt by the bed. Richard's pulse was still even. Good. "How do you know him?"

Éléonore sighed. "I've met him before. His first cousin married my grandson-in-law's adopted cousin. We're family."

Family, right. "Is he a blueblood?"

"No. He lives in the Weird now, but he's an Edger like us, from the Mire. When I first saw him, I thought the same thing—some sort of noble house. But no, he's an Edger."

"Who is Sophie?" A wife? Perhaps, a sister?

Éléonore shrugged. "I don't know, dear. But whoever she is, she must be very important to him. I can tell you that Richard is a skilled swordsman. He was teaching my grandsons how to fight the last time I was in the Weird. Whoever ran him through is likely dead."

Charlotte let her magic slide over Richard's body. A skilled swordsman. She could believe that—his spare body was strong but supple, honed by constant exercise. His blood pressure was still too low. In time, his body would replenish the blood he lost, but it would take a while, and she didn't want to gamble.

He had called her beautiful.

She knew she was a reasonably attractive woman, and he had been delirious, so it shouldn't have mattered, but for some reason it did. She had stayed away from romantic relationships in the Edge—one Elvei was enough—and she had almost forgotten she was a woman. A single word from a complete stranger touched off something feminine inside her. She felt unreasonably pleased when she remembered his saying it, as if he'd given her a gift she really wanted but didn't expect. He would never know it, but she was grateful for it.

Charlotte rose and got her cell phone.

"Who are you calling?" Éléonore asked.

"Luke. Richard will need a blood transfusion, the sooner the better."

"Should we leave?" Daisy asked.

Éléonore held her finger to her lips.

"Yes?" Luke answered.

She put him on speaker. Holding the phone to her ear was really awkward. "It's Charlotte. I need A+." It had taken her a few weeks to learn the Broken's medical terminology, but with the help of books, she had eventually prevailed. She'd identified Richard's blood type when her magic slid through his veins.

The EMT fell silent. "I can get you two bags. Five hundred."

Two pints. It would have to do. "I'll take it."

"Meet me at the end of the road in twenty." Luke hung up.

"Five hundred dollars?" Daisy's eyes were the size of saucers.

"Highway robbery," Éléonore said.

"He's the only source of blood for Edgers, unless we do a person-to-person transfusion." Charlotte shrugged. "It's just money." She could always make more.

"Do you want us to leave?" Daisy asked again.

"I have to meet him and get the blood, but if you don't mind waiting, I can work on Tulip when I come back." She was tired, but she couldn't very well send Tulip out with one cheek clear and the other pockmarked with acne.

Daisy pursed her lips. Tulip pulled on her sleeve. The older sister sighed. "We'll wait."

"Please make yourself welcome," Charlotte said. "There is tea and snacks in the fridge. I'll be back in half an hour or so."

The girls went into the kitchen.

"Thank you for doing this for him," Éléonore said.

"It will help him heal. Like you said, he's family." Charlotte smiled and pulled a medical dictionary off the shelf. In the hollowed-out space inside lay her cash reserve. She plucked the stack of twenties and counted out five hundred. "Will you keep an eye on him?"

"Of course. Charlotte, take a gun."

"It's just down the road."

Éléonore shook her head. "You never know. I don't have a good feeling about this. Take a gun just in case."

Charlotte took a rifle from the wall, chambered a round, and hugged Éléonore.

"I'll be back."

"Of course."

Charlotte went outside, crossed the lawn, and got into the truck. The truck had belonged to Rose, and she had finally learned to drive it last year. It lacked the elegance of the Adrianglian phaetons, but beggars couldn't be choosers.

She turned the key. The engine started. There was something about Richard's face that called to her. She wasn't sure if it was the handsome masculine lines or the fiery intensity in his eyes. Or maybe it was because he thought she was beautiful. Whatever it was, she had become invested in his survival. She wanted to see him open his eyes again and hear him speak. Most of all, she wanted him to safely recover.

Five hundred was a small price to pay for that.

TWO

ÉLÉONORE checked Richard's pulse. It was even. Charlotte was a miracle worker, and the poor girl had no idea. Most people in her place would be rolling around in money. None was more desperate than a mother with a sick child or a husband with a dying wife. They'd give you their last dollar. But Charlotte healed them all for a pittance and acted like she was nothing special.

They had done something to her in the Weird. She was like a bird who'd had her wings broken once, and wasn't willing to take the risk and try flying again. She fought against wealth and recognition on purpose, as if she was hiding. She never said from who or why. Éléonore sighed. Well, she, for one, was content to let her have a safe corner of the Edge to hide in.

A knock made her turn. Daisy and Tulip stood in the doorway.

"I've got a call from work," Daisy said. "They want me to come in. Is it okay if I bring Tulip by tonight instead? Do you think Charlotte would mind?"

"I don't think she would. Go on. Work's more important." Éléonore smiled.

"Thank you," Daisy said.

"Thank you," Tulip echoed.

She was such a sweet, shy girl. "Don't worry. Charlotte will clear your face right up."

"Do we need you to move the stones?" Daisy asked.

That's what living in the Broken does to you, Éléonore

thought. Daisy had no clue how basic magic worked and wanted nothing to do with it. "No, the stones only prevent someone from coming in. Once you're in, you can move them or just step over them to go out."

"Thank you!" Daisy said again. The girls went out. Éléonore heard the screen door slam shut.

She checked the time. Charlotte had been gone for twenty minutes. She couldn't cross the boundary into the Broken. Her magic was too strong, so she would likely just wait at the end of the road, before the boundary, until Luke came through and delivered the blood.

A hint of anxiety squirmed through her, an unpleasant premonition that left unease in its wake. She couldn't tell if it was her magic warning her or if she'd become paranoid in her old age. It was terrible to get old. But then the alternative wasn't much better. Besides, Charlotte would sit in the truck with the doors locked. She had a rifle, what little good it would do her. Not that the girl wouldn't defend herself, but she didn't have that steel-hard core Éléonore's granddaughter did. Rose's resolve carried her through life's rough waters. Charlotte had weathered some storms, but she lacked that primal viciousness of a born Edger. That's what made her so special, and that's why she liked her so much, Éléonore reflected. She too hadn't been born in East Laporte. Charlotte's presence reminded her of a different time and a gentler place.

Éléonore brushed Richard's hair from his face. "Who is Sophie, Richard?"

He didn't answer. It could've been anyone, a wife, a lover, a sister. Éléonore knew very little about him. She'd only met him once, but he'd made an impression. It was the way he carried himself with quiet dignity. His brother was all flash, charm, and jokes, but Richard had that sardonic, sharp wit. He didn't speak much, but occasionally he said clever things with a completely straight face . . .

"Mrs. Drayton!" The scream rang out, high-pitched and vibrating with sheer terror. Tulip.

Éléonore ran to the door. Tulip stood at the wards, her face skewed by fear into a distorted mask. "Mrs. Drayton! They have Daisy!"

Éléonore hurried across the lawn. Move faster, legs. "Who? Who has Daisy?"

"Men." Tulip waved her arms. "With guns and horses."

A long, ululating howl rolled through the Edge. The tiny hairs on the back of Éléonore's neck stood up. She grabbed a stone and pulled Tulip into the protective circle. "Inside, now!"

Tulip ran for the door. Éléonore replaced the stone and hurried after her, across the grass, onto the porch steps.

The sound of hoofbeats made her spin. A rider came down the road. His head was shaved. He wore black leather, and as he rode, the sun glinted off the long chain shackles hanging from his saddle.

Slavers.

The realization lashed her like a whip. Éléonore dashed across the porch into the house, shut the door, and locked it.

Tulips stared at her with huge eyes. "What's going on?"

"Shhh!" Éléonore moved to the window and peeked through the gap in the curtain. The rider paused by the house, turned his horse, and tried to ride up to the porch. The ward stones shivered. The horse backed away, nearly throwing its rider. He glared at the house, stuck his fingers in his mouth, and whistled.

More riders followed, joining the first. They wore dark clothes, and their faces were grim. Some bore tattoos, some were painted up, some wore human bones in their hair. Half a dozen wolfripper dogs, big, savage-looking creatures, flanked the horses. A man on the left, scarred, with the face of a bruiser and long blond hair pulled back into a braid rode up and dumped a body onto the ground. Daisy. *Mon dieu.* She was pale as a sheet.

The men surrounded the lawn. One, two, three . . . Sixteen that she could see.

Éléonore's heart sank. There would be no mercy.

"What happened?" she whispered.

"We were walking down the road to the car. Daisy was

looking in her purse for the keys. That blond guy rode out and kicked her. He just kicked her right in the face!" Tulip's voice squeaked. "She fell and yelled at me to run, so I ran—"

The scarred blond man pulled Daisy forward.

"Hush now," Éléonore whispered.

"Do it," he barked.

Daisy reached for the nearest stone with a shaking hand. Her cheek was bleeding. She touched the stone and tried to lift it. Magic pulsed. Daisy yelped, jerking her hand back. The slaver sank a kick into her stomach. Daisy screamed and curled into a ball. Tulip cried out, and Éléonore clamped her hand over the girl's mouth.

The leader's voice carried over, harsh and grating. "We don't want you. We don't care about you. We want the man you're hiding inside. Daisy here says she can't open the ward, and given as she tried, I'm inclined to believe her. It's up to you, then. Give me what I want, and I'll go away. It's that simple."

Sixteen men. Far too many. One or two, even four, she could deal with. She'd let them in and curse them, but sixteen was just too many. Thoughts skittered around in Éléonore's head. She had to get help.

"Do you have a phone?" she whispered.

Tulip pulled a cell phone out of her pocket.

"Call Charlotte," Éléonore whispered. "Two-two-seven twenty-one thirty."

Tulips dialed the number with shaking fingers and thrust the phone at her.

"This is Charlotte," Charlotte said, her voice calm.

"Where are you?" Éléonore whispered.

"At the end of the road. Luke was running late, and I just got the blood."

"Don't come back to the house!"

"Why? Éléonore, what's wrong?"

"I need you to go down to the Rooneys'. Take the second fork left, then go to the end of the road. Tell Malcolm Rooney there are slavers at our house. There are sixteen of them, and they want Richard. Tell him he owes me, and that he's got a pretty daughter and he doesn't want them showing up at his house next. If he knows what's good for him, he'll get the militia together and run them out of the Edge. Go, Charlotte. Go now."

The phone beeped, and she thrust it back at Tulip.

"All you have to do is walk down and move one of these ward stones." The slaver called out. Éléonore looked through the gap. He had pulled a knife out. The large curved blade caught the sunlight. "You know how this goes," he called out. "I'm a peaceful man. Don't make me do this."

CHARLOTTE took a turn at breakneck speed. Slavers? It made no sense. Slavery had been outlawed in both Adrianglia and the Broken for centuries. But the fear in Éléonore's voice was vivid and real.

She had to get to the Rooneys'. East Laporte had no police force, but when something threatened the entire town, the Edgers sometimes came together into a militia to meet it.

Trees flashed by her. Come on, she willed. Go faster, truck. Go faster.

"LISTEN to me." Éléonore grasped Tulip's bony shoulders. "They will hurt Daisy now. There's nothing we can do about it. The ward keeps me from using magic on them, and if we try to shoot them, they'll kill her."

"She's my sister!" Tulip whispered back. "If we give the guy to them—"

"They'll murder us all. They're lying, dear heart. They're lying, bad, awful bastards. We have to wait until help comes." Éléonore hugged her, wrapping her arms around the girl's bony shoulders. "No matter what you hear, no matter what you see, you can't go out there. We have to wait it out."

"Hold her," the slaver said.

Daisy whimpered.

Éléonore clamped Tulip to her. "Don't listen. Cover your ears."

"Last chance. Move the stone, and everyone walks away from this."

Éléonore held her breath.

"Fine," the slaver said.

Daisy shrieked, a high-pitched sound suffused with pain.

Éléonore chanced a look at the window. The blond slaver was holding something pale and bloody between his index finger and his thumb. Daisy writhed in the hands of two other men.

"That was an ear," the slaver announced. "Next we'll do fingers."

"WE have to go." Charlotte stared at Malcolm Rooney, towering over her by eight inches.

Around them, the Rooney house was a flurry of activity: short, plump Helen Rooney dialed one number after the other on her cell, going down the list of contacts, while their two teenage sons stockpiled weapons on the porch. As soon as she'd arrived, their oldest son and daughter had left to carry the message down to the neighbors, and now armed men milled about at the house.

"Now you listen to me," the big man leaned closer. "They're safe behind the wards, and Éléonore is a tough old lady. She can handle herself. Sixteen men is a lot of firepower. We sure as hell aren't going to ride out there unprepared, or we might as well just slit our own throats and be done with it."

"They're alone in the house!" She saw a dozen men ready to go.

"It will be fine," Malcolm said.

She looked into his eyes and knew arguing was useless. He would do this at his own pace or not at all.

"Another hour, and we'll be good to go."

"An hour?" He was out of his mind. You could get the entire town up and moving in thirty minutes.

"It will be fine," Helen Rooney said, the phone still to her ear. "It just takes time to get everyone together, that's all. Everything will be okay."

The sickening, nagging feeling in the pit of Charlotte's stomach said otherwise.

Malcolm pulled a shotgun off the wall. "You're lucky East Laporte is a different place now than it was six years ago. Back then, you would've gotten no help, but now people will come together."

He turned his massive back to her. She realized what was happening: the Edgers were delaying on purpose. Nobody wanted to confront sixteen armed men, so they were dragging their feet, hoping things would resolve themselves.

Charlotte took a deep breath and let go of her persona as an unassuming Edge healer. She raised her head, sinking the icy, unmistakable tone of command into her words. "Mr. Rooney."

He turned, surprise stamped on his face. He had expected the Charlotte who lived down the road. Instead, he got Baroness Charlotte de Ney, the Healer of Ganer. She stood before him, the full power of her magic in her eyes, her power radiating from her. The house was suddenly silent.

"Your wife is developing osteoporosis, you have an enlarged prostate, and your youngest son doesn't have ADHD, as your wife told me; he has hyperthyroidism. If you want any of these problems to be treated in the future, you will stop patting my shoulder and telling me not to worry my pretty little head about it. You will get this mob together now and follow me out there, or so help me gods, I will make your life hell. You think those aches and pains you feel now are bad. After I get through with you, you will be a broken man. Move."

TULIP went rigid in her arms. "Don't look," Éléonore whispered.

Daisy flailed, throwing all of her weight. "No! No, no, no . . ."

The slavers dragged her to the ground and pinned her hand to the edge of the sidewalk.

Knife flashed. Daisy screamed, a wordless, sharp shriek of pain.

"Left pinkie," the slaver announced. "You planning on getting married? Because I'm about to take the ring finger."

Tulip jerked, trying to get out of Éléonore's arms.

"Stop!" Éléonore tried to hold on, but the girl bucked like a wild beast, suddenly too strong to hold. Éléonore gripped her, holding on, Tulip's panicked kicking pushing them against a window.

A shot rang out. Glass shattered and something bit Éléonore in the shoulder, right into the bone. Her fingers slipped, suddenly weak. Tulip shoved her back and scrambled toward the door.

"No!" Éléonore screamed.

Tulip burst out of the door and onto the lawn.

Éléonore jerked the door open. "Stop, Tulip!"

A hot, piercing pain struck Éléonore in the chest, pitching her back. She lost her balance and fell onto the porch, half-hidden by the wooden rail. Suddenly it was so hard to breathe. The air turned bitter. They had shot her, she realized. She began pulling power to herself. The magic came slow, like cold molasses.

At the ward stones, Tulip turned and was looking at her with wide, panicked eyes.

"Tulip, is it?" the scarred slaver said. "Don't look at her. Look here. Is this your friend? Sister maybe, no? Sister, then."

"You open the ward, and they will kill you," Éléonore called.

"I give you my word," the slaver said. "Nobody will kill you."

The magic kept winding around her. Not enough. Not nearly enough. She was too old, she realized. Too old and too weak. She'd outlived her power. "Don't do it!"

"Do you want to go home, Tulip?" the slaver asked.

Éléonore tried to rise, but her legs wouldn't hold her.

"Move the ward stone, and it will be all over," the slaver

said. "You and your sister can go home. I'll even give you her parts back. See?" He held out a bloody stump of a finger.

Tulip cringed.

"Don't!" Éléonore called out. Her voice was going hoarse. Blood stained the porch boards, and she realized it was hers.

"I said to shoot her," the slaver said. "Do I have to finish her myself?"

Bullets whistled around Éléonore, biting into the wooden rail around the porch.

"Stop!" Tulip cried out.

The blond slaver raised his hand. The shots died.

"See? I'll stop for you. I can be reasonable. You don't listen to her," the slaver said. "She's old and selfish. You have to do what is good for you and your sister. Move the stone, we'll get our guy, and we go our separate ways. Otherwise, I'll have to cut off something else. Maybe your sister's lips or her nose. She'd be disfigured for life."

Tulip stood, frozen.

"Hold her down," the slaver said.

They flipped Daisy over on her back. He leaned over her the knife in his hand.

"Don't!" Éléonore cried out.

Tulip grabbed the ward stone and jerked it aside. The circle of protective magic broke.

Oh, you foolish child. You foolish, foolish child . . .

The large thug next to the scarred man stepped over the useless stone and backhanded Tulip out of the way. She fell on the grass.

A gun barked twice. Éléonore jerked and saw the scarred slaver raise a smoking gun. The back of Daisy's head was a bloody mess. She wasn't moving.

Tulip screamed, a high-pitched desperate shriek.

She had to save her. Éléonore gritted her teeth. She was old, but she was still a hedge witch.

The larger slaver moved on to Tulip.

Éléonore hurried, pulling magic to her in a desperate rush.

"Leave it," the leader said.

I'm so sorry, Rose. I'm so sorry. I just wish we could've visited one last time.

"It's free merchandise."

"Have you seen her face? You've got to think before you act, Kosom. Who's gonna buy her with that face? You can fuck her once, if you put a sheet over her head, but nobody's going to purchase that. The buyers don't want ugly women. You have got to develop some business sense. Go kill the old lady on the porch and drag the Hunter out of this damned house."

Tulip sat up, her eyes wide.

The last strand of magic wound itself about Éléonore. It was all she could hold.

The big thug pointed his gun at Tulip's face.

Éléonore let go. The magic shot across the lawn, sticking to the thug with the gun and splashing to the other three men near him, surrounding them like a swarm of dark bats.

"Run!" Éléonore screamed. "Run, Tulip!"

Tulip scrambled backward, rolled to her feet, and dashed across the road into the woods.

The four thugs fell, contorted by spasms, but the leader and more than two-thirds of the slavers remained standing. Her magic had fallen too short.

The leader with the pale hair ran up onto the porch. "You old whore."

She got away. At least the child got away.

The slaver pulled a gun from a holster. "You fucking bitch."

Éléonore glared at him. She would die here, on this porch, but she would take him with her. Éléonore spat blood from her mouth and spoke the words, binding the last of her power into them, drawing on the very magic that anchored her to life. There was no cure from a death curse. "I curse you. You won't see the sunset . . ."

"Fuck you." He raised his gun. The black barrel stared at her.

In her mind she was hugging the boys, George on her

right and Jack on her left. Flowers bloomed all around them, and Rose was waving at her from across a sunlit garden. ". . . And you'll suffer before you die."

The last words left her mouth, taking her life with it. The world vanished.

CHARLOTTE checked the dashboard clock. Fifteen minutes past noon. She had been gone for close to an hour. The makeshift militia left the Rooneys' ten minutes after she made her stand. Three trucks filled with armed people traveled in front of her, and on the sides, half a dozen Edgers rode on horses.

It was taking too long. Please, Dawn Mother. Please don't let it be too late.

The leading truck sped up. So did the next two. She frowned.

In the truck bed in front of her people were looking up and to the right. Charlotte bent forward, trying to get a better view through the windshield.

A column of black greasy smoke rose above the treetops. Oh no.

She laid on her horn.

The trucks hurried up the road. Charlotte clenched the wheel. Come on. Come on!

The trees parted.

A torrent of fire devoured the house. Orange-and-red flames billowed out of the roof, blackened support beams thrusting out like bones of a skeleton. Fire filled the doorway, boiling within the house, winding about the porch posts, and belching smoke. The orange flames surged through the windows, licking the siding.

Charlotte jerked the truck into park, shoved the door open, and ran across the lawn. The heat slammed into her, pushing her back, and she jerked her hand up, trying to shield her eyes from the worst of it. Ash swirled around her.

Corpses sprawled on the grass, four armed men, their

bodies contorted, their faces grotesque masks. Her skin crawled. Suddenly, she was both hot and cold.

A high-pitched mewling sound made her turn. At the edge of the lawn, Daisy's body lay on her stomach. A wet red hole gaped in her head. Tulip slumped by the body.

Charlotte's magic burst out of her, sliding over the girls, checking . . . Tulip was unhurt. Minor bruising on the face but no major injuries. Daisy was dead. Irreparably, irreversibly dead. Not a hint of life remained.

Cold shot through her. She wasn't fast enough. They called her for help, and she wasn't fast enough.

Tulip sat on the grass next to her sister, her hands bloody, her face smeared with tears and dirt, and wailed. Her pain stabbed at Charlotte, hot and acute, overwhelming. There was nothing she could do to help it. All her magic and all her power was useless.

Helen Rooney dropped on the ground by Tulip, trying to hug her, but Tulip pushed free and kept crying. The black-and-gray ash rained on her face. She wailed and wailed, as if she was trying to expel her heart and all of the ache in it out of her body with her voice.

"Where is Éléonore, sweetie?" Helen asked.

Tulip pointed at the fire.

Charlotte turned to the house. A charred figure lay on the porch, little more than a scorched husk.

Charlotte's world screeched to a halt.

She couldn't bring herself to move. She just stared at the broken, burned body. Éléonore . . . Éléonore was dead. How could this be? Her mind refused to accept it. Éléonore was alive and vibrant less than an hour ago. She was alive, she was talking and walking, and now she was dead, and Daisy was dead with her.

Éléonore would never smile again. She would never catch the cuckoo clock as it fell out of her hair. No more stories about Rose and the boys. No more of anything.

"What about the man?" Helen asked.

"They took him," Tulip sobbed.

Helen leaned toward her, murmuring something. Malcolm bent over them.

I need to move, flashed in Charlotte's head. She needed to do something, say something, but she just couldn't. She just stood there, locked into a painful haze.

Malcolm Rooney walked across the lawn to her. She saw his lips move, but no sound came.

The roof beams crashed down with a loud crack and tumbled in an explosion of sparks. Charlotte jerked. Her hearing returned, and she heard Malcolm's deep voice: ". . . slavers." He shook several pairs of shackles at her. "Found this on the bodies. Haven't seen their kind in ten years. Must've hit quick. Looks like they popped Daisy in the head, shot Éléonore, took your fellow, and set the house on fire. Tulip hid in the woods and watched the whole thing, poor kid. The house was gone in minutes. It's an old building. Went up like kindling. They're on horses, looks like a dozen, maybe more, besides those." Malcolm nodded at the bodies. "That's Éléonore's work. They call it the Broken Stick curse, because it locks them into weird shapes like that. The old lady had a lot of power in her."

Her mouth finally managed to make a word. "Why?"

"That's what slavers do. They raid towns like ours, steal kids and pretty women, and take them off to the Weird to sell as slaves there. This Richard fellow must've pissed them off somehow."

Richard . . . The slavers had taken him. Her mind started up slowly, as if rusted. She was too late for Éléonore and Daisy, but there was still a life they could save. "We have to go after them."

Malcolm shook his head. "Slavers are a nasty lot. They got what they wanted, and they're gone. This Richard, he's no kin to me. Hell, he didn't even grow up around here. He stirred them slavers up like a hornets' nest, and they chased him here, but now they're gone, and this thing's done with. Take a long, hard look at what he brought down on you. I say good riddance."

She stared at him, shocked. He would not do anything.

He had already made up his mind—she saw the decision in his eyes. Malcolm Rooney, the big, strong bull of a man, was afraid. He would walk away.

"Those bastards shattered four lives. Éléonore took me in. She made me welcome, she gave me a second chance at life, and they murdered her and burned her body and her house." Her voice rose. "They killed Daisy, who was barely twenty, and her fifteen-year-old sister watched her die. And you're just going to let it go?"

Malcolm clamped his mouth shut.

Charlotte looked past him at the Edgers. Guilt and sadness stamped their faces. Not a single one would meet her eyes.

Dear gods. The tiny hairs on the back of her neck stood on their ends. They agreed with Malcolm. They would all just walk away and pretend that this horror never happened. She had known that in the Edge every man was out for himself, but this? This seemed inhuman.

"Éléonore lived here all her life." She pointed to the charred corpse. "Her body is still smoldering over there. Don't you understand? If we don't stop them, they'll do this again. Look at Tulip. Look at her!"

People looked at their feet, at the grass, anywhere but at her or the child crying her heart out.

"Chasing them will only get more people killed, and none of us have children or relatives to spare," Malcolm said quietly. "We'll find a place for Tulip. Hell, looks like Helen won't let go of her, so I guess she'll be coming home with us. You ought to come on down, too."

Charlotte looked at him because looking at Daisy's and Éléonore's bodies hurt. Grief filled her to the brim, bitter and overwhelming. She was choking on it. Oh gods, Rose and the boys would eventually need to know. What would she even tell them? I'm sorry I didn't get there in time? I'm sorry I went on with my life as if it didn't matter and let those bastards spread their misery?

"We can fix a bedroom for you," Malcolm said gently. "The more the merrier, they say. It will be okay, Charlotte.

It will all work out. You've done helped many people here. We'll find you a new place to live, don't you worry about that. What do you say?"

The pain, sadness, shock, and guilt churned inside her. She couldn't contain it. She had to do something.

The slavers thought they could stomp out people, and they would keep going, killing, burning, and hurting children. They would crush other lives just as they had crushed her little comfortable world. Even now they rode away, unpunished, carrying off the man she had healed, and she didn't even know why any of this had happened. They would hurt him, torture him, and likely kill him.

Somebody had to make a stand. If none of the Edgers would step up, she would have to be that somebody. There was nobody else.

Charlotte reached deep inside herself, into the darkness, carefully hidden and locked away, and found a single crimson spark. She forged a tentative connection. Need flooded her, the magic so hungry, so desperate to break out, and feed, and kill. Fear shot through her. She almost recoiled. If she let it loose, there would be no turning back. She'd worked so hard to bind this part of herself. She had almost succeeded.

Charlotte looked at Tulip's face, at the wet streaks of tears stained with ash.

"Tulip!"

The girl looked up.

Charlotte held on to the spark. "I can't bring Daisy back to life, sweetheart. But I can make sure that they don't hurt another girl the way they hurt you. I'll make them pay. I promise you, they won't take anyone else's sister away."

Tulip's face quivered, and she sobbed.

"Charlotte?" Malcolm asked.

Charlotte took a deep breath and blew on the spark.

"Are you listening to me?"

The crimson and darkness exploded inside her, twisting into a hungry, furious inferno.

She looked at him, and her face must've been terrible,

because Malcolm Rooney took a step back. Charlotte turned and strode across the grass to her truck.

"If you go, you're going alone!" Malcolm yelled.

She kept walking, her magic raging inside her.

"It won't bring Éléonore back! They'll just murder you. Charlotte? Charlotte!"

She got into her truck and started the engine. The fire inside her burst out, winding about her in tendrils of deep, angry red.

These bastards would never hurt anyone again. She would make sure of it.

THREE

WHEN a man found himself in difficult circumstances, it always paid to assess the situation. Especially if he woke up and found he couldn't move.

Richard opened his eyes.

Let's see. First, he was in a cage, a fact made painfully apparent by the pattern of steel bars imposed on the riders, silhouetted against an old forest. Second, his hands were tied behind his back. Third, a heavy chain shackled his legs to the steel ring in the bottom of the cage. Fourth, a thicker chain secured the cage to the cart, making several loops, as if the weight of the cage wedged into the cart's hold wasn't enough to hold it in place. Ergo, he was captured by the slavers, and they were afraid that he would sprout wings and take off with the three-hundred-pound cage around him.

He couldn't remember how he got into the cage. At some point he must've been beaten—his face ached and was likely bruised. He tasted mud on his lips, probably from someone's boot. Also, judging from a less than pleasant odor, someone had taken the time to urinate on his chest. Slavers, a charming breed, always happy to treat their guests to their fabled hospitality.

The wound in his side didn't hurt at all, and despite all of his expectations, he was still alive.

How in the world was he still breathing? He had taken enough wounds to recognize the stab to his liver was life-threatening even if he had been magically transported to a surgeon's table the moment after he had received it. Instead, he'd made it fatal by running for hours.

He recalled falling by some road. There was something in between that and the cage, something murky. For some reason, he had a feeling it involved Éléonore, Rose's grandmother, whom he'd met once. Another memory surfaced, a woman with gray eyes and blond hair. Her face was a blur, but he remembered her eyes under the sweep of dark blond eyebrows, intense and beautiful—his foggy memory made them luminescent—and the concern he read in their depth arrested him. Nobody had looked at him like that for years. It was such a beautiful memory that he was half-sure it was a product of his hallucinating brain yearning for something radiant in his grim, blood-drenched life.

Except that someone had healed him because his injury was gone. Stab wounds didn't just vanish on their own. It gave his muddy recollection of the woman with gray eyes some credence, but healing magic was exceedingly rare and highly prized. Finding someone in the Edge with it was extremely unlikely. The Edge was the hellish place you went when neither the Weird nor the Broken would have you. A healer with talent like that would've been treasured in the Weird.

This was getting him nowhere. He had no plausible explanation why he was alive, so he'd have to set it aside for the time being. His more immediate problem was the cage and a crew of slavers guarding it.

There was no way to tell how long he'd been unconscious, but it was unlikely he'd been out for too long. They were traveling through the Weird's woods, and the magic flowed full force. The forest crowded them in, the massive tree trunks, fed by magic and nourished by rich Adrianglian soil, rose to improbable heights. Against that backdrop, the riders on the barely visible trail seemed insignificant and small. The horses moved at a slow walk, hampered by the wagon carrying him.

Richard cataloged the familiar faces. A few were new, but he knew about half of them, prime examples of scum floating in the gutter of humanity. His memory served up their names, their brief biographies, and their weaknesses.

He'd studied them the way others studied books. Some came from families, some were born psychotic, and others were just greedy and stupid. Most carried rifles and blades, their gear worn and none too clean. He didn't see any wolf-dogs and didn't hear any either. Where had all of the hounds gone?

CHARLOTTE stepped out of the truck. Ahead, the over-grown dirt road ended, turning into a forest path. The boundary loomed before her. She felt it in the very marrow of her bones, a strange disturbing pressure that threatened to squeeze the breath out of her.

The slavers had passed through it. The brush still bowed, disturbed by the riders. She saw the traces of hoofprints on the ground and the twin grooves of wide wheels. They had a cart, and not magic-powered like the modern phaetons, but an old-fashioned, horse-drawn cart, the kind country people still used in the provinces. The trail led through the boundary, so she would have to pass this way, too. The last time she had crossed it, the feeling of her magic being peeled away nearly made her turn back.

Charlotte took a deep breath and stepped into the boundary. The magic clutched her, squeezing at her organs as if trying to wring the lifeblood from them. The pressure pushed her, propelling her forward. Each step was a conscious effort. Sweat broke on her forehead. Another step. Another. The pressure crushed her. Charlotte hunched over. She would crawl if she had to.

Another step.

Suddenly, the grinding burden vanished. Magic flooded her, rejuvenating her body. It was an absurd sensation, but she felt herself opening up like a flower greeting the morning sun. If she'd had wings, they would've unfurled. She inhaled slowly. There it was, the familiar potent power she was so used to wielding. During her years in the Edge, living with half magic, she had forgotten how wonderful it felt.

She had never understood why Éléonore didn't move to the Weird . . .

Éléonore.

She had to keep moving. She was at least half an hour behind the slavers, probably more. The old Adrianglian forest stretched before her. The forest path forked ahead. Which way, right or left?

Charlotte knelt to the ground, trying to follow the hoofprints. A carpet of old pine needles blanketed the floor of the woods and the path, obscuring the trail. She had learned some tracking when she was a girl from an old veteran scout living at Ganer College because she thought it was interesting. But those lessons were long ago, and she had never taken them very seriously.

A high-pitched, labored whine came from under the brush on her left. She turned. Two brown canine eyes looked at her from a large black muzzle.

Charlotte froze.

The dog dipped its big head and let out another thin whine. She smelled blood. It lashed her healer instinct like a whip. The dark magic raging inside her vanished, as if snuffed out.

"Easy now." Charlotte crouched and moved toward the dog. "Easy."

It lay on its side, panting.

She reached for it.

The dog's lips trembled, betraying a flash of fangs.

Charlotte stopped moving, her hand outstretched. "If you bite me, I won't help you." The dog couldn't understand her, but it could understand the tone of her voice.

Slowly she reached forward. The dog opened its mouth. Jaws snapped but fell short of her fingers. It was too weak.

"If you were healthy, you'd tear my hand off, huh?"

Charlotte touched the fur, sending a current of golden sparks through the furry body. Male, low blood pressure. A bullet wound passing through the abdomen. Someone had shot the dog.

"This world is full of terrible people," she told him, and began to repair the damage. The bullet had entered the chest, cut through the left lung, and tore out of the dog's side. Judging by the state of the wound and blood loss, it had happened about five to six hours ago.

Charlotte knitted the injured tissues, rebuilding the lung.

The dog leaned over and licked her hand, a quick, short lick, as if embarrassed by his own weakness.

"Change your mind since it doesn't hurt as much anymore?" She sealed the wound and petted his withers. Her hand slid against a spiked collar. "You wouldn't be a slaver dog, would you?"

The dog rose. He was a massive beast—if they both stood upright, he could put his paws on her shoulders.

Charlotte got up. "Where are your owners?"

The dog looked at her, sniffed the air, and turned to the right.

She had nothing better to go on.

"Right it is," Charlotte said, and followed the dog down the path.

THE wagon rolled over a root, creaking.

"That's far enough," a grating voice called out. Voshak Corwen, a seasoned slaver with over a dozen raids under his belt. Hardly a surprise, Richard reflected. This was the man Tuline had promised to betray. They must've agreed to set that little trap together, and when Richard had cut his way through Tuline's crew, Voshak took his men and went after him.

"We make camp here," Voshak said.

"We're only two hours from the boundary," a tall, redheaded man called out. Richard didn't recognize him. Must be a new hire. The slavers needed to replenish their herd regularly—he kept thinning it out.

Voshak rode into view. Of average height, he was built with a gristle-and-tendon kind of strength: lean, with high endurance. He wasn't the fastest or the strongest, but he would go the distance. A network of scars sliced his face. No doubt he had some romantic story about how he got them instead of admitting that a stablehand had raked his face with a pitchfork during a failed slave raid.

Voshak's hair, a pale blond braid, which he bleached, was his trademark. It made him memorable. That's how the slavers operated. They adopted costumes and personas, trying to make themselves larger-than-life and hoping to inspire fear. They counted on that fear. One could fight a man, but nobody could fight a nightmare.

Voshak focused on the redhead. "Milhem, did I make you my second?"

Milhem looked down.

Ceyren, Voshak's second, was likely dead; otherwise, he would be here pulling Milhem off his horse and beating him to a bloody pulp. Interesting.

"Then don't open your trap," Voshak said. "If I want your opinion, I'll beat it out of you." He surveyed the riders. "If any of you morons are worried, nobody's following us. These are Edgers. They look out for number one, and none of them want to catch a bullet. It's been twenty hours since we last slept, and I'm tired. Now make the damn camp." He turned to an older, one-eyed slaver. "Crow, you're my second now. See they get it done."

Crow, a broad-shouldered, weather-beaten bastard, roared, "Get a move on!"

Reasonable choice for a second, Richard reflected. Crow was older, had experience, and he worked hard to inspire fear. If his eye patch and height didn't do it, the heavy black leather and ponytail of jet-black hair decorated with finger bones would.

Voshak turned his horse. His gaze paused on Richard. "Awake, my gentle maid? You've got something right here." The slaver touched the left corner of his mouth. "What is that? . . . Oh, that's shit from the bottom of my boot."

Laughter rang out.

Richard smiled, baring his teeth. "Always brightening the day with your humor, Leftie."

A muscle jerked in Voshak's face. He clenched his reins. "You sit in your cage, Hunter. When we get where we're going, you'll sing like a bird when I start cutting through your joints."

"What was that? I didn't quite hear." Richard leaned forward, focusing on Voshak. A hint of fear shivered in the slaver's eyes, and Richard drank it in. "Come closer to the cage, Voshak. Don't cower like a little boy hiding from your daddy and his belt."

Voshak dug his spurs into his horse's flanks. The animal jumped, and he rode off. Coward. Most of them were cowards, cruel and vicious. Brave men didn't kidnap children in the middle of the night and sell them to perverts to earn their drinking money.

The riders dismounted. Two secured the horses, keeping well away from his cage. Others began pulling tents from the saddlebags, olive and gray, with a red logo spelling out COLEMAN sewn on one side. The tents must've come from the Broken. A few slavers piled together some branches. A dark-haired man soaked them in fluid from a flask, struck a match, and dropped it on the fuel. Fire flared up like an orange mushroom. He shied back, rubbing his face.

"You got any eyebrows left, Pavel?" Crow called.

Pavel spat into the fire. "It's burning, ain't it?"

A slaver stopped by the cage. He was thin, with dirty brown hair and pale eyes. He climbed onto the wagon, opened a small door near the top of the cage, barely large enough to pass a bowl through, and dipped a ladle with a long handle into a bucket.

Richard waited. His mouth was so dry, he could almost taste the water.

The slaver passed the ladle through the window. "Why Leftie?" he murmured.

"It's what his father used to call him before he beat him in his drunken rages," Richard said. "His right testicle never dropped."

The slaver held the ladle closer. Richard drank, three

deep delicious gulps, then the man retracted the ladle and latched the window shut.

The slavers began to settle down. A pot was set over the fire; a couple of rabbits had been dressed and chopped into it. Voshak came to sit by the flames, facing the cage. He bent to poke at the coals, and Richard pondered the top of the man's blond head. The human skull was such a fragile thing. If only his hands weren't tied.

He had to survive and bide his time. The slavers were taking him to the Market, he was sure of it. Left to his own devices, Voshak would've strung him up on the first tree he saw. Richard grinned. And after his neck snapped, Voshak would probably stab his corpse a few times, drown it, then set it on fire. Just in case.

Someone near the top of the slaver food chain must've recognized that the rank-and-file slaver crews feared the Hunter. They wanted to boost morale by making a production out of killing him. Richard might have worked for a year to get to the Market, but he had no intention of arriving there on their terms. An opportunity would present itself. He just had to recognize it and make the best of it.

If he failed now, Sophie would take his place. The thought filled Richard with dread.

Revenge was an infectious disease. For a time it gave you the strength to go on, but it devoured you from the inside like a cancer, and when your target was finally destroyed, all that remained was a hollow shell of your former self. Then the target's relatives began their own hunt, and the cycle continued. He'd learned that lesson at seventeen, when a feuding family's bullet exploded in his father's skull, spraying bloody mist all over the market stall. What he had lost was irreplaceable. No amount of death would bring his father back to life. Back then, Richard was already a warrior, a killer, and he continued to kill, but never out of revenge. He severed lives so the family would be safe, and the new generations would never feel the pain of having their parents ripped out of their lives. He fought to keep the rest of them safe.

He failed.

Richard's memory resurrected Sophie the way she used to be—a funny, beautiful, fearless child. The muddy swamp flashed before Richard. When he had finally found Sophie in one of the holes, she was standing on the body of a slaver she had killed. As he pulled her out, her eyes burned with a fear and hate that had no place on the face of a twelve-year-old child. She had survived the slavers, but she would never be the same.

He'd hoped the years would cure it, but time only nurtured it. He watched, powerless, as that fear and hate germinated into self-loathing. When she came to him asking to be taught to work with the blade, he viewed it as a diversion. Sophie had never taken her lessons seriously before, neither from her own father nor from her sister. He thought she would get bored. He had no idea.

Her self-hate grew and matured into steely determination. He saw it in Sophie's face every morning when she picked up her sword to meet him in practice. He was running out of things to teach her. One day, she would decide she was good enough, take her blade, and go hunting instead. He wouldn't be able to stop her, so he had chosen to beat her to the punch. What he was doing wasn't revenge, but justice. The world had failed Sophie by allowing slavers to exist. He had failed her by letting her suffer at their hands. He hoped to restore her faith in both.

A woman walked out of the forest. She was tall, about five-foot-eight, and pale. Mud splattered her faded jeans. Her lavender T-shirt had a scoop neckline and was smudged with something dark, dirt or possibly soot. Her blond hair rested on top of her head in a loose knot. Her mouth was full, her eyes were wide and round, and the line of her jaw was soft and feminine. She was beautiful, refined, but iced over by a lack of emotion and an eerie, unnatural calm.

Their stares connected. Every cell in his body went on alert. He couldn't see her eye color from this distance, but he was sure her eyes were gray.

She was real.

His stomach tightened in alarm. *What are you doing here? Run. Run before they see you.*

The conversation died. The slavers stared.

Crow picked up his rifle and rolled into a crouch.

"Now that's what I call free merchandise," Voshak murmured from his perch on a fallen log.

"There are no towns around here," Crow said quietly. "Where did she come from? I say shoot her now."

"What's your hurry?" Voshak leaned forward. "No gun, no knife. If she could flash, she would've hit us by now."

"I don't like it," Crow said. "She might be with him."

Voshak glanced at the cage. Richard turned to look him in the eye, and the slaver captain shrugged.

"Hunter is the Weird's animal. She's wearing jeans. And if she's with him, then he'll enjoy watching me fuck her brains out." Voshak raised his voice. "Hey, sweetheart! Are you lost?"

The woman didn't answer. She was still looking at him, and her eyes told Richard she wasn't lost. No, she was exactly where she wanted to be. She had some sort of plan. How did she get here?

"Where are you from?" Voshak asked. "Talk to me. Are your folks worried about you?"

The woman said nothing.

"She's mute," someone offered.

"A pretty woman who doesn't talk. My God, we can charge double." Voshak grinned.

Appreciative laughter from half a dozen throats rang out.

"I don't like it," Crow repeated.

"I've seen this before." Pavel spat into the fire. "She's a loonie."

"What's a loonie?" A younger slaver asked.

"An Edger or someone from the Broken," Voshak said. "Sometimes they blunder halfway through the boundary into the Weird and get stuck. Not enough magic to go either way. Eventually, the boundary spits them out, but they're not quite right after that. The lights are on, but nobody's driving. They just wander around until they starve to death."

"Too much magic." Pavel waved his hand around his ear. "Fries their brains right up."

"I don't—" Crow began.

"Yes, we know. You don't like it." Voshak grimaced and turned it into a smile. "Don't worry, sweetheart," the slaver captain called out. "We'll take good care of you. You come sit by me." He petted the log next to him.

The woman didn't move.

"Come on." Voshak winked at her. "It's all right."

The woman approached, moving with innate grace.

Richard watched her. She glanced at him briefly as she took her seat, and he saw a smart, agile mind behind her eyes. No, she wasn't fried. Not at all. But Voshak was right. She had no weapons. Even if she was a flasher, the slavers were too spread out. Someone would shoot her before she got them all. He had to get out of this cursed cage.

"Pass me that puppy chain," Voshak said.

Pavel passed the twelve-foot chain to him. The slavers used them as human tie outs—just enough length to let slaves shuffle off to the bushes to relieve themselves. Voshak smiled and locked one iron cuff on the woman's ankle, above her shoe. He locked the other on his own ankle. "There we go. Just like marriage."

The woman gave no indication she understood what had just happened.

Voshak leaned closer to her and brushed a small tendril of hair from the back of her long, graceful neck. "That's a good girl."

Richard wished for a sword, a knife, a nail. Anything he could stretch his flash on. He'd slice through the bars with the first cut and sever Voshak's fingers from the rest of him with the second. Watching him touch her was like seeing filth smeared on her skin.

Voshak let go of her neck. "If only you were fifteen years younger. You'd be worth double."

"That'd make her what, like ten?" a young man asked from the right.

"More like fifteen," Voshak said. "She's fared well, but

you've got to look closely. See, no baby fat left. No wrinkles yet, and her lips are still full, but the face doesn't have that fresh look. Buyers like them young. She's thirty, if she's a day. She'll still be worth a good chunk of change, but in our trade a woman past twenty-five is past her prime. And some of those bitches look like hags by thirty. It all depends on how gently they were used."

The woman sat still, her gaze fixed on the flames.

Voshak leaned over and checked her face.

"Told you," Pavel said. "Nobody's home."

"That's not a bad thing," Voshak said.

Richard locked his teeth. It had taken incredible courage to walk into the camp like this, to surrender herself into their physical custody. She had to know what they would do to her. He'd seen the aftermath of what happened to pretty women in slaver camps. They would pass her around and rape her, and he wouldn't be able to stop them. He would have to watch, helpless. He had seen worse things, but never from inside a cage with his hands tied.

He wanted to scream and throw himself against the bars, but he couldn't even move.

She had to have some sort of a plan. Please, whoever you are above, let her have a plan. Perhaps she planned to wait until they went to sleep and bury a knife in Voshak's throat. She couldn't hope to survive after that. Was this a suicide mission?

Voshak half turned to him and ran his hand down the woman's back. "Friend of yours, Hunter?"

Rage boiled inside him. Richard pictured cutting Voshak into pieces. "No."

"I bet you don't have any friends, Hunter. Did we kill them all, or are you just an asshole?"

Magic brushed against him, a subtle, delicate current. Richard forced himself to sit completely still. The magic touched him again, nipping gently on his body, draining him. He focused and felt other currents sliding to wind around the slavers. He followed their source back to the woman. Their stares connected.

Her face was so placid, but her eyes burned. The woman looked away. The magic current slid away from him to find another victim.

His magic sensitivity was off the charts—one of the benefits of being born into an old Edger family—but he had no idea what she was planning. Whatever it was, she could use a distraction, and he was the man for the job.

"Let's talk about *your* friends," he said, leaning back as casually as his restraints would allow. "Jeremy Legs. Chad Gully. Black Nil. Isabel Savage. The Striker Brothers. Angelo Cross. Germaine Coutard. Carmen Sharp. Tempest Wolf. Julius Maganti."

Voshak's face skewed with rage.

The mysterious magic currents weaved back and forth among the slavers. Anger and fear stamped their faces, but he couldn't see any adverse effects. The brush of the current that had slid by him was too light to cause any real harm. Maybe she needed more time.

Richard kept going, hammering each name in.

"Ambrose Club. Orville Fang. Raoul Baudet. My personal favorite, Jackal Tuline. Where are your friends, Voshak? Or rather, I meant to say 'your cronies,' since a lowlife like you doesn't have friends. My mistake."

The woman stared into the flames. Perhaps her magic wasn't working.

Inwardly, Richard swore. He took a risk and provoked the slavers. They glared at him like a pack of mongrel dogs. If he kept aggravating them, he'd be in real danger of getting shot. He had to get out of this damn cage before they killed him and her, and he didn't have any idea how to do it.

Richard feigned indifference and shrugged. "Do you want me to keep going? Would you like to know what each of them looked like when they died?"

"What the hell did we do to you?" Voshak snarled. "Did we rape your wife, did we take your children, what? What the hell is it?"

"You trade in human lives, which makes you an aberration. Your kind shouldn't exist. You're a wrong, and I decided to correct it. Or perhaps I'm just bored, and you're stupid and easy to kill."

Voshak swore.

The magic was getting thicker. She was still working on it, whatever it was. He needed to create some strife. As long as they fought among themselves, they wouldn't pay attention to other, subtler changes. He picked a familiar face. Daryl Long, bad-tempered, neurotic, and jumpy. Perfect.

"Daryl?"

The dark-haired, lanky slaver startled.

"Two weeks ago, I killed your brother."

Daryl recoiled.

"Every time I end one of you, I hope for some backbone, but your brother didn't die like a man. Before I cut his head off, he offered to set you up for me if I let him go. I killed him anyway because there was nothing I needed from him. You see, I know everything already, Daryl. I know about the old man. I know about the barn. I know what the two of you did to him before you slit his throat, and I know why you had to set the fire to the place."

Daryl's meager control snapped. He lunged at the cage. "I'll kill you. I'll fucking kill you!"

Crow swung the butt of his rifle and slammed it into Daryl's face. The blow knocked him backward. The slaver crashed to the ground, blood drenching his face.

"Nobody touches that bastard!" Voshak thundered. "The orders are he goes to the Market, and we'll deliver him there even if I have to blow your brains out."

Nobody said anything.

"We got him." Voshak pointed to the cage. "He's chained up! All he can do is talk. Let him yap. You touch him, I kill you. Anybody have anything to add?"

On the left, Pavel, the one who'd started the fire, coughed.

Voshak spun to him.

The man next to Pavel coughed, too.

Pavel coughed again, harder.

"Do the two of you think this is funny—" The end of the word dissolved into a wet hack. Voshak strained. "What the hell?"

Across the clearing, another slaver coughed, then another and another.

"All of you, stop it," Voshak barked. "I said stop!"

The coughs died.

Pavel strained, obviously trying to contain his hacking.

Voshak pointed his finger at him. "Don't you do it."

Pavel clenched up, gagged, holding it in . . . The cough exploded out of him in a gush of red. Blood burst from his nose and the corners of his mouth. The slaver dropped to all fours, retching. A clump of something wet, soft, and bloody fell out of his mouth.

Voshak grabbed his gun.

Across from Pavel, at the other side of the fire, another man collapsed, coughing and bleeding. People gripped their weapons, looking around.

"What the hell is going on?" Voshak roared. His voice caught, he sneezed and stared at his hand, covered with red mist and tiny chunks of flesh.

The slavers fell, as if cut down at once by an invisible sickle. Voshak spun, looking left, right, his eyes wild.

"The woman," Crow croaked, dropping to his knees. "The woman!"

Voshak whirled to her. She still sat on the log.

"You bitch!" The blond slaver lunged at her and fell back, staggering under another fit of coughing.

Crow struggled upright, raising his rifle.

A familiar wolfripper hound burst from the bushes and rammed Crow. A rifle shot popped, going wide into the sky. The dog bit into the slaver. Crow screamed once, writhing on the ground, and fell silent.

A stream of translucent darkness flickering with red sparks spiraled around the woman. An identical stream twisted in the opposite direction, winding about her body. She turned slowly to look at Voshak, hacking his lungs out on the ground.

Richard saw her eyes, and her gaze chilled him all the way to the bone. Power luminesced within her irises.

The woman rose. The dark streams of her magic widened and collided. The sparks flashed with deep crimson. The streams split into dozens of small tendrils and shot out like striking snakes, biting into the slaver captain.

Voshak screamed. His knees gave, and he crumpled to the ground.

"Help me!"

The bodies didn't move.

Voshak tried to roll to his feet, but his legs refused to support his weight, and he crashed down, coughing blood. "What do you want?"

She didn't answer.

Voshak cried out. Tremors wracked his body.

"Do you want money? I have money!"

The woman said nothing.

"What is it? What do you want?"

"You killed Daisy," she said. Her hoarse voice trembled with barely contained anger. "You murdered Éléonore."

So his memory of Rose's grandmother wasn't a dream or hallucination. Regret washed over Richard. Indirectly or not, he'd caused another casualty. The boys would be heart-broken.

He put it away, in the same place he put his guilt for the other things he had done.

Voshak squirmed on the ground. "I hate you. I fucking hate you. I'd do it again. I should've killed that skinny bitch, too."

A tendril of dark magic streaked from her, stinging the slaver captain. He shuddered, gurgling.

"Éléonore was like a mother to me. You cut a hole in my life. You murdered a young woman. She had her whole life ahead of her. You just ended it, and now her sister will have to live with her death," the woman said, her face iced over. "I want you to understand how much suffering you've caused. I want you to hurt before you die."

Voshak flailed, as if she had whipped him.

She watched, her pain plain on her face. Richard wondered why she didn't prolong the torture for the rest of the slavers. Considering the circumstances, instant death was a mercy.

Voshak drew one last shuddering breath and lay still. The odor of putrescence flooded the clearing. Nausea choked Richard. Voshak's body began to decompose.

The dark currents of magic shrunk, once mighty dragons, and now just pet snakes, sliding over the woman's skin.

She stepped forward. The chain from the shackle around her ankle pulled at Voshak's leg. The slaver's bones fell apart, rotting flesh rolling off them, and suddenly she wasn't chained to anyone. She walked toward him, picking her way among the bodies, beautiful and terrifying, like an angel of death.

She reached his cage.

They looked at each other through the bars.

Her eyes were just as he remembered: luminescent with power and heartbreakingly beautiful, but this time he saw no concern in their depths. His cage had changed owners. Whether it was for the better remained to be seen.

Richard weighed his options. One of three things would happen: she could kill him; she could walk away, letting him die slowly; or she could let him out. If he had any hope of getting out of this mess alive, he had to talk her down. He had to survive and finish what he started.

The dark currents of her magic licked the bars of the cage, sparking with red on the metal. Richard braced himself. He could tell by her eyes that whether he left this cage a free man or died of starvation and thirst inside it depended on what he'd say next.

THEY were dead. All of them. It had felt so unbelievably good to experience their dying. The darkness sang inside her, triumphant, while the rest of her trembled, repulsed and terrified. She was painfully aware of the corpses littering the clearing behind her.

It had taken all of her will to sit quietly and siphon off their life force, weakening their bodies and building up her own reserves. She'd thought it was the only way to kill them all at once and quickly. Finally, she had infected them and used their own magic to feed the disease within them. They felt nothing until the magically accelerated disease finally bloomed and severed their lives in a few painful instants. They didn't deserve mercy, but she didn't want their suffering as much as she wanted their lives. They couldn't be allowed to continue, and so she ended them fast.

All except their leader. Something had compelled her to kill him slowly. She'd monitored his body, as it surrendered to the disease, and the feeling of intense satiation that came over her as he lay there dying terrified Charlotte to the very core of her being. She had to cut it short and kill him before she began to revel in his pain.

The magic pulled on her even now, whispering into her mind, begging her to continue. She locked the magic in the cage of her will, forcing it to subside. She had broken her oath as a healer, but she wasn't a mindless abomination. Not yet. She could still hold it in check.

Richard leaned closer to the bars of the cage, his long, dark hair falling over his face. She almost took a step back.

His color was good, Charlotte noted. Stable vital signs. His body was strong and fit but still, he was recovering with surprising speed. His face was muddy and bruised, and the stench of old urine rose from his clothes. The thugs had tried to batter and debase him, but it made no difference. He refused to notice it, the way most people made a conscious decision to ignore light rain when they were in a hurry. He wasn't humiliated. He wasn't cowed or beaten down. A calculating mind looked at her through his eyes. He was like an old wolf on a chain, lethal, cunning, restrained for the time being but biding his time. Danger rolled off him. In her years as a healer, Charlotte had treated many threatening people: soldiers, agents, spies. Her instincts warned her to stay away from him.

Richard opened his mouth.

Her pulse spiked in alarm.

"You're real," he said.

What? "I am."

"When I woke up in the cage, I thought I dreamt you."

She wasn't sure what to make of it. "You were delirious when we met."

"Did you heal me?"

She nodded.

"Thank you."

She forced herself to sit down on a pile of bags on the ground. The slaver dog trotted over and lay by her feet between her and the cage. Richard raised his eyebrows.

"Éléonore is dead," she said. "They killed her, and they killed a young woman, Daisy. Then they set my house on fire."

"I'm sorry," he said.

There was an unexpected sincerity in his voice.

"You brought this nightmare on me," she said.

He nodded. "I did. It wasn't my intention, but the responsibility is mine."

"I want to know why. Why did they do this to us?"

Richard shifted in the cage. His hands were tied behind his back. It must hurt, Charlotte realized.

"These men are slavers. They raid the isolated settlements in the Weird and the Edge and sometimes even in the Broken. They kidnap men and women, and deliver them to the coast to the secret meeting points, where ships pick them up. From there, the captives are taken to the Market, a hidden auction house where they are sold off to the highest bidder. Slavery has been outlawed for three hundred years, but they prosper."

"How? If slavery is illegal . . ."

"The border barons always need fodder for construction and armies. Mine owners use slave labor. The magic users who tangle with outlawed applications of magic theory buy subjects for their experiments. And others, well, when you see a rich man with a young, beautiful woman on his arm, would it occur to you to ask if she was free?"

"That's barbaric."

Richard's eyes turned hard. "You would be surprised how many 'servants' come from the Market."

He was right. It would never have occurred to her to ask anyone if their attendants were slaves. She simply assumed they weren't.

"The slavers feed their own legends," he said. "They dress in black, they arm themselves with wolfripper dogs, they ride dark horses. They appear from nowhere in the middle of the night, reap their human harvest, burn the settlements to the ground, and vanish like ghosts."

"Like a night terror," she said. *Bastards.*

Richard nodded. "They want to be the stuff of nightmares because fighting one's fear is always harder than fighting another man. They see themselves as outside the law, as wolves who prey on sheep. Most of them didn't amount to much, and they cling to their illusions of grandeur both because they have nothing else and because they find cruelty empowering. So if you wish an honest answer, here it is. They killed Éléonore and Daisy, and burned your house because that's what they do. It wasn't personal or planned. They didn't give it a second thought. They simply did it because that's the way they do business. Other people's lives matter to them not at all. They're slavers."

His words only fueled her rage. "And you?"

"I hunt the slavers. I've killed dozens over the past months. They think themselves wolves, so they call me Hunter. They're not fond of me."

"I can see that."

"I made a mistake, and they finally caught me. They were taking me to the Market for a public execution."

That explained things. The slavers had beaten him not to hurt him—he was unconscious—but to make him less frightening. They were terrified of him. If they were the night terrors, he was their legendary killer, and when you kill a legend, you must make it as public as possible, or it might not take.

"Are there more of them?" she asked.

"Many more." Richard grimaced. "No matter how many I kill, there are always more."

Many more. That meant many more dead Daisies and Éléonores, many more Tulips, weeping over bodies. Many people like her, left with a gaping hole ripped in their lives, not sure how to pick up the pieces and move on. Her magic seethed within her. Her body was nearing exhaustion, but she wanted to scream in outrage. Why did this go on? Who allowed this to keep happening? Did they think nobody could stop them? Because she could, and she had, and she would do it again. It wasn't finished. She wasn't finished.

"Tell me more," Charlotte said.

He shook his head. "Not through the bars of the cage."

She leaned back. "I'm not sure it's a good idea to let you out. I don't know what you might do."

His eyes met hers. "My lady, I assure you, I'm not a danger to you."

"Says the Hunter of wolves."

"You view me as dangerous, but you allow a slaver dog with bloody teeth to lay by your feet."

"I've known the dog longer than you."

He grinned at her. "'Can two people ever truly know each other through the bars of the human cage?'"

Charlotte blinked. He'd quoted the *Prisoner's Ballad*, a work that was considered to be one of the pinnacles of Adrianglian literature. She was sitting on some dirty bags in the middle of a clearing filled with corpses, and a man who, by his own admission, was a serial killer just quoted a philosophical masterpiece to her. This had to be some sort of surreal absurd dream.

"I can simply walk away and leave you in the cage," she said.

"I don't think you will," Richard said.

"What makes you so sure?"

"You healed me," he said. "I remember your eyes. You wouldn't sentence a man to slow death."

He'd called her bluff. Leaving him to starve to death was

beyond her now, no matter how dangerous he was. "If I open this cage, you'll answer my questions."

"As honestly as is in my power."

"Before I let you out, typhus, malaria, red death, Ebola, tuberculosis . . . Do you have any preference? I have others, as well."

"Where?" Richard asked.

"I carry dormant samples of them within my body. To cure a disease, you must first understand it, and sometimes a deliberate infection is necessary for vaccination. If you attempt to attack me, I will end you, Richard. Look around you if you have any doubts."

"I'll strive to keep it from slipping my mind."

Charlotte rose. The white-haired slaver was the leader. He would likely have the key. She crouched by his body— it smelled awful—and searched his clothes, briskly turning out his pockets. Money, bullets . . . "No key."

"Thank you, but we don't have to have one," Richard said. "I only need a knife and free hands."

She pulled a blade from the sheath on the slaver's waist, reached between the bars, and sawed through the tough cord binding his wrists. The rope snapped. He rolled his shoulders and held out his hand.

She might regret this, but she couldn't just leave him in the cage. Charlotte put the blade into his hand. Richard flipped it. She felt magic flow toward the blade. It drained from his body onto the metal, stretching in a thin glowing line of pale white along the edge.

Richard sliced at the chain wrapped around his feet.

The metal fell apart.

She'd seen concentrated flash sever a body before but never metal. Not like this.

He struck at the chain securing the cage's door, and it crashed to the ground. Richard pushed the door open, slid out, and swayed, catching himself on the wagon. She hadn't realized how tall he was, almost six inches taller than she. Charlotte waited for him to sit down, but he remained standing. It was an obvious strain.

Then the light dawned on her. She sat back on the bags, and Richard sank to the ground as well, leaning against the wagon wheel. Ridiculous. Richard might not have been a blueblood, but he behaved like one, and the ingrained manners of the Weird wouldn't permit him to take a seat if she was standing.

"You had questions?" he asked.

"Tell me about your involvement with the slavers," she said.

"Are you familiar with the Marshall of the Southern provinces?" Richard asked.

"Earl Declan Camarine? Rose's husband," Charlotte said. "Éléonore spoke of him quite often. I never met him in person, but I do know of the family."

"The Office of the Marshall of the Southern Provinces has fought slavery for years," Richard said. "Unsuccessfully. The slavers have an elaborate organization, and the slaver crews like this one are just the lowest rung of it. The slavers employ shippers, accountants, brokers, and guards. The list goes on. In the last decade, the Marshall of the Southern Provinces has led several operations against the slavers and failed. Somehow, they knew exactly when and where he would strike."

"Someone is protecting them," Charlotte guessed.

"Someone highly placed and well connected, with access to the inner workings of the Ministry of State. A little over a year ago, Declan invited me in for a conversation. Declan needed someone on the outside, a man who could act without the constraints of his office. He asked me if I would be that man, and I agreed."

"Why?"

Richard paused. His eyes grew darker. "My family is from the Edge. I have my own motivations to want the slavers dead. Suffice it to say that my reasons are highly compelling."

There was trauma there, she could sense it. Some great injustice had been done to Richard. She wanted to know what drove him, but his eyes told her that was the one question he wouldn't answer. And Sophie, whoever she was, had to be a part of it.

"I spent eight months collecting information and gathering people I could trust and another four pursuing the slavers. I studied them, then I killed them. I slaughtered them in the open against overwhelming odds. I killed them in their sleep. I destroyed their camps. Four slaver captains are dead by my hand. It made no difference. They simply recruit more thugs. I knew I had to climb up their food chain and sever the head of the organization. And for that, I needed to find their Market, where the kidnapped are sold. During my latest raid, I obtained a map. It's the record of where the slaver ships are landing, but the map is in code, and I couldn't break the cipher. I needed the key."

"Is that how you ended up in the cage?"

"I bargained with a man and fell into a trap," Richard said. "It was a miscalculation, and I won't repeat it. They chased me, and I ran. I knew the Edge was my best chance. Unfortunately, I was too delirious to know where I was going or to deliver a warning when I got there."

He leaned forward and bowed his head. It was a bow that would've been a credit to any blueblood lord. "I'm sorry I brought this on you. I will make them pay. It's all I can offer you."

He was about to end this conversation and leave, taking her chance to matter with him. No. No, she wouldn't stand for it. The wounds inside her were too raw, the memory of the fire too fresh. "Not all," Charlotte said. "I'm coming with you."

"It's out of the question," he said.

She gathered herself and looked down on him with all of the haughtiness her upbringing could provide. "You mistake me, my lord. I'm not asking."

"My apologies. In that case, I should advise you that I don't respond favorably to threats."

The dog raised his head and bared his teeth.

"You're not my enemy," Charlotte said. "I don't want to kill you, Richard. I want to end this." She pointed to the cage behind him.

He sighed, and for the first time, she saw the signs of weariness in his face.

"Perhaps, I should explain further. I mentioned that I needed a cipher key."

"Yes."

"Jackal Tuline, one of the slaver undercaptains, had a sister. A month ago, she was serving drinks at a tavern. Voshak bashed her over the head with a bottle and forced himself on her in full view of a dozen witnesses. He flattened her nose and dislocated her jaw. I've seen her personally, and the woman is almost unrecognizable. The experience left her deeply damaged, and her face is the least of her injuries."

Charlotte glanced at the decomposing corpse. He wouldn't force himself on anyone again. That knowledge filled her with a frightening, savage joy.

"The word on the street said Tuline wanted revenge but was too afraid to take Voshak on directly. I approached him and offered him a chance to get even. We bargained."

His voice dripped with derision, as if he were describing swimming through sewage.

"We came to an agreement. He would sell me the cipher, and I would see to Voshak's death. When I met Tuline in the woods to deliver the payment, six of his men ambushed me." Richard smiled. It was a hard, humorless grin. "Tuline took a few moments to astonish me with his cleverness. He had deliberately engineered the rape of his own sister." Richard paused. "He thought this plan up, talked it over with Voshak, then he did it. All to draw me out. The level of depravity is mind-boggling."

It made her want to retch. "What happened?"

"I left him in two pieces." Richard leaned forward. "When Declan came to me with this proposal, he told me that this mission would consume me—and it has. He chose me for many reasons, in large part because I have nothing to lose. My family doesn't need me now. My wife left me. I'm childless."

An old pain stirred in her. She was childless, too. "I'm sorry."

He paused, momentarily off-balance. "Thank you."

An awkward silence stretched between them.

Richard cleared his throat. "I chose this road deliberately, and when I started, I thought I was worldly. I wasn't. I've seen atrocities along the way that would horrify most people, and I committed some because I had to be as ruthless as my enemy. There is no room for mercy or compassion in this quest, and there is no turning back. It changes you, and should I survive, I'm not certain that I'll be capable of normal life. Make no mistake, my lady. I'm a monster. Don't follow me. It's a one-way trip. Sane, kind people aren't meant to take it."

"How about mass murderers?" she asked. "What's the policy for us?"

Richard shook his head. "Go home, my lady."

"My home is burned to the ground."

"These people are ruthless, cruel thugs. Think of what you must become to hunt them."

He didn't understand. "Look around you," she said softly. "I came to the Edge to hide from my magic. I ran because I have an obligation as a healer to contain it and prevent it from hurting anyone. I needed to be someplace where my power was weakened and nobody knew me. Someone had injured me, and I wasn't sure I could hold my emotions in check and not seek revenge. I came to the Edge alone, and I had nearly starved to death when Éléonore found me. She saved me, Richard. I rebuilt my life. I was content and this"—she indicated the corpses with the sweep of her hand—"had fallen dormant. And then they killed her, and they killed Daisy."

Her voice snapped, and she swallowed. "She was only twenty-three, Richard. Twenty-three. She had barely started her life, and they crushed her and ripped out her sister's heart. Every time I close my eyes, I see Tulip wailing over her sister's body. I can't undo it. I can't just let it go."

"You have to try," he said. "Vengeance will eat you alive."

"It's not about vengeance." She shook her head. "It's about stopping them. You're trying to warn me about the road, but I'm already walking it. Have you heard of the Healer's oath?"

"'I swear to hold the human body sacred,'" he quoted. "'I will apply all my effort, all my magic, and all my knowledge of procedure and remedy to preserve life, to treat malady, to ease suffering. I swear to knowingly do no harm through the use of my magic or craft. I will prescribe no remedy when none is needed. I will not seek to improve on Nature's design for the sake of vanity, knowledge, or human passion.'"

"How do you know that?"

"One of my relatives was a certified Physician," Richard said.

"There is more," she said. "'Should I break this vow through my ignorance, I will surrender myself to the mercy of my peers. I will accept their judgment and my dishonor, and should they convict me, I will cease to practice medicine. Should I break this vow by deliberate action, I will know that I have betrayed myself. I will have drowned my teachers in guilt and cast doubt and suspicion upon my students. Let my name be a bitter taste on the lips of those who knew me, let my countenance be that of dishonor, let me fade into nothingness and be forgotten, save as an example of failure and weakness, for I would become an abomination in the eyes of the world.'"

He waited.

"I'm a certified healer from the Ganer College. Today I killed human beings through the use of my magic. I did it willingly." The words tasted foul on her tongue. "My life is over. Do you understand? I sacrificed everything I was so I could do this because it's my responsibility as a peer of the realm and a human being to destroy this human cancer before it hurts anyone else."

She pointed to the dead bodies. They lay there, silent and accusing, evidence of her fall from grace.

Charlotte turned to Richard. "I own the consequences of my deeds. I have nothing to lose. I need your knowledge and expertise, but I'll keep going, with you or without, and I won't stop until the slave trade is broken. You can benefit from this alliance, as can I. Think what an asset I can be. Don't let my sacrifice be wasted."

RICHARD leaned back. She was looking at him, waiting for an answer.

He had done his best to persuade her to leave, but everything about her, from the coldness in her eyes to her wary posture, convinced him she would not. He had no idea who she was. He only knew that they had the same purpose.

She was beautiful and radiant. He remembered the concern in her eyes. The same concern drove her now, pushing her toward acts of violence. On the surface, he'd be a fool to turn her down. She was driven by tragedy, just like him, and she would be incorruptible, just like him. He needed a blade to kill, but she could kill dozens at once empty-handed. She was Death, and she had just asked to be his ally.

Walking next to him would break her. He'd fought so hard to spare Sophie from this grisly soul-eating burden. He couldn't bring himself to say yes to this woman.

"How often can you do this?" He pointed at the corpses, delaying his need to answer.

She frowned. "The process is complicated. When I healed you, I used the reserves of my own body to speed your regeneration. When I injure, the method is similar. It takes very little magic to introduce a pathogen to the body, but to make it kill with unnatural quickness requires a lot of power and control. To kill this many, I infected them all, then siphoned off the natural life force of their bodies until I was overflowing with it. There is a high degree of risk: had I poured too much of myself into the process, I would've died, but I am very angry, and I've never killed with my magic before, so

I took the chance. Given ample rest and the right circumstances, I can do this again tomorrow."

"Would you risk it without rest?" Richard asked.

"If the incentive was high enough," she said.

So she valued her goal higher than her life. He would have to take that into account. She was likely to overextend herself on her own.

"What about doing this on a smaller, individual scale?"

The woman shrugged. "Infecting a single target is much easier."

"Are you still capable of healing?"

She reached over and drew her hand across his cheek, letting the tiny golden sparks penetrate his skin. The ache in his face dissolved.

"Does the bruise still hurt?" she asked.

"No." It was in his best interests to keep his mouth shut, but he couldn't help himself. "What you do . . . it's a gift. Reconsider."

Bitterness dripped from her voice. "Too late."

"Are you able to control your magic? Can you rein it in?" Richard had to account for all possible contingencies.

"Yes," she said. "What I do requires a very deliberate intent and concentration. I won't be infecting you in my sleep because I had a nightmare."

"Do you have any family? Anyone who could be used to compel you to do something against your will?" Anyone he could use to talk her out of this madness.

"No."

"Do you have any enemies?"

"Yes. Elvei Leremine, my ex-husband. He's terrified of me and will take every opportunity to obtain revenge. Also, by using my art and magic to murder, I've broken the healer's oath. If I'm discovered by the realm, Adrianglia will execute me. If you don't want this to happen, the use of my magic must be more covert."

He was running out of questions.

"There is one more thing you should be aware of," she

said. "I can't heal myself. If I'm injured, I'll have to recover by normal means unless we can find another healer."

She had committed herself to it. She would embark on this path with or without him, but her chances of survival were much higher if he took her with him. She had great power, but she was vulnerable. This time she got lucky. If he abandoned her now, eventually she would walk into the wrong camp. It would take just one man to shoot her dead or knock her unconscious. She had saved him twice, once from the wound and the second time from the cage. No matter how much he didn't want to witness her transformation into someone like him, he owed it to her to safeguard her.

Richard held out his hand. "Last chance to turn back."

"No." She put her hand into his.

"These are my terms. You will accept my authority. If I say to wait in a certain place, you will wait. If I say to kill someone, you will kill them. You understand that your life is secondary to our cause. If your compassion jeopardizes our mission, I may not be in a position to be merciful. If you choose to hinder me, I'll cut you down."

He waited, hoping he'd scared her off.

Her face showed no hesitation. "Agreed."

They shook.

"My name is Richard Mar."

"Charlotte de Ney," she said with a sigh.

A noble title. She had mentioned she had one, but even if she didn't, he would have known simply by the way she held herself. Blood itself, noble or no, didn't confer any special benefits. He was living proof of that—an Edger mongrel, yet he could and had passed for a blueblood many times. But he had years of education, and he recognized in Charlotte the grace and poise that training imparts.

Propriety dictated that he should let go of her hand. He did, although he didn't want to.

"We start with the bodies," Richard said. "Voshak should carry a copy of the cipher. One more thing."

"Yes?" She raised her eyebrows.

"The dog."

"What about him?"

"You can't possibly mean to take him with us."

She raised her eyebrows at him.

"He's a wolfripper. Born and bred to hunt wolves, and since he was owned by the slavers, he was trained to hunt men. You're looking at 170 pounds of cunning and vicious predator."

"I'm so glad you think he's smart." Charlotte smiled at the dog. "The dog stays, Richard."

He sighed.

Charlotte pushed herself up from the pile of bags. He read exhaustion in the slump of her shoulders. Her magic had come at a cost. He decided not to argue.

"As you wish." Richard handed her his knife. "We have some corpses to strip. It's easier to cut pockets than rummage through them. We may have to ride hard once we find what we're looking for. Can you do it?"

Charlotte raised her head, her gaze regal and proud. "Of course I can."

FOUR

JEANS definitely had their advantages, Charlotte decided. For one, they provided a nice protection for one's thighs when in a saddle. Unfortunately, they did nothing for the ache in her core muscles. It had been two and a half years since she had last ridden a horse, and although her posture and balance were still good, after eight hours, her inner hip muscles and her butt had turned into painful mush. The reality of expending so much magic so quickly had crashed into her a while ago. Her head felt fuzzy. Her eyes wanted to close.

"Almost there," Richard murmured.

"I'm fine. Please don't worry."

Considering that he was near death less than twenty-four hours ago, of the two of them she was in much better shape.

They rode side by side on the Salino-Kelena Adrianglian highway. Around them tall oaks dripped long beards of moss. The day had long since burned down to night, and the moon shone from the sky, drenching the road in silver light. Darkness hid between the tree trunks. Strange noises came from within the woods: a deep guttural grunting, followed by the distant snarls of a predator, the high-pitched squeaking of some rodent, and the eerie hooting of the great twilight owls trying to flush out their prey. Somewhere between the shrubs, the dog glided, silent despite his bulk.

They had searched Voshak's bags and found the cipher and another map, hidden in the false bottom of his canteen. Richard translated it while she chose the best horses and searched for useful weapons. The map indicated a pickup point just north of Kelena, a large harbor city. The map gave a specific date and time, eleven o'clock, evening, the day after next. The moment they had finished gathering supplies and Richard finished stuffing some of the more outlandish pieces of leather into their saddlebags, they had ridden out.

Richard slowed his horse.

"What's wrong?"

"My wound is aching," he said.

Her magic told her that his wound was no worse than it had been hours ago. He was giving her an opportunity to rest, and she was too tired and too grateful to fight him on it. Still, she had to. "I appreciate it, but please don't make allowances for my sake. I'll manage."

"We're only a few miles away," he said. "Have you ever been to Kelena?"

"No."

"It is a noisy, garish hive of a city. We'll be walking into the Cauldron, one of the most dangerous neighborhoods in Adrianglia. They call it the Cauldron because that's where the worst humanity has to offer is thrown together and allowed to boil until the scum floats to the top."

Charlotte laughed softly. She hadn't thought she would ever laugh again after what she had done, but her body had passed the point of pain, and she felt weightless and disconnected. "You've missed your calling."

"I'm a complete failure as a poet," he said. "When I was fourteen, I wrote a long ballad about the bleakness of my life and the heaviness of the burden that was being me. My brother stole it and read it out loud at a family gathering. That was the first and the last time I managed to make the entire family laugh."

The laugher kept coming. She heard the hysterical tone in her own voice but couldn't stop it.

Richard halted his horse and dismounted.

The back of her eyes grew hot. She had to get ahold of herself.

Richard took her reins and led their horses off the road.

She slid out of her saddle, her body whining in protest. Her limbs were shaking. A big poplar loomed in front of her. Charlotte circled it and sat on the ground, wrapping her arms around her legs and gathering herself into a ball the way she used to do when she was a homesick little girl.

It was all over. *If you were more grounded, you'd sprout roots, Charlotte.* She wasn't grounded anymore. All of her trials, all of her self-imposed exile, all of it had been for nothing. She murdered people. She held their lives in her hands and snuffed them out. It brought her joy. And Éléonore was dead, and there wasn't a damn thing Charlotte could do about it. Éléonore was gone, and she must've suffered before she died. *I'm sorry. I'm so sorry.*

Charlotte bit her lower lip, trying to hold back the flood. Oh Dawn Mother. How did it all go so wrong? *Please,* she prayed silently, *please, please make this all into a nightmare. Please let me wake. I just want to wake up. Please . . .* She would have given anything to turn back the last twenty-four hours. Anything to keep Éléonore and Daisy from dying. Anything to shield Tulip. Poor Tulip. She was all alone now. The slavers wrecked her life. One moment she had a sister and a future, and the next she had nothing, only grief.

The warmth behind her eyes turned into tears. They rolled, wetting her cheeks. Her chest hurt. She sobbed. Suddenly, she couldn't hold it any longer. The tears tore out of her.

A dark shadow emerged from the bushes. The dog lowered himself on the ground by her feet and licked her ankle. She slumped over her bent knees and cried like a child.

Please. Please let me wake up.

She cried and cried, praying in her head even though she knew nobody heard her. It was godsdamned unfair. Why? Why did they have to die? She'd killed the bastards who killed them, but it didn't make things right. It was just a circle of pain and death, and she was trapped in it, angry, grieving, and helpless.

The sobs turned into dry heaves. There was no balm, no poultice, no pills she could create to make things better.

Dead would remain dead. Nothing could take back their suffering or hers.

Finally, even her dry heaves died. Exhaustion smothered her.

She felt alone. So utterly, completely alone. She raised her head, straightening, and realized that fabric was touching her shoulders. Richard had draped his cloak over her. She hadn't even noticed.

"Thank you." She pulled the cloak tighter around herself. It was a kind gesture, completely at odds with his confession of being a killer and the air of danger that still emanated from him.

He was sitting next to her, leaning against the rough bark, his profile etched against the moonlit sky. Had she met him under different circumstances, she might have felt fear at his proximity. Now she was too numb and too beat-up emotionally to muster any anxiety.

"I suppose you're regretting bringing me along," she said.

"I've regretted it from the moment I decided to do it."

Her pride was stung. "I won't be a burden."

He turned to her, dark eyes filled with concern. "I never viewed you as a burden."

"Then why?"

He looked up to the moon. "In this life, some of us are killers, born with a predatory instinct. I'm one, but you're not."

He must've forgotten she had just murdered a dozen men. "Why? Is it because I'm a woman?"

"No, it's nothing so obvious as gender. My aunt was the best killer I've met. For whatever reason, some of us are born to kill, and others, men and women both, are born to nurture. Your instincts drive you to help others. My instincts drive me to end lives."

She sniffed. "You don't know me."

Richard smiled. Despite the dirt, he really was a strikingly handsome man. Arrogant, predatory, but handsome.

"Those of us who are killers learn to recognize others of our kind. We know rivals because they pose danger."

"And I don't?" Charlotte asked quietly.

He smiled again, and this time his face was almost mournful. "Even the most peaceful and kind person will become dangerous if backed into a corner. I don't question your power, but you don't have the innate aggression or the predatory drive of a natural-born killer. I've been one all of my life, and what I've done and seen during these past months haunts me. I know what lies ahead. I know it will be very difficult for you. You think now that you're dealing with grief and purging it from yourself, but it's only the first taste of what's to come. Are you sure you don't want to return? I would consider it an honor to escort you to the Edge."

"No."

"Do you think the Edgers wouldn't take you back?"

She sighed. "They would, but I can't go back to East Laporte. When the slavers surrounded the house, Éléonore called me. I drove to our neighbors to ask for help. They gathered about twenty people together, all carrying guns, then they stood around."

"Nobody wanted to fight," Richard said. "They probably delayed until the slavers were gone. Typical."

She turned to him. "Yes. Éléonore lived among them all of her life. She helped many of them, and they just abandoned her and left her to die. And when I asked them for help to go after those bastards, not one of them would meet my eyes. I can't go back there. I've made my decision. I don't know what your motivations are, but mine are just as valid. Please respect my need for justice."

"My apologies," he said. "I won't mention it again."

Charlotte wiped her face with her sleeve and rose. Richard got up.

She held out his cloak. "Thank you for your cloak."

"My pleasure."

Richard held her horse's reins while she put her foot in the stirrup and mounted. He handed them to her, got into his saddle, and they rode out.

Half an hour later, the forest parted. Charlotte halted her

horse. A wide field of waist-tall grass spread in front of her, rolling into the distance, where a nacre sea lapped at the shore under a bottomless dark sky. To the left, bathed in the salt water of the ocean, rose impossibly tall towers. Built of pale gray stone, they were triangular in shape, smoothly curved at the corners. A turquoise metal wave tipped each tower, sending rivulets of metal down the pale stone sides, like climbing plants that had sprouted a network of thin roots. The moonlight played on the metal, and its gleam matched the reflections on the placid ocean. The towers stood in a perfect semicircle, enclosing most of the city, like wave breakers.

"Kelena's Teeth," Richard said. "During hurricanes the towers send out a magic barrier, shielding the city from the storms and the worst of the surge."

"It looks as if the city is halfway in the water."

"About a third. There are canals running all through the city, so when the tide rises, the water simply passes through Kelena into the salt marshes. All that grass is deceptive. That's not solid ground under it, it's marsh flats with a thin layer of water over mud. An ideal home for horned turtles. They grow to five feet wide and can snap a human femur in half with their jaws. Fortunately, they are slow and rarely venture on the road. Shall we?"

Charlotte nodded and they trotted down the highway toward the city. She could see between the towers now, and from her vantage point in the saddle, the interior of the city looked like a mess of roofs, balconies, and bright, frayed banners. A human hive, just as Richard had described it: messy, chaotic, filled with strangers. A vague anxiety rose in her. From here, the city appeared too large, too full of people. While at the College, she had dreamt of traveling, but once she left it, the marriage and the house had taken precedence.

Now she was riding toward this teeming city through the night, accompanied by a man born between the worlds who cut steel with his sword and had flawless manners. It felt surreal.

"My brother says the Broken has a city in this exact same

spot. According to him, its citizens have an unhealthy fascination with pirates," Richard said.

She found his voice strangely reassuring. "The same brother who stole your ballad?"

"Sadly, yes."

"What does he do?" she asked to keep the conversation going.

"He's an agent of the Mirror."

Charlotte turned to him. "He is a spy?" The Mirror was Adrianglia's intelligence and espionage agency, the realm's main weapon in its cold war with the neighboring Dukedom of Louisiana. It operated in the shadows, and the exploits of its agents were legendary.

Richard grimaced. "He steals anything that's not nailed down, cons people into going along with his improbable schemes, and possesses a unique talent that lets him win when he gambles. It was the Mirror or a prison cell."

His distaste had a false, put-upon quality about it. "You're proud of him," she said.

A narrow smile lit Richard's face. "Extremely."

"I've never been to the Broken," she told him. "I tried, but my magic was too strong."

"Neither have I," he said. "I also tried to cross and nearly died. The Edge is my limit. I would love to see the Broken."

"I would, too."

The Broken's gadgets fascinated her. Some, like microwave ovens, had their equivalent in the Weird, but others, like plastic wrap and cell phones, were completely new to her. When she had received de Ney manor, she had climbed into the attic. It was filled with strange things from the previous owners' travels, and she loved to sort through their abandoned treasures. Each item was a little discovery, wrapped in echoes of adventure. She felt the exact same way about the swap meets she'd gone to in the Edge. She rarely bought things, but accompanying Éléonore on one of her treasure hunts was an experience in itself. Éléonore would find some strange gadget from the Broken, and her face would light up.

Grief stabbed her. Charlotte stared ahead at the city. She would make them stop. They would regret the day they ever came to East Laporte.

"Do we have a plan?" she asked.

"The slaver ship docks tomorrow night," Richard said. "They will expect a crew of at least ten men and a group of slaves, usually twelve to fifteen, typically adolescents and young adults. If they don't see that on the shore, the ship may not dock. It's imperative we get on that ship."

"Because it goes to the slave market?"

"Yes. The slavers are run by a board of trustees, like a business. The individual slaver captains don't know who the trustees are."

"You seem very sure of that," she said.

"Once you hang a man over an open fire, he usually answers your questions honestly," Richard said. "The slavers don't know the identity of the trustees, but they do know that once the slaves board the ships, they are taken to an island. There are sixty-seven islands along the Adrianglian coast. The slaves are sold at the market, and the sales are recorded and presided over by a bookkeeper. He's directly accountable to the trustees. He will know their identities and faces."

"So where are we going to get a crew of slaves and slavers?" she asked.

"We're going to bargain with Jason Parris," Richard said.

"Who is he?"

"The most vicious crime lord in the Cauldron."

The anxiety she'd been feeling since coming into view of Kelena returned full force. "Ah," Charlotte said, forcing her voice to sound light. "I'm so relieved. I thought we would be doing something dangerous."

RICHARD strode down the wooden boardwalk along the Cauldron's Sharkmonger Canal, aware of Charlotte walking next to him and the dog trotting a few yards behind. To the right, two-story buildings rose in a continuous wall, built

of anything from stone to discarded lumber, each story with
its own faded, weather-beaten awning. The awnings hung
over the boardwalk, shielding it from the rain and sun. It
was late evening, and the numerous colored lanterns hanging from chains and ropes seemed almost to create more
shadows than they banished.

Beyond the buildings, even higher structures stretched
upward, making the canal resemble a river running along
the bottom of a deep, man-made canyon. The water, the
color of milk tea, was completely opaque. Small docks punctuated the canal here and there, marked with bright orange-
and-green sail-like banners that stretched all the way from
the top story to the ground.

The air smelled of bitter salt, seaweeds, smoke, and a
confusing, slightly nauseating amalgam of odors particular
to the Cauldron: incense; cooked meat; alcohol fumes; the
distinct reek of sumah, an illegal narcotic; and the ever-
present stench of fish guts.

They passed a small square dock. A body floated facedown, bumping against the wooden supports. Next to him,
Charlotte stopped for a short moment and then kept walking.

She had probably never been to a place like this before,
but if she had, he wouldn't know. She obviously didn't
belong here, in the vicious human gutter. In her place,
Cerise, his cousin, would've put her hand on her sword and
stalked like a predator in unfamiliar territory. Rose, Declan's
wife, would've been wary, alarmed, at the very least cautious. Charlotte floated. The way she held herself with assur-
ance and slight indifference, as if she were strolling through
a garden listening to the slightly boring droning of a friend,
made it impossible to question her right to be here. She made
herself belong, and when she saw a bloated corpse in the
water, she'd merely paused for a moment, as if it were an
odd flower, and resumed walking.

Her training was so strong that even here her poise was
flawless. Charlotte must've had a mentor, someone with an
ancient bloodline and an instinctual understanding of etiquette. He recognized it because despite being a poor Edge

rat, his own education had come from such a man. His mentor was his granduncle, an exile from the Dukedom of Louisiana, and he was sure that if Vernard were still alive, he would've offered Charlotte nothing but praise.

Who could've hurt her so much that she had abandoned everything and fled to the Edge?

DAWN Mother, there was a dead person floating in the water.

Ice rolled down Charlotte's spine, an alarming mix of revulsion, fear, and anxiety. The sight of a single corpse after she had created so many shouldn't have been so unsettling, but somehow this lone bloated body, discarded like garbage and ignored by everyone, nearly made her gag.

"Tell me about this crime lord," Charlotte said, hoping for a distraction before her stomach rebelled and emptied itself on the boardwalk.

"Jason Parris was born in the Broken, in a small mountain town," Richard said. "His family was poor, so after he finished high school, he joined the Marine Corps. It's one of the elite branches of the Broken military. He survived a war in a foreign country and decided to leave after his four-year term of service was completed. When he returned home, he couldn't hold a job. He worked for a series of businesses doing manual labor and was either fired or quit—he didn't last long at any of them."

"Why? Wouldn't being in the military teach him discipline?"

"Oh, he has discipline." Richard shrugged. "He also has very definite ideas about who is and isn't worthy of his loyalty. He listened to his sergeants and officers because they had done what he did and he was smart enough to recognize that they were trying to keep him alive. In his mind, they had earned the right to give him orders. His civilian employers weren't worthy of the same respect. They understandably took a rather dim view of his attitude. Jason found himself often unemployed. He was used to having his own money, and suddenly he had to depend on relatives for a roof over his head. It made him angry. One night, in a bar fight, that anger boiled over, and he severely injured a man. A relative took him to the Edge to keep him out of jail. He was just coming to terms with the idea that magic existed when slavers raided the Edge settlement. Jason was fit and healthy, prime merchandise from their point of view. They overpowered him. He proved to be a difficult captive and attacked them every chance he got. Voshak tried his best to break him but couldn't. Jason went through the Market and was sold to a garnet mine. A month later, I raided that mine and found him in a hole in the ground. It was my second raid, and knowing what I know now, I would've had doubts about pulling him out of that hole."

"He didn't want to go home?"

Richard grimaced. "No. He asked for directions to the nearest city instead. I dropped him off at Kelena. He started calling himself Jason Parris and said that this city would become known as his island. An allusion, if you will, to the place where he first received his military training. Now, a year later, he owns everything you can currently see. The old crime lords that ran the Cauldron had established certain boundaries. They had families and business interests, and were unwilling to risk them. Parris had nothing. He tore through them and took over all of their territory. He kills whoever whenever however he feels necessary, without reservation or remorse."

"Why would anyone follow him?" Sooner or later, someone like that would turn on his own people.

Richard shook his head. "Jason isn't a psychopath. He's vicious, but he kills selectively, with a strategy in mind. His people fear him, yet they also know that as long as they comply with his demands, they will be safe and rewarded. He respects strength. He can be charming, but no matter what he says or how he greets us, don't trust him or his second, Miko. In fact, don't trust anyone in that building. Jason is the drive and the muscle, but Miko is his mind, and that mind dreams up plans with high body counts."

Richard stopped, and Charlotte paused next to him. The continuous wall of buildings here was particularly ramshackle, the awning pale and weather-bleached from a once deep rust to a pale, sad orange. Loose lumber had been nailed to the wall in every direction.

"Why did we stop?" Charlotte murmured.

"There are sentries watching us," he said. "Across the street on the roof, one on the right in the boat, and there is one directly above us on the balcony, listening to everything we say. They will report to Jason, and we'll wait here and see if he decides to see us."

She leaned closer to him. "And if he doesn't?"

"Then I'll knock," Richard said.

The wall of the house behind them slid open. An old woman emerged, wearing a shapeless red dress and a red scarf on her hair. She waved at them with a wrinkled brown hand and disappeared inside, into the gloom.

"We've been invited." Richard smiled.

"Indeed."

"Follow me, please."

He strode through the narrow hallway. The dog trotted in after him. She was last through the door, in command of Rear Ward, or whatever the proper military term was. Charlotte followed the dog up a short flight of narrow dark stairs, into a hallway, and through another doorway. A spacious room stretched before them, illuminated by the familiar Weird-style lanterns. Shaped like bunches of delicate glowing flowers, the lanterns cascaded from the hooks between the windows near the tall ceiling. An expensive rug stretched across the polished wooden floor to the stone fireplace. In the center, a tea table waited, surrounded by soft chairs upholstered in light leather.

A man sprawled in the largest chair. His broad shoulders stretched the fabric of his gray shirt. His chest was broad, and his arms, revealed by the short sleeves of his tunic, bulged with muscle. He had to be over six feet tall, and his huge frame dwarfed the chair. His head had been shaved in a series of meticulously spaced strips of various widths that ran from his forehead to the nape of his neck; the effect was alternating stripes of glossy hair and smooth, shaved, light brown scalp.

His features would've been handsome in a masculine, square-jawed, leader-of-the-pack way, but a scar covered most of the left side of his face. A burn, Charlotte diagnosed. Not by direct application—either from steam, or more likely, flash-magic heat. Deeper lines crisscrossed the scar. Probably from a grate of some sort that had covered the heat source. So this was Jason Parris. She had expected someone older, but he appeared to be in his mid-twenties.

The man's eyes, startling green against his darker skin, surveyed Richard and paused on her. Intelligent eyes. He radiated power and menace, and when she met his stare, his eyebrows crept up a hair. Perhaps he had expected her to flinch.

A girl stood next to him, as lean and slight as he was bulky. She looked too young to be here, seventeen, perhaps eighteen. Her face was smooth and a shade darker than his. Her hair hung over her face in stiff, straight locks, the result of some sort of hair product. She wore close-fitting jeans and a gray sweatshirt with HARVARD printed on it in red letters. It had to have come from the Broken.

"The Hunter," Jason said. His voice was deep and resonant, and he spoke in an unhurried manner. "I feel honored. Do you feel honored, Miko?"

Miko said nothing.

"See, she feels honored." Jason spread his massive arms. His voice had a slight mocking quality to it. "You smell like piss and you look even worse."

Jason's stare slid over to her. His light eyes widened. "Richard, you have a girl. And you got a dog together. Where are you registered? I will buy you a toaster."

"The dog is hers," Richard said.

The wolfripper showed Jason his big teeth.

"So, what can we do for the mighty Hunter?"

Richard reached into his bag.

Miko leaned forward, focused.

A man stepped from the doorway, a crossbow in his hands.

Richard extracted Voshak's bleached-blond braid from the bag and tossed it to the crime lord. Parris snatched it from the air and looked at the blond strands. "When?"

"About ten hours ago."

"Anybody left from his crew?"

"No."

Parris glanced at the crossbowman and tossed the braid into the air. A bolt whistled and bit into the opposite wall, pinning the braid securely in place.

The crime lord turned to Richard. "You bring me such fine gifts, Hunter. What do you want?"

"There is a slave ship docking north of the city at eleven tonight. They expect a crew of slaves and slavers to board it," Richard said.

Parris leaned forward, his eyes suddenly predatory. "They will take them to the Market."

"Yes. One small problem: the slaver crew is dead, and they'd failed to capture any slaves. If someone was in charge of a rough crew, that someone could take their place."

The crime lord smiled. It was a chilling smile. "If only we knew a man with such a crew."

Richard shrugged. "He might be a valuable man to know. He would become quite wealthy, but more importantly, he would be the man who sacked the Market."

Parris raised one eyebrow.

"The security on the island is geared toward dealing with runaway slaves and irate customers. They won't expect an assault from a couple of dozen armed fighters. It's an opportunity for money from the slave trade, wealth from the buyer's agents, and a chance for revenge."

"Risky," Parris said. "We don't know how well the place is guarded. I was half-dead when they dragged me through it, but I remember guards."

"'No guts, no glory,'" Richard quoted.

Risky was an understatement, Charlotte reflected. This plan Richard had hatched made a hardened criminal pause, yet he didn't even mention it to her beforehand. Unquestionable obedience was one thing, not being used to her full potential was another. She would have to point this out to him when they were alone.

"What share do you want?" Parris asked.

"None. I want the bookkeeper, and I want him alive."

The crime lord pondered it. She could sense Parris's hesitation. They needed to offer him something to tip the scales in their favor. What could they possibly propose to him? What would a crime lord be interested in? Money, of course, but even if she could get access to her finances, she doubted money alone would make him risk his life and his people.

Her gaze paused on his face. The scar stood out against his skin like a brand. It must've made it difficult to look in the mirror every morning.

"How did you get your scar?" Charlotte asked.

Parris turned to her. "A gift from Voshak. I'd broken out of the cargo hold. The plan was to take a swim, but the plan failed, and Voshak had his boys hold me against the ship's heating unit. Tried to teach me a lesson." He flashed his teeth at her. "I'm a hard learner."

"Would you like me to remove it?" she asked.

Parris raised his eyebrows. "You can do that?"

"Yes." The skin was the easiest of all body tissues to heal.

Parris pondered the idea for a moment. "Thanks, but I think I'll keep it. It's part of me now."

Miko leaned over to him and whispered something, her face urgent.

Jason frowned. "Yes, but you'd have to make it look old."

Miko whispered again.

Parris considered it. "If she heals me and I get all profits from sacking the Market, you have a deal."

"Before she does anything, she needs rest and food," Richard said.

They were talking about her as if she weren't even in the room.

Parris stared at him. "Do I look like a Holiday Inn to you?"

"Eight hours of uninterrupted rest behind a solid door, a

fresh change of clothes, food, and clean water to wash up," Richard said. "Those are our conditions."

Parris sighed. "Fine. But if my face isn't fixed by noon, you'll be resting six feet under for a lot longer than eight hours."

CHARLOTTE followed Richard and a woman armed with a sword up the stairs. They walked into another narrow hallway, and the woman stopped by a door and swung it open. Richard stepped inside, and Charlotte and the dog followed him into a small suite. Perfectly clean, with pale, almost golden wooden paneling on the walls and large windows framed by green curtains, the room could've belonged to any of the nicer hotels. A large bed dominated the floor, its linens and bedspread an inviting light yellow. Two stacks of clothes lay on the bed. To the right, another door opened to a small bathroom.

A single bed in a single room. Jason was assuming they were a couple.

The dog flopped on the rug and sniffed at the floor. Richard shut the door, locked it, and lowered a heavy wooden bar in place, securing the door as if it were an entrance to an old castle.

His skin had turned sallow. Grime stained his face. An abominable stench rose from his clothes. He had to be squeezing the last drops of energy from his exhausted body to remain upright.

"I don't mind waiting for the bathroom," she said.

He bowed his head slightly. "Neither do I."

She crossed her arms.

"You agreed to follow my orders," he said.

"The order of our bathing has nothing to do with our mission."

"Charlotte," he said, his voice tired. "I'm not going to shower before you."

The sound of her name coming from him startled her. Something about the way he said it touched off the same feminine flutter she had felt when he called her beautiful. It was the strangest feeling, a mix of anxiety, surprise, and pleasure, soaked in excitement. But nothing about this made sense. She was covered in blood and dirt. Not only that, he had recently watched her kill people, then go through their pockets. Romance had to be the last thing on his mind and should have been the last on hers.

"Richard," she said, her voice firm. "You smell awful. Please have mercy on my nose."

"You deserve the first turn at the bathroom. Offering to fix his face was a stroke of genius."

"Thank you, but I'm perfectly happy waiting."

Richard stared at her. They were at an impasse.

"While I have your attention," Charlotte said, "I'd appreciate it if in the future when you come up with a plan that makes a hardened criminal pause, you could at least give me the gist of it ahead of time. In broad strokes. While I don't have your expertise in dealing with the criminal underground, I'm a woman of reasonable intelligence, and I react badly when surprised. I understand that you're used to being the lone swordsman, but I promise you that I can be an asset at the planning stage and can assist you better if I know where you're going. Use me as your, what's the Broken expression? Sounding door?"

"Sounding board," he said, his voice dry.

"Exactly."

Richard's face had a most curious expression. Two parts exasperation, one part shock, and three parts politeness so ingrained in him that it was keeping the rest of his emotions in check. "Will there be anything else, my lady?"

"Yes. It would bring me great pleasure if, when both of us are present during a conversation, you could occasionally acknowledge my presence and allow me to speak for myself instead of referring to me in the third person."

Richard locked his jaw. She waited patiently to see if he would explode.

"The next time we have to talk to a violent psychopath, I'll strive to keep that in mind," he said.

The next time you don't, I won't stand there quietly.
"Thank you for indulging me."

"My pleasure."

He bowed his head, managing to put enough exasperation into that bow to fuel a small ship for a voyage across
the ocean. Very well. She curtsied. The effort of bending
her legs nearly took her off her feet.

They straightened.

"We still have the question of the bathroom," she said.

He reached into his pocket and pulled out a silver doubloon. "Heads or tails."

"Heads." She took the coin from his palm. "And I will
do the tossing."

"You don't trust me."

"You told me not to trust anyone. Besides, I'm not the
one with a brother who magically wins bets."

She flipped the coin and slapped it onto the back of her
wrist.

"Tails." Richard smiled. "I win. The bathroom is all
yours, my lady."

Accusing him of cheating wasn't just illogical, it was
silly. Charlotte took her stack of clothes and walked into the
bathroom. The dog followed her.

"No," she said firmly, and shut the door. A disappointed
whine answered her.

Inside an Adrianglian-style drencher shower waited for
her: a wide showerhead positioned directly above, over her
head. Charlotte turned the handle and warm water cascaded
down in a welcome waterfall. Charlotte stripped and stepped
under the flow.

The water splashed over her in a cleansing stream. Her
legs buckled a little. Her muscles ached all over, and the
shower did nothing to wash the encroaching drowsiness
from her. Charlotte washed her hair with detached thor-
oughness. It felt like someone else was driving her body. If
she didn't hurry, she would collapse before she reached the
bed. She washed all the dirt off, wrapped a towel over her

hair, dried herself with the larger towel, and picked up the
first garment from the stack of clothes.

RICHARD heard a muffled word from the bathroom. His
body was giving out from fatigue, and the bathroom door
was relatively thick, but he was absolutely sure that Charlotte de Ney had just called someone a prick.

Considering her latest stand, he shouldn't really be surprised. Their partnership was less than a day old, and he
had already received a dressing-down. *Your own damn fault,*
he congratulated himself. *You took her with you.*

The dog rose from his spot by the bathroom door, trotted
over, and flopped by him with all the grace of a sack of
potatoes. Big shaggy paws rose in the air, and he was presented with a canine chest.

"Really?"

The dog looked at him. Fine. Richard reached over and
rubbed the fur. He couldn't possibly smell any worse. The
wolfripper dogs weren't trained to kill humans, only to find
them and keep them put. The slavers didn't wish to unduly
damage their merchandise. Aside from their size and their
teeth, the wolfrippers were just dogs, and this shaggy idiot
seemed starved for affection.

Richard scratched the dog's belly. He wasn't sure why he
hadn't thought to tell her what he was planning. It was simply force of habit. He had been on his own for too long.
Being chewed out for it, like he was a child who had committed a lapse in manners, however, wasn't in his plans. She
would have to get over it. Nor would he be obeying her
orders. In fact, he would address it the moment she came
out of the bathroom, to prevent future misunderstandings.

The door opened slowly.

"It appears our host has a sense of humor," Charlotte
said, and stepped out.

Her hair fell down over her back in a combed wet wave.
She wore a flowing robe of pale pink that ended a few inches

above her knees. The robe was completely, decadently sheer. He could see every curve of her body, from the elegant neck to the swell of her breasts, barely obscured by the folds of the fabric, to the supple bend of her waist and widening of her hips . . .

He was staring. All of his years as an adult male had vanished, wiped away as if they never existed, and he was a teenage boy again, awkward and dumbstruck. He gaped at her, unable to glance away, unable to make a sound, unable to do anything but stare.

He wanted her. She was an erotic dream.

This wasn't real, he decided. He was still in a cage or lying by the road dying, and his feverish brain had conjured up a beautiful fantasy to taunt him one last time before he passed on into the afterlife.

A pale pink blush spread over Charlotte's cheeks.

Look away, you fool.

Richard closed his mouth and forced himself to turn to the bed and pick up his own stack of clothes. "It appears you're right. Jason does have a sense of humor. Let's hope I don't come out in a leather loincloth."

He headed to the bathroom, forcing himself to look anywhere but at Charlotte as she crossed the room and climbed under the covers.

In the shower, he leaned against the wall, bracing himself with both arms, and let the water splash onto the back of his head and over his back, massaging his tired muscles. Richard closed his eyes and saw Charlotte in his mind. *Get a grip. You're the man she sprung from a cage, covered in filth, piss, and blood.* She took pity on him and healed him. She had no idea that it was more kindness than he had seen from a woman in years. For her it was merely common charity.

She was a beautiful, refined woman. A man would have to be dead not to respond to her. He had come so close to death, and now his body was rejoicing in the fact he'd survived. Acting on it was out of the question. She trusted him, and he wouldn't break that trust. Even if she opened that door, which she would not, Charlotte had just suffered an emotional catastrophe. Only a lowlife would take advantage of that, and he wouldn't be the mistake she regretted first thing in the morning.

Richard shut his mind off, soaped up the sponge, and scrubbed himself until he could detect no odors other then the crisp, spicy scent of soap. The shower was almost more effort than he could take. As he stood under the water, he briefly considered simply sitting down on the floor and not getting up. But he was pretty sure she would come looking for him, and being found naked slumped on the shower floor would be truly disastrous.

Jason had left that outfit on purpose. The man was smart and perceptive. He would've read their body language, deduced that they were traveling together but weren't intimate, and taken this opportunity to taunt him. If Richard was keeping score, this one would go to Jason Parris, but he wasn't interested in side battles.

His clothes turned out to be plain Weird attire: simple dark gray underwear, a tunic, and brown cotton pants. It would do until he could acquire new ones. He exited the bathroom. Charlotte lay on her side, hidden under a sheet. Her eyes were half-closed, and he wasn't sure if she was asleep or watching him through the curtain of her soft eyelashes.

Richard took his sword from where he'd left it, by the door, and sank down against the door, crossing his legs, his blade resting against his shoulder. Generations of his ancestors had slept just like this, and some of them had woken up with their blades in their attackers. If Jason had a moment of insanity and decided to disrupt their rest, he would join them.

"Richard," Charlotte said.

"Yes?"

"Are you worried we may not survive the night?"

There was no point in lying. "I prefer to be cautious."

"Would you like a blanket and a pillow?"

He would've liked to join her in bed. *And what would*

you do if you did? You're so tired, you can't see straight.
"No, thank you. I'm used to sleeping like this. It gives me comfort."

She stirred on the bed. "Thank you."

"For what?"

"For guarding the door, and for taking me with you."

There were many questions he wanted to ask her. He wanted to know where she was from, why she had run away to the Edge, and how her ex-husband had hurt her, but the fatigue smothered him. Richard closed his eyes and surrendered to sleep.

FIVE

WHEN Charlotte awoke, sunlight was spilling through the windows into the room, the delicate and pale radiance of the late morning coloring the light yellow bedding a faint peach.

Richard stood by the door, with his bare back to her. He'd changed into dark trousers and was holding a white shirt. Muscle corded his back, hard and powerful, bulging under bronzed skin, as if he had absorbed the sun's warmth and now was suffused with it. He was built like a predator, lean, strong, fast, and perfectly balanced. Frightening in his potential for violence yet irresistibly compelling. She wanted to run her hand up his back, tracing the contours of the muscle underneath. It was a completely sensual desire, a physical need free of rational thought. He was so different from her, so very masculine, and she wanted to reach for him.

Richard raised his arms, pulling on the shirt. The muscles flexed under his skin, bulging on his broad shoulders. She watched, mesmerized. Last night, when she had crawled into a strange bed, feeling half-dead, it occurred to her that she was in the house of a criminal, deep in the worst part of the city. If Jason Parris wanted to murder them, he could at any time and with complete impunity. Nobody even knew where they were. Her fear had spiraled, threatening to explode into a panic attack. Then Richard had sat down with his back against the door last night, and her anxiety had faded. Somehow she was completely sure that nothing would make it past him to harm her. It was selfish, but she closed her eyes knowing he wouldn't move till morning, and she slept well.

No woman could mistake the way he had looked at her last night when she had stepped out of the shower. She had looked at him too, through the curtain of her eyelashes, when he emerged, his skin clean, his hair damp. She looked at him even though she knew she shouldn't have. He embodied strength, and she felt weak, despite knowing otherwise. Further, she had survived terrible things, and she was tempted to remind herself that she still lived in the most primal of ways. She wouldn't do it to him, however. First, it was simply not done, not in this fashion and not after a mere two days of knowing each other. Second, Richard made it plain that his effectiveness depended on having no attachments. He would resent her.

Neither of them were in their right mind. People who had nothing to lose often did crazy things, and she had to listen to the voice of reason.

He turned.

She'd remembered that he was handsome, but his face caught her by surprise. His intelligent, intense eyes took her measure, and she had to fight not to stammer.

"Good morning," Richard said.

She called upon her years of training, and when she spoke, her voice was completely even. "Good morning."

"Jason's people brought us new clothes," he said, pointing to a stack of clothing in the chair. "They're old and probably not quite as nice as what you're used to, but we mustn't attract attention. In the Cauldron, new clothes are likely to get us killed, and we probably want to avoid that, if at all possible."

He should've slept a lot longer, considering his injury. "How long have you been up?"

"Not that long."

"Come here, please."

He approached the bed. Charlotte sat up, holding the sheet over her chest, raised her hand and touched his neck with her fingers. His skin felt hot under her fingertips. An excited flutter dashed through her. She smelled the light scent of soap emanating from his hair and skin, a hint of spice and citrus.

Really now. She was thirty-two years old. She could hold her libido in check. Charlotte focused. Her magic slipped out of her fingers and sank into his skin. The wound had almost completely healed. His temperature was normal. Mild dehydration, slightly elevated pulse. In fact, it rose in the brief seconds she touched him. Of course, she told herself. He'd seen her butcher sixteen people. Naturally, he would be alarmed when she touched him. Charlotte dropped her hand.

"Clean bill of health," she said.

"Glad to hear it."

He was looking at her. The daylight streaming through the gap in the curtains painted a light gold stripe across his face, tinting his skin gold and bringing a rich russet tint in his irises. He was handsome, his body was strong and fit, and the danger he radiated just enhanced his pull. When Charlotte looked at him, really looked at him as she did now, he was striking.

And she had no business looking at him. Both of them were on a mission, and it left no room for softness or attraction.

"We never talked about the plan," she said.

"It's simple," he said. "We impersonate slavers and their catch, board the ship, and ride it to the Market. Once we near the port, you may have to eliminate the crew. It will have to be done quickly and silently, so as not to alarm those on land."

"Can Jason's people operate the ship?" she asked.

"He assures me that they can. Whatever his other faults are, Jason is efficient and competent. This is a port city, and there are many former sailors in his crew. We'll dock and let Jason and his cutthroats do what they do best. Meanwhile, you and I will go and find the bookkeeper. We must eliminate the people at the top of the slaver's food chain, and for that we will need the bookkeeper alive. Once we know the identity of his superiors, we'll go from there."

She would have to kill again. She knew what she had signed up for when she demanded to come with him. Now wasn't the time to get squeamish. "It's a sound plan," she said. "How large a crew do you expect me to kill?"

"The ship they will be using is likely fast, maneuverable, and unremarkable. I'm betting on a brigantine or albatross, which means fifteen to twenty people at most. Will it be an issue?"

That was a complicated question. "No. No issue," she told him.

Richard stood up. "I'll wait outside the door for you."

He took his sword and stepped out.

In that moment, when she found that red spark inside, she had known exactly what the consequences would be. Her life as a healer was over. Her life as an abomination would be brutal and devoid of sympathy or warmth, but probably short. It would be worth it, she told herself. If no other child ever had to cry the way Tulip had because the slavers had taken someone from her, it would be worth it.

THE corpse lay on a table, a large male about ten years older than Jason but with a similar skin tone. The flesh on the corpse's cheek bore the same pattern as the scar on Jason's face.

The corpse looked fresh. Was it a rival, a long-standing enemy? Or more likely, some man off the street who happened to resemble Jason Parris. Charlotte exhaled quietly. She had walked into this world on her own. She would deal with it.

Richard leaned against the wall, his arms crossed. The crime lord sat next to the corpse in a chair. Miko leaned against the wall as well, as if mirroring Richard, one leg bent, her foot propping her up. She was a strange girl, quiet, her narrow face calm, but there was this odd hint of unpredictability about her, as if she was just waiting for the right moment to stab someone.

The disfigurement on the corpse's face looked red and fresh. The marks on Jason's face were more than a year old.

"How will you age the burn?" Charlotte asked.

"We have a necromancer," Jason said. "She will age it. Is there anything you need to heal me?"

She shook her head.

The aftereffects of fatigue were still there, pooling in her bones, but she'd recovered much faster than she had expected. If she had healed sixteen people yesterday, she would be in bed, unable to move. But now, she felt . . . refreshed. Relieved, as if some heavy physical burden had been lifted off her shoulders. The irony.

Healing is a noble sacrifice, Lady Augustine's voice instructed from her memories. *Harming is a selfish perversion.*

The burden wasn't truly gone, Charlotte reflected. She had simply traded the pressure created by the imbalance in her magic for the weight of murder on her mind.

"So this healing, is it a special talent?" Jason asked.

"Yes."

"Some magic can be taught."

Charlotte nodded. "Yes. Flashing can be taught and improved through practice, even for someone from the Broken, assuming they have any magic at all. Healing can be made more efficient, but you must be born with the talent."

Jason was looking at Richard. "Your sword thing is a flash, isn't it?"

Richard nodded.

Jason looked at her. "I've seen a lot of strange magic shit here but never what he does. I asked him to teach me, but he won't."

"You do enough harm as it is," Richard said.

Jason grinned. "Aww, you hurt me, old man."

Richard raised his eyes to the heavens. "I've unleashed you on this poor unsuspecting city. I simply feel sorry for

the cutthroats of Kelena. If I teach you to flash, there will
be none of them left."

"I don't need flash for that." Jason touched his scar. "Let's
get on with it."

Charlotte took a chair and set it in the beam of light spilling through the high window near the ceiling. "Sit, please."

He sat down. Charlotte stepped closer, turning his face
with her fingertips to better view the scar in the light. A
second-degree burn, extending into the reticular dermis, the
deep layer of skin that cushioned the body against stress.
She'd healed worse.

She raised her hand and let the golden sparks of her magic
sink into his skin. He held completely still, his unnerving
gray eyes steady.

The damage was extensive. She sank into the task of
repairing the tissue destruction. When a body sustained an
injury, specialized cells, which the Broken doctors called
"fibroblasts" and the College healers called "suture cells,"
sprang to the rescue. They moved into the wound and began
secreting collagen, traveling within the clot until finally they
anchored and closed the gash. The moment this anchoring
took place was determined by many factors, and when the
process went on too long, it led to the buildup of fibrous tissue and sometimes, if the scars formed on organs, fibrosis,
which could be fatal.

The scar itself was comprised of the same collagen fibers
as the regular skin, but instead of crisscrossing, these fibers
aligned in the same direction. She had to soften the stiff
tissue of the scar and then painstakingly shift the collagen
fibers within the skin to approximate its normal basket-
weave pattern. It was slow, methodical work. Facial scars
required precision—the symmetry of the face was at stake.
The room, Richard, Jason, all of them faded. Only the
injured tissue remained, and she focused on realigning it.

As if through a wall, she heard muffled voices.

"You're getting your scar healed, and you've procured a
body double," Richard said. "Why the sudden need to appear
dead?"

"The Mirror is taking an interest in me," her patient answered.

"What did you do?"

"Many things, none of them good, but none of them concern the spooks either. They're watching me, and I don't like it."

"I warned you, Jason," Richard said.

"Don't lecture me, old man."

"You're expanding too fast and killing too many. Violence attracts attention."

Jason sighed. "In case you failed to notice, I've been doing pretty well."

"The Five Gangs are frothing at the mouth trying to put you on the bottom of the ocean, Rook has placed a bounty on your head, and now the Mirror's agents are watching your house. Your definition of 'well' is troubling at best." He suddenly smiled and affected a slight accent. "'I do not think that word means what you think it means.'"

He was obviously quoting something he and Jason seemed to know that she did not.

Jason grinned. "Ha, she ain't a princess, and you wish you were that good a swordsman." He turned to Charlotte. "How do you stand him?"

"He sleeps by the door with his sword to keep me safe," she told him. "Don't move."

Finally satisfied, she withdrew her magic and took a step back.

He looked good. It was one of her finer restorations. Relief washed over Charlotte. She could still heal. She had lost none of her skill or power. She hadn't realized until now that she'd been afraid taking lives might come at the cost of the primary purpose of her magic. She knew it didn't preclude her from healing; she just wasn't sure if her control or precision had been compromised.

The post-healing fatigue wrapped around her, making her dizzy. Jason touched his face. The scar had aged him, but now she could see his face more clearly, and Charlotte realized he was still a young man.

Miko stepped up and offered him a mirror. Jason looked at himself. His eyes widened.

"Magic hands," he said. "That's a very valuable talent. Almost makes a man regret that he doesn't own it."

"Touch her and lose your fingers," Richard said, his voice casual.

Jason looked at her. "Come work for me. I'll take better care of you."

"No."

"See, the problem with Richard is, he doesn't know how to treat a woman. You have to take care of women properly. A woman is like a horse."

Dawn Mother, not one of those. "How so?"

"When you want to tame a horse, you offer her an apple. She has to get used to your scent and your delicious apples before she'll let you put the bridle on her. Soon, if you ignore her, she'll follow you waiting for a handout. If you keep bringing her treats, eventually she'll let you ride her."

Mhm.

Richard was leaning against the table like a dark shadow, his pose relaxed, his lips smiling, but his eyes watched Jason with complete focus. Like a wolf sighting his prey, she realized.

Jason smiled, displaying even white teeth. At her position on the wall, Miko rolled her eyes.

"All I'm saying is I have plenty of apples," the crime lord said. "You should give it some thought. You'd like my apples."

Charlotte leaned closer to him. "Jason, whoever told you this nonsense isn't your friend. Women aren't horses, or dogs, or cats. We're human beings, and the sooner you figure that out, the less likely you will wake up with Miko's knife in your throat."

He stared at her.

"You asked me what I want. I want to crush the slave trade. Having a fling with you doesn't appeal to me. You're handsome, but you're too inexperienced and too arrogant to be good in bed. Having ridden many horses doesn't make you a good rider; it just proves that you can't recognize a good one or don't know how to keep her. You're too young for me, and in ten years, when you improve, I will be too old for you. So let's not speak of this again."

A thin, high-pitched sound came from the wall. Miko was snickering.

Jason turned in his chair and looked at her, outraged.

She giggled some more.

The crime lord blinked and turned back to Charlotte. "Some people would be worried. Words like that can get your throat slit."

"Some people don't realize healing can be done in reverse," she told him. "Why don't you ask Voshak what he thinks about that?"

Richard stalked across the floor and came to stand by her side.

"You're as crazy as he is," Jason growled.

"Now you're getting the idea," Richard said.

"Even if we sack the Market and you get your information, what can you do?" Miko said suddenly. "You're only two. The slavers are hundreds."

Richard grimaced. "I know. It's a shame, really. I would've liked to give them a sporting chance, but sometimes life simply isn't fair."

Charlotte smiled. You had to admire the man.

"Your face is restored to its former beauty." Richard turned to Jason. "Are you going to hold up your end of the bargain?"

Jason rose and pulled the hood of his cloak over his face. "I'm on it, old man. I remember. You said the ship lands at midnight. Where is he planning to dock?"

"Teal Inlet."

"Meet me two miles north of it tonight at ten."

He left the room, Miko in tow.

"What now?" Charlotte asked.

"Now we go to the city," Richard said. "I have contacts here. We'll need them for tonight."

*   *   *

IN the daylight, Kelena didn't look any better, Charlotte reflected, walking with Richard along the canal. It smelled the same, too. At least the dead body was gone, probably swept out to sea by the tide. They had left the dog at Jason's house. She didn't the see the harm in his coming, but Richard pointed out that if he bit someone, they would likely be drowned in the nearest canal. They locked him in a room with a cow femur from Jason's kitchen.

Richard turned into the narrow alley between the houses, barely wide enough to let them move side by side. The alley opened into a small courtyard, formed by the tall walls of surrounding buildings. Another, much wider alley to the right led from the courtyard, and three men blocked it. They didn't look friendly.

Her throat tightened. Her pulse sped up, and an uncomfortable heaviness filled her chest. Charlotte swallowed, but the tightness refused to dissolve. There was going to be a fight.

It's just a physical reaction, she told herself. *It's just fear.* Her anger and outrage had numbed her yesterday, but that armor had melted during the night. She was very much aware she was alive. She was afraid.

Charlotte squared her shoulders. She had to handle it.

The front man, hard, large, bald, with swirls of dark tattoos running over his pale scalp, grinned. His lips stretched unnaturally far, showing a mouthful of two-inch-long fangs. Spiked strips of metal covered his knuckles.

His magic washed over her, grating against her skin like a handful of sharp sand. A familiar revulsion drowned Charlotte. Her fear spiked in response. The man had been modified with illegal magic, the kind the Dukedom of Louisiana used for the Hand, its covert agents. She'd dealt with it before. A modification made its recipients stronger, faster, and more deadly. It also robbed them of their humanity and was nearly always impossible to reverse.

Charlotte focused on the two friends of the alligator-mouth. The one to the left was tall, armed with a short mace tipped with a fist-sized chunk of metal. The one to the right, leaner and probably faster, carried two knives. The red rash on the knife fighter's neck indicated a case of advanced luries, which is what happened when one had sex with unhealthy partners without protective measures.

Of the three, the modified alligator-mouth man posed the biggest threat. Charlotte felt the magic stir inside her. It yawned, stretched, like a cat rising from a nap, and licked its teeth. Infection wouldn't be fast enough. She'd have to tear into them and try to cause organ failure.

"The man with the strange teeth is enhanced with illegal magic," she murmured for Richard's benefit. "The one with knives has a swollen groin."

He blinked. "Thank you. I'll take it under advisement."

She'd never done a direct unhealing before. Infection, yes, but nothing that caused internal bleeding with the exception of her slip with Elvei. A coppery taste appeared on her tongue. Adrenaline.

The alligator-mouth realized that his toothy display wasn't having the desired effect. "You're lost," he called, his voice deep.

Richard kept walking. She followed him, the dark currents spinning inside her.

"Don't worry, we'll show you and your bitch the right direction."

"So kind of you," Richard said, and then he *moved*.

One moment he was next to her, the next he had smashed his hand into the alligator-mouth's throat. The man jerked back, and Richard twisted him over his arm, driving the full weight of his opponent to the ground. Before the leader landed, Richard hammered a kick to the macer's knee. The cartilage crunched, the leg bent the wrong way, and the man crumpled. Richard caught the mace, pulled it from the falling man's hand, and pivoted to the knife fighter. The handle of the mace danced in his hand, sinking solid blows—head, solar plexus, groin—and the knife fighter dropped to the ground, curling into a ball.

Alligator-mouth surged to his feet and lunged at Richard, hands out, jaw gaping. Richard knocked his right arm aside, locked his hand on the man's wrist, jerking it down, smashed the mace handle against the nerve cluster at the base of the man's exposed neck, and hit him again just below the jaw.

The big man staggered, as if drunk, waved his arms, fighting desperately to remain upright, then half sat, half fell on the ground, his eyes dazed.

Charlotte closed her mouth.

It happened so fast, she didn't even help. She had simply stood there. The healer in her cataloged the injuries: one traumatized throat, one tear to the posterior cruciate ligament of the knee—a partial at the very least. A full tear was more likely with impaction of the anterior aspect of the femoral condyle against the anterior aspect of the tibial plateau. Richard had kicked the attacker so hard he knocked the bones of the leg together, bruising the femur and tibia. A full tear would mean a healer like her or a ligament graft, because once that ligament ripped completely, no surgeon could sew it back together. Two concussions—one mild, one severe—one sprained neck, one sprained arm, multiple bruises, and three dignities irreparably damaged. All in less than five seconds. And he hadn't even unsheathed his sword.

Richard approached her and held out his hand. Shell-shocked, she rested her fingers on his, and he helped her step over the bodies into the narrow alley leading from the courtyard.

Talk, she told herself. Talking makes you appear confident. She couldn't afford to let him know that he'd shocked her. She had to appear cool and collected because that's what he needed in a partner. "I thought Jason would better control his territory," she said. Her voice sounded normal. She'd expected it to shake.

"They were probably his men," Richard said.

"What do you mean?"

"You humiliated him," Richard said. "This was the way he showed his displeasure."

"I suppose you'll now point out that this is the result of me speaking for myself." Just try it . . .

"That would be satisfying for me, but not entirely accurate. I've visited the city on four occasions since he took control of the Cauldron, and he prepared a lovely surprise for me every time. The hardest was an Erkinian woman. We fought for three full minutes, and I thought she'd kill me."

They seemed to have a love-hate relationship. Jason admired Richard—she'd read that much in his face and the way he looked at him—and wanted his approval, while at the same time resenting Richard for it. "Jason has father-figure issues, doesn't he?" she asked.

"Yes." Richard sighed.

"In that case, it's good that you're a human Cuisinart," she said.

"I'm sorry?"

"A Cuisinart. It's an appliance from the Broken. You put vegetables into it, push a button, and it chops them into tiny pieces."

Richard frowned. "Why would you need an appliance to chop vegetables? Wouldn't it be easier to chop them with a knife?"

"It's meant to save time," she explained.

"Does it?"

"Well, cleaning it usually eats up most of the time you save on chopping."

"So you're telling me that I'm useless."

"It's a neat gadget!"

"And I'm hard to clean, apparently."

She checked his face. Tiny sparks danced in his eyes. He was pulling her leg. Well. If that's how it is . . . "Considering last night's argument, I think that you're remarkably difficult to clean."

"There probably is a retort to this that's not off-color," he said. "But I can't think of one."

They reached the middle of the alley. A street person sat on the filthy pavement, a sad, hunched-over figure swaddled in rags. His hair hung over his face in an oily gray tangle. A bitter stench of rotting fish rose from his clothes. He looked old and tired, his face a mess of grime. The dirt was caked so thick she could barely see his eyes, his pupils milky white. He was suffering from cataracts.

The beggar raised his cup and shook it at Richard.

Richard glanced at the beggar. His expression didn't change, but his eyes turned darker. Richard bent down and dropped a coin into the cup. "Third tooth," he said, his voice barely above a whisper. "Two hours. Bring your brother."

The beggar pulled back his cup, his head drooping lower.

Richard straightened and took her firmly by the elbow. His touch was light, but Charlotte realized she wouldn't be able to get away. Richard drew her away from the beggar, down the alley.

"Don't look back," he murmured. "That was George."

The urge to turn around was overwhelming. "George Drayton? Éléonore's George?"

He nodded.

Her heart beat faster. The boys would have to be told what happened to Éléonore. She was their grandmother. They deserved to know. Her throat closed up. What would she say? There was no way to soften the blow. It would be devastating. She was a grown woman, and seeing Éléonore's body burning had torn a hole in her life that filled with grief, guilt, and anger. They were children who had known Éléonore all of their lives. She was the safe haven of their childhood, the one person besides their sister who loved them no matter what and would never abandon them. She made their world safer, and now that illusion of safety would be ripped away. Charlotte swallowed. She had to find the right words somehow.

It occurred to her that George sat in filth on a street. "Why is George dressed as a beggar? I thought the Camarine family had adopted the boys?"

"He and his brother work for the Mirror."

They're spies? Wait a minute. "Richard, George's only sixteen. Jack should be fourteen."

He took a second to glance at her. "Yes?"

"Aren't they too young? They're barely in their teens."

"Some children are less childlike than we like to pretend," he said. "At George's age, I had killed two people and watched my father's head explode as he was shot dead in a market. What were you doing at sixteen, Charlotte?"

The long field filled with moaning people surfaced from her memory. The coppery scent of blood, mixed with the toxic stench of warped magic, and the smell of smoke rising from the town a few fields away.

"At sixteen I was healing the victims of the Green Valley Massacre."

"And George is being inconspicuous to—"

A boy shot into the alley ahead, slid on garbage, caught himself, and dashed toward them. Reddish brown hair, cropped short, handsome face, dark eyes, completely wild with excitement. She'd seen this boy before in a photograph . . . Jack!

"Run!" Jack yelled. "Run! Go, George!"

Behind him a mob of enraged people spilled into the alley, brandishing knives and clubs.

The beggar-George jumped to his feet. "What did you do?"

"There he is!" the man at the head of the mob roared. A rock whistled past their heads, ricocheting from the side of the building.

"Run!" Jack yelled.

Blue lightning shot out of the crowd—someone had flashed. *Oh no.*

Jack jumped six feet in the air, avoiding the glowing ribbon of magic by a hair, bounced off the wall, and sprinted straight at them.

"Hi, Richard, hi, pretty lady!" Jack dashed past them.

Richard grabbed her hand. 'We have to go!"

They broke into run and chased after Jack, running fast on the cobbled stones. George swore and tossed something over their heads at the crowd. A dry pop burst behind them.

Charlotte glanced over her shoulder. A plume of dense white smoke filled the alley. People coughed.

The blue-glowing whip of someone's flash struck out of the smoke, licking the cobbles. Someone in this mob was throwing magic around blind. This city was insane.

They cleared the courtyard and the narrow alley, burst out onto the boardwalk, and pounded down the street. The entrance to Jason's hideout flew by. The air grew hot in Charlotte's lungs.

A small wooden dock rose on their left. "Go right!" Richard yelled, too loud, and leaped off the boardwalk into the dark water, pulling her in with him. The tepid water swallowed her. Charlotte gulped a mouthful of salty liquid and nearly choked. Gods alone knew what sort of contamination was in that water.

Charlotte kicked her feet and surfaced, spitting the water out. Richard pulled her under the dock, just as two other bodies hit the water a foot away. A moment, and George and Jack broke the surface next to them. The four of them huddled under the dock, their backs against the canal wall, among dirty foam and garbage.

The mob spilled onto the boardwalk. Charlotte held her breath.

"They went right!" someone yelled. "To the Reed Alley!"

Boots pounded above them, shaking drops of water from the dock's boards onto them.

The filthy wet creature that was George raised his hand, gave his brother a death stare, and drew his thumb across his neck. Jack grinned.

A dead fish floated up from the depths right next to Charlotte. Ew. She pushed it gently aside with her fingers.

The last of the stragglers ran past, the noise of the mob retreating. Richard waded to the left, walking along the canal wall at a brisk pace. She waited to make sure the kids followed and went after him.

Fifteen minutes and two canals later, they climbed out onto the boardwalk. Jack shook himself. Filthy water ran from George's rags in dirty streams. His hair dripped. He stared at his brother, his face grim. If stares had temperature, Jack would've turned into a burned-out match.

Charlotte gulped a breath, hoping for some fresh air and finding none. Her own soaked clothes smelled like rancid seaweed. Water filled her shoes, and something slimy had wedged itself under the toes of her left foot.

Richard ducked into another alley, and she followed, limping and making squishy noises on the cobbles. The boys brought up the rear.

Nobody said anything for the next ten minutes until Richard stopped before a warehouse. The small wooden door swung open. A woman stepped out in front of them, carrying a metal bucket filled with bloody water. She hurled the contents into the canal.

Great. Fantastic. Once they were somewhere safe, she would sit everyone down and check them for infection.

Richard held the door open, his eyes scanning the board-walk.

Charlotte ducked inside and stepped into a large gymnasium. Men and women, stripped down and sweaty, punched and kicked heavy sandbags. A man and a woman, both muscled with crisp definition, sparred on the reed mats; another pair of fighters squared off, their hands raised, in the roped-off ring raised on a wooden platform. A din hung above the muscular bodies: the rapid staccato of smaller bags being hit, the thuds of kicks hammering at the heavier bags, guttural cries, and rhythmic breathing.

Charlotte took a step forward. Everything stopped. The gymnasium went completely silent. As one, the fighters looked at her. None of the faces were friendly.

Not good. She straightened her shoulders, raising her head. Behind her, Jack took a deep breath.

Richard stepped through the doorway and strode ahead of her, oblivious to the hostility in the room.

A middle-aged, overweight man stepped away from the ring and walked toward Richard, his steps unhurried. A scar cut across his tan face, just a hair shy of his left eye. Half of his right earlobe was gone, the edge of the old wound ragged and uneven. Bitten off, Charlotte realized.

If there was a problem, she'd push the teens outside and block the door. At least she'd buy them a few minutes.

Richard and the overweight man met in the middle of the floor. The man's eyes were grim.

Here we go.

The overweight man hugged Richard, turned, and went back to the ring. The punches and grunts resumed. Richard nodded at them. "Back room."

As soon as they were alone, she would punch him, Charlotte promised herself. No, no she wouldn't, because resorting to physical violence wasn't proper. Then again, it might be considered self-defense. If she died as a result of this journey, it wouldn't be because of slavers. It would be because Richard's inability to communicate would give her a heart attack.

RICHARD closed the door of Barlo's back room and glanced about: a long table, two benches, a sink with a freezing unit next to it, and a scale . . . empty. Barlo had used this chamber as one of the two rooms where fighters warmed up before bouts.

His heartbeat slowed. So much of his life in these past months had been spent waiting, calculating, watching. Moments like this, born from excitement and danger, when he ran along the steel edge of his sword, matching his wits against opponents, were when he felt truly alive. His heart pumped, the world seemed brighter, the experiences sharper, and he loved every bit of it.

"Richard!"

He turned.

Charlotte faced him. Her wet tunic molded to her figure, and her hair, which she'd put up into a neat knot, had come undone and hung over her face. That air of detachment and civility had been washed away, as if someone had taken an elegant cat, groomed to within an inch of its life, and dumped a bucket of water on it. Her expression had the same shock, outrage, and promise of violence.

If he laughed, she'd probably kill him. Quite literally.

Charlotte opened her mouth, clamped it shut, opened it again . . .

He strained to keep his face solemn. "My lady?"

"Words."

She seemed on the verge of breaking down or screaming. It was best to tread carefully. "Words are good," he agreed.

She raised her hands. "I want to punch you."

Richard almost doubled over. He'd driven the quintessential aristocrat to crude violence. It had to be about the canal. Oh, the indignity. "I know the water isn't the cleanest, but we had no alternative." He let the mask drop a little and smiled. "I promise you, it will be okay. Before you know it, we'll be warm and dry."

"I don't care about the bloody canal! Simple words, Richard! Like 'We're safe' or 'They won't harm us!' Or 'He's an old friend.'" She made a short cutting motion with her hands. "Something! I thought we were about to get pummeled."

Pummeled here? At Barlo's? Did she think he would bring her to somewhere where she would be unsafe? "Of course you were safe. I took you in here."

"You also took me to Jason's, where you then slept holding your sword."

Oh, really now. He took a step toward her. "I assure you, my lady, that you were perfectly safe. If anyone put a hand on you, they'd lose it, and everyone inside that place knew it."

Charlotte clenched her hands. "Aargh!"

"I'm just trying to clarify." He knew he should've let it go, but the idea that he would stupidly put her in danger irritated him beyond belief. "So you want me to tell you if we're in danger or if we're safe. You do realize that there may not be an opportunity to warn you every single time?"

Charlotte dropped onto the bench. "I would settle for some of the time at this point."

Richard couldn't stop himself. "As shocking as it seems,

occasionally you may have to rely on your own judgment. For example, if we're running from a mob, we're probably not safe."

Charlotte's gaze was sharper than a knife. "One more word of mocking, and I'll infect you with papillomavirus."

She had graduated to actual threats. What was it with this woman? "Pray tell, what would that be?"

"Warts," George said.

Laughing was out of the question, he reminded himself. "My apologies. Please allow me to remedy the situation by using words: we're safe here. Barlo's an old friend. His fighters know me. We can speak openly here."

She hung her head.

George yanked the sodden mass of hair off his hand and hurled it across the room at his brother. Jack dodged, and the wig splattered against the wall.

"You moron!"

"Me?" Jack blinked, an expression of angelic innocence on his face.

"You!" A white glow sheathed George's eyes. "Two weeks! I spent two weeks watching Parris, and you screwed it up for me. All you had to do was stay out of the way and watch for his people coming out. What the hell did you do?"

Jack shrugged. "I stole a fish."

Richard hid a laugh. If he had a doubloon for each time he and Kaldar had had this precise conversation . . .

George's blue eyes went wide. "Why?"

"I was hungry. And bored. But mostly hungry." Jack spread his arms. "Look, I took one small fish, then the guy started screaming, so I slapped him with it. It wasn't my fault he tripped and fell into a stall of fruit. So I laughed, and they all started chasing me."

The rage written on George's face imploded into icy determination. His voice was suddenly calm. "And so you had this pissed-off mob chasing you. Why did you lead them my way?"

Jack widened his eyes in mocking sincerity. "Because you needed a bath."

George pulled his rags over his head and dumped them

on the floor. He wore a gray-and-black tunic and pants. Good choice, Richard decided. The clothes hugged his body, while allowing ample freedom of movement. In the few years he had known him, the boy had filled out. George would never be a large man, but he had that devastating combination of lean muscle, quickness, and discipline that made one a lethal swordsman.

"Two weeks in that alley. Rain, heat, people kicking me as they passed by. And you decided I needed a bath."

"Water is good for you. Really. You were filthy."

"Mhm," George said.

"Do you have any idea how badly you smelled?" Jack wrinkled his nose.

"I was supposed to smell. I was pretending to be a beggar. You blew my cover."

"Your cover was already blown," Richard said. "Parris knows the Mirror has been watching him."

"See?" Jack said.

"That's beside the point. You ruined two weeks of work because you were bored. Now I'll be pulled off this assignment, and someone else will have to take my place."

Jack shrugged, slightly less sure of himself. "Good. It's summer. All you do is work. Maybe we can finally have some fun."

"I'm going to kill you," George said calmly.

Another familiar emotion. This had to run its course, or it would fester.

"Boys," Charlotte began. "I really don't think—"

A glowing yellow sheen rolled over Jack's irises. He was two years younger but already the same height as George and wider in the shoulder, with the beginnings of a powerful musculature. Benefits of his changeling blood. Of course, it came with many drawbacks.

Jack motioned at George. "Bring it."

George lunged forward, swinging his arm. Jack moved to block. Midway through the punch, George twisted, picking up speed, jumped, and kicked his brother in the chest. Jack flew out the door and into the gym.

Nicely done!

Charlotte gasped.

George strode to the door with a determined look on his face.

"George!" Charlotte called.

He turned on his toes, produced an elegant bow, said, "Excuse me, my lady. This won't take long," and walked out.

Charlotte looked at Richard. "Why are you just standing there?"

"They're young men. It's quite normal," he told her, and held the door open for her. "It's better they resolve it now and be done with it."

She sighed, stood up, and went out into the gym.

The two boys danced across the floor, launching a flurry of kicks and punches, blocking, spinning, jumping. The other activity stopped, and the fighters watched them. Jack clearly had superior strength and speed, but George had studied harder. His movements had the surety born from many hours spent training, while Jack fought on instinct. His instinct was rarely wrong, Richard reflected, as George slid across the floor after taking a powerful kick. But it was no substitute for practice. Still, since William, his cousin's changeling husband, had taken over Jack's hand-to-hand education, the boy showed a marked improvement.

George rolled to his feet, lunged, getting inside his brother's guard, and locked his hands on Jack's arm. Northern three-point flip, Richard diagnosed. Jack tried to counter with the Lower Sud drop—William's influence—but the three-point was nearly impossible to stop, and George had gotten a good hold. Trip, turn, flip. Jack flew through the air, and George slammed him onto the ground. Jack's back slapped the floor.

Ugh. Richard grimaced in sympathy. That had to hurt.

George landed on him and locked his arm into a bar. The fighters cheered.

Next to him, Charlotte winced again. Watching it from the healer's point of view was probably more trying. He decided to reassure her. "They're actually quite careful with each other. For example, this takedown was designed to incapacitate the opponent. A quarter turn to the right, and Jack would've landed on his neck."

She gave him an unreadable look.

He felt compelled to explain. "George could've broken Jack's spine . . ."

She raised her hand. "Richard, stop trying to make me feel better. You're making it worse."

"Don't be an idiot," George said, putting pressure on Jack's arm. "You're done."

"I'm just resting," Jack told him through clenched teeth.

"You're done," George said.

They were at an impasse. Jack wouldn't admit defeat, and George, despite all his anger, wouldn't dislocate his brother's arm. He took a step forward to break them up, but Charlotte beat him to it.

She walked across the gym and crouched by the two teens. "That's enough, George." She gently put one hand on his fingers, gripping his brother's arm. "I have something very important to tell both of you, and it won't wait."

"Is it good news?" Jack ground out.

Profound sadness reflected on Charlotte's face. "No. It isn't."

George released Jack's arm. The boys rolled to their feet.

"Come," she said, linking one arm with George, the other with Jack, and led them both back into the room.

SIX

"MY name is Charlotte." Dear Goddess, there were no right words. Charlotte took a deep breath. "Your grandmother might have mentioned me."

"You rent our house," Jack said.

"Yes." She nodded.

George leaned forward. "Something happened to Grandmother." It wasn't a question.

"Yes," she answered anyway. "I'm a healer. Richard was injured and running away from slavers. He'd reached East Laporte and lost consciousness. Someone found him and brought him to me so I could mend his wounds." She swallowed. "Your grandmother and I were very close. She was always kind to me. She was my friend."

The words stuck in her throat. She forced them out, each sound cutting her from the inside. "She was with me when Kenny brought Richard to us. There was also another young woman and her sister with us at the time."

Her chest felt heavy. An ache set in, rolling around her heart like a ball of lead. Both George and Jack were looking at her, and she couldn't look away. Her voice sounded strange to her.

"I healed Richard. He had lost a lot of blood, so I left to buy some. While I was gone . . ."

She couldn't do it. She couldn't bring herself to say the words.

"The slavers burned the house and murdered one of the young women and your grandmother," Richard said. "Éléonore is dead."

She saw the precise moment when the meaning of the words sank into George. He took a small step back. His face jerked, and his shoulders slumped forward, as if he had been stabbed and wanted to curl into a ball to protect the wound.

"No," Jack said. "There are ward stones around the house. There are fucking rocks around the house! Nobody can get in."

George's eyes blazed with white. The glow built, spilling like tears of lightning onto his cheeks. He chanted something savage under his breath. She felt the magic swell around him. The tiny hairs on the back of her neck rose. So much power. So *much* power. It built on itself, like an avalanche.

"Stop!" she called. "George, no . . ."

The magic crested and broke. White light shot out of his eyes and mouth, shining from within him out of his every pore, setting his skin aglow. Éléonore had told her the boy was a necromancer. She'd said nothing about this.

His feet left the ground. He hung suspended a foot in the empty air. His magic smashed into Charlotte like a blast wave. She gasped and saw him through the lens of her own power. He glowed like a radiant beacon of light, his magic focused into a beam, searching the darkness.

His ghostly voice echoed through her mind.

"Mémère. Mémère, it's me. Answer me. Please answer. Please, Mémère."

The desperation in his words flooded her. The tears heated her eyes. He was reaching far, past the edge of the Weird, past the boundary. It was impossible, but he was doing it.

"Please, Mémère. I love you so much. Please answer."

That voice, suffused with so much love and hope, pulled tears out of her. Hot moisture wet her cheeks. Someone put his arms around her, and she realized it was Richard. He steadied her. She knew she had to pull away, but she needed the warmth of his arms, the link to another human being, because she was adrift in the sea of George's anguish, and it was tearing her apart.

"Mémère . . ." George's ghostly voice pleaded.

The darkness didn't answer.

"Please don't leave me.
"Please . . ."

His glow dimmed. The magic let go, and George fell, dropping into a crouch. His legs gave way, and he sat clumsily on the boards.

"She's gone," he said, his voice so young.

She slipped away from Richard, onto the floor, and hugged him. "I'm so sorry. I'm so, so sorry."

Jack's skin tore open. A wild tumble of muscle and skin spilled out, and a huge lynx landed on the floor. The big cat snarled and ran out the door.

Richard jumped to his feet. "I'll watch over him." He took off after the lynx.

George stared at the floor, his gaze dull. No words would fix it. Nothing she said would make any difference, so she sat next to him and held him. It was all she could do.

RICHARD ran out the door. The boardwalk was empty. He'd paused for a precious second to grab a set of spare clothes from Barlo, and now Jack was gone. Changelings like Jack weren't exactly welcome in society. Their minds worked differently from normal people's. They had trouble understanding human relationships and rules of behavior, but they felt every slight deeply, and it often drove them to violence. The Dukedom of Louisiana murdered them at birth, while Adrianglia treated them as its dirty secret, turning them into soldiers in its prisonlike military schools.

Jack hadn't been given up to the realm at birth, like most of his kind. He grew up in a loving family, which made allowances for his nature. Kelena wouldn't be so kind. If he was spotted and identified, someone would try to kill him.

Richard turned, scanning the buildings. The boy was fast, especially on four legs, and wasn't thinking clearly. Lynxes were tree cats; they pounced on their prey from the branches above. He would want to be someplace high, where he could be alone.

The warehouse across the canal was too low. The distant high-rises of the Business District were too far away and too populated. Where could he have gone?

To the right, the tall, pale tower of the nearest Kelena's Tooth scraped the sky. Tall and isolated. A perfect hiding spot.

Richard jogged through the tangled labyrinth of the Cauldron, along the boardwalks to the edge of the water, then continued past it along the docks stretching into the ocean. The day was overcast, and the water mirrored the gray sky.

He had experienced plenty of loss in his life. His mother was the first to go, dead at twenty-eight of an aneurysm. He remembered the way she had looked in the coffin, a pale, bloodless imitation of herself. He'd wondered for an absurd moment if someone had replaced her with a doll. His father was next. Marissa. Then Aunt Murid and Erian . . .

He wished he could've spared George and Jack the same fate. Once again he was watching children suffer and unable to do anything about it.

The last dock ended. In the distance, waves broke against Kelena's Teeth, splashing against the stone bases of the towers. The tide was low, and crests of sand surfaced here and there. Richard took a chance and jumped. The water came to his knees.

He waded through to the nearest stretch of sand, heading toward the closest tower. A trail of paw prints pockmarked the sand. Cat footsteps, no claws. The trail led to the tower.

Kelena's Teeth had keepers, who monitored the weather and activated magical defenses when storms came. They stood watch in shifts inside the towers. Richard broke into a run, moving at full speed, devouring the sand in long strides.

Ahead, a stone block slid aside in the tower wall, about twenty feet above the water. More stones slid from the walls, winding in a spiral around the tower, leading down. A man ran out, his eyes wild, and sprinted down the newly formed stairs.

Richard reached the tower. Finally.

The keeper splashed through the water toward him. "There's a changeling in the tower!"

Richard reached into his pants and pulled out a half doubloon. "There is no changeling."

"I saw him!" The older man waved his arms. "A huge cat as big as a horse!"

A horse was pushing it. A pony at best. Richard took the man's hand, put the coin into it, and looked into his eyes. "There is no changeling," he repeated slowly.

Understanding dawned in the man's eyes. "I didn't see anything."

"That's right. I'll need to borrow your tower for a few minutes, then I'll leave, and it will be safe for you to go in."

Richard started up the stairs.

"If he breaks anything, you'll pay for it!" the keeper yelled. "And don't touch anything either!"

Richard clambered up the stones that formed the stairs and ducked into the entrance. It was amazing how quickly fear subsided when gold became involved.

A spiral staircase wound about the stone inner core of the tower, illuminated by the light from many windows. He climbed the steps, higher and higher, until he saw a gaping door at the end of the stairway.

A raw, pain-filled sound came from upstairs. It wasn't a feline snarl or any other sound one would expect a lynx to make. Halfway between a howl and a cry, gut-wrenching and brutal, it vibrated through the air. If Richard had hackles, they would've risen in response.

Richard sat down. There was no need to go in. The boy required privacy.

Another cry followed, wordless and filled with grief and guilt.

Richard leaned his back against the wall. Jack and he, they were both men, and men had unspoken rules.

Many years had passed since his father died, and for many of these years his aunt Murid had taken care of him and Kaldar. He was almost an adult when she took him in, but he remembered how much it hurt. He felt abandoned, terrified, guilty for not being there, but the only emotion the rules allowed him to display was anger, and so he raged like a lunatic. Aunt Murid handled his pointless fury with the same expertise she'd handled Kaldar's obsessive stealing. Both of them had gone out of their way to do dumb shit just to remind themselves they were alive. But even in their darkest moments, both of them knew they were loved. They had a home. It wasn't the same as the one before, but they were grateful for it.

When he was thirty-two, the Hand had attacked the family. In the final battle with Louisiana's spies, Murid fell. He hadn't seen her die, but Kaldar had. Richard vividly remembered looking at her savaged body. He remembered his chest hurting and the look on Kaldar's face, the glassy-eyed gaze of a man whose every emotion had drowned in profound grief. They didn't talk about it. They stood next to each other at the funeral, stone-faced, because that was the thing to do. After the funeral, they drank together as was proper for a Mire family and went their separate ways within the Mar house.

He'd come up to his room, thinking he would read a book. Instead, he sat in his chair, catatonic, staring into space, until he realized he was crying. Kaldar must've mourned, too. Neither of them would ever admit to his grief. They'd never spoken about it.

The woman who had taken care of them, sheltered them, and guided them, filling the shoes of both parents at once, had died. But he couldn't bring himself to comfort his brother even though he knew both of them desperately needed that comfort.

Now Jack and George had lost a woman who loved them and sheltered them, and they followed the same pattern. Jack's running out was probably for the best. If George wanted to grieve freely, he could, because Charlotte was a woman, and her presence wouldn't be a deterrent. And Jack . . .

Another forlorn howl rolled through the tower.

He would talk to Jack when the boy was done. There were things he had to say, things he wished someone had said to him or Kaldar years ago.

Whatever differences he and Kaldar had, they were brothers, Richard reflected. They had dealt with their guilt and pain in the same way. Kaldar channeled it into an insane obsession with destroying the Hand. Even marriage to the woman he clearly loved beyond all reason did nothing to knock his brother off his path. Richard, on the other hand, had chosen to go after slavers. There probably was a hint of insanity in what he did. No, perhaps not insanity. Fanaticism.

"Fanatic." It was an old word originally meaning "inspired by god," and its first meaning was to describe a person possessed by a god or a demon. It was a very accurate description, he reflected. He was possessed, not by a demon, but by the need to correct a wrong. He was a true believer, his cause was just, and he had given all of himself to it without regret. But at the core, it was about helplessness. When Sophie had stopped showering, then stopped talking, then ran away when he tried to ask her why, he could do nothing. He had never felt more helpless in his life, not even when his wife, Marissa, walked out on him.

He'd loved Marissa completely, with absolute devotion, and when she'd left him after two years of marriage, his whole world shattered. He had decided it was a good lesson, eventually, once he had crawled out of the deep, dark hole where he'd existed for months. He thought the experience had cured him of the longing for female company just as he'd thought that the road he was on had burned all capacity for emotion out of him. But here was Charlotte, and she stirred something inside him that compelled him to respond. He couldn't help himself.

If he'd met Charlotte before this started . . . It was an intriguing but fundamentally stupid thought. If he had met her, she wouldn't have given him a second look. She was a blueblood and a healer, probably highly respected, while he was a Mire rat with no name, no status, no rank, and very modest means of support.

And yet he couldn't stop thinking about her. That's how it started, Richard reflected grimly. Thinking about a woman, wondering what it would be like, picturing it. A purely physical attraction he could handle, but he'd seen her in a moment of vulnerability. He knew exactly what it cost her to follow him. She was courageous, in the true sense of the word. Experience and training had given him an edge, and he rarely experienced acute fear when facing an opponent. Most of the time, he didn't even feel anxiety, as if his soul had developed calluses. Perhaps he simply didn't have anything to lose.

Charlotte had no combat experience. She hid her fear well, but he was learning to read her. When she raised her chin and squared her shoulders, Charlotte was afraid. She had been alarmed when they met Jason Parris, scared when they faced the thugs, and frightened when the mob chased them. Yet she kept going, overcoming her fear every time. That strength of will was worthy of both his admiration and his respect. Her very humanity made her fascinating and drew him to her. He wanted to know more about her. He wanted to spare her that fear. He wanted to remove whatever was causing her discomfort. Yet there was no way to do it without cutting short her involvement, and he had made a promise to respect her mission.

Jack emerged from the room. He was nude, and his eyes were red.

Richard offered him the clothes. The boy dressed.

Richard rose. "There is no shame in grief. It's human. You didn't do anything wrong. It doesn't make you weak, and you don't have to hide it."

Jack looked away.

"You couldn't have prevented your grandmother's death. Don't take any of the guilt or blame on yourself. Blame those who are actually responsible."

"What happened to the slavers?" Jack asked, his voice hoarse.

"Your grandmother killed some of them. Charlotte killed the rest."

They went down the stairs side by side.

"I want in," the boy said.

"In on what?"

"You're the Hunter. You're hunting the slavers. I want in."

"And how would you know that?" If someone had opened their mouth, he would be really put out.

Jack gave a one-shouldered shrug. "We overhead you and Declan talking."

"Declan's study is soundproof."

"Not to reanimated mice," Jack said. "George wants to be a spy. He listens in on everything, then he tells me."

Fantastic. Declan and he had taken extra measures, like activating soundproof sigils and meeting during late hours, and two teenage boys could still undermine all of their careful security precautions. How comforting. And he wasn't feeling like a complete moron, not at all. He was sure Declan wouldn't feel like a moron either.

"I'm coming with you," Jack said.

"Absolutely not."

Jack bared his teeth in a feral grief.

"No," Richard said. "This isn't a fun adventure."

"Kaldar let us—"

"No." He sank enough finality into his voice to end all arguments.

Jack clamped his mouth shut and walked sullenly next to him. They left the tower and headed toward the city.

This battle wasn't won, Richard reflected, looking at the stubborn set of the boy's jaw. And once they got back, George and Jack would tag team him. If worse came to worse, he'd talk Barlo into keeping them under lock and key while he and Charlotte dealt with the ship.

"GEORGE," Charlotte murmured.

George remained slumped in her arms, catatonic. She scanned him again. No physical injury. Too much magic, expended too quickly. She had no idea if he was slipping into a permanent coma or just resting, exhausted.

I shouldn't have told you. She realized she'd spoken the words aloud.

"She was our grandmother," George said. "We have a right to know."

Charlotte exhaled. *Conscious. Finally.*

The boy pushed away from her very gently, got up, and offered her his hand. She took it and stood up.

"Richard values family above all else," George said. "He would've told us if you didn't."

"Do you know what he does?" she asked.

George nodded.

"Then you know he will do all he can to get justice for your grandmother, and so will I."

"She liked you," George said. "She told us a lot about you. We saw your picture."

Charlotte swallowed. "Your grandmother was very kind to me."

"Is that why you're with him now?" George asked.

"It's complicated," Charlotte said. "But yes."

"We will join you."

He said it matter-of-factly, as if it was the most natural thing in the world for a sixteen-year-old to become a killer. No. Not on her watch.

"There is no place for children in what we are about to do. Richard will tell you the same thing."

"I'm sixteen," George said. "I'm less than a year away from being an adult. I need this. I need to get my own justice. You know how I feel. You must've cared for her. Why would you stop me?"

"Look at me." She waited until he met her gaze. "No. We will do our part, and the two of you will take care of Rose. You have my word that the slavers will pay for what they've done. I'll fight them until I end them, or they end me. This is my battle, and you will stay out of it."

"Exactly," Richard said, opening the door.

Jack slipped into the room.

"Your sister will need support." Richard stepped inside and shut the door.

"She has Declan," Jack said.

Richard turned to him, his face suddenly hard. Charlotte fought an urge to step back, and Jack tensed.

"It's your duty to take care of your family, and Rose and your brother are the only family you have left now. A man doesn't avoid his responsibilities. Do I make myself clear?"

"Crystal," George said.

"Tonight, a slaver ship will dock in a secret location," Richard said. "You will watch us board it, and you will deliver the name of the ship to your brother-in-law. He will trace it. In the event things don't go as planned, he will at least have that information. That's as much as I'm willing to let you do."

Jack opened his mouth.

"Think before you say anything." Richard's voice held no mercy. "Because unlike my brother, I have no qualms about hogtying the two of you and paying Barlo to sit on your bodies until we're out to sea."

Jack clamped his mouth shut.

"We'll take it," George said.

"Smart move. Do I have your word?"

George's face showed no doubt. "Yes."

"Wait for me outside."

The children left.

"What are you doing?" Charlotte peered at him. "Why involve them at all?"

"Because their grandmother is dead, and they feel helpless and angry. Letting them have a token part in this revenge will ease that anger. Otherwise, their grief will drive them into doing something rash, and neither of us will have an opportunity to save them from the consequences."

It was obviously a mistake. "How are you planning to keep them from getting on that ship?"

Richard smiled. "George gave me his word. Honor is important to him."

How can a smart man be such an idiot? "Richard, did you feel how much magic that boy expended? If he cared about his grandmother that much, some faint notion of manly honor isn't going to stop him from getting his revenge."

"My lady, we agreed you wouldn't question me."

"My lord, this will end in disaster."

He smiled, a narrow sardonic smile. "Then you'll get to tell me, 'I told you so.'"

Like arguing with a brick wall. Charlotte opened the door and walked out.

She had to remember why she was doing this: she sacrificed and killed so nobody else would suffer the way these children were suffering now. She would deal with Richard, and she would get on that ship. When she was done, the slavers would be little more than a scary story.

SEVEN

NIGHT came far too quickly, Charlotte reflected, patting the muzzle of her horse. She stood under an oak. The wolf-dog sat by her feet and showed his teeth to anyone who came too close. In front of her, about forty people assembled in the clearing. The moon hid behind the ragged clouds, and what little illumination they had came from the tall torches thrust along the edge of the clearing.

About half of Jason's people, the "slavers," wore an assortment of leather and carried weapons. The other half, mostly women in filthy clothes, busily tied knives and cudgels under their skirts and shirts. A few had on the Broken's jeans, others wore the Weird's dresses. Here and there clothes were being strategically ripped. A young woman walked around the gathering with a bucket of blood and a paintbrush, and smeared the red liquid on random bodies.

Richard was somewhere out there, getting ready. George and Jack had concealed themselves at a good observation point, ready to play their role in the mission. She and Richard had dropped the Draytons off half a mile away, with Richard giving them strict directions to stay out of sight, to which both teens informed them that it wasn't their first time.

"Beautiful," Jason said next to her.

The dog growled low. She petted the big black head.

She hadn't heard Jason walk up. He wore a monk's cowl. Stripes of white paint crossed his nose and cheeks, while a horizontal black stripe darkened the skin around his eyes. He looked terrifying.

"Shouldn't you be joining them?" He nodded at the slaves.

"I suppose I should." She walked over and took her place between two "slave" women. The redhead with the bucket of blood stopped by her and casually painted some blood on her neck.

"Whose blood is it?" Charlotte asked.

The redhead shrugged. "No clue. Got it at the butcher shop." She moved on.

At least it wasn't human.

"You got a knife?" a slender, filthy girl asked her. There was something familiar about her . . . Miko.

"I don't need one, thank you."

"Take a knife." Miko offered her a curved, wicked-looking blade. "It might save your life."

"What about you?"

The girl grinned at her. "I have several."

Charlotte took the blade, slid it into the waistband of her trousers, and pulled her tunic over it. She looked up and saw a ghost striding through the crowd toward her. Wide-shouldered, wearing a padded leather jacket, his hair in a ponytail, an eye patch covering his left eye, leading a black horse. His name was Crow, and she'd killed him. She had watched him die in that clearing with the rest of the slaver crew.

Her heart hammered. She took a step back.

Crow kept coming.

That was fine. She would kill him again. The dark tendrils slipped out of her.

"Charlotte?" the one-eyed slaver said in Richard's voice.

She had always prided herself on excellent control of her magic. Between the moment her magic slithered out to kill him and the next instant, her brain made the connection, and she withdrew her power, aborting his murder in midstrike.

"Yes?" she asked, sounding as normal as she could.

"Are you all right?" he asked.

"Yes." No. No, please take me away from here. "You look older," she said, to say something. His face was covered with wrinkles.

"Liquid latex," Richard said. "Processed tree sap mixed with water. If you slather it on your face, it will shrink as it dries, wrinkling the skin."

He resembled the dead man so much, it was uncanny.

Richard leaned toward her. "Once we get to the island, things will be chaotic. It's essential that we aren't separated. We must find the bookkeeper. He's our only lead to the top of the slaver ring."

A shrill whistle made them turn. Jason had mounted a horse.

"Wretches, scum, and villains," he called out. "Lend me your ears!"

Light laughter rippled through the crowd.

"Every single one of you is owed a debt by the slavers. Tonight we collect. We'll board their ship. We'll sack the Market. We'll be legends." He paused and smiled. "We'll be rich."

An enthusiastic riot of catcalls and guttural grunts answered him.

He tilted his head. "But we don't do this just to get rich."

"We don't?" someone asked with pretended shock.

More laughter followed.

"No, we don't. Look around you." Jason spread his arms. "Go ahead, look."

Heads turned as people looked at the woods and the night sky.

"Tonight, we're the masters of all we see. Tonight, we will triumph and grind those bastards under our boots. We'll take their money and their lives." His voice gained a savage intensity. "We'll listen as they scream and beg us for mercy. We'll smell the gore as we cut them open and bathe our hands in their blood. We'll gouge the light out of their eyes. Tonight, we'll truly live!"

Silence claimed the clearing.

"Hell, yeah!" Richard barked in a deep voice.

"Yeah!" another male snarl echoed.

The crowd erupted in shouts, shaking their fists.

"He gets carried away sometimes," Richard told her under his breath.

"You don't say." More violence. More murder. More joy as her magic devoured lives. Charlotte swallowed. She vividly remembered the seductive rush of pleasure she had derived from killing the slavers, and experiencing it again terrified her to the very core. Her teeth chattered. She clenched them, and her knees began to shake.

"We move!" Jason roared.

Around her, people picked up their gear. She wanted to turn around and run the other way.

"May I?" Richard asked, holding a pair of cuffs.

She raised her hands. Carefully, Richard placed the pair of handcuffs on her wrists. "Twist like this, and they'll open."

The cuffs felt so heavy on her wrists. Charlotte forced herself to nod.

His fingers brushed her hands, the rough sword master's calluses they bore scraping her skin. His hands were warm. She looked up at him, asking for reassurance.

He met her gaze. "I won't let anything happen to you, my lady."

He said "my lady" as if it was a term of endearment. There was such quiet conviction in his voice that, for a moment, the clearing and everyone around them faded away. It was just the two of them, and he was touching her hands and looking at her in that particular way, concerned, almost tender. Such a strange emotion in the eyes of a man who was a killer. Her worry melted into the air. If only she could walk right next to him, with him holding her, nothing could hurt her.

"Form two lines," Jason called out. "Slaves in the middle, slavers on the sides."

Reality rushed at her in a terrifying avalanche. What she was doing, standing with him like this, was wildly inappropriate. She didn't care.

"Stay safe," she said.

"You, too."

Richard released her and nodded to the dog. "Come."

The beast hesitated.

"Come," Richard ordered. The big beast rose off his haunches and trotted over to Richard. Richard locked a long chain on the dog's collar, mounted his horse, and took position next to Jason. The women formed two lines behind her and Miko, and they started down the road, the "slavers" on horses around them.

They trudged down the trail. The oaks ended, and the marsh began, a perfectly uniform field of low grasses. The trail veered left and right, cut in the grass. The horses clopped through the slushy, oversaturated soil, their hoofs splattering her clothes and face with mud.

The anxiety returned full force. Charlotte knew they'd only been walking for a few minutes, but this trek through the vast field of mud seemed endless. It felt like she was marching through some extended nightmare to her death. The wind rose up, flinging the salty smell of the ocean into her face.

She thought of Tulip's ashen eyes, and Éléonore's charred body, and George's haunting voice. *"Please, Mémère . . ."*

She would stop it. No matter how much it cost her.

An eternity later, the marsh gave way to sandy dunes rough with clumps of sea-oat grass and blanketed with patches of short, creeping grass with wide leaves. Thin spires, like the stamens of a water lily, rose between the leaves, glowing with green, and as the breeze touched them, they swayed, sending dots of brilliant emerald into the night.

"Don't step on those," Miko said next to her. "That's fisherman's trap grass. It will burn your legs."

They crossed the dunes and finally stepped onto the beach. In front of her, the ocean stretched, dark and menacing. To the left, the coast curved, forming a small peninsula, cutting off her view with trees. To the right, the distant turquoise lights of Kelena shimmered, like a mirage above the water.

"Three torches," Richard said. "One in front, two in the back, about twenty feet apart."

A "slaver" on her right slid off his horse, took three

torches out of his saddlebag, ran forward, thrust the first
torch into the sand, and lit it.

"It's a dark night," Jason said.

"Dark works for us," Richard said.

The third torch flared into life. They waited.

The dog strayed back, the chain stretching, and licked
her hand.

The dark silhouette of a brigantine slid from behind the
peninsula.

GEORGE lay on his stomach atop a sand dune. A small
black box rested on the sand in front of him. Below, the false
slavers and their "captives" waited on the beach. In the distance, the brigantine dropped anchor. It was a Weird-style
ship, with six segmented masts that rose in a semicircle from
the deck, like the wings of a water bird about to take flight.
The masts bore panes of gray-green sails. In the open sea,
the sails melted against the sky, making the ship harder
to see.

Mémère was dead. It had been six months since he'd last
seen her. She had come up to visit for a week at Midwinter.
He remembered her face as if he'd seen her yesterday. He
remembered her smile. The scent of lavender that always
floated around her. He knew that scent so well, that years
later catching a whiff of it calmed him down.

When he was younger, Mémère was a constant presence
in his life. He barely remembered his mother. She was a
distant smudge in his memory. He recalled his father better,
a large, funny man. When he was eight, he was invited to a
friend's house in the Broken. He was given a choice of mov-
ies to watch, and as he flipped through the cases, he saw a
man in a leather jacket and a wide-brimmed hat, holding a
whip. The title read *Raiders of the Lost Ark*. He'd read the
description and realized that this strange man, Indiana
Jones, did the same thing his father did. He hunted treasure.

He'd watched the movie twice in a row, which was probably why he was never invited back. But as he'd grown older,

maturity had given him a new perspective. His father wasn't Indiana Jones, no matter how much he wanted it to be true. His father had abandoned them when they needed him most, forcing Rose to take on all the responsibility of caring for them. There were days she'd come home so tired she could hardly move—once she even fell asleep in the kitchen while peeling potatoes.

But Mémère was always there. Her house served as their safe haven. No matter what trouble he would get into or how much Rose was mad at him, Mémère was always there with hugs, cookies, and old books. She was there the first time his magic showed itself. He was three years old. He'd been playing in the yard when he saw a squirrel. She had a bushy tail and fluffy red fur, and she didn't seem afraid of him. She just sat on the trunk. He wanted to pet her, so he started moving closer and closer, one tiny step at a time. He was almost there; and then she fell off the trunk and died.

He'd picked up the fluffy body. He didn't really understand death. He just knew that she wasn't moving. He wanted her to move, but she wouldn't. She just hung in his hands, limp, like an old toy. He remembered a feeling of stark terror. For a second he'd thought he would die too, just like the squirrel, then something pulled on him, hurting, and the squirrel turned and looked at him.

He'd dropped her and ran, across the yard and up the porch. He must've screamed because his grandmother had run out onto the porch and scooped him up. He'd buried his face in her shoulder, and she hugged him. A ghost of her voice fluttered from his memory: *"It will be all right. It's a gift, Georgie. Nothing to be afraid of. It's a gift . . ."*

George locked his teeth. Six months ago, he'd asked her again to move to the Weird. They had been sitting on the balcony drinking tea. She was leaving to return to the Edge later that day, and a feeling of dread had smothered him, heavy, like a wet blanket. In his mind, she looked exactly the same as she had been when he was little, but now every time she visited, he noticed incremental, alarming changes.

Her hair was thinning. Her wrinkles cut deeper into her face. She seemed smaller somehow. It made him ill with worry.

"Please stay," he asked.

"No, dear. I live in the Edge. That's where I belong. This is very nice, but it's not for me."

He'd helped her get into the phaeton that morning. She'd kissed him good-bye.

He should've done more. He should've insisted. He should've compelled her to stay. If he really had begged, she would have. How could he have been so careless and stupid? Now she was dead. He didn't even know how she died, if she had burned alive in that damn house . . . he closed his eyes tightly, stopping the tears from welling up.

He would have to tell Rose.

The brigantine was lowering two boats. The people on the beach waited patiently.

"We should be down there," Jack said next to him.

But they weren't. Of the two Mar brothers, Kaldar was the more malleable. His ethics had flexible boundaries, and he bent, if the wind was strong enough. But George had taken sword-fighting lessons from Richard over the past year. Richard was like a granite crag in a storm, immovable and resolute. The look in his eyes had told George he wouldn't be getting his way. Not this time.

His Mirror assignment was over. George had failed. Jason Parris had identified him as an Adrianglian agent, and he'd already sent the dispatch to the Home Office. Erwin wouldn't be pleased, but right now his handler's disappointment was the least of George's worries. He would watch Richard and Charlotte get on the ship; and then he and Jack would be forced to go home like good little children. Inside, he was screaming.

The boats pulled away from the vessel, speeding across the water, driven by magic-fueled motors. The magic residue slid off the propellers, turning their wake into a glowing trail of yellow-and-emerald radiance.

Small tongues of green lightning flared at the brigantine's aft. They had a cloaking device, and they were priming it.

Of course. The South Fleet of Adrianglia possessed three
corsair-class vessels, five hunters, and an aerial-support
dreadnought. Each carried pulverizer cannons as well as a
host of other deadly toys. A fast and light civilian brigantine
like this one couldn't take more than one or two shots. Its
best strategy lay in speed and in not being detected in the
first place, which is where the cloaking device would come
in handy.

A cloaking device was also hellishly expensive. The slave
trade must've served them well. He ground his teeth again.

Jack bared his teeth, his voice a vicious whisper. "Stop
grinding your teeth."

"Shut up," George whispered back.

"It bugs me."

"Cover your ears, then."

The crooked ribbons of magic lightning built. George
opened the box he'd brought. Inside was a single glass bub-
ble. He twisted it open, plucked out a glass lens edged with
tiny metal cilia, and slid it into his eye. The lens's delicate
metal tendrils moved, searching, and locked onto his nerves.
The pain shot straight into his brain, as if someone had hammered a wooden spike through his eye socket. The Mirror's
gadgets could do incredible things, but they always came
with a price. He shook his head and looked up. The brigantine slid into clear, sharp focus, as though he were standing
right next to it. He could see the carved sides and the slender lines of the ship's rigging. If this brigantine followed the
Adrianglian Maritime Code, the name would be near
the bow.

Next to him, Jack growled. "Are we just going to lay here
like idiots?"

"Yes, we are."

Lightning dashed from the stern toward the bow, dancing over the vessel's sides, illuminating the ship. That was
the moment he was waiting for. He trailed the lightning with
his gaze.

"This is wrong," Jack said.

"We stay put."

The green sparks illuminated the name, written in thick black letters on the bow, and faded into darkness. George sucked in his breath.

No. No, he must have read it wrong.

He waited for another flash.

"George, breathe," Jack growled into his ear.

The lightning flashed, illuminating the letters once more. It still said the same thing. George went cold. There could be only two possibilities for this ship to be here now, and he couldn't deal with either.

Again. He had to see it again.

"What the hell is the matter with you?" Jack hissed.

The magic sparked off the boards, and he read the name again, for the third time, each letter like the stab of a sword into his gut.

George yanked the lens out of his eye. "We have to get down there."

"You said we had to stay put."

"And now I'm saying we have to get down there."

He slithered backward off the dune and took off running toward the beach.

Jack caught up with him. They went to ground again just behind the "slaves."

"Why?" Jack whispered, barely audible.

George paused for a second, weighing Jack's right to know against his explosive temper. If Jack blew up, they would never get on that ship.

He deserved to know. Better do it now.

"Because that ship's name is *Intrepid Drayton*."

Jack recoiled. For a moment he thought it over, and then the right gears caught in his mind. He made the connection between their last name and the name of the ship. His eyes sparked with fire. "Did they kill Dad?"

"I don't know."

"Is Dad selling slaves?"

"I don't know."

"He left us to rot in the Edge so he could sell slaves?" A snarl roiled through Jack's voice.

George grabbed his shoulder. "Hold it in. Not until we're on board and know exactly what's going on."

Jack ducked his head, hiding the changeling glow of his eyes, and sucked in the air through his nose.

They would have only one shot at this. The boats had to be close enough for Richard to be unable to do anything about their presence but far enough away that the sailors wouldn't see any commotion.

George took a deep breath.

The leading boat rolled over the surf, its crew distracted. Now.

George lunged forward, and Jack followed. They dashed into the line of slaves and thrust themselves behind Charlotte.

"What the devil are you doing?" Richard growled under his breath.

He didn't even turn. The man must have eyes in the back of his head.

"Changing the plan." George ripped off a piece of his shirt and twisted it around Jack's hands into a makeshift tie.

"Go back," Charlotte hissed.

Richard dismounted and walked toward George, pulling a pair of handcuffs off his belt. They stood face-to-face, Richard glaring down from the height of an extra four inches. It was a furious glare suffused with so much menace, it could end a riot. George stared straight into it. Today, he had the will to match it.

"You gave me your word," Richard ground out.

George took a step forward, his voice barely above a whisper, meant for Richard alone. "The vessel's name is *Intrepid Drayton.* Before Earl Camarine adopted me, my last name was Drayton. There is a painting of that ship in my dead grandmother's house."

He took the cuffs out of Richard's hands and slipped them onto his own wrists with a click. "It's my father's ship. Either the slavers killed my father and took his vessel, or he's working for them, and he's responsible for his own mother's death. I need to know which it is. If you stand in my way, I will move you, Richard."

FOR a moment Richard stood there, glowering, then he checked the cuffs on George's wrists. "Don't do anything stupid."

He turned around and strode to the front, next to Jason.

George exhaled. To Richard, family was everything. He understood blood debts and the right to exact justice for one's family, but it had been a gamble.

His father couldn't work for the slavers. Even he couldn't have sunk that low. Even Rose, who bordered on hating the man, always said that he was never mean or violent. Opportunistic, unwise, and selfish, yes. Could he be selfish enough to work for the slavers? George was thinking in circles. He had to get a grip.

The boats landed, their flat bottoms scraping the sand with a soft sibilance. An older man stepped out first, followed by four other sailors. Tall and broad-shouldered, he walked like a sailor, lurching slightly with each step, planting his feet firmly on the ground.

George peered at him, noting every detail. Gray eyes, dishwater-blond hair, cut short, older face, once probably handsome, but puffy from lack of sleep and likely too much alcohol, graying stubble on the cheeks . . . Was it him? He strained, trying to remember, but in his memory his father's face was a vague blur. He used to remember. He used to know what his dad looked like, but the years had passed, and now the memories were lost.

"Crow," the man said. "Where's Voshak?"

"Hunter got him," Richard answered, his voice a ragged growl. "Shot him on the edge of Veresk as we were riding out."

"And Ceyren?"

"Got him, too. Arrow to the eye. A fucked-up thing to see."

The man sighed. "That's what he usually does. Somebody should take care of that fucker. He's cutting into our profits."

"Someone will take him down," Richard-Crow hacked and spat in the sand. "Ain't gonna be me, I tell you that."

"I hear you." The man looked past Richard at the slaves. "You did well for yourself."

"Did all right," Richard-Crow agreed.

Maybe it wasn't him. Maybe the slavers had killed him and someone else captained the ship. It would be far better if their father was dead than profiting from the murder of his own mother. *Say your name,* George willed silently.

"I take it you'll be coming on board instead of Voshak," the man said.

"Me and everyone you see here," Richard-Crow growled.

The man raised his eyebrows.

Richard stepped forward, leaning in as if ready to punch. "I've been on a crew for four years. First, they gave the crew to Bes. Then, when his old lady killed him, they gave it to Carter. After Carter got his dumb ass shot, I went to them and told them to give me a crew. They said I ain't got leadership potential. They gave it to Voshak instead. Well, their damn leadership potential is rotting in the woods. This is my crew, and I'm taking my wolves in to let them see that."

The sailor raised his hand. "Okay, okay. I got it, spitting wonder. I don't get involved in politics. I just ferry the merchandise. You want a ride to the island, you got it. Load them up."

"Move them," Richard snarled.

A whip snapped above George's head. The slavers started forward, toward the boats. He was being herded like human cattle.

George moved, following Charlotte. He was hot and cold at the same time, every cell of his body keyed up, as if the core of his body were boiling. Sweat drenched his hairline.

The sailor's gaze snagged on Charlotte. "Nice. I was always a sucker for a blonde with a good rack."

George shut his eyes for the tiniest moment, trying to recall what little memories remained from his childhood.

Was Mother blond? He strained, searching through the vague recollections . . . His eyes snapped open. She was blond. He was sure of it.

It didn't mean anything. Many men liked blond women.

The sailor was looking directly at him. "Good-looking boys. Aren't they too old for the Market? They like their kids younger."

George's stomach churned with acid. Next to him, Jack clenched his fists. A drop of blood slid between his fingers onto the pale scrap of fabric tied around his hands.

Hold it in, George prayed.

"Special order," Richard said.

The sailor grimaced. "Never understood that myself."

"As long as they pay me." Richard spat again.

George climbed into the boat, Jack at his heels, and stared at the sailor on the beach. *Say your damn name.*

The sailor grinned. "Hello, my lords and ladies. My name is John Drayton. I'll be your captain this evening."

A hot, invisible knife stabbed George straight in the pit of his stomach. The world gained a red tint. Logic told him it was the capillaries in his eyes expanding in reaction to his increased blood flow, but that logic spoke from some distant place in his brain, and he shut it off. Grandmother was dead, and the scumbag who was her son and his father made his money from playing captain to her murderers. John Drayton trafficked in slaves. He had abandoned his children, so he could get rich off of other people's misery. He might as well have killed his own mother with his own hands. He was responsible.

"Welcome aboard *Intrepid Drayton* for your island cruise. You'll notice bluefin sharks following our ship. If you make any trouble, we'll tie a line around your neck and toss you overboard. The bluefins like a little chase before their dinner. You behave, and they'll go hungry. Personally, I hope you don't—I enjoy a little spectacle. Brightens up a boring voyage."

He had to kill his father, to bring him to justice. It was the only right thing to do.

A soothing current of magic prickled his skin. His heartbeat slowed.

"Sit by me, George," Charlotte called, her voice like a rush of cold water onto his scalding anger. "Please."

He forced himself to turn around. She sat in the bottom of the barge, her hand resting on Jack's forearm. His brother's head was down, the mass of brown hair hanging over his face. A hoarse, strained sound, a muted, controlled snarl, emanated from Jack with every breath. His brother was teetering on the verge of losing his human form.

They still had a job to do. They had to get to the island. His vengeance would have to wait. His legs felt wooden. He couldn't make himself move.

A hard wooden baton smashed in the back of his knees. George crashed down.

"Sit the fuck down," one of Jason's slavers said.

"I see we have the first candidate for the shark feeding," his father called. "One more, boy, and I'll personally shove you off my deck."

George forced himself to sit next to Charlotte. She was watching the rest of the slaves board, her face calm.

"There will be a time later," she said, her quiet voice laced with menace. "We won't have to wait long."

EIGHT

CHARLOTTE closed her eyes and listened to the waves splash against the hull. Two hours ago, they had been loaded inside the hold of the ship, slaves first, then the slavers. John Drayton was a careful man who locked up his passengers, willing and unwilling. Richard and Jason were the only two men who had remained above on deck.

George and Jack sat on the floor near the bulkhead. Jack's shoulders, rigid with tension, slumped forward. He hasn't said a word since they boarded, but she had seen his eyes. A violent, furious thing stared at her through his irises. Something savage lived inside Jack, and he was using all of his power to hold it at bay. She wanted to tell him she knew exactly how he felt, but her instincts warned her that any stray word could tip the balance in that thing's favor. She had treated changelings before, or rather she'd treated the changeling soldiers, the hardened, barely human killers who had come out of the crucible of the Adrianglian changeling academy. If Jack lost control now, in the hold, none of them would survive it.

George knew it, too. He sat next to his brother, hovering protectively over him. His eyes were clear with determination, his face sharpened with grief and anger. He felt betrayed, and he wanted revenge, and she didn't blame him one bit.

Anger filled her too, and she held on to it, letting herself steep in it, solidifying her resolve. John Drayton, Éléonore's long-lost son. Not so lost anymore. She pictured his smug smile. *"Good-looking kids." They are your children, you heartless bastard. It wasn't enough their grandmother is dead, now you're indirectly responsible for her murder.* She wished she could strangle the swine, but he was upstairs. This one life she would've taken with pleasure. She glanced at the boys again. Yes, with pleasure.

Charlotte glanced out the narrow porthole, little more than an air vent. The ship had activated a cloaking device the moment they raised anchor. A dense cloud of magic-infused fog slid over the vessel, wrapping it like a blanket. The myriad tiny droplets of water that created the mist acted as countless minuscule mirrors, busily reflecting the ship's surroundings. An outside observer wouldn't see the ship. He might perhaps notice a smudge against the perfect line of water and sky. In bright daylight, this distortion would be quite obvious, but at night, with the mist rising from the water, the *Intrepid Drayton* was practically invisible. Unfortunately, from the inside, the reflective fog was opaque and all she saw now was a dense curtain of mist.

They must've been sailing for at least an hour or two. Time stretched here, inside the hold.

"I want out of this damn ship. How are we gonna get out of here?" a blond woman next to her murmured to Miko. "We can't kill the sailors until we get to port, and if we kill them when we get there, there will be a commotion."

The slender girl nodded at Charlotte. "She's our key."

The blond woman stared at her. "You don't look like much."

"Looks can be deceiving," Charlotte told her.

"They better be." The blond woman bared her teeth. "Because if they lead me out of this bucket in chains and into the slave pens, you'll be the first I come after. You've got a skinny throat. Easy to cut."

Charlotte's magic stirred in response to the menace in the woman's voice, bubbling to the surface. She kept it in check and stared back at the blond woman with disdain.

The woman yanked a knife from inside her rags.

Miko stepped in her way and hissed. "Don't be stupid."

"Did you see the way she looked at me? Like I'm gutter

trash, and she's the Marchesa of Louisiana. I'll cut her throat!"

Miko moved and suddenly there were two slender blades in her hands. "You *are* gutter trash, Lynda. Jason has a plan. You fuck with his plan, you fuck with me."

"You got a big mouth for such a dumb bitch. About time someone shut it for you."

Lynda lunged forward. Miko spun, thrusting, and the woman crumpled to the boards, gurgling on her blood.

Miko turned, one arm held high, the other low, blood dripping from her knives, and surveyed the hold. "Anybody else want to fuck with the plan?"

Nobody volunteered.

Lynda writhed on the floor, hot, dark blood spreading around her on the wood. Charlotte let her magic lick at her. External jugular vein cut, internal jugular vein partially nicked, rapid blood loss, estimated time of death: two to three minutes. A familiar sense of obligation tugged at Charlotte, but this time it wasn't backed by kindness, only habit.

"Do you want me to heal her?" Charlotte asked.

"No. One less psycho."

"Then finish it. She's suffering."

Miko dropped down on one knee. The knife rose, plunged down, and Lynda stopped struggling.

The door swung open, revealing Richard. About time. He motioned to her. Charlotte approached.

"We're about to make landfall," he whispered. "There are nineteen sailors on this boat."

"What about the captain?" she asked, glancing at the boys.

Two pairs of eyes stared back at her, one of them glowing amber.

"He's ours," Jack said, his voice a ragged, inhuman growl. People backed away from him.

"Wait until I call you," Richard said, and looked to her. "Sailors only."

She raised her chin. "Very well. Let's get this over with."

Richard turned and climbed the ladder up to the deck.

She followed. The ship sliced through the blue-green waters and the salty breeze, barely skimming the surface of the ocean, its grandiose sails spread wide. The dense barrier of magic fog surrounded it on all sides except for the prow, where the curtain parted. Orange and blue lights winked through the gap—their destination.

Sailors moved along the deck. Some sat, some talked quietly. Richard pulled her against the cabin and braced her with his big body, hiding her from the rest of the crew. She rested her hands on his leather-encased body, feeling the comforting strength of his muscular shoulders. It felt so intimate standing like this. It was almost an embrace. She knew she was reading too much into it, but she needed an embrace so badly.

Something brushed against her. She glanced down. The wolfripper hound leaned against her legs.

"How fast do you need them to die?" she whispered. She was so angry, and they were scum who ferried slaves and fed children to sharks. She would extinguish their lives.

"At the speed we're going, we'll dock in fifteen minutes. They're about to light the colors," he said. "The port is likely armed with cannons. They will send a challenge signal. We must send the proper reply, or they'll consider us hostile. Once the reply is accepted, they're yours. Kill them as quickly and quietly as you can."

"Challenge!" someone called out.

Richard leaned over to glance at the bow of the ship. She did, too.

A pale green flare shot upward from the port. Charlotte held her breath, waiting.

"If it's green again, they grant us safe passage," Richard whispered in her ear, his breath a hot cloud.

"Light the colors," a deep voice bellowed from the deck above them. "One two, two two, one three!"

Magic dashed up the masts. Arcane symbols ignited on the surface of the sails, one each in those on the middle mast and the third in the sails of the center mast on the left side.

A second green flare blossomed in the night sky.

The deep voice barked a string of nautical nonsense. The crew sped about the ship, spinning wheels, adjusting metal levers in the control consoles by the masts. The sails shrunk. The segmented masts began to straighten slowly.

"Now," Richard said.

The monstrous magic in her chest stirred, waking. She listened to it, sorting through the plagues she carried within, until she found one that felt right.

A sailor brushed by them. "Hey, Crow, who have you got there?"

Charlotte reached out above Richard's shoulder and gently caressed the man's weathered face. Her magic rose from her in narrow dark streams, like the tentacles of an octopus, and bit into him. He barely noticed. His skin fractured under her fingertips, sloughing off in tiny white scales of epithelium glistening with magic, and the breeze carried them on, down to the rest of the crew. The man stared at her, seemingly mesmerized but really just dying very quickly. The skin of his face turned to powder, as if he'd dipped his head into a bucket of silvery flour.

Her magic wrapped around him, draining his reserves, and withdrew. The wind stirred the powder that used to be the top layers of his skin, blowing it off. The tiny particles caught on his eyelashes. He sighed and crumpled down softly.

Richard turned, still shielding her, to look over his shoulder. The sailors began to fall one by one, silent, soft, each releasing a cloud of scaly powder as they sank unmoving to the deck.

They were bad people who deserved their deaths, yet she felt a crushing sadness at their passing all the same. She buried it away, deep inside, wrapping it in the layers of her anger and resolve. There would be time for self-pity later.

Richard had the strangest expression on his face. Not quite shock, not quite panic, but an odd mix of awe and astonishment, as if he couldn't believe what he saw.

At the far end of the ship, Jason Parris turned, his eyes wide, as the sailors around him folded like deflated balloons.

The dog raised his muzzle to the moon and howled, his lonely cry floating above the waves like a mourning wail.

Above them something thumped quietly. A man tumbled from the upper deck, his face ashen with powder. Richard lunged at him, trying to catch the body to keep it from making a loud thud. But a gust of wind beat him to it—four feet from the deck the body broke into a cloud of particles. They slid harmlessly from Richard's skin and melted into the breeze.

He turned to her. "What is it?"

"White leprosy," she said. It was a terrible disease. She had fought it before, she knew all its little habits and quirks, and she had twisted them with her magic just enough to turn it into her silent assassin. He would think twice about letting her touch him now. Something inside her contracted at that thought.

"Jack," Richard said, his voice low. "Tell them the ship is ours."

"He can't hear you," she told him.

"Jack has good ears," Richard reminded her.

Sure enough, Jason's crew poured out of the cargo hold and spread across the deck, people taking up positions where the sailors once stood. People kicked the fallen bodies overboard. The corpses broke in the wind.

Someone gasped. She saw panic in some faces.

"Tell Silver Death thank you for the pretty ship," Jason said to them. "And stop gaping. We still need to bring this baby to port."

There was no escape. Death was now a part of her name.

George and Jack emerged from the crowd.

"I need you to guard your father," Richard said. "There are things he knows that we need. If you can't help yourself, tell me now."

"I'll do it," George said. "Jack will need a few moments to vent."

"I'm counting on you, George. This is your only second chance. If I come back and he's dead, you and I are done. Do not harm your father."

The boy reached behind his neck and pulled a long, slender blade from inside his clothes. "Understood. I'll keep him in perfect health."

Richard rapped his hands on the door of the cabin.

"What is it?" Drayton called.

"There's a problem," Richard replied in his normal voice.

The door swung open, revealing Drayton with a rifle in his hands. He saw Jason's people and jerked the gun up.

Magic pulsed from George, dark and potent. A woman charged out of the crowd and grabbed the gun. Charlotte saw her face and nearly gagged. Lynda, her slit throat a red ribbon across her neck, her face still splattered with the spray of her own blood.

Drayton yanked the gun, but she hung on, blocking the barrels with her stomach. The slaver captain pulled the trigger. The muffled shot popped, like a dry firecracker, blowing small chunks of flesh from Lynda's back. The undead woman jerked the rifle out of Drayton's hand and broke it in half like a toothpick.

Drayton stumbled back.

Lynda dropped the broken rifle at George's feet. "Maaaster," she whispered, her voice a sibilant mess. Her neck leaked tiny droplets of blood. She stared at George in complete adoration, like a loyal hound gazed at her owner. "I love you, master."

Behind her, Jack snarled like some nightmarish monster.

George's face showed no mercy. "Hello, Father." He took a step forward, pushing the bigger man into the cabin. "Let's visit."

Lynda ducked in after him. The door swung shut.

Oh, George . . .

"To the bow," Richard said, resting his fingers lightly on her arm.

She followed him to the front of the ship and came to stand by one of the control consoles, all bronze and copper gears encased in glass and enveloped by magic.

Her magic sang within her, the monster satiated but not fully satisfied. The more she fed it, the more sustenance it wanted. It wound and curled around her in dark currents, almost as if it were an entity of its own, and it loved her, like a loyal pet, existing to serve her and bring her comfort. All those endless hours of cautionary lectures she'd heard within the walls of the College were right. Destruction was seductive and self-rewarding, while healing was an arduous chore.

She had taken a chance this time. Instead of siphoning off their lives to fuel her magic, she simply killed them, feeding the disease with her own power. Stealing other lives to feed her magic had felt too good. If she tasted it again, there was a chance she wouldn't stop, and she didn't want to risk it. Strangely, even though she had relied only on her own reserves, she didn't feel that drained. Killing was easier than the last time—and the next time it would be easier still. She was on a slippery slope. She had to fight to keep from sliding down.

One of Jason's men came to stand by them, saw Charlotte still wrapped in magic, and halted in midstep, maintaining his distance. He looked at her, looked at the console, shifted from foot to foot uncomfortably . . .

"Would you like me to move?" she asked.

"Yes," he exhaled.

Charlotte took two steps to the right, away from the console and toward two other men near Jason, both looking like they crushed skulls for their living. The cutthroats shied from her, backing up. Jason held his ground, but his face locked into a hard, impersonal mask. He was deeply afraid and determined not to show it.

She felt utterly alone. So that's what it was like to be a pariah.

"My lady." Richard's fingers touched her arm.

She almost jumped.

He offered her his arm. "May I?"

Charlotte rested her fingers on his forearm and stood next to him, painfully aware that their legs were almost touching and the streams of her magic wound about him. She dared to glance at him. His face was relaxed. He looked back at her and smiled, as if they had stopped during a stroll in a park to admire some flowers. It made her feel human.

Why, why didn't she take Éléonore up on the invitation to visit her family? Had she met Richard a year ago, things might have been so different. He was the kind of man she had always wanted to meet. Strong, honorable, and kind. *He is also a killer,* an annoying voice whispered in her mind. Well, so was she.

Too late now. They were on a ship sailing to deliver death. Romantic fantasies would get her nowhere. She'd given up that luxury.

Charlotte looked straight ahead. A large island loomed in the distance. Two ports hugged its coast. On the right, handsome piers of cut stone thrust into the ocean, flanked by graceful yachts and private boats. Picturesque palms spread their fanned leaves and wide roads, lit with blue and yellow lanterns, ran deeper inland, toward pastel-colored houses in shades of turquoise, white, yellow, and pink. To the left, rougher piers offered refuge to tugboats and barges, leading to a seedy boardwalk and hostile, dark streets. Farther to the left, a naval fort of gray stone stabbed the ocean, overseeing both ports.

"Where the hell are we?" someone asked.

Richard swore, a quiet, savage sound under his breath, and caught himself. "My apologies."

"What is this place?" Charlotte asked.

"The Isle of Divine Na," he said. "It's an independent barony—the Baron of Na purchased it from Adrianglia when the continent was being colonized. The entire place is one big luxury resort, full of tourists in the late summer and fall. See, the luxury port is in the north, and the commercial port, where we're heading, is to the south. We're barely three hours from Kelena. I've looked at this island as a possibility for the Market but dismissed it because I thought it would be too risky to run a slave operation on an island full of vacationers. It was here all this time under my nose, and I missed it."

"Don't beat yourself up, old man." Jason grinned, patting Richard's shoulder. "Happens to everyone."

Richard glared back at him, his composure slipping, and for a second she thought he'd rip Jason's arm off and beat him with it.

She leaned closer to Richard, and murmured, "If you decide to throw him to the ground, I promise to kick him. Vigorously."

"Thank you," Richard said. "I may take you up on it." He sounded sincere.

A green flare went up at the dock to the left.

"They want us to dock," one of the older men said to Jason.

"Then dock us. Gently. We'll need this ship in one piece to get the hell out of here."

The man barked some orders. The ship slowed, approaching the dock in a graceful arc.

"One fort," Jason murmured, his face thoughtful.

"It has five long-range, flash-load cannons," Richard said.

The slaves formed up in two lines on the deck. Jack moved to the front.

"Who the fuck put the kid on point?" Jason took a step toward the lines.

"Leave him where he is," Richard said. "He sat in the hold for two hours, holding himself in check. He needs to vent, and none of us needs to be in front of him."

The crime lord looked at Richard. "He's a kid."

"He's a changeling," Richard answered. "You've never seen one fight. Give him the benefit of the doubt."

The faint hum of the cloaking device stopped abruptly. The fog dispersed. Charlotte hugged her shoulders, feeling suddenly exposed.

A metal chain clanged—they'd dropped the anchor. The ship slowed further, approaching the dock carefully, almost gently.

"Once we disembark and take the fort, take her out a few hundred yards," Jason said to one of his men. "I don't want to strip this island and come back to a sunken ship."

Three dockhands waited on the wooden pier. Behind them, a crew of slavers waited, no doubt ready to receive the merchandise. Some of the slavers were female. Women were no less capable of cruelty than men.

Lines flew from the ship to the pier. The dockhands secured them.

"Lower the gangplank," Jason said.

Two men cranked a large wheel. A metal ramp slid from the ship's side toward the dock.

The moment it touched the stone, Jack started down the gangplank. The women followed him in two lines, still keeping their hands bound.

"You're eager for the slave pens, sweetheart?" one of the slaver women asked.

Jack swayed. A psychotic grin stretched his lips. His face jerked, his expression feral.

A tall slaver stepped forward. "Come her—"

Jack spun, leaping so fast, Charlotte barely saw the knife in his hand slice through the slaver's neck. Jack landed, catching the man's severed head by the hair, and hurled it at the slavers.

"Holy shit," Jason said.

Her mind reeled at the amount of force it must've taken to slice through the muscle and bone of a thick human neck with a knife.

The slavers froze, shocked, and Jack ripped into them like a pike into a school of minnows. Blood sprayed, people screamed in pain. The slaves abandoned their fake shackles and charged down to join the slaughter. The dog shot down the gangplank and into the thick of the fighting. She tried to keep up with Jack, but he darted in and out of the bloodbath. She caught a flash of his face—he was smiling.

In two minutes, it was all over. Eight bodies lay on the ground. Jack shook himself and dashed down the dark street, melting into the gloom. The dog chased him. The women started moving after the two of them.

"Stop!" Jason roared.

The pretend slaves halted.

"Fall in! Find your squad captain. Now."

The criminals separated with almost military discipline, forming four groups.

"Squad one, slave pens," Jason barked. "Let everyone out, set it on fire, kill whoever comes to put it out. The slaves will run wild, let them. Don't follow them. Squad two, hit the barracks and burn that shit to the ground. Kill as many as you can. Squad three, with me. I want these cannons, and I want them yesterday. Once we have the fort, a double green flare will go up. Squad four, hold the line here. Cut this port off from the city. Everyone, you see a red flare, we abort, and you get the hell out. Blue flare, haul ass to where it came from. Don't loot until I give the all clear. You stop to stuff your pockets before I tell you to, and I'll kill you myself. You get me?"

The criminals howled in agreement.

"Go!" Jason yanked a large sword from under his cloak. "Good luck, old man. Try not to get in my way."

He strode down the gangplank, his monk's habit flaring. The criminals dispersed.

Richard held out a ragged gray cloak to her. "I'm wearing a disguise, but you aren't. Someone might recognize you."

It was unlikely, but there was no need to tempt fate. She put on the cloak, hiding her face in its deep hood, and adjusted her bag of first-aid supplies under the folds.

Richard unsheathed his sword. The slight curve of the long, slender blade caught the light from the lanterns.

"Our turn," Richard said. "We must find the bookkeeper. Stay close to me."

RICHARD marched down the gangplank, keenly aware of Charlotte following him. The Broken was forever closed to him, but its books were not, and he'd read extensively about the Broken's military traditions. As a Marine, Jason was trained in the art of small wars. His particular branch of the military evolved to respond to an enemy employing asymmetric warfare, the tactic that involved striking against the vulnerabilities of the opponent rather than seeking to eliminate the bulk of its force. Jason would take a page out of that playbook: he would deliver brutal precision strikes against the vital points of the island, he would drown the island city in chaos and confusion, demoralizing the enemy and severing communication, then he would eliminate the fractured opposition. He would be ruthless and impossible to rein in, but he couldn't blockade the entire island.

They had to hurry, before the bookkeeper caught on and attempted his escape. They *needed* his information.

He veered left, following the cobbled streets at a rapid walk. He would've liked to run, but Charlotte's face had turned chalk pale after she'd eliminated the crew, and the color still hadn't returned. He didn't want to push her.

What she had done to the crew of the *Intrepid Drayton* shocked him to the core of his being. There was a kind of terrible beauty to her magic, and when he stood in the epicenter of her silent storm, a feeling of otherworldly awe claimed him, as if he became part of a mystical event that couldn't be explained, only experienced. It was a peculiar, mesmerizing serenity with a touch of fear, the kind he sometimes felt when walking alone through the towering woods of Adrianglia or staring at the rough ocean and its sky, pregnant with a storm. He had encountered something greater than the limits of his ordinary life, and he was both alarmed and drawn to it.

Jason was right when he called Charlotte Silver Death. The name fit. Horror and beauty mixed into one. But underneath it she was a living, breathing woman, and when he'd looked at her, standing alone at the bow of the ship, vulnerable despite the potent magic swirling around her, while the rest of the people hugged the sides, afraid to step even an inch closer, he felt her isolation. He wanted to shield her, and he had.

He still wanted to protect her now. Despite everything he had gone through, despite his goal being in sight, if someone

had offered him a chance to instantly transport her somewhere safe in exchange for having to relive the last six
months over again, he would've taken it in a heartbeat. And
she would deeply hate him for it.

Three people shot out of a side street, two men and a
woman. Good weapons, good clothes of a similar cut—town
militia or the Market's slavers. They charged him.

He lent a part of himself to his blade, feeling the magic
slide along the edge of his sword. In the Edge, becoming
one with the blade took time and effort, but here in the
Weird, where the magic was at its strongest, it required a
mere fraction of a second. His flash surged along the blade,
pure white, fed by the adrenaline coursing through him.

The first man stabbed at him with a short, utilitarian
sword. Richard swayed out of the way and thrust into the
man's armpit. The sword slid into his flesh, cutting bone and
gristle like it was warm butter. He felt the faintest resistance
when the heart ruptured and freed his blade with a sharp
tug in time to slam the pommel into the second man's face.
The second attacker stumbled back. The woman jumped
into his place, swinging the heavy mace in a devastating
sideways blow aimed at Richard's shoulder to incapacitate
his sword arm.

Richard leaned back, letting the mace whistle past him
and sliced his sword across her throat. A shallow cut, all
that was needed. She gulped her own blood and fell.

He grabbed the remaining man and hurled him against
the wall, holding the blade an inch from the thug's throat.
The man's eyes told Richard he was drowning in sheer animal terror.

"The bookkeeper?"

"House on the hill," the thug said, his voice shaking.
"Columns. White columns."

Richard released him, and the man took off down the
street at a dead run.

Charlotte stood unharmed, taking short, shallow breaths.
An expression of deep frustration touched her face.

"Come, we have to hurry," he told her.

She caught up to him, and together they started up the street, toward the low hill.

"Why do I always do that? Why do I freeze instead of helping you?"

"No killer instinct, remember?" he said. "It's a natural reaction. When in danger, we fight, flee, or freeze."

"You don't freeze."

"I'm too busy trying to impress you," he said. "Is it working?"

She gave him an unreadable look. Perhaps now wasn't the best time for levity.

The street ran into an eight-foot-tall stone wall. Small rocks, each paler than the gray stone making up the bulk of the wall, guarded its top, embedded about twenty feet from each other.

"Ward stones," Charlotte said.

Climbing the wall was out of the question. The ward wouldn't let them pass.

"New plan." Richard turned, and they trailed the wall, heading down. Somewhere there had to be a gate or an opening.

Ahead and to the right, screams cut the silence. An orange-and-red glow lit the night, punctuated by a column of smoke. Jason's crew had set something on fire.

The side street curved, and they followed it around the houses, closer to the fire and to another wall. An iron gate lay wrenched to the side. Richard ducked through the opening. A wide courtyard spread before him. To the right, near a blocky building, a fight raged between the slavers and a ragged mob armed with shackles and rocks. The slaves struck out, their haggard faces contorted with bestial fury, their bodies, gaping through the holes in their rags, bearing whip marks. They had no weapons. They ripped into the slavers with their nails and teeth like wild animals.

These weren't the freshly acquired, to be sold as slaves. No, they were the rejects, probably used for manual labor on the island, little more than beasts of burden. No human being should have been treated this way, but they had been, and now they were finally venting their rage. They would kill anyone in their path.

Straight ahead, a raised platform with seven sets of metal posts stood, each post widening at the top. The slaves' shackles would be fixed to the post, under that wide top, so they could be evaluated. To the right, another gate gaped open, and another group squared off for its control. Nine armed slavers in leather on one side and four of Jason's people on the other. Neither was willing to make the first move. Jason's people were good and looked desperate, but the slavers outnumbered them two to one.

He had to get through that gate.

Richard grabbed Charlotte's hand and squeezed it. "We'll have to cut our way through. Stay behind me."

He strode toward the fight. A slave spun into his way. Richard knocked him aside and thrust himself between the two lines, holding his sword lightly at an angle.

The slavers surveyed him, spreading out. He heard Jason's people move back.

Here, poised on the threshold between violence and peace, was his true place. Generations of warriors, stretching back through time to the fierce native clans that had first fled into the Mire to escape a magic catastrophe, had stood just like him, balanced on that sword's blade between life and death. Here he was in control, serene and at peace.

In that brief moment, when their lives and his came together, he truly lived. But for him to experience life, his opponents had to die.

The first slaver moved to his right. Richard struck, piercing and cutting with a surgeon's precision and speed honed by countless hours of practice. He spun in a fluid movement and stopped, his sword held at a downward angle.

The slavers looked at him.

The second, fourth, fifth, and seventh of them fell. They made no noise; they simply crumpled to the ground.

The remaining slavers froze for an agonizing second and rushed him. He melted into the moment, striking without thought, completely on instinct. *Gash across the chest, reverse, throat cut, abdomen cut, stab under the rib cage to the right, free the blade cutting across a chest in the same move, reverse, cut across the throat, thrust forward . . . and it's over.*

Too soon. It was always over too soon.

The last slaver stopped short of his sword. The thrust never connected. The man lingered upright for the space of a breath and sank to his knees, struggling for air. Behind him, Charlotte's magic coiled back into her body.

She stood very still, her eyes opened wide, looking at him as if they had met for the first time. *This is it,* he wanted to tell her. *This is who I am.*

He couldn't tell if she was surprised or horrified or perhaps both or neither. Regret stabbed at him, but then it was better that she knew his true nature. They had to move. He took her hand, and they ran to the gate.

"Thank you," he told her. "That was brave of you, but also unnecessary. Please don't do that again. I don't want to accidentally injure you."

She pulled her hand out of his fingers. "I'm not helpless, Richard."

Did she find his touch repulsive? He sliced through the lock securing the gate. "I know you're anything but. But you've done your part, and it's my turn. Save your reserves. We may need them."

They went through the gate, and Charlotte gasped. Above them a corpse hung from a pole. A boy, Jack's age. His eyes had been gouged out. His mouth was sewn shut. His nose was a broken mess of flesh and cartilage on a face scoured with burn marks. A sign hanging around his neck read, "We're always watching."

He had seen this before—the slavers' favorite visual aid to discourage escape. He had pried Jason out of a hole in the ground just before he was about to end up on such a pole. Anger, hot and furious, burned in him, then died down to a simmer.

"He was alive," Charlotte whispered.

"What?"

"He was alive when they mutilated him. Those are pre-death wounds."

Darkness whipped out of her. The hair on the back of his neck rose.

Charlotte clenched her fists. "I'm going to kill every slaver we find."

He noticed the set of her jaw and the thin line of her lips. Her eyes burned. He recognized this fury. It and he were old friends, and he knew it was useless to get in its way. "As you wish," he told her. "All I ask is that we move up the hill toward the bookkeeper."

Ahead, the streets unrolled before them, climbing up a low hill. They marched upward together.

THE house sat recessed from the street, a stately, respect-able, two-story mansion, flanked by carved columns and palm trees. A brown horse was tied to the side, flicking its ears and casting nervous glances at the street.

Richard glanced back behind them. No movement. They had left a trail of dead bodies, and half of them belonged to Charlotte. She killed again and again, driven by an over-whelming need to stop the slaver savagery from happening. He was like that too, at the start of this mess. Back then, every new mutilation and atrocity infuriated him. He had seen things so wrong and shocking, that the only reaction he could manage was to destroy those who committed them. It had become his moral imperative and the only possible human response.

He saw it now in Charlotte. She was trying to cleanse the city. He wasn't a mind reader, but he knew exactly what went through her head. If only she could manage to kill every slaver in their way, the pain would stop. If she didn't kill, she would have to process the full horror of what she had seen in the past five days, and it would rip her to pieces.

It had taken him several months before he realized that killing slavers accomplished nothing. They were the imme-diate tormentors, but no matter how many he cut down, as long as somewhere, someone wealthy was getting wealthier from that torment, new slavers would always take the place of the old. Charlotte would come to realize this too, but for now she needed to act, and act she did. He had known that many plagues existed, but seeing them in all their terrifying glory was an educational experience.

She was walking oddly now, as if her feet hurt when she rested her weight on them. Her lips were pressed together into a thin, hard line. Her skin was pale, her eyes very bright. She looked feverish. She must be expending too much magic. There were only two ways from here: she would stop exerting herself and recover, or she would drain herself and die.

"We're almost done," he told her. "No more, Charlotte. Save yourself."

Charlotte nodded.

He cut into the door, carving the lock out of it with precise strikes, and pushed the heavy wooden halves open, revealing a large hall with a staircase curving to the second floor.

His mind barely registered the three crossbowmen crouched behind an overturned chest of drawers. He saw the crossbow bolts coming at him and automatically flashed, throwing his magic in a pale shield in front of him. The bolts bounced off. He dashed forward.

"Die," Charlotte ordered, her voice exhausted.

The three crossbowmen choked. He jumped over the chest and cut them down with three strikes.

Behind him, Charlotte slumped over and leaned against the column. Damn it all.

SHE was spent. The last spark of magic burned dimly within her. If Charlotte let it go, her hold on life would slip. She was almost tempted to do it.

How had it snuck up on her so quickly? She had expended a lot of magic, but she never felt tired. She felt light and all-powerful, as if her body had become a burden, and she was disconnected from it. And then, in the last five minutes, as she climbed the steep street to the house, reality crashed back into her. Her body felt so heavy, so constraining, as if every pound of her flesh and bone had become three. Her feet ached. She wanted to vomit just to lighten the load.

The moment her magic flowed out to strike at the bowmen, her legs failed. Too much of herself had gone out with the magic. She had to lean against the column, or she would fall.

Richard loomed over her. She glimpsed anger in his eyes.

"No more." His clipped voice held an unmistakable command.

She felt the magic of his body, a vibrant life force shivering just inches from her. All she had to do was reach for it. Her magic whimpered, eager for sustenance. That's how plaguebringers were born—the exertion drove the healer to seek an alternate source of fuel and siphon off the nearest life to keep on killing.

He dipped his head to meet her eyes. "Charlotte!"

She wasn't ready to give up on life yet. "Do not raise your voice at me, my lord. I know where my limits are, and I have no intention of fainting or dying. I won't use my magic anymore. You're on your own."

A lean, dark-haired man walked out from behind the staircase. He carried a sword.

THE man held a Sud sword, a long, slender length of steel. Young, fit, walking with perfect balance, and carrying his sword with complete confidence. An adept, probably a professional fighter.

Richard flicked the blood off his blade.

They looked at each other.

The sword master attacked. Richard parried and lunged. The blade met a wall of blue flash and slid off. Magic burned his arm. The Sud used the flash to reinforce his blade. Fantastic. And here he thought this would be easy.

Richard ignored the pain and spun, delivering a short

barrage of strikes. The Sud parried, dancing and spinning. They moved across the floor. Richard attacked. Strike, strike, strike. His blade bounced from the Sud's sword. Normally, his flash-sharpened blade would've severed his opponent's weapon.

The man was good, Richard gave him that.

Richard backed away. He walked the path of the lightning blade, relying on that first, faster-than-sight strike to instantly incapacitate his opponent. Failing that, he fought with precision, banking on his power and control. The rapid melee of parrying and trading blows while covering a lot of ground was his weakness, while the Sudanese swordsmen reveled in it.

The Sud attacked in a flurry of blows. Richard parried, lunging, thrusting, looking for an opening and finding none. The Sud coated his entire sword in a protective magic sheath, making it nearly impossible to break and using it as a shield. It was down to skill and speed, and the Sud had plenty of both.

The man feinted to the right. Richard pulled away, avoiding the trap. As he dodged, the man hopped forward, turning the feint into a spin, and kicked. Richard saw it, but he had no way to avoid it. He spun into it, flexing, taking the hit on his left shoulder. The kick hammered into the muscle, and Richard staggered back. Like being hit with a club.

The Sudanese swordsman landed and spun on one foot, showing off. "My technique is superior."

Vanity. The Sud was young, hungry, and eager to prove that he was better. *Thank you for showing me the chip in your armor.*

"Keep hopping around," Richard said. "Your dance teacher isn't here to clap for you, but I'm enjoying the show."

Most men would've begun to tire by now. He doubted this one would. The Sud seemed to take putting spring into one's step literally. His sword was unbreakable, his technique flawless. But the man himself was flawed.

A hint of movement tugged at Richard. He turned his head slightly. Charlotte pushed away from the column. He had to keep her from doing anything rash. Charlotte was a proud woman. If she had any strength at all, she would've remained upright, so she must've been at the end of her rope. If she thought he was desperate, she'd try to save him. Letting her die for his sake wasn't in the plan.

He shrugged, nonchalant. "My lady, I'll be with you in a moment. I just need to pull the wings off that pretty butterfly."

The Sud clenched his teeth, making his jaw muscles bulge. It wouldn't take too much more to nudge him in the right direction.

"Don't mind me," Charlotte said.

"First I'll kill him, then you," the Sud promised.

"I don't think so." Charlotte sat on the overturned chest. "He's better."

"I'm better and faster," the Sud said.

She shook her head, her voice matter-of-fact. "Not only is he better, but you fight for money. He has more at stake."

No panic, no tremor in her voice. Just a calm statement. She hit the Sud right where it hurt, and she did it as if the outcome of the fight were already a foregone conclusion. Damn, but that was impressive.

Charlotte had no doubt he would win. Richard shifted the grip on his sword. He couldn't disappoint.

He motioned to the Sud with the fingers of his left hand. "Come on, let's have the finale. I can't waste any more time on your prancing. The lady is waiting, and I don't want to be rude."

The Sud leaped, unleashing a flurry of strokes, too fast to keep up. Richard parried the first, the second, the third, and counterattacked, holding his sword with both hands, sinking all of his strength into the overhead blow.

The Sud flashed, shielding his blade, but the sheer power of the impact staggered him.

Richard struck again, bringing a barrage of blows onto the Sud's sword, forcing him back with every strike. Sweat broke out on Richard's forehead. This attack was draining all of his reserves, but he was betting on the Sud's ego. If he was lucky, the younger man would rise to the challenge. A wiser swordsman would simply wait Richard out and, once he tired, kill him at his leisure, but youth and wisdom didn't always travel together.

The Sud lunged forward, grinding his blade against Richard's, flash against flash. They struggled, locked. The Sud twisted, trying to catch Richard's leading leg with his foot, aiming to trip him. Richard shoved him back. The younger man stumbled, off-balance. Richard hammered a front kick to his chest.

The Sud fell back and rolled to his feet like a cat. His face was a furious mask. He screamed and charged. Richard sidestepped his barrage of strikes, dodging, parrying, knocking the blade aside when he could. He knew the wall was behind him, but there was no place to go.

His foot touched the stone of the wall. The Sud whirled like his joints were liquid and thrust, aiming at the heart, so fast he blurred. Richard parried on pure instinct, sliding his blade under the strike. Their magic ground against each other, blue against white. The man's entire weight pressed onto Richard's blade, tearing a ragged snarl from him.

The swordsman's blade slid up, gaining an inch.

Richard pushed back, his arms shaking from the strain. Holding the younger man's deadweight was squeezing the last drops of strength from his tired body.

Another inch. The Sud's narrow blade slid along Richard's sword. He saw it move but was powerless to stop it.

The sword cut his left biceps, slicing through the muscle in an agonizing slow burn.

Sonovabitch. There was no way out of this position that didn't end with his being hurt. Even if he could summon enough strength to shove the younger man back, the effort would leave him exposed for a counterstrike, and with his back to the wall, he had no way to maneuver.

The Sud grinned.

If he lost, Charlotte would die. He would fail, and Sophie would be left alone with her demons. He had to kill the other man.

He would endure pain if it meant he would win.

Richard dropped his blade. The Sud's sword, abruptly free from resistance, slid forward and cut deeper across his arm, biting into the bone in a flash of pain. Thrown off-balance, the Sud pitched forward, and Richard hammered his fist into the man's throat. The swordsman rocked back from the blow. Richard tore the sword from his opponent's hand, flashed, coating it in his magic, and thrust it upward, under the rib cage. The blade carved through the lungs and heart like a knife through a soft pear. The bloody end emerged from the Sud's breast and sliced into the underside of his chin.

The man opened his mouth, surprise making his face look young . . . Blood poured out from between his teeth, drenching them in red. Richard pushed him back, and the Sud fell, his unseeing eyes staring at the ceiling.

Richard slumped forward, trying to catch his breath. His left arm hung useless, the gash in his muscle burning as if someone had poured molten lead into wound. He stared at the man by his feet. What was he, twenty-five? Twenty-eight? His whole life ahead of him, good looks, talent, and now he was dead. Such a waste.

Richard gritted his teeth and looked at the cut. Blood drenched his skin and dripped on the floor. He didn't have much of it to spare as it was.

Gods, it hurt like hell. He breathed in deeply through his nose, trying to separate himself from the pain, forced his face into a calm mask, and turned to Charlotte.

She sagged on the overturned chest, her shoulders slumped, her spine bent. "Let me see it."

"No." If she saw it, she would try to heal him, and he couldn't let her do that.

"My lord—"

"I said no."

"—don't be a baby."

A baby? He ripped a sleeve off the Sud's shirt and wrapped it around his arm. "There. It's fixed."

"Don't be ridiculous."

He picked up his sword. His left arm felt like it was on fire, and it hurt to move.

"Richard, don't ignore me. You just wrapped a filthy rag over an open wound, which is surely infected now."

He walked over to her. "I'm fine. You're spent."

"At least let me look at it!"

"Are you well enough to go upstairs?"

She pushed herself up from the chest, that familiar ice flashing in her eyes. "Without my magic and with my eyes closed, I'm a better field medic than you are. You *will* let me look at your wound and dress it properly instead of wrapping some soiled sleeve around it. It will take two minutes, then we can go upstairs and hunt down the bookkeeper. Or we can do it your way, and you can faint from blood loss, in which case we're both dead because I can't carry you or protect you. Your arm, my lord. Now."

He turned, presenting her with his left arm. It was easier than arguing. She pulled a bag from under her cloak, opened it, and a took out a plastic first-aid kit, complete with the Broken's familiar red cross on it. Charlotte opened the kit, took out a small vial, and handed it to him. "Drink this."

He pulled the cork out with his teeth and gulped the bitter liquid. Cold rushed through him, down the injured muscle, right to the source of pain. A welcome numbness came. It felt heavenly.

Charlotte splashed something on the cut and began wrapping his arm. "He cut the bone."

"Mhm."

"This stone-faced routine isn't necessary. I know the pain is excruciating."

"If my rolling around on the ground and crying would make things easier for you, by all means I will oblige." It finally sank in. He had won and lived, and so did she.

Charlotte rolled her eyes. "We're lucky his sword was so sharp. The cut is very clean. If you give me an hour or two to recover, I will heal this. Was it necessary to let him slash you?"

Argh. "Yes, it was. He was very good, and I didn't have

a choice about it. Since when are you a connoisseur of martial arts?" He was actually arguing that he was a lesser
swordsman. How did it even make sense?

"Since my life started depending on them."

"The next time I'm in a fight for my life, I'll be sure to
ask your advice, my lady."

"If you do, I'll advise you to not throw away your sword."

He almost growled, but it would've frightened her, and
he held himself in check. An infuriating, impossible woman.

She tied the final knot and wrapped white tape around
the bandage. "What's next?"

"We go upstairs."

"Very well." She leaned toward him to tie a sling around
his shoulder. Her hair brushed against his cheek. Desire
stabbed him, sudden and overwhelming. His irritation only
made him want her more.

Charlotte slid his arm into the sling and put the kit back
into the bag. "If you promise not to get yourself cut or skew-
ered with anyone else's sword, I promise not to faint."

Delightful. "I'd be a fool not to take that generous offer."

They started up the stairs, agonizingly slow.

"Did you really think I would win?" he asked.

She turned to look at him, gray eyes so beautiful on her
lovely face. "Of course."

Richard imagined stepping forward, pulling her to him
with his uninjured hand, and kissing her right there on the
stairs. In his mind, her lips were warm and inviting. In his
mind, she loved it and kissed him back.

His mind was a place of many dreams, most of them dead
and abandoned. *She's walking next to you,* he told himself.
*She saw the true you, and she's still willing to care for you.
Enjoy what little you have while you have it.*

They made it into the hallway. A faint light painted the
floor under the door on their right. Richard pointed at the
wall by the door. Charlotte pressed her back against it.

He kicked in the door, spinning to the side. Bullets pep-
pered the opposite wall, biting chunks out of the plaster.

He'd seen the inside of the room for a fraction of a second, but it was enough: a red-haired woman sat behind a desk and a tall man stood next to her, armed with one of the Broken's guns. Richard yanked a throwing knife out of the sheath on his belt, thrust himself into the doorway, and hurled the blade. The knife bit into the gunman's throat. The man stumbled back and fell.

The woman stared at him with cold, clear eyes. She had a heart-shaped face, with the high, contoured cheekbones bluebloods often found desirable. Her flame red hair coiled around her head in a complex braid. Her tunic was silk, cut in what was assuredly the latest style. An oval pendant hung from her neck on a thin gold chain: a pale, aquamarine stone the size of his thumbnail. She looked to be near Charlotte's age.

Behind her were two large windows. Rows of shelves supported an assortment of books on the right wall while a large white limestone fireplace occupied the left. An *arithmetika*, a magic-powered calculator, sat on her desk, next to stacks of paper. No weapons appeared to be in the vicinity.

"We found the bookkeeper," Richard said. "Come inside, Charlotte."

She walked into the room. She saw the dead gunman. Her eyebrows rose briefly, then Charlotte sank into the nearest chair.

"If you had a knife, why didn't you throw it at the swordsman downstairs?"

"It would've been a waste. He would've knocked it aside." Richard nodded at the woman. "Place both hands on the desk."

She did so. Delicate fingers, adorned with thin gold rings studded with stones. Wealth and taste were sometimes unlikely bedfellows, but in this case, they were clearly bosom buddies. A familiar anger flared in him.

"You're wealthy, probably well educated," he said. "Juliana Academy, perhaps." Juliana's was considered the best place for blueblood girls with money to receive their education.

He'd became very familiar with Adrianglian school selection for Lark's sake. He shouldn't have bothered. His niece shot down all of his careful choices.

"Winters College," Charlotte said. "Her tunic perfectly matches the shade of her eyes. Juliana's encourages more creativity."

The woman arched an eyebrow and looked Charlotte over, pausing on her dirty, bloodstained clothes. His urge to injure her shot into overdrive.

"And where did you study, if I may ask?"

"I had personal tutorship from one of the first ten," Charlotte said, her voice glacially cold and cutting with scorn like a knife. "Don't try to belittle me; you're hopelessly outclassed. I see shortcomings in your every single aspect, from your lack of taste to your rotten morality. You've involved yourself in the basest of crimes. You facilitated murder, rape, and the torture of children. Your conduct is unbecoming a peer of realm."

He almost winced.

The woman drew back, her cheeks turning red. "Please, spare me the rhetoric. We're a higher breed. You know this as well as I do. You simply put on blinders and call it altruism. I call it willful ignorance. Those of us who are blueblood became so because our ancestors rose from the ranks of unwashed mobs. They were the thanes, the chiefs, the leaders of their people. The betters of the rest by virtue of their abilities and will. We're their descendants. They climbed to power, and we maintain it. It's that simple. These people you're accusing me of crimes against live like animals. In many cases, being stripped of their freedom is the best thing that ever happened to them."

Charlotte stared at her. "The function of a noble title is to serve the people. Seven blocks from here, there's a body of a boy whose eyes have been gouged out with his mouth sewn shut. He was still alive when they did it. What is wrong with you? Are you human at all?"

"A regrettable but necessary casualty." The bookkeeper crossed her thin arms on her chest. "But you are right, perhaps we should've left him with his lovely family to live in squalor while his parents drank themselves senseless in an effort to forget their own laziness and beat him when his existence reminded them of their baseness. Those who are capable act. They amount to something in life. They don't live in filth, gorging themselves on cheap food, drowning in addictions, and rutting to produce yet more of their ilk. We rescue children from that. We provide a valuable service."

Unbelievable.

Charlotte made a choking noise.

"Your condemnation means nothing," the bookkeeper said. "This enterprise was conceived by a mind far superior to yours or mine. Think about it, when a blueblood buys a pretty young girl, she has a shot at a better life. If she's smart, she will elevate herself by having his child. Just the other day, we fulfilled a special order for a childless couple. They wanted a pair of twins, a boy and a girl, between the ages of two and four, resembling both of them. Do you have any idea how difficult it was to find suitable children? Yet we've managed. Slavery is an opportunity. It's regrettable you can't understand that."

Nothing either Charlotte or Richard could say would ever make this woman see reason.

"Kill her," Charlotte said. "If you don't kill her now, I'll do it myself."

"We need her testimony and information." He approached the table. He had no idea how they would make it down the hill and to the port with a captive, but by gods, he would try.

"Killing me won't be necessary." The woman raised her chin. "Unlike you, I know my duty to the spear."

She grasped her pendant.

Richard lunged to stop her.

The stone crunched under the pressure of her fingers. A blinding spike of light shot out into her chin, through her head, and out of her skull.

Charlotte gasped.

The bookkeeper sagged in her chair, dead, her head drooping to the side. The whole thing took less than a second. She had been wearing an Owner's Gift necklace. He should have seen it, gods damn it.

The world screeched to a halt. He felt like he was falling.

All this time, all this work, and the arrogant scum killed herself. Was there no justice in the world?

Maybe Charlotte . . . He pivoted to her.

"Very dead," she said, her face disgusted. "Irreversibly dead."

"Damn it."

His mind whirred, trying to reassess the situation. Wallowing in defeat never served any purpose. No, he was kidding himself. Even if they had managed to take her alive, neither of them could have gotten her to the ship in their present condition, and if they did, by some miracle, manage it, she would never testify. But it wasn't over, he reminded himself. Not yet. They might not have the bookkeeper alive, but they still had her office and everything within it.

Duty to the spear. Only one spear came to mind. "Gaesum," he thought out loud. The symbol of the Adrianglian royal family.

"That would explain her devotion," Charlotte said. "If she thought she was serving the crown in some capacity, she couldn't permit herself to acknowledge that they could do something base, or her entire worldview would come crashing down."

They looked at each other. In Adrianglia, the crown was revered. The power of the royal bloodline had its limitations, but the monarch still held the presiding position over the Council, wielding much of the power within the executive branch. The royal family was looked upon as the epitome of behavior and personal honor. The idea that the crown could be involved in the slave trade was unthinkable.

"There has to be a trail somewhere. She was a bookkeeper; she had to have kept financial records." Richard strode to the shelves and pulled a stack of books out. He handed them to Charlotte. She leafed through them while he rummaged through the desk. His search of the drawers turned up a wooden box, unlocked. Inside, necklaces lay in a row, each with a simple large gemstone in a variety of colors. Unlike the bookkeeper's pendant, their chains were short. Once fastened around the neck, they couldn't be removed by slipping them over the head.

"Is that what she used to kill herself?" Charlotte asked, her voice dry.

He nodded. "They're called Owner's Gifts." He picked one up, dangling the false ruby pendant. "They're given to young attractive slaves who are used for sexual gratification. They have a one-time lock: once fastened, they're impossible to take off without cutting through the chain. Each contains a small magic charge designed to kill the wearer. The necklace detonates if the chain is cut or the stone is damaged. A pointed reminder that if you disobey or displease, your life can end in an instant. They work much better than shackles and are a lot less obvious."

She clenched her teeth, and he read a mix of horror and disgust in her face. "Every time I think I've reached the limit, this place shocks me."

And that was true, Richard realized. He thought she'd grow callous or numb, but every new evidence of cruelty cut a new wound into her. Again, he wished he hadn't brought her here. There were only so many wounds one could take.

"What do you make of this?" Charlotte showed him a hollowed-out book.

Hope stirred in him. "Was there anything inside?"

"No."

And the newborn hope plummeted to its death. "We have to keep looking."

Twenty minutes later, they looked at each other across the table. The office was a wreck. They had left nothing untouched. The ledgers, if they existed, eluded them.

Richard braced himself on the table. He felt another bout of dizziness coming on. He'd gotten through the first one a few minutes ago, but now the vertigo was back. Taking wounds came with a price.

"Richard," Charlotte said.

He turned.

A bloody figure stood in the doorway, his hair and clothes stained with gore and soot. His eyes were tired, and he was carrying a bloody crowbar. A huge black dog panted by his side.

"Jack?" Richard said.

"Hi." Jack dropped the crowbar. It clanged on the floor.

"How are you?" Charlotte asked.

"Good," he said, his voice dull. "I'm all funned out. I think we should go to the ship now. The city is burning, the fire's coming this way, and the smoke is making my throat itch."

"We can't leave yet." Charlotte sighed. "We've looked everywhere, but we haven't found the ledgers. We have to find them, or all this was for nothing."

"Did you look in the safe?" Jack asked.

"What safe?" The room had no safe, only a table and the shelves, and he had knocked on all the clear walls looking for a hollow spot.

"In the fireplace."

Richard turned to the fireplace. It was a typical Weird limestone fireplace without a mantel. No fire was laid out and the fire pit was perfectly clean. No soot marks. It definitely hadn't been used, but this far south it might have been conceived as decorative. Richard moved to it, probing the stones with his hand. "What makes you think there is a safe in it?"

Jack sat by Charlotte on the floor. "There's no chimney. It smells like the dead woman's perfume—I can scent it from here. Also, there's a doorstop."

"Where?" Charlotte asked, brushing debris from Jack's hair.

Jack pointed to the ground. A small ornate doorstop designed to be slid under a door sat by the desk. If the front of the fireplace swung open like a door, it was in the perfect position to be grabbed and wedged under it.

There was no reason for the bookkeeper to spend time at the fireplace. She wouldn't have gone anywhere near it.

Richard knocked at the stones. If there was some mecha-
nism to unlock it, he couldn't see it. He picked up his sword.

"Maybe there is a hidden switch," Charlotte said.

"It would take too long." He concentrated, feeding magic
into the blade, forcing it toward the tip of the sword. The
flash-coated edge glowed brighter and brighter, until it blazed
like a tiny star. Richard raised the sword and forced the tip
into the limestone, testing it. The blade sank into the fireplace, cutting through the rock with surprising ease. No more
than half an inch, he decided. If there was a safe, he didn't
want to damage the contents. He dropped to one knee,
slashed horizontally across the fireplace, rose, and slashed
again at his eye level.

The front of the fireplace slid half an inch. Richard
stepped back. The cut section crashed down and fell with a
loud thud, its back exposed—wooden boards with a thin
layer of limestone affixed to its front. Inside the gutted fireplace, shelves gaped, containing five small black books and
one red one.

He turned to Jack. "Well done."

"You're a genius." Charlotte hugged the boy.

Richard pulled out the books and brought them over to
Charlotte. His hands shook.

She opened the first black book, and her eyes widened
as she read.

He flipped through the red volume, scanning the pages
filled with neat rows of accounting figures. Investments and
payments, to and from five names. Here they were, the people
directly profiting from the sale of human beings. Lord Casside, a rich blueblood who'd made his money in the import
and export trade. He'd seen him once at Declan's house during a formal dinner. Lady Ermine. He had no idea who she
was, but he would find out. Baron Rene, another unfamiliar
name. Lord Maedoc, a retired general, a decorated war hero.
And . . .

"Viscount Robert Brennan."

"The king's cousin?" Charlotte asked.

Richard nodded. So it was true. The bookkeeper truly served the spear. Robert Brennan, the seventh person in line for the throne. Never in his calculations had he ever thought that the chain of command went that high.

"You're shocked," Charlotte said.

"I don't understand." Richard leaned against the desk. "He was born wearing a silk shirt. He has wealth, status, the privilege afforded to his bloodline, the best education one can buy . . ."

All the things that had been denied to Richard. An education was a double-edged sword: it broadened his horizons, and, at the same time, it made him painfully aware of the opportunities he would never have. There was a time when he felt trapped in the Mire, aware of the world outside the Edge but unable to get to it, chained to the swamp. He had neither the breeding, nor the money, nor the opportunity to make it past the Louisiana troops guarding the border with the Edge, but he had the intellect and the education to understand the full futility of his position. He would've killed to open just one door and escape. Brennan had all the advantages. Every door was open to him.

"Why? Why do this? He's like a millionaire who's robbing beggars."

"Who knows," Charlotte said. "Maybe it's the thrill of doing something criminal."

She sounded exhausted. Worry stabbed at him. He had to get her and the boy out of here.

He cut a section of the gauzy curtain, stacked the books on it, and tied it into a makeshift bag. Stealing was criminal. This was an atrocity. More so, because Brennan, born into privilege, had a duty. He had a responsibility to wield his influence for the benefit of the realm, and instead he spat on it. Whatever sickness drove Brennan to rule over the slave trade, Richard would make sure he paid. He would make certain. He had promised it to Sophie, and he would see it through.

Richard sheathed his sword and handed the bag of books to Jack. "This is vitally important. Guard it."

The boy nodded.

Richard offered Charlotte his right hand. She rose from the chair, swaying a little. They walked downstairs and out of the front door. Below them, the city stretched down the hill to the harbor. Orange flames billowed from two different sides of the town, far to the left and closer to the right, devouring the structures. Here and there, isolated shots rang out, followed by screams. A single ship waited in the middle of the harbor, like a graceful bird on a sea of black glass, and above it all, in the endless night sky, a pale moon rose, spilling its indifferent light onto the scene.

Richard turned to the left, behind the house. The horse still waited. He untied the reins and brought it over to Charlotte.

"I can walk."

"Charlotte." He hadn't meant to put all of his frustration into that one single word, but somehow he did.

She blinked, startled.

"Please, get on the horse."

She climbed into the saddle. He took the reins and started down the street, Jack at his side. The dog took position ahead of them. Richard's face itched mercilessly. As soon as they got down to the coast, he would wash all the gunk of his disguise off his skin.

"George has been alone with dad for a long time," Jack said.

It was a lot to ask, but he had confidence in George, and the boy needed to redeem himself. "He will be fine."

"Are you going to kill our dad?" the boy asked quietly.

"It's not for me to decide what to do with your father." John Drayton deserved to die, and if Drayton weren't connected to the boys, he would dispose of the man like the piece of garbage he was. But family took precedence, and the children's claim superseded his.

"If you're going to let us handle it, don't let George do it," Jack said. "I'll kill him for grandma. I don't care. I don't even remember him, but George waited for him all this time. It would be bad for him."

It was said that changelings didn't understand human

emotion. They understood it just fine, Richard reflected. They simply couldn't figure out why others chose to mask what they truly felt. Jack wanted to spare his brother. Even in the Mire, where things like betrayal and punishment were kept in the family, no child was expected to kill his parent.

The boy, no, the young man was looking at him.

"Don't worry," he told Jack. "That's one burden neither of you will have to carry."

NINE

"YOU look good," John Drayton said from the opposite end of his cabin. "Solid. All grown-up. I remember when you were sickly. You kept raising animals because you couldn't stand to watch something die. I take it you've gotten over that."

George examined the man in front of him. The key was to cordon off his own anger and evaluate him as he would any other opponent. The years had banged John around, but he was in good health. He ate well and carried a few extra pounds. The air in the cabin hinted at the spicy notes of his cologne. His clothes were well cut from good fabric. His hair was professionally shorn to flatter his face. John Drayton was a vain man, and he liked spending money on himself.

George remembered him as being big, a tall shadow. He remembered him being funny. He would make jokes.

The thought spurred the vicious part of him into a gallop. Jokes. Right.

For the first hour and a half, John had kept his mouth shut, probably waiting for him to talk. Waiting for "How could you abandon us, Father?" and "I've waited for you to come back, Father!" Waiting for some tell, some clue or lever to push. *Keep waiting, scumbag.*

Most people didn't handle silence well, and John had banked on it and lost. George had no problem with silence. It was an effective tool, and he'd seen his Mirror handlers use it to great effect. Having finally realized that no clues would be coming, John decided to start talking and probe for weaknesses. George had sat in on enough of the Mirror's interrogations to guess the most likely course this conversation would take: John would try to bridge the gap between the six-year-old sickly child he left behind and the sixteen-year-old he saw now.

"You remember what I told you when I left?"

Like an open book.

"I said—"

You mind the family, Georgie. Keep an eye on your sister and brother for me.

"—for you to keep an eye on your sister and brother for me. You've done good. Jack's still alive, that's something. Couldn't have been easy to make that miracle happen."

What do you know about it? What do you know about Jack, about his rages, about his not understanding how people think, about Rose spending hours to coax him back to humanity? What do you know, you slimy weasel? You know nothing of our family. You chose to know nothing.

"How's Rose?"

Where were you when she worked herself into the ground? Oh, that's right, getting rich from misery, rape, and pain.

"You afraid to speak to me, George?" John slapped his palm on the desk. "Damn it, boy. Tell me how my daughter is!"

George moved Lynda a step closer. "Do that again, and I'll let her gnaw on your neck, slowly, one bite a time. Rose will be delighted when I bring her your head."

John leaned back. Fear shot through his eyes. He hid it fast, but George had seen it. Yes, he knew the type. John would do anything, say anything to avoid physical pain and punishment. He feared being held accountable more than anything.

"You wouldn't do that," John said. "Not the Georgie I remember. The Georgie I remember was kind."

"The Georgie you remember had a father." Argh. He knew he shouldn't have responded to the bait. Too late now.

John's face brightened. "You still have one. Look, I know I haven't done right by you kids. And it's not like I set out to haul slaves for a living. I just kind of fell into it."

"Do tell. How does one fall into slavery?"

"The same way one falls into anything." John spread his arms. He was becoming more animated, happy he'd found some common ground. "You're hard-up for cash, and one day in port, a man asks you if you want to make some easy money."

Easy-breezy. No need to worry about paltry things like honor, integrity, and sleeping well at night.

"That's the only kind of money you were ever interested in, isn't it? The easy money."

"Hey, I work hard just like anybody else. I just had a stretch of hard luck there for a while." John leaned forward. "Georgie, listen to me. Whatever else happens, I'm still your father. I've done pretty well for myself here, and I wanted to come and find you guys. I kept thinking, just do one more run, get a little bit more money, then I'll split. But I'm in a good place now, and I'm sick of these slaver assholes. We can take off, you know. You and me. I can show you the ropes, bring you into the family business. I'm a good sailor, Georgie. Let me tell you, when you go out on the ocean and leave the shore behind, it's something. Just water everywhere, sapphire blue for miles and miles. Water, wind, and sky. You can taste the freedom. There is adventure there. Mystery."

He was good.

"What about Jack?"

John shrugged. "What about him? Jack's a good kid. Didn't go nuts like his people do."

"His people?"

John leaned closer. "Oh, come on, Georgie. We all know it. Rose is mine, you're mine, but Jack was never mine. For him to be what he is, one of his parents had to be a change-ling, and there ain't no changelings in my family or your mother's. I checked. My father wasn't one, my mother isn't one . . ."

George fought against grinding his teeth.

"Their parents weren't changelings, and on your mother's side, nobody was one for three generations back either. Your mother, she wasn't a bad woman, but she was troubled. You think it was easy knowing she opened her legs to every bastard that came through town? It hurt me. Really hurt me, but I've come to terms with it. And so should you. You always looked out for Jack. Rose and your grandma, they put that burden on you, and I never thought it was fair. Everyone deserves a break, Georgie. Everyone. Come with me. Jack can look after himself. And later, when you're older and I'm ready to retire, you can take over. This ship isn't just named after me. It's named after you, too."

No, it isn't. He looked into John's eyes and saw a cold calculation there. In that moment George realized he would be dead the moment they left land behind. They'd find what was left of him later, bobbing on the waves with his throat slit and his body torn by fish. *My own father.*

"Thank you, but I already have a career."

"What sort of a career is that?" John pointedly looked over his rags. "If you got one, it doesn't pay too well by the looks of it. No offense to you, boy, but you can do better. Or are you talking about those bandits over there? That's no good. We picked you up near Kelena, that means it's either the Rook, the families, or Jason Parris, and it has to be Parris, because the families know better, and Rook likes running his show personally, and I haven't seen him. Am I right? I am right. Parris is a ravenous shark, that's what he is. Cutthroat. Can you take a man's life, Georgie? You think about that because you've got to be a cold, calculating killer to be in his company."

"I'm not with Jason Parris." George leaned back.

"Who are you with, then?"

George reached inside his sleeve, peeled off the coin he kept taped on his forearm, and tossed it to him. "I'm with the people who fish for ravenous sharks."

John caught the coin. The magic charge bit his fingers with tiny sparks. He flinched. The surface of the coin flowed, turning into a miniature mirror. Every agent of the Mirror carried one. Some wore rings, some had earrings, and some embedded it into a knife's hilt. He'd chosen a coin. It seemed appropriate.

John stared at his own reflection. Blood drained from his face. John dropped the coin like it was hot.

"I'm an underagent of the third degree, Father. I started when I was fourteen. My mission count is at twelve, ten successes and two aborts. My kill count is at seven, and I'm very good with a rapier. In two years, when I complete my training, I'll be the youngest full-fledged agent in the Mirror's recent history. Coincidentally, in two more years I'll also graduate from Brasil's Academy, since I've taken their entrance exams and passed them with a perfect score. There is a place for me waiting in the Diplomatic Corps."

John Drayton stared at him, his face slack with shock.

"So you see, Father, if I ever feel the need to play at being a sailor, a vessel will either be provided for me, or I'll purchase one. Given that my name is now George Camarine and the Duke of the Southern Provinces thinks of me as his grandson, I can afford an entire fleet. A small one, but it will be sufficient." George smiled, a controlled baring of teeth. "I've already accomplished more in my life than you could ever hope to achieve. Your promises of a grandiose smuggler life hold no attraction to me, so do be quiet, Father. I'm fighting a strong urge to kill you, and I'd hate to slip up and do you in before Jack comes back."

Knuckles rapped on the door.

"Enter," George said.

The door swung open. Richard shouldered his way in, favoring his left side. His left arm rested in a sling. He had washed off his disguise and looked like himself. Jack followed, supporting Charlotte. She, on other hand, looked like a shadow of her former self: pale, exhausted, and sickly.

"Did you run into trouble?" George asked.

"Some," Richard said. "Any problems?"

"None. Just talking to the dead man."

John licked his lips. "What have I ever done to you that you hate me so much?"

"The crew you were supposed to be meeting by Kelena was chasing me," Richard said. "I'm the Hunter."

John drew back.

"I ended up at your mother's house," Richard said. "We're distantly related by marriage, and she recognized me and tried to help me."

"Grandmother is dead," Jack said. "The slavers burned our house. You killed grandma, Dad."

John's hands shook. He swallowed. "I wasn't there."

Oh no, you don't get to weasel your way out of this one.

"Not directly, but you made it possible," George said. "You contributed."

John dragged his hand over his face and through his hair.

Richard took a piece of paper off the desk, wrote something on it, and pushed it across the desk to John. "Five names. What do you know?"

John looked at the list. His voice lost all emotion. "They're called the Council. That's where the real money goes. Maedoc is the muscle; he supplies the slavers. Casside is the main investor. I don't know what the other two do. Brennan runs the whole show. That's all I've got. I'm low on the ladder. If you expect me to testify, I won't. I'll never make it. Brennan will have my throat slit before I ever get a word out, and even if I did, it's all rumors. I never met any of them. We never talked. I follow the schedule, pick up slaves, bring them here, and get paid. That's the end of it."

"I'm done with him." Richard turned to him. "He's yours."

Finally. He rose.

"George," Charlotte said softly.

He turned to her.

"Think about what you're about to do. He is your father. Think about the cost." She glanced past him. "Think about the guilt."

It dawned on him: Jack. Jack always wanted their father to return. When they were small, he used to sit in a tree, watching the road, waiting for him to come back. In elementary school, in the Broken, Jack would fight anyone who dared to say anything bad about their dad, and he would beat them bloody. George had no problem with his hands being bloody, and neither did Jack in the heat of the moment, but he might regret it later. Jack tended to brood, and sometimes his brooding took him to dark places. He was only fourteen.

John Drayton had to die. He had to pay the price for the inhumanities he helped commit, but George couldn't let John's death ruin his brother. The scumbag wasn't worth a single minute of Jack's self-loathing.

"You're right," George said. "It's not worth it. We'll get a boat, take him to the mainland, and have him put away. You'll be in prison for so long, you'll forget what the sun looks like."

"Do what the boy says," Richard said.

John rose. "Right." He reached out to ruffle Jack's hair. Jack pulled back, avoiding the touch.

John dropped his hand. "Right."

They went out, Richard first, then John, and George, with Lynda in tow. Jack was the last.

Outside, the stench of smoke assaulted George's nostrils. The island town burned, the orange glow of its fire reflecting in the waters of the harbor. A cleansing fire, George decided. And a warning. Richard had unleashed Jason Parris on the island like a tornado. The news of the Market's burning would carry, and soon every slaver along the Eastern seaboard would know he wasn't invincible and his paycheck wasn't safe. It was a brilliant move. Richard was a born tactician. George would have to remember that.

The cabin door swung open behind him. Jack emerged.

Richard stepped closer to him. "I need you to watch Charlotte for me. She overspent herself."

"Why me?" Jack asked.

"Because Jason's crew is full of bad men, and she's alone and vulnerable."

Jack glanced first at Richard, then at George. He wasn't quite buying it.

"Can you just do one thing without arguing?" George tossed his hair back. "Just do it."

"You do it."

"You owe me for the canal."

Jack growled something under his breath.

"Don't worry," Richard said. "I haven't forgotten."

Forgotten what?

Jack shrugged and went into the cabin.

"Into the boat." Richard pointed to a small barge waiting by the side of the vessel. They must've used it to come aboard.

They got into the barge, Richard at the nose, then John Drayton. George sent Lynda in next, added insurance. Everyone sat. George took a seat at the stern, passed his hand over the motor, starting the magic chain reaction, and the boat sped across the harbor to the shore. Midway through it, George let go of Lynda. She pitched into the waves, softly, and sank into the cool, soothing depths to finally rest. He didn't need her anymore. Half a minute later the boat plowed into the soft sand of the beach. The two men stepped out. He followed.

"Still protecting your brother," John said.

The frustration he had been holding in finally broke free. "Shut up. You don't know him. Don't talk about him. Because of you, Mémère is dead. It's good that she's dead— because if she knew what you've become, it would kill her."

John inhaled. "Fine. Let's get this over with."

Richard pulled out his sword.

"He's my responsibility," George said. "My family and my shame."

John winced.

Richard held out his blade. George took it. The lean, razor-sharp sword felt so heavy. The hilt was cold. He concentrated, channeling his magic like a current of molten metal from his arm into his fingers, into the sword, and finally letting it stretch across the edge. The blade sparked with white. He'd trained for months to learn how to do it, but now the magic coated the steel as if on its own.

He couldn't bring himself to raise the sword.

George was trapped between guilt and duty. The indecision

hurt, deciding hurt more, and he was so monumentally angry at his father for making him choose. Was he really that weak?

"C'est la différence entre lui et toi." Richard switched to the language of Louisiana.

This is the difference between you and him.

"If you raise that sword, you're letting his actions determine yours," Richard continued in Gaulish. "You're simply reacting to what he has already done. We are forever linked with those we kill. If you end his life, you will drag his corpse with you for the rest of yours. When your brother and sister look at you, they will see the killer of their father; when you look in the mirror, you will see a murderer. Had he lived with you and abused you or those close to you, ending his life might be cathartic, a sign of rebirth. But this man is a stranger to you. You barely know him. There is no empowerment in his death by your hand. He has no right to govern your life. Let your own actions define who you are."

He was right. Killing John Drayton simply wasn't worth it. If he forced himself to do it, he would regret it. It would eat at him, and why should he sentence himself to the same burden he tried to spare Jack?

George swallowed and slowly lowered his sword.

"Can't do it, huh?" John smiled. "I'm still your father, boy."

The very fact that he was goading him meant killing him would be a bad idea. "No," George said. "You're not. You're just some swine that slept with my mother and ran off."

Richard pulled a gun from inside his clothes. It was a firearm from the Broken, a large heavy hunk of metal. He flipped it and offered it to John butt first.

"You're free to go. Use it to protect yourself."

What?

John Drayton had killed, tortured, and raped. If set free, he'd sell them out the first chance he got. He'd go on stealing, hurting, and profiting from other people's misery. It had to end, here and now, so he would never darken his brother's or Rose's horizon.

George turned to Richard.

"Trust me," Richard said. "It's the right thing."

John hefted the gun in his hand, taking a couple of steps back. "Loaded."

"Six bullets," Richard said.

"More than enough."

John raised the gun. George stared down the black barrel, as big as a cannon. Everything around him stopped. The world gained a crystal clarity, and George saw everything in minute detail: the individual leaves of the palm behind his father, the bead of sweat on John's temple, the tiny red veins in his father's eyes . . .

The sound of the safety being released rocked George like the blow of a giant hammer against his skull. He knew the bullet would hit him between the eyes. He was staring death in the face.

"You're an idiot," John said to Richard.

"He's your son," Richard said. His voice was calm, so calm.

He should do something, George realized. He should—

"Yeah, about that," John grimaced. "Sorry, boy. I never thought you were mine either."

John squeezed the trigger. A bolt of white tore out of the gun and bit deep into John's chest. He convulsed soundlessly, like a marionette jerking on invisible strings, and fell into the sand.

George felt the moment his body crossed the threshold between life and death and into his domain. *It's done, Mémère. It's done. He won't hurt anyone else.*

The relief washed over him, replaced instantly by shame. "How?"

"An Owner's Gift necklace," Richard said. "I loaded a stone into the chamber instead of a bullet. When he tried to fire, the stone shattered and released its magic."

"And if he had walked away?"

"I would've stopped him and taken the stone out."

George couldn't tell if it was a convenient lie for his sake or the truth. The terrible thing was, he didn't even care. He was simply relieved that John Drayton was a corpse. *What does that say about me?*

Richard clamped his arm around him. "He died the way he lived. That's the kind of man he was."

"I waited for him." George barely recognized the hoarse, dull sound as his own voice. "I waited for him for years. When Rose was working a crappy job in the Broken, I'd sit on the porch, waiting for her to come home, and pretend I saw him walking up to the house. He would come up with a big smile and tell me, 'George, come sailing with me. We'll look for treasure together.'"

His eyes watered. He forced the tears back. "He tried to get me to abandon my own brother. He tried to kill me. I looked into his eyes. They were cold, like a shark's." He wanted to cry and scream like a child.

"None of what he did or what he had become is your responsibility," Richard said. "He was a grown man, and he's responsible for his own sins. Everything he did in his life led him to this point. I knew he would pull the trigger. It was as inevitable as the sunrise."

George stared at him. "I should've done it. I should've ended it . . . him."

"You feel that way in the heat of the moment because you look at your father and see the legacy of his crimes. It brings you deep shame. You want to wipe it clean and right the wrongs, but killing him wouldn't undo them," Richard said.

"My youngest brother betrayed our family and our relatives died because of it. His cousins, his nieces, nephews, children, people who loved him and cared for him. He broke bread with us, he shared in our sorrow and happiness, then he betrayed us. He was a deeply selfish human being. He watched our father being murdered; he was hurt, and he wanted revenge. That was all that mattered to him. I looked into his eyes, when he told me he'd done it deliberately, and it was like looking into the soul of a stranger."

"What happened to him?" For some reason the answer seemed vitally important.

"We forced him to walk with us into the final battle. I saw him on the battlefield. I thought it was my fault, because he was *my* brother and he had put the family at risk. But I've realized he'd made his own choices. I could've killed him, but I chose to walk away. I've ended a lot of lives, but I'm relieved I didn't take his. He wasn't among the dead when we were done, so he's still out there somewhere."

Richard bent to look into George's eyes. "Your father made his own destiny, and the weight of it crushed him. He was fated to die here, by his own hand. No regrets, George. No guilt, no shame. Leave it here on this beach. If you carry it, it will poison you. Come. We must get back to the ship."

Richard led him back into the boat. They sped across the harbor back to the ship.

George stared at the water. He hurt, and he cradled that knot of pain in the pit of his stomach and tried to grow a callus over the wound.

RICHARD stepped onto the deck of the ship. Ahead of him George ducked into the cabin. Richard turned and looked at the inferno claiming the island. Orange flames raged, sending plumes of greasy black smoke into the sky. Distant screams echoed, some of fury, some of pain. A ship sank slowly to the left, the lone vessel that had attempted to escape the slaughter. Jason's cannons had fired a single shot from the fort, and the glancing blow had crippled the stately yacht. The magic-operated pumps had managed to keep it afloat, but they were slowly losing the battle, and now the elegant vessel careened, serving as a warning to anyone else contemplating a quick escape.

This is what hell must look like.

A small flotilla of boats departed from the docks and sped across the water, their magic-fueled motors leaving pale trails of luminescence in their wake. Jason's crew was coming back.

The door of the cabin swung open behind him. "Richard!"

He turned.

Charlotte marched at him, buoyed by anger, the outrage so plain on her face, she nearly glowed. She had drained all of her reserves on the island. She couldn't have recovered in the scant fifteen minutes it took them to ride to the beach and back. Worry squirmed through him. If she wasn't careful, the exertion would kill her.

"Did you let that child kill his father?"

He marveled at her fury.

"Answer me, you heartless bastard!"

This place, this hell on earth, should've broken her. Charlotte should've given up by now, beaten down by the horrors and fatigue. But she must've seen the pain in George, and it propelled her to confront him. She would never compromise herself, Richard realized. She would never become jaded or lose her resolve. No matter how many dead bodies she walked by, it would always bother her. She had the nobility of spirit to which he aspired and which he so sorely lacked. She wasn't naive or blind; she simply chose to do what was right, no matter the personal cost.

He wanted this woman more than he had wanted anything in his entire world. Life with her would never be easy, but he would be proud of it.

He wanted her so much, it almost hurt.

In his mind, the ship split, she on one end of a chasm, he on the other. Between lay all the things he had done and she had seen him do. They had too much to overcome. It would never happen. When all was said and done, she wouldn't want a hardened killer with blood on his hands. She would want someone who'd make her forget this hell.

"Richard, don't just stand there. I deserve an answer!"

"John Drayton took his own life," he said. "George had no part in his death. He did witness it. It was good for him. It brought things to a conclusion."

She looked at him for a long moment, her gray eyes bright, almost silver. Maybe there was some chance of something . . . ?

"I'm a heartless bastard," he told her, wishing he could close the distance between them. "But even I wouldn't let a child murder his own father. Is that how you see me? Am I a complete monster in your eyes, Charlotte?"

She turned and walked away. He closed his eyes, inhaling the smoke from the funeral pyre that was the Isle of Divine Na. Well, there it was. He had his confirmation.

She would be free of him soon. They had the ledgers. It would all be over in a matter of days.

"Richard!" Charlotte called.

He turned.

She stood by the cabin. "You're not a monster. You're the most noble man I've ever met. In every sense of the word. I wish . . ."

His pulse sped up.

Jason Parris bounded onto the deck. "Am I interrupting something?"

Charlotte closed her mouth.

Gods damn him. He would strangle that moron and throw his lifeless body overboard.

"Yes."

Parris grinned. "Well, too bad. We need to haul ass out of here."

Jason's crew flooded the ship, lowering the nets to haul up bags of plundered goods.

"If I had fifty extra men, I could own this island." Jason swept the burning city with his hand. "I'd make it into my own Tortuga."

A pirate port of the Broken. He'd read about it in books. "Adrianglia would hardly tolerate Tortuga so close to its shores. What are you planning to do when the Adrianglian Navy blockades the island and starts pounding it with carriage-sized magic missiles?"

"Duck and cover?" Jason flashed his teeth. "What happened to your arm, old man? Did the mighty Hunter actually get hurt this time?"

Charlotte's knees folded, and she slid along the cabin's wall to the deck.

He shoved Jason out of the way, cleared the distance between them, and dropped to his knees. "Charlotte?"

She looked at him, her eyes clear. "Well, this is embarrassing."

"Are you all right?"

"I'm fine," she said. "Mortified, but fine. I shouldn't have marched out here. I've overextended myself. I don't think it's anything life-threatening, but I'm probably going to lose consciousness. Please don't leave me here on the deck."

"I won't." He wrapped his right arm around her. She leaned against him, her forehead resting against his cheek. He couldn't believe he was touching her. "I promise."

"Look at the two of you," Jason said above him. "You're a sorry-looking mess. Maybe after this, you should plan something less tiring. A tea party or a book club or whatever you senior citizens do in your spare time. Look at me—six men dead, the city looted, and I'm good. Look at my crew. Are y'all tired?"

"No!" a dozen people roared.

"See? Fresh as daisies."

Richard growled low in his throat. One day . . .

Charlotte caressed his cheek. Her lips brushed his, and he forgot where he was or what he was doing.

"Thank you," she said.

He held still for a full minute before he finally realized that she had drifted off into sleep.

WHEN Charlotte awoke, she was lying on a cushioned seat, under a blanket. Around her, the polished walls of the horseless phaeton glowed in the sunlight filtering through the gauzy curtain. Sealed behind smooth, transparent pseudo-resin, the structure of the phaeton consisted of gears and delicate metalwork, with glowing, hair-thin threads of magic running through it all. Faint lights of warm amber-and-green magic slid along the threads once in a while, melting into the metalwork, like man-made will-o'-the-wisps. Drowsy and comfortable on the soft seat, she watched the soothing interplay of magic and metal. It occurred to her that she had no idea how the phaeton actually worked. She had ridden in them a hundred times and never thought to find out.

Someone was watching her. Charlotte turned her head. Across from her, Richard sat in the contoured seat. He still wore the same clothes, smelling of smoke. His hair was a mess. His arm rested in a sling. He was ridiculously handsome, and his dark eyes were warm, almost inviting.

Last night was a blur. She remembered being so tired, waiting for Richard and George to return. George's story made no sense, and she chased Richard on the deck and demanded to know if he let George kill his own father. Her mind boggled at the idea that he would force the child to live with that kind of guilt. It would scar George in a way nobody could heal.

Richard looked her straight in the eye, standing there against the backdrop of the burning city, like some beautiful demon, and said nothing. Then she raged at him and accused him of being heartless. He had the strangest look in his eyes, then he told her John Drayton killed himself. She believed him. Richard didn't lie.

And then he'd asked her if she thought he was a monster.

She wanted to tell him then. She wanted to explain the rush of gratitude she felt when he offered her his arm on the bow of the brigantine. She wanted to tell him that she admired him for making a stand and that she wished she could've met him before all this happened, before she had thrown her life away.

Then Jason's crew boarded the ship, and she had nearly fainted like some weak-nerved fool. Her legs refused to support her, and she went down like a cloth doll. Somehow, she had gone the entire thirty-two years of her life without fainting once, and now she'd managed to almost do it twice in a day. It had to be some sort of record. So shameful. Some partner she turned out to be. It's a wonder she didn't die of sheer embarrassment.

Richard had come to her rescue. She remembered his scent as he wrapped his arm around her, the smell of sweat

and smoke and sandalwood, a rich, smooth, earthy, powerful redolence that took her to places she had no business
going. She had said something in her addled state she
couldn't remember.

"Where are the boys?"

"In front," he said. "They insisted on driving."

"And the dog?"

"He's with them. You will have to name him at some
point."

"Where are we?"

"Half an hour from Camarine Manor," Richard was still
watching her with that warm look in his eyes. "We're almost
there."

"Already?"

"It's late afternoon," he said. "We left Kelena at dawn
and rode nonstop through the day."

"Do you still have the ledgers?"

He reached into a bag lying by his feet and pulled out an
edge of the small red leather book.

It slowly dawned on her then. The horrors of last night
were over, and she could let them fade from her, as if it were
all a terrible nightmare. They had their proof. They would
take it to the Marshal of the Southern Provinces, and the
slave trade would be no more. She'd been too spent and
traumatized to recognize it last night, but now she finally
understood.

They had won.

She looked at Richard. "We won."

"We did." He smiled. It was a genuine, beautiful smile
that pulled her as if she were a speck of iron and he a powerful magnet, its lure so sudden and strong, she pressed her
back deeper against the carriage seat. She'd kissed him last
night before passing out. She was almost sure of it.

"Are you all right, my lady?" he asked.

That "my lady" slid over her soul like soft velvet over
skin. "Fine, thank you."

She waited, but he said nothing more. He made no move
toward her. He was probably letting her collect her wits. She

thought he wanted her, but maybe she'd read too much into a look. Maybe there was no mutual attraction. Charlotte searched her memory, trying to scrounge up some definitive evidence that he was drawn to her. She could find none. She thought she heard something in his voice or saw something in his eyes, but she barely knew him. They'd been together for a mere two days. She could've been mistaken.

She had thrown away everything she was taught and willingly walked into hell, where she had murdered countless people. It filled her with self-loathing. She hated what she'd become, and she wanted reassurance that she still deserved to be loved. It was coloring her judgment. Richard had made it clear where his priorities lay. True, he always addressed her with complete courtesy and tried to protect her from harm, but she was a useful tool. Any man with exposure to the Weird's customs would afford her that courtesy, because she was a blueblood and a woman.

She had to stop deluding herself. She had let her fantasies carry her away once, and she was now perfectly aware of the monsters and heartbreak that lay in wait on that path. She'd made a fool of herself already. If he had any tact—and Richard had tact in spades—he wouldn't mention it.

She summoned whatever poise she could muster. "How's your wound?"

"Better. It's so kind of you to ask, my lady."

And why in the world did his "my lady" sound like an endearment to her ears? Charlotte scanned his injury. It was regenerating well, but a budding infection promised to blossom into a serious problem. "I'll need to heal you when we stop."

"Why not now?" He touched the curve of the seat next to him.

She blinked. He was sprawled on the seat, tall, handsome, dangerous, and he was smiling. It was a wicked smile, inviting, no, seductive, as if he was promising her that if she sat next to him, he would claim her, and she would enjoy it.

Get a grip. You're not some schoolgirl. Charlotte forced

a shrug and invited him to the seat next to her with a nonchalant wave of her hand. "Why not?"

Richard rose and sat next to her. She caught a hint of the same scent she remembered from last night, a rich, slightly spicy sandalwood mixed with smoke. Gods, this wasn't any better.

Don't look at his eyes or his smile, and you'll be fine. Her gaze paused on the sharp line of his jaw, his lips . . . She wanted to kiss him.

Argh.

She forced herself to concentrate on the injury, which was hidden by his doublet. His arm was out of the sling. "Why did you put your doublet back on?"

"It seemed like a bad idea to travel surrounded by cutthroats with my bum arm on display. Jason's people are like sharks, you see. A hint of weakness, and they'll rip you to pieces."

"Take off your shirt."

"I'm afraid I may need some help."

She could've sworn there was a hint of humor in his voice. Perhaps he found her attraction amusing. It seemed out of character for him to toy with her, but then, men did strange things when women were involved. Perhaps he was laughing over her discomfort in his head.

She had to stop letting her thoughts run around like wild horses. They were carrying her off to crazy places. He needed help getting the jacket off? Fine. She would assist him. Charlotte stood up and gently helped him pull the doublet off, revealing a long-sleeved dark tunic underneath. She would've liked to yank it off of him, just to make her point, but her professional pride wouldn't permit her to purposefully cause pain to a patient.

His arm was still covered by the sleeve of the tunic. Would she have to peel it off him? Her mind conjured up images of his body beneath the tunic, the tight, strong muscle under the bronzed skin. No. No, that was completely out of the question.

"Do you have a knife?" Charlotte asked.

He pulled a knife out and offered it to her, handle first.

"Perfect." She took the knife and slit his sleeve, exposing the bandage. She handed the knife back to him. He reached for it. His fingers brushed hers, and every nerve in her stood at full alert. Utterly ridiculous.

She removed the tape and the bandages. The cut hadn't bled as much as she expected. Richard had a remarkable talent for quick recovery. She touched the gash, letting the current of golden sparks wash over it. Richard held completely still.

"You're permitted to wince," she said.

"Only if you promise not to tell anyone."

"Your secret is safe with me."

She placed her hand over the wound, her fingers touching his carved biceps, and channeled her magic, repairing injured tissue, melding the blood vessels, and purging any hints of infection. She sealed the skin, painfully aware that he was sitting right there, only inches away. She wanted his tunic off. She wanted to touch that bronzed skin and slide her hand up the hard ridges of his stomach to caress his chest.

"All done," she said.

"Thank you."

An ugly mess of a burn scar crossed his shoulder a couple of inches above the wound. The edges of the scar were perfectly straight as if someone had heated a rectangle of metal and pressed it against the flesh.

"May I?"

"Of course."

She touched it. The heated metal had to have been held to the skin for at least a few seconds. "Were you branded?"

"In a manner of speaking."

Barbaric, to inflict this sort of pain on a human being. "Who did this?"

"I did it."

She looked at him. "You did this to yourself? Why?"

He sighed. "I had a tattoo on my shoulder. I wanted it gone."

"And you thought disfiguring yourself was the best way to go about it?"

"It seemed fitting at the time."

"What in the world was on your shoulder that you wanted it gone so badly?"

"My wife's name," he said.

"Oh." She pulled back. "I'm sorry. I didn't mean to pry."

"It's all right," he said. "I've come to terms with it. I was young and very much in love. I did ridiculous things like pick wildflowers and leave them on her balcony, so when she woke up, she would see them first thing in the morning."

No man had ever brought her flowers. Elvei favored more substantial gifts. It must've been so sweet to wake up to a balcony filled with wildflowers. It was at odds with who he was now: a grim swordsman who killed so efficiently, it could've been an art.

"I wrote dreadful poetry. After we were married, I'd hide small gifts for her around the house."

"I haven't known you that long, but that doesn't seem like you, Richard. You are . . ."

"Bitter? Fatalistic?"

"Practical."

He grinned at her. "As I said, I was young and romantic. Or a sappy moron, as my brother put it. Marissa hated the Mire. She hated everything about it. I wanted her more than anything, so I became what I thought she wanted in order to win her. It worked. She married me."

"She must've loved you." How could you not love him?

Richard sighed. "She decided I was the best she could get under the circumstances. The Mire is sectioned off from the rest of the Edge: impassable swamps on both sides, the State of Louisiana on the border with the Broken, the Dukedom of Louisiana in the Weird on the other. The trek to the Broken is long and dangerous, and a lot of us from the old Mire families can't pass through the boundary. Too much magic in our blood. On the other hand, the border with the Dukedom is heavily guarded. Louisiana is aware that the Edge exists, and it uses the Mire to dump its exiles, so they don't want anyone coming back across the boundary. The swamp resources are limited, and the number of people keeps rising as Louisiana shoves more and more of its undesirables across the border."

"It sounds hellish," she said honestly.

"It has a certain primeval, savage beauty. In the morning, when the mist rises above the water and the giant alligators sing, the swamps have an almost otherworldly air. My family was . . . better off than some. We were numerous, we owned land, and we had a reputation of retaliating fast and hard."

She could believe that. A whole clan of swordsmen like him would give anyone pause. "And your wife?"

"She was born in the Mire, a daughter of an exile from the Dukedom of Louisiana and a local woman." He leaned closer. "You see, our family also had Vernard. He was an exile, a blueblood of the finest bloodline. His entire family had been sent to the Mire with him, and my uncle married his daughter. Vernard took over our education. I was his finest pupil."

So that was it. Like she, Richard had had the benefit of personal instruction from a blueblood peer of the realm. That's why his manners and poise were so polished. Living in the Mire must've been terrible for Richard. To have the self-awareness and know that there is a better place out there that was out of reach.

"I wasn't like most men of the Mire, and that appealed to Marissa. She had grown up on her father's stories of mansions and balls, and I was as close to that as she could find in the swamp. She was very beautiful, and I was like a blind man who suddenly saw the sun." A mordant smile stretched his lips. "Kaldar almost never stops and thinks about the consequences of his actions. Something is fun or not fun, and my brother's fun often lands him in interesting places such as jails or castles belonging to California robber barons. Where other people see certain death, my brother sees an opportunity for a hilarious, thrilling adventure. But when

I got the tattoo, Kaldar warned me that marrying her was a bad idea."

"Wow."

"That should've stopped me in my tracks, but it didn't. I married her. She wanted a clean house free of the swamp's mud, and I gave it to her. She wanted clothes from the Weird. I bought them when I could find a smuggler."

"So what went wrong?" It was inappropriate to pry, but she couldn't help herself.

"Her grandmother died."

"Was it very traumatic?" Sometimes the death of a family member caused an irreversible shift in one's life. She was a prime example of that.

"No. Marissa's grandfather had passed away earlier, and her grandmother left the entirety of their savings to her. It was enough to buy her passage out of the Mire into the Broken, purchase false documents, and start a new life there."

Charlotte recoiled. "But you couldn't go."

Richard nodded. There was a shadow of old pain in his smile and in his eyes. She had an urge to throw her arms around him and kiss him until it went away.

"She waited until I was out in the swamp on a family errand and left. When I came back, there was a note on the kitchen table and a collection of the things I'd given her. Jewelry, books, her wedding ring. She took nothing that would remind me of her or the house. The note told me that I'd been a good husband, but this was her way out of the swamp, and she had to take it."

She left him? She had left this man? Unbelievable. Charlotte almost shook her head. She would give anything to have Richard bring her flowers.

"Did you go after her?"

"There was no point. She had made it clear she didn't want me, and I still had some pride. I got drunk. At some point I burned off her name. I recall doing it, but I couldn't tell you when. I was drunk for a long time."

"Did you ever find out what happened to her?"

"Yes. Kaldar came across her on one of his excursions to Louisiana. She's married to a man who owns a store that sells man-made ponds and fountains for people's yards. She works in the store as well. They have three children, two of their own and a boy from his previous marriage. Kaldar asked me if I wanted him to ruin their little haven. I knew at that moment that despite all my efforts, I was a flawed man because for a few minutes I seriously considered taking him up on it. But I managed to walk away from it." Richard grimaced. "And now I've told you my sob story, and it wasn't my intention."

"You have my word that I won't share it," she said.

"It's not that."

"Then what is it?"

He clamped his jaws shut, the line of his mouth resolute. "Richard?"

"I don't want to seem like a pathetic, moonstruck fool," he said quietly. "So far, you've seen me as a killer, you've seen me as a monster, and now I've added a doleful sentimentality to it, setting myself up to be pitied or laughed at. I keep missing the mark."

Her pulse sped up. Charlotte caught her breath. "And what's the mark?"

"The mark is where I seem capable and confident. A better man than I am."

He was looking at her again with that intense male need. She couldn't possibly be imagining it. It was right there. She wondered if he even realized what his stare communicated. No, probably not.

He wanted to seem better for her sake. He wanted her to like him, and he'd told her something he hadn't meant to share. She wanted to tell him she understood, to share something equally intimate . . .

"I almost murdered my ex-husband." It just popped out of her. Dawn Mother, why in the world did she say that? Of all the things she could've told him, that was the last one on the list.

Richard's eyes widened.

"I'm such an idiot," she whispered.

The phaeton came to a stop. She glanced out of the window in reflex. A beautiful manor lay before them, three stories of beige stone walls, arched windows, and a grand cascade of pale stairs rolling onto the green lawn.

George opened the door. "Welcome to Camarine Manor."

He held out his arm to her. She rested her hand on it and stepped out. Three people waited for them at the top of the stairs. The man was unquestionably a blueblood: tall, wide-shouldered, built for battle. His face was classically beautiful, even more so because he'd chosen to pull back his long, pale blond hair into a low ponytail and the hairstyle accentuated the masculine cut of his jaw.

The woman next to him had to be Rose. She had a perfect figure, not obviously lean, nor voluptuous, but rather fit. Her face was delicate, with fine features and big eyes framed in dense natural eyelashes, for which at a certain point of her life, Charlotte would've given her right arm. Her Edge heritage was obvious. It wasn't her lack of beauty or poise that gave her away, it was her choice of styling. She was off ever so slightly, but to high society, she might as well have hung a sign around her neck that said "Amateur."

Her gown was probably cut in the latest fashion—the fabric was of good quality, and the workmanship looked flawless—but the pale yellow, an attractive color on its own, wasn't flattering to her skin. Her hair was overly elaborate for an evening at home, and the style her curls were arranged in was decidedly winter instead of late spring. The entire package seemed more suited to a slightly older woman, one who had earned the right to veer from the latest trend by virtue of her status, accomplishments, or reputation. Rose was still in the age bracket where women were expected to be on the cusp of fashion. She was likely modeling herself after another woman's example, perhaps the earl's mother or his much older sister.

The Camarines surely had hired a stylist, but no woman wanted to be consistently told that her taste in clothes was flawed. If Éléonore's stories of Rose's character were true, she either got exasperated and fired the stylist, or more likely, consulted him only on special occasions. She didn't commit any fashion crimes, by any means, but she wouldn't be held up as an example of what to do either.

On second look, the earl favored a slightly older cut to his clothes as well. He knew, Charlotte realized. He understood that Rose was off by half an inch and adjusted his attire to match. She was so loved. A familiar pain, dulled by time, stabbed at Charlotte. They had that thing she so wanted and was denied. Rose was so very lucky.

A young girl stood on Rose's left's side, no more than fifteen. Charlotte looked at her face and had to fight to keep from staring. The girl was exquisitely beautiful. Not just pretty, beautiful, almost shockingly so. Her face, a perfect oval, had the coveted high cheekbones and the small yet full mouth. Her nose suggested a touch of something exotic, its lines straight but slightly unusual for Adrianglia, and her eyes reinforced it. Large, wide, yet lightly elongated at the inner corners, they hinted at some mystery, some uncommon heritage and the promise of a dangerous edge. She wasn't just stunning, she looked interesting, which was infinitely more important than classic perfection or beauty. She could've walked into a ballroom filled with people, and every single one of them would pause for a second look.

That dark haunting beauty seemed familiar, but they hadn't met before. Charlotte was sure of it.

Richard opened his arms.

The girl dashed down the stairs.

He picked her up and hugged her, and Charlotte realized where she had seen her before: there were echoes of Richard in that beautiful face. Did he have a daughter? No, it couldn't be—he'd said he was childless.

"Richard," Declan said. "Good to see you in one piece. Why are the boys with you?"

Rose was looking past them to her brothers. "Did something happen? Why do the two of you look like that?"

George took a deep breath.

"You'll just draw it out." Jack pushed forward, past his brother.

Oh no.

"Grandmother is dead. Dad was working for people who killed her. George killed Dad, although he won't admit it."

Charlotte was looking straight at Rose, and she saw the precise moment when the other woman's world broke to pieces.

CHARLOTTE sat in the soft chair in Declan Camarine's study. Richard rested in the other one. The girl sat at his feet on the floor like a loyal puppy, her pose completely at odds with her clothes or age. They should've been introduced, but everyone had more important things to do. Somewhere in the house, Rose was trying to make sense of what happened. Her brothers were with her. Charlotte had tried to offer some consolation, but it was pretty clear that Rose needed her privacy, so she came with Richard instead.

At his desk, Declan closed the red ledger. "The evidence is damning."

"It shows a direct financial trail," Richard said.

"That it does." Declan's face wore a grim expression. She had expected him to be more celebratory. Perhaps he was shocked by the contents or maybe the raw impact of the tragedy his wife was trying to overcome still stunned him. "It fits perfectly. Brennan's position with the Department of the Interior would permit him to keep tabs on my office. He oversees internal security. My people are legally bound to inform the Department of the Interior of any operation that requires the transport of more than ten marshals. He knew where we would strike before we had a chance to get there."

Declan fell silent.

"And, my lord?" Charlotte prompted gently.

He looked at her. "And if it was anyone but Brennan, I would act on it immediately."

Richard leaned forward, focused. "The numbers don't

lie. Audit his accounts. You'll see the record of payments made to him."

"If it was anyone else, my name and position alone would be sufficient to instantly gain access and isolate the suspect from any channels of influence. But in this case, he is the cousin of the king," Declan said. "His favorite cousin, the man whom the King sees as his younger brother. I know Brennan. He is smart, and he navigates the waters of the Department of the Interior like he owns them. He doesn't make mistakes.

"If I request an audit based on the existence of this led-ger, I would have to throw all of my pull and all that of my father's and mother's reputation just to get a foot in the door. The ledger will be reviewed by half a dozen people, none of whom want to pin a target to their own chests. Brennan will know about it almost immediately. Someone will tell him simply for a chance to be invited to the next royal pic-nic. I'll be asked how I came into possession of the ledger, a question, like many others, I'll have to dodge.

"Days will pass, the investigation into the ledger will drag on, until he'll finally come forward and offer to simply settle this because he has nothing to hide. We will perform the audit and find nothing. The ledger will be denounced as a fake. Apologies will be rendered, throughout which he will appear magnanimous and gracious, while I will be painted as overeager, earnest, and naive at best, and jealous and harboring a deep vendetta against Brennan at worst. My credibility will be shot, forcing me to step down, and with me out of the way, Brennan will be free to rebuild his vile enterprise at his leisure."

Charlotte sat in stunned silence. The shreds of their vic-tory floated about her, melting into nothing.

"So this is it? It was for nothing?"

"No," Declan said. "We know who he is now, which means we can more effectively cut him off from access to our antislaver operations. He's suffered a catastrophic loss from the sacking of the Market. If we consistently dismantle the slave trade, ruining his profits over the course of the next few years, he may decide that continuing his oversight is too expensive . . ."

Tulip's tortured face flashed before her. "No."

The two men looked at her.

"No," she repeated. "Not good enough. A few years? Do you have any idea what I've seen? Do you know at what cost those few years will come?"

"Charlotte," Richard said quietly. The adolescent girl was staring at her, dark eyes alarmed.

She checked herself and saw the dark streams of her magic splayed around her. Her control was beginning to slip. She pulled her shame back into herself.

"You have my deepest respect and admiration for the depth of your sacrifice, my lady." Declan rose and bowed to her. "I'm merely pointing out the facts."

"What do you need to end him?" Richard asked.

"A confession," Declan said. "Preferably in front of a dozen infallible witnesses."

It would never happen. Something inside her was dying bit by bit. Perhaps it was hope.

"Then we'll have to obtain it for you." Richard rose. Declan did, too. She regained her feet.

"You're welcome to stay at the house," Declan said.

Richard glanced at her. Charlotte shook her head gently. They needed to be alone with their grief and deal with it as a family. Richard and she were not a part of it, and she wanted to be left to her own despair.

"Thank you. It's most gracious of you, but I believe it would be best if we moved on," Richard said. "The less we're seen together, the better."

Declan escorted them out of his office.

Outside, dense clouds the color of lead had overtaken the sky. A gust of wind pulled at her hair—a storm was coming. Charlotte realized for the first time that she was still wearing the same clothes she'd worn on the island. A blood splatter stained her pants, a castoff from Richard's sword.

She could smell the stench of smoke on her tunic. She looked like a wreck. It was a wonder they had let her into their home at all.

On the stairs, the girl stared at Richard with a wordless desperation.

He hugged her and kissed her hair gently. "I will be at the Lair." He handed her a folded piece of paper. "Give this to George. Don't leave the manor. I may have need of you."

She nodded.

Richard started down the stairs toward the phaeton, and Charlotte followed. What else could she do?

The doors swung open, and Rose rushed outside. "Wait!"

Charlotte paused.

"How was she before she died?"

"Your grandmother was well," Charlotte said. "She spoke of you and the boys often. She kept all of your presents. The glasses you'd sent her were the envy of the whole town. Mary Tomkins almost took sick from sheer jealousy."

A haunted look passed over Rose.

"She was healthy," Charlotte continued. "I made sure to keep up with her aches. She was respected. Her biggest worry was trying to keep a cuckoo clock in her hair. She knew you and the boys loved her, Lady Camarine. She stayed in the Edge of her own choosing, and a pair of wild horses couldn't have pulled her out. Your grandmother never saw herself as a victim. It is perhaps presumptuous of me, but I would suggest that you shouldn't see her that way either. If anything, the blame belongs to the people who killed her— and me, because when she needed help, I wasn't fast enough."

Charlotte turned and walked toward the phaeton. She felt spent and empty, scraped completely dry.

"Lady de Ney," Rose called out.

Charlotte turned again.

Rose bowed. It was a deep, formal, Weird bow. "I don't blame you. I blame them. Thank you for taking care of my grandmother."

"You're welcome," Charlotte told her. She just wanted to get away.

Richard swung the door of the phaeton open for her, and she climbed in.

"The ride won't be long," he promised, and shut the door. She heard him get in the front, in the driver's seat, where an instrument panel waited. The horseless phaeton took off down the road.

Two years, she reminded herself. That's how long it took Richard to get to this point. She had only been at this for less than a week. It had been the most difficult week of her life, but it was only a week. Even if it felt like a lifetime.

Rain drenched the phaeton. She looked outside the glass window and saw a gray haze of water. The raindrops bombarded the roof, sliding along the smooth resin walls of the phaeton, as if she were under a waterfall and yet remained completely dry. Charlotte covered her face and cried. It was a wordless, silent sobbing born of pure pressure that squeezed the tears out of her eyes, more a stress relief than true mourning.

The phaeton came to a halt. The door swung open again, and she jumped out into the deluge, grateful that it would wash the signs of her weakness from her face.

Tall trees surrounded a narrow driveway. In front of her, a house crouched in the rain, like a shaggy bear. She could barely make out the dark log walls under the roof green with moss. Lightning flashed above. A moment later, thunder tore through the hum of the rain. Richard grabbed her hand, and they dashed across the driveway to the house. Charlotte ran up the stairs onto the narrow porch, Richard swung the door open, and she ducked inside gratefully.

TEN

"LIGHTS," Richard said.

Pale yellow lanterns ignited on the walls, bathing the cabin in their soothing light. Delicate frosted spheres, they dangled from the wood like bunches of glowing grapes. The layout of the cabin was open and simple: in the center, two large couches faced each other, flanked by an overstuffed chair, all in handsome, masculine brown. A classic Adrianglian fire pit sat between the couches, a rectangular construction of stone with a grate partially overshadowed by an exhaust hood venting outside the house.

To the left, wooden stairs led to a small loft supporting a bed. Under the stairs, a desk stood, filled with stacks of paper. A large map of Adrianglia decorated the wall, with hand-drawn arrows and annotations written in Richard's hand.

At the right wall, a kitchen occupied the far corner, complete with the ornate box of an icer unit and a small stove.

Richard walked past her, struck a match, and dropped it into the pit. Immediately, the flames surged up. He must've laid out the fire before he'd left.

Long windows offered a view outside the house, all of the forest soaking in the gray deluge of cold rain. Every inch of the wall free of windows was filled with bookcases. Volumes of all shapes and sizes sat on the shelves, interrupted by odd objects. He liked books. So did she.

The space felt warm and inviting, the crackling of the logs a soothing counterpoint to the rain. For some odd reason, she had expected the house to be austere, almost grim, but it was comfortable and inviting. He was letting her into his personal space, into his home.

"A towel?" he asked, offering her a green towel.

"Thank you." She took it and stood there, looking at the towel like an idiot.

"Would you like to take a shower? The water is heated by the icer's coils, so it should be hot," he told her. "It's through that door on the right. There are clean clothes in the cabinet."

She could wash the Isle of Divine Na off her skin.

The bathroom was equipped with a standard Adrianglian shower. When the first drops of water hit her, Charlotte exhaled.

Ten minutes later, she rummaged through the cabinet and found a tunic that was too long on her and a pair of soft woolen pants, which were tight on her hips. She twisted the towel into a turban on her head and slipped out of the bathroom. Richard waited until she was settled on the couch by the fire pit and entered the bathroom with his own towel.

She watched the flames and tried not to think. If she didn't feel so broken, she would've walked along the shelves, caressing the spines with her fingers. She wanted to know what he liked, what books he had read, but defeat wrapped around her, like a thick, dull blanket, and she couldn't fight it off.

The heat of the fire warmed her skin, and she forced herself to enjoy the simple, meager pleasure of being clean, warm, and safe, at least for the moment. When she looked up, Richard had left the bathroom and was coming toward her. She pulled the towel off her hair and let it down.

He sat down across from her. For a few minutes, they sat silently, the fire crackling between them.

"Are you all right?" he asked.

"We lost," she said, hating the failure in her voice.

"We lost a battle. I intend to win the war."

"How?" she asked.

"We know who runs the slavers. We have the names of five people. We study them, then we go after them," he said.

Go after them? After the bluebloods with money, after the peers of the realm with power, after the cousin to the king . . . "You make it sound so simple."

"Charlotte?" he asked quietly. "Are you giving up?"

"No. I have to see this through to the end. I just . . . I feel spent. I thought it would be over."

"But it isn't."

"No." She faced him. "The truth is that I'm weak, Richard. Despite all my determination, the moment I saw a way out, I leaped at it. When we found the ledgers, I felt this overwhelming relief. I felt hope. I haven't gone over the edge yet. I could stop and never use that side of my magic again. I glimpsed a new chance at life, but now it's gone."

"It's a strength, not a weakness. Despite everything you've seen and done, you retained your humanity. I admire that."

She shook her head. "There is nothing worthy of admiration here. I'm simply a very selfish woman. We've been robbed of our victory, and even though I barely began the fight, I'm already in despair at the first setback. How can you keep going? I thought you would be more dejected."

"I am. I'm used to setbacks by now, but this one is crushing." His damp hair, almost black with moisture, fell over his face. The light of the fire played on his skin. "I struggled with it, but I'm also a very selfish man."

"What does that mean?"

He glanced at her. "I realized that if this were over, you would leave."

The slavers, Brennan, and the insurmountable obstacles to bringing them to justice faded from her mind. He was right there. All she had to was get up and take two steps forward or invite him in. He could be hers.

Charlotte raised her chin. "I'm here now. In your house."

Richard stopped moving. She had his complete attention.

She leaned forward and ran her hand through her long blond hair, letting it fall over her shoulders to frame her face. He focused on her completely. She read admiration, desire, and a touch of hard male possessiveness in his gaze. It made her giddy.

"The question is, are you going to do something about it, Richard?"

Richard cleared the distance between them in one rapid step, then his arms were around her. She saw him leaning down and closed her eyes. The first touch of his lips made her shudder, not in fear or excitement, but in desperate, all-consuming want. His lips told her everything she needed to know without making a single sound: that he wanted her just as desperately, that he hoped, that he wouldn't force her. That he thought she was beautiful.

His tongue brushed her lips, and she tilted her head and opened her mouth, letting him know that she wanted him, too. He tasted her, kissing deeper, seducing with a promise of more but holding back. Her body tightened. Her breasts pressed against his chest. A deep-seated desire sparked inside her. Suddenly, she felt empty, and she wanted to be full of him. He sensed it, as if they were perfectly attuned, and pulled her tighter, possessive.

His hands stroked her back, under her tunic, and the roughness of the calluses on his fingers scraping lightly against her skin sent aftershocks through the sensitive muscles of her back. Wrapped in his heated strength, she let go of words and self-awareness, and just kissed him, delighting in the simple pleasure of having him. He tasted of sandalwood and smoke and the promise of bliss.

"So beautiful," he whispered in her ear, and kissed her lips, her cheeks, then her neck, coaxing her to melt. It was too slow. A sudden fear that he would change his mind gripped her.

"Bed," she whispered to him.

He picked her up like she weighed nothing and carried her up the stairs to the loft, depositing her on the covers.

The bed was huge.

The full reality of what she was about to do dropped onto Charlotte's shoulders, like a crippling burden.

She swallowed. The blood spatter on her clothes flashed before her. She wanted to forget it. The clothes she wore now were clean, but she still wanted them gone because she knew her skin was free of blood.

She started to pull the tunic off herself, then his hands touched the bare skin of her stomach and slid up, along her back, stroking places she never thought erotic but which now sent small pulses of desire through her. He kissed her neck, slipped her tunic off, and kissed her chest, moving down in a slow, confident seduction. Her husband used to do this.

She swallowed and pulled away.

Richard stopped.

Her confidence evaporated. She felt so vulnerable sitting there with her shirt off, painfully self-conscious.

Richard swallowed. She sensed he was about to step back and grasped his hand. "No."

He stopped.

"I want you," she told him. "I . . ." She tried to make sense of the tangled ball of feelings.

Richard crouched by the bed. "A woman once told me to use words."

"I'm barren," she said with brutal honestly. "Sex was about making children. I want to be loved." She sounded so needy and desperate. "I'm afraid."

"Of me?"

"Of intimacy." She swallowed. "I need it to be different than it was with him."

She killed it. She ruined it, she brought the shadow of her ex-husband into the bedroom, and now Richard would have the burden of being different from him without knowing what it was like. It was unfair and selfish. He would walk away from her.

"Do you want me?" Richard asked.

"Yes." He had no idea how much.

Richard pulled off his tunic. Underneath, his body rippled with strong, carved muscle, his bronzed skin lightened with old scars. She watched mute as he took off his shoes. His pants followed. He was aroused.

Oh gods, he was so aroused.

Richard sat on the bed, leaned against the carved wooden headboard, and rested his muscular arms on its top edge. His spare, hard body looked almost decadent against the sheets.

"Come," he invited.

She stared at him, her eyes wide.

"You want it different. Come, make it different."

"Me?"

"You."

He was giving her control. She wasn't sure what to do with it.

She would do *something*.

Charlotte stripped, shook her head, letting her blond hair fall over her in a cloud, and sat on the bed.

He was looking at her with such unrestrained, almost feral need, that she blushed. All of his brakes were gone. This was Richard without manners, without proper etiquette, without restraint. She thought he was ice. She had no idea he was fire.

The awkwardness fled, leaving sheer excitement.

"What can I do?" she asked him.

"Anything you wish."

Anything she wished. She raised her hand and touched his chest, drawing her fingers along the narrow hollow between the hard panes of his pectoral muscles. He strained, his body tightening under her touch, but kept his hands on the headboard. She felt so free and . . . wanton. Yes. That was the word.

Charlotte slid her fingers lower, caressing the hard bulges of his abdominal muscles, sliding her hand lower, past his navel, tracing the long line of dark hair pointing down.

"Richard?"

His voice was strained. "Yes?"

"How good is your control?"

"How good do you need it to be?" His voice sounded strained. His biceps bulged as he gripped the headboard.

"Can you keep your hands on that headboard?"

"If you want me to, yes."

She touched the smooth head of his shaft, and he flexed in response, raising himself slightly off the covers.

"Let's find out," she whispered.

She stroked the hard length of him and lowered her head to kiss his neck. The rasp of his stubble scratched her tongue. She tasted a hint of sweat and soap. He groaned. She smiled and kissed him again, his lips, his chest, running her tongue over his nipples, over his hard stomach. An insistent liquid heat spread between her legs. She really could do anything. He would let her. She had complete control. Her excitement spiked.

She trailed a line down from his navel with the tip of her tongue, feeling the muscles tense, like hardened steel under the skin.

She slipped his shaft into her mouth.

His back arched, as he flexed his arms, lifting himself and her. The headboard creaked.

She licked him, testing his discipline. His body shuddered. He groaned again. "You may not want to . . . do . . . that. It's been a while for me."

"For me, too." She straddled him, her breasts inches from his lips. She felt him press between her legs. He was looking at her, his gaze like a heated caress. Everything about him was so unbelievably erotic, from his strong muscular body, to the way his skin, warmed by the fire, burned under her touch, to the way he looked at her.

She tilted her hips. The hot hard length of him slid inside her in a rush of pleasure, stretching her from the inside. Charlotte gasped, arching her back, feeling the full extent of him inside her. She felt tight, but flexible, pliant, warm, and so impatient for more.

"Gods, I want you," he growled.

She began to rock forward, sliding over him. It felt like heaven, but she wanted more.

"Touch me now," she whispered. "Please."

He pushed off the bed, grasping her hips, grinding up, deeper into her. His mouth found her breast, then her nipple, still cool from the shower. His tongue slid over it, and she tightened in response, the rush of sensation so intense it almost hurt. He sucked on her, and she shivered atop him, bending back, riding him faster. Her joints turned liquid.

He slipped his hand down between her legs and touched the sensitive knot of nerves there. Bliss cascaded through her.

"Please," she moaned. "Please."

He kept caressing her, his fingers skillful, adding just the right amount of pressure, matching her movement. The combined sensation overwhelmed her, lifting her higher and higher. Her head swam, but she felt every moment, every caress, as she was hovering on the precipice.

Her breath was coming in quick whimpers. His body was so hard under her, each muscle taut with strain. He let out a masculine half growl, born of pure lust. It triggered some deep feminine instinct inside her that told her his pleasure was as intense as hers.

And then the waves of euphoria crested inside her, met, and she fell over the cliff. All the strength went out of her spine. She slumped forward, her eyes wide, lost in erotic bliss.

He flipped her back onto the covers. She kissed him, running her hands down his back. He pinned her down, pretending to keep her from moving, and looked at her, her mouth, her breasts, the swell of her hips. There was something so deeply gratifying in the look of male satisfaction on his face. She realized that he must've wanted her for a long time, and now he had finally gotten her.

"I want you," she whispered.

"Are you mine, Charlotte?"

"Yes."

"You should've said no. Now you're mine, and I won't let you go."

He thrust into her, building to a smooth, rapid rhythm. She melted, matching his thrusts, once again desperate for that peak of pleasure. She didn't close her eyes. She watched his face, drinking in every moment of his pleasure. He kept thrusting, his whole body taut with tension, the muscles of his back strong like hard cables under her fingers. He reveled in her. Moments later, she climaxed again, the aftershocks of an orgasm rocking her. His body went hard, a tremor gripped him, and he emptied himself into her with a satisfied male groan.

She held on to him, not wanting to let go. He turned, shifting his weight onto the bed, and they lay wrapped in each other. She felt so happy, so heartbreakingly happy.

"Can it be like this again?" she asked.

"It can be however you want it to be," he told her, and kissed her lips.

She closed her eyes and smiled.

"YOU never told me why you do this. Why you went after the slavers."

Richard turned his head and looked at her. Charlotte lay on her stomach on the covers, still naked and completely his. That glorious hair spilled over her back like a silken waterfall. Her face, neck, and arms had a tan, but her breasts and the swell of her butt were pale, and the intimate bare stretch of that pale skin seemed intensely sexual. She lay next to him, content, perhaps even happy, completely at ease, looking at him with her silver eyes. Like sunlight shining through the rain, he thought.

Mmm. Mine. My Charlotte.

He'd made her happy, he'd made her moan and ask for more of him. If it was at all in his power, he would make it so it would always be like this.

It could always be like this, a quiet voice whispered inside him. He could take her with him and disappear. Just walk away. Nobody would blame him. Nobody but the ghosts in his memories.

Richard reached over and stroked her shoulder.

"Do you remember the girl at the Camarine Mansion? The one who met us?"

"You look alike. Is she your daughter?"

"She's my niece. Her name is Sophie."

"The Sophie? The one you were saving when you were delirious?"

He nodded. "My grandparents had several children. My father was the oldest son, and Gustave, my uncle, was the second oldest. Our family was involved in a feud. In the Mire, everyone feuds with somebody. Our feud was old, with deep roots."

"Is that why your father was shot in the market?"

"Yes. I was too young to take care of the family, still a child by the Mire's standards, and Gustave was a much better fit. He became the head of our clan. He had two daughters, Cerise, who is now married to Earl Camarine's best friend, and Sophie."

"So you're her cousin?"

"Technically. Our relationship was always more that of an uncle and niece. I'm old enough to be her father. Gustave was often busy. One day, he had gone out and taken his wife and Cerise with him. Sophie came to see me. She wanted to take a boat down the river to Sicktree, the nearest town. Her mother's birthday was coming up, and she wanted to sell some wine and buy her a gift."

Telling the story was like cutting open the old wound deep inside him. He was surprised it still hurt that much, after so many years. "Celeste, my second cousin, was going with her. I didn't see the harm in it. Celeste was a capable young woman and a good shot. In the Mire, everybody knows everybody, and our family had a dangerous reputation. Nobody except for the feuding family would dare to bother them, and our feud had cooled to a smolder. I told them to go ahead.

"About twenty minutes out, a group of slavers found them. They put a bullet into Celeste's head. She pitched into the water, and Sophie went in after her. When Sophie broke the surface, the slavers hit her over the head with an oar and hauled her into their boat."

Charlotte moved closer to him, wrapping her fingers around his.

"Slavers were unheard of in the Mire. The border with

Louisiana is the only place they could enter, and it's guarded too tightly. Someone on the Dukedom's side had to have let the slavers in for that raid. We never found out who or why. The girls didn't come home, and that evening, we went out on the river and found Celeste's body. We began combing the swamp, but we had no idea who had taken Sophie or why."

"Where did they take her?" Charlotte asked.

"To a hole in the woods. They wanted children, specifically. They put her into a hole in the ground. Sophie said on the second day a man climbed down to visit her. He groped her and tried to rip off her clothes."

Charlotte's eyes shone with outrage.

"Sophie can flash. She's properly trained like most of us. Her training wasn't complete then, but she defended herself. She flashed through the man's eyes and killed him. In punishment, they stopped feeding her or giving her water. It took us eight days to find her. I remember that camp like I saw it yesterday. Half-flooded holes, starving children, some dead, some dying. We slaughtered the slavers. I got into the hole to pull Sophie out. I stood on the slaver's corpse to lift her. Some of him was missing."

"Dawn Mother, did she eat him?"

"I don't know. I never asked. She didn't know when we would be coming for her, and she did what she had to to survive. But she was never the same. First, she stopped brushing her hair. Then she stopped wearing nice clothes. She decided that she didn't like her name and she wanted to be called Lark. She spent most of her time in the woods and stopped talking. She would hunt small game or just find carrion and hang it on a tree in the forest because she was convinced that she was a monster, and we would run her off into the woods to fend for herself."

Charlotte sat up. "Did you get her help?"

"There are no healing colleges in the Mire," he said. "Every time I tried to speak to her, she would run away as if I were one of them. One of my cousins is a physician. Not like you, but she is talented in her own way. She examined

Sophie several times. There was nothing physically wrong with her. But Sophie was always close to her mother, and as long as some connection between her and her family remained, I thought that, given time, she would slowly heal. But the Hand came calling."

"The Louisiana spies?" Charlotte's eyes widened.

"They wanted something our family had. Do you recall the exile I mentioned? Vernard?"

"Yes."

"His last name was Dubois. Does it mean anything to you?"

Charlotte frowned. "Vernard Dubois was a celebrated medical scientist in the Dukedom of Louisiana a few decades before my time. I've read some of his work—he concentrated on applied medical botany. Contrary to what some people think, the College healers don't just limit their medical education to the use of magic. We study pharmacology, herbology, and other disciplines just like any other medical . . . I'm rambling. Was he the same man?"

"Yes. He's Sophie's grandfather."

Charlotte blinked.

"Louisiana exiled him into the Mire because he had crossed the line into the forbidden territory of magic alteration."

"That's rich." Charlotte snorted. "They turn their spies into magic monstrosities. You wouldn't believe some of the things they do to the human body."

"I would," he told her. "I've killed many of them."

She leaned over and brushed a kiss on his lips. "What does Dubois have to do with all of this?"

"He built a device. He meant it to be a healing apparatus, but instead it turned the human body into an indestructible monster. The Hand wanted it. Louisiana sent a unit of their magically altered spies into the Mire led by a man who calls himself Spider. They kidnapped Sophie's parents. It cost us two-thirds of our family, but we wiped them out."

"Sophie's parents?"

"Spider fused her mother."

Shock slapped Charlotte's face. That's how Richard had reacted when he first found out. The process of fusion melded human tissue to that of plant, creating a symbiotic entity with all of the memories of the human being but none of the will. Irreversible and agonizing, it had robbed both Cerise and Sophie of their mother.

"Gustave survived," he said. "So Sophie has one parent. When the Mirror relocated our family to Adrianglia, I hoped she would leave Lark behind. She traded rags for dresses, and now she takes etiquette lessons. The rest of the time she trains."

"With her sword?" Charlotte guessed. She was beginning to get an idea of how their family worked.

Richard nodded. "I've never seen her level of dedication. She practices constantly. Three years ago, she had no interest in it. If you asked me back then, I would've told you she would be a mediocre fighter at best. Today, I'm running out of things I can teach her. She developed the killer instinct, she's ruthless, and I worry about her lack of restraint. Something drives her."

"Do you think she wants to go after slavers?"

"I don't know. I told you about my brother. I have, *had*, another, our half brother Erian. He was just a child when my father died. He was standing right next to him. It irreparably damaged him. He hid it for years, but eventually his hatred consumed him. I don't want that for her."

"You think that by killing the slavers you can heal her?" Charlotte asked.

"No. But I can spare her the need to take revenge herself. She's a good fighter, but she's still a child. If she goes after the slavers, she will die. Even if she doesn't, seeking vengeance will damage her more. Slavery is an aberration. It shouldn't exist in our time, yet it does, and I decided I won't permit it. I can't stop it on the entire continent, but I will stop it here in Adrianglia. Sophie will never have to see what I saw. I won't let their atrocities scar her any further." His voice degenerated into a snarl. He caught himself. "I let her go on that boat. I was the one who said, 'I don't see any harm in it. Go ahead.' "

"You couldn't have known."

"It doesn't change the fact that it happened."

"Richard, it's not your fault. It's not her fault either. I can take her to Lady Augustine. She is my surrogate mother at Ganer College. She's a mind soother, and she's as good at healing the soul as I am at healing the body. If anyone can assist Sophie, she can, and she will."

"I'm not certain she wants help." It wasn't their way. One didn't rely on strangers.

Charlotte raised her arms. "Of course she doesn't want help. None of us want help when we're fifteen and the world has victimized us. That's why we have adults in our lives who make that decision for us. She may not want it, but she needs it. Promise me that once we're done, one way or the other, you will take her to the College. If neither of us survives, her sister or Rose should make sure she visits there. I will write a letter. If you take it with you, Lady Augustine will see you. Promise me?"

"I promise," Richard said.

"I'll hold you to it."

A sad whine echoed through the house.

Charlotte blinked. "Is that the dog?"

"Couldn't be. We left him with the boys." Richard slid off the bed. "I'll be right back."

He went down the ladder and opened the door. A black shape shot by him, smelling of wet fur and dripping rainwater.

"I thought I was rid of you," he growled.

The dog shook, causing the fire pit to hiss.

"He's decided he's ours," Charlotte called from the loft.

Richard took the towel she had left on the couch and spread it down for the dog. The big mutt flopped on it.

Richard climbed back up the stairs, stretched out on the bed, and pulled her closer. "Your turn."

She raised her eyebrows.

"Tell me why you wanted to kill your ex-husband."

Charlotte turned on her back, looked at the ceiling, and sighed. "Turnabout is fair play?"

"Yes."

"I was taken to the College when I was seven. It's the only life I knew until I was twenty-seven years old. I've read books about adventures and love. I flirted. I even made out with boys."

"Shocking."

"Oh, it was. In the last years of my being there, I couldn't wait to escape. I was going to travel. I would have all the adventures I could possibly want." She sighed again. "At twenty-seven, I received my land grant, my house, and my noble title for my decade of service. I moved in, and soon I realized that I had no idea how big the world really was. I was going to travel, I really was, but the house needed work and the garden needed to be tended, and there were good books . . ."

She made big eyes at him.

"You were scared," he guessed.

She nodded. "I had all the training and confidence I would ever need, but I just couldn't bring myself to do anything with it. And then Elvei Leremine walked into my life. He was a blueblood, flawless, handsome . . ."

"I hate him already," he said.

Charlotte smiled, a sad parting of lips without humor. "I was besotted with the idea of falling in love and having a family. Here was my prince, so considerate, so together. The whole thing seemed like a perfect shortcut to happiness. Instead of combing through men and dealing with rejection, I found the ideal husband right away, and I married him because I was so utterly stupid. He stood in line to inherit his family's lands, but until then we decided it would be best if he came to live with me. He started speaking of children right away. We tried for six months, and he grew more and more alarmed when I didn't conceive. Then, finally, I went to be diagnosed. For another year and a half I denied the inevitable. I went to the best healers I knew. I underwent procedure after procedure—the memories still give me nightmares. I refused to give up. I was always taught that if you strive hard enough, you will achieve what you desire. I'd read all those romantic books, where a woman can't conceive, then she meets the right man, and the power of love or his magic virility or what have you overcomes her problems, and she has gorgeous triplets. My magic cure was just around the corner, I was sure of it."

She turned to look at him. "I'm barren, Richard. Irreversibly. I will never have a child. There is no cure."

"I'm sorry," he said.

She hesitated. "Does it matter to you? I can never give you a child."

She was thinking of staying with him. Don't read too much into it, he warned himself. They came from completely different worlds. She was a blueblood, and he was a fraud, with hardly anything to his name.

"There are sixteen adults in my family, all that remains of over fifty, and almost twenty children, most of them with one dead parent or both," he told her. "I have many children to take care of. My worth isn't tied to having one specifically my own."

Charlotte sighed and caressed his cheek. Her finger traced his lips. "Funny, had you asked me that before I'd married Elvei, I would've told you the same thing. But somehow the quest to have a child became the most important thing in my life. I felt deficient. Almost as if I were somehow not female if I couldn't conceive. Somewhere in the middle of all of this, I realized that Elvei required a child so he could inherit the family estate. He was in competition with his younger brother, and he was trying to race to the finish line and produce a bouncing baby to claim his land, house, and leadership of the family with it."

"He sounds like an idiot." *Who the hell would care about the lands and house when he had her?*

Charlotte gave a one-shouldered shrug. "I was very naive. And my blinders were firmly in place. Elvei was always attentive. He came with me on some of my procedures. This journey toward getting a child was something we took together. It was a quest we had in common, and I thought it would bring us closer. Really, we were both at fault. He should've made his position clear before the wedding, and I shouldn't have mistaken his courtesy and attention for love. I think it took a toll on him as well. He'd grown obsessive. We had to have sex in a specific position because someone had told him it was most likely to result in conception. He'd help me chart my ovulation. It was a kind of insanity that took over both of us. Looking back at it, all of that seems . . . creepy."

Richard stared at her, speechless. Her husband was an ass. He wanted to find him and skin him alive. Saying it out loud, however, probably wasn't the best strategy.

"In the end, when all options were exhausted, I came to him with the news. I had expected him to hug me and tell me it would all be fine and that he loved me anyway. He presented me with an annulment."

Charlotte laughed bitterly. "My world had collapsed. I wanted to hurt him, and I almost did. I came this close." She held her index finger and thumb a hair apart.

"What stopped you?" he asked.

"It was wrong," she said simply. "I was a healer. I was meant to heal people, not to hurt them because they crushed my heart."

And that's why she would always be the ray of light in his darkness. He had to hold on to her. He couldn't let her go. He had to not screw this up.

Charlotte closed her eyes. "We, the healers, have two sides to our power: one prolongs life, the other cuts it short. We're conditioned to use only one. It's repeated so often, you have it chiseled in your mind by the time you reach your teens: do no harm. Healing is hard work. You feel the magic leaving you. But doing harm is easy. You feel powerful and strong. It's almost euphoric. You don't realize how much magic you've spent until it's gone, and you collapse dramatically and make a complete fool of yourself."

"You may swoon as you wish. I'll always be there to catch you."

She laughed.

He grinned.

Charlotte turned on her side and looked at him. "Two things can happen when a healer stops being a healer. One, they drain themselves of all of their magic and die. And two . . ."

She hesitated.

"Two?" Richard prompted.

"They become a walking plague. They spend their magic, realize they require more, and began to feed on those around them, converting other lives into fuel for further killing. They cease to become human. The first time I killed, when I infected Voshak and his slavers, I wasn't sure I had enough power to kill them all. So I fed on them. You have no idea how wonderful it felt."

Her voice shook.

"You're terrified of it," he guessed. Alarm wailed in the back of his head. He was certain he read an article describing something very similar a few years back. The book claimed it was a death sentence to the magic user.

"Yes. Since then I haven't done it. Once you start, the temptation to keep going is too strong. In the bookkeeper's mansion, when I was near my limit, I felt you. I could sense your life force. It made me hungry." She touched his face. "Are you scared?"

"No." He wasn't afraid of her; he was afraid for her.

She cleared her throat. Her voice was quiet. "Some people think they are better than others at what they do. I don't think, I know. I'm the most powerful healer of my generation. I wouldn't become a plaguebringer, I would unleash a pandemic on this world. I'd become a living death. I would rather spend all of my magic and die than kill thousands of people."

She closed her eyes. "I shouldn't have ever done it. You have to understand, back at the clearing I saw you in the cage, battered and bruised, and they were lounging about as if they were on some picnic. It made me so angry. Draining them seemed like the only way, and I did it. I knew the risks, I just didn't realize how strong the pull of the magic is."

"You were in shock," he told her. "Trust me, I was there. I saw your face."

"It's not an excuse. A lot of healers disappear after a few years. I always thought it was because they burn out. Maybe they don't. Maybe they succumb instead and have to be put down like rabid dogs."

"Stop," he said. "Don't do this to yourself. You won't be put down. I won't let anyone touch you."

"Richard, if I ever lose myself, you have to stop me." Her lips touched his, warm and pliant, and he savored her taste. "I know it's a lot to ask, but promise me."

Something inside him went dead and cold at the thought. "I'll take care of it."

He would do it because she asked him. At the very least, he would try. He wrapped his arms around her and pulled her to him, wishing he could protect her from everything, wishing he could keep her safe. Men, creatures, beasts, he could end them. But how could one fight magic? He couldn't cut it, he couldn't kill it, and if it took Charlotte from him, there was nothing he could do about it.

She hugged him, sliding next to him. "Some twisted romance we have going here."

He forced a smile. "I don't know. It could be worse."

"How?"

"We're still fighting our war. We could simply give up."

"We can't give up," she said. "If we did that, everything we have done until now would be for nothing."

"Does it pull on you? Your magic?"

"It's almost as if it has a life of its own. I picture it as a dark beast or a nest of snakes. Sometimes it sleeps, like now, perfectly content. And then I use it, and the beast awakens and scratches from the inside, trying to claw its way out."

"I wish you had told me sooner." He squeezed her closer and kissed her lips. She tasted so sweet. "I shouldn't have asked you to kill the crew. I shouldn't have let you get off that ship, period."

"You don't get to tell me what I should or shouldn't do." She smiled.

"Yes, I do. You promised to obey me."

She rolled over and climbed on him, her face full of mischief. "And if I disobey you, mighty Sir Richard, what shall you do?"

"I have no idea. I suppose I'll growl in a ferocious, manly way." He put his arms behind his head. Her hair spilled over her left breast. Her right was bare, a perfect, glorious breast tipped by a small dark nipple, almost pink against her soft, pale skin.

She was so beautiful. He was amazed she let him touch her. That he had her here with him was some sort of miracle of the universe.

"You're ogling my breasts."

He raised his eyebrows. "Of course."

She leaned over him, her locks falling around them like a shimmering curtain. Her nipples brushed his chest, cool peaks against the heat of his body. He smelled the delicate scent of citrus from her damp locks.

"Are you afraid loving me will make you weaker, Richard?" she whispered.

"No." She had no idea how much he wanted her. If someone right now offered him a guarantee that she would stay with him in exchange for walking away from his mission, he wasn't sure what his answer would be. *You've fallen too hard and too fast, fool.*

No, loving her didn't make him weaker. It made him desperate.

"You're mine," he said, and wrapped his arms around her. "I have no intentions of letting you go."

She smiled, a wicked sexy smile.

"I mean it," he told her. "You can't escape."

The logical side of him warned that a hope of a future together would only hinder them. It would make them hesitate. It would cause them to avoid danger and abandon caution for each other's sake. They were able to do what they had to do precisely because each of them had nothing to lose. But that wasn't true anymore. He shut down the logic. It didn't help.

"Maybe I don't want to escape." She caught his bottom lip between his teeth, pulled gently, and let go. Her eyes were luminescent. "My deadly noble swordsman."

He was so hard, it was making him crazy.

"I want to have you again," she whispered. "Can I have you again?"

He rolled her over on her back and pinned her down. She widened her eyes. "Oooh, I'm trapped. What will happen to me?"

He bent down, relishing the softness of her body under him. "Let me show you . . ."

ELEVEN

CHARLOTTE swept the cabin floor, chasing the dust and tiny particles of ash into a neat pile. It had been three days since they had arrived at the cabin. Richard called it his Lair, but even lairs could stand a sweeping. Three days of nothing but conversation, savory meals, and sex. Unrestrained, amazing sex. She smiled to herself.

A delicious aroma of frying meat floated up from the kitchen, accompanied by the sizzle of food in a hot pan. She wasn't sure what Richard was cooking for breakfast, but whatever it was, it smelled divine. He liked to cook, she'd discovered.

A faint hissing announced a phaeton arriving. They had been waiting for it.

"We come in peace," a male voice announced from the outside. "Don't shoot us."

Richard leaned away from the stove. "It's my brother."

"I'll let him in," she said.

Charlotte unlatched the door and swung it open. A man in his early thirties stood on the porch, carrying a very thick leather file. The resemblance was definitely there: similar hair, except Richard combed his and Kaldar left it in a disorganized mess; similar faces, both handsome with contoured jawlines and pronounced cheekbones; similar height. And yet they were different. Richard's features had nobility and pride, while Kaldar was handsome in a roguish way, with a wild glint to his eyes and a charming grin. She had a feeling he smiled frequently and lied easily, while each of Richard's rare smiles was a gift.

Kaldar blinked. "Who are you?"

"I'm Charlotte," she told him.

"A pleasure. Say, Charlotte, have you seen Richard? A brooding fellow about as tall as me, but much uglier and incapable of humor?"

"Uglier?"

"Well, perhaps not uglier per se, but definitely more melancholy. His trouble is that he thinks too much. It keeps him from enjoying life. Have you seen him?"

"He's inside cooking."

"Cooking? He hates to cook."

Kaldar stepped over the threshold and ducked left. A knife sprouted from the doorframe where his head had been a moment ago. Kaldar flicked his fingers at the blade. "See? Incapable of humor."

"What are you talking about?" Richard raised his eyebrows. "I thought the look on your face was bloody hilarious."

"Who are you, and what have you done with my brother?"

A young man followed Kaldar through the door. An impeccably tailored jacket hugged his fit, slim frame, and he moved with the casual elegance so many bluebloods strived to achieve through dancing lessons. He walked with supple grace but a certain surety, not a dancer, but rather a swordsman. His blond hair, cut long, which usually indicated a mage, accentuated the precise cut of his features, still touched with boyish softness. He turned to her. Familiar blue eyes looked at her from a face that was already arresting and in a few years would be devastating.

"George?" she gasped.

"Good morning, my lady." He took the broom from her. "I'll finish this."

She tried to reconcile the filthy urchin with the flawless blueblood prince and failed. The pieces simply didn't fit together.

"Terrible, isn't it?" Kaldar shook his head in mock resignation. "Look at the caliber of the competition I have to deal with. You know, women under twenty-five don't even notice me anymore when I tow him around."

George rolled his eyes.

"You're married," Richard reminded him.

"I was complaining in a purely hypothetical sense." Kaldar turned to Richard. "What are you cooking? Did you make enough for everybody?"

"You won't be left unfed, don't worry." Richard jerked the pan up in a sharp motion. A pancake flew in the air and flipped back into the pan.

"The least you can do is feed me. I brought your information." Kaldar shook the file. "My wife stole it for you from our illustrious spy agency, and we spent the whole night copying it by hand, then taking it back to the Mirror . . ."

"He has an imager at his house," George said. "It took him less than half an hour to copy everything."

"Traitor child." Kaldar dropped the file on the counter. "A gift for you, my ever-so-serious elder sibling." He made an elaborate flourish with his hand, and a piece of paper popped into his fingers out of thin air. Richard put the wooden spoon down and opened the paper. His face showed nothing. He looked at it for a long moment and passed it to her.

It was Richard's image captured with an imager and printed on paper with the word HUNTER printed at the top. The shot had caught him in a moment of battle. He'd just swung his sword, and the body in front of him was still falling. Blood spatter stained his skin. His hair flared, moving from the momentum of his turn. His face looked serene.

"Where did you get this?" Richard asked.

"While I was procuring your information, I happened to be by Rodera. She's a hell of a city, and I made an excursion into her gutters and ruffled through her skirts. The slavers are passing this around. You are busted. How many times have I told you to wear a mask? Why don't you ever listen to me?"

Half an hour later, when they finished the omelet Richard made, Kaldar had made at least ten jokes, told them a funny story about his wife, and made fun of Louisiana's ambassador. She understood why Richard got a slightly tense look on his face when he mentioned his brother. They were polar opposites. Kaldar, being the life of the party, had no urge to explore the virtues of dignity and restraint, while Richard had no desire to entertain others with his wit or draw attention to himself.

"I suppose we should start," Kaldar said.

George dragged a large freestanding corkboard into view.

Mirth drained from Kaldar's face. "Now then."

He opened the leather file and began pinning images to the board, five in all. Charlotte felt a pang of regret. She still saw Tulip in her dreams, but now, when she awoke, Richard held her, and the feeling of lying next to him was indescribable. He never said it, but the way he looked at her, the way he listened, the way they gave pleasure to each other made her feel loved, and deep inside her, a pathetic little hope had reared its head. She hated herself for that hope. It chipped at her resolve and at his. This path demanded sacrifices. They both knew it. They had both agreed to accept it. But each moment she had him to herself felt like a gift. Now that hope was dying, and its death throes brought her at once relief and a sickening fear.

"Lord Casside."

Kaldar pointed to the first image. A dark-haired man with a strong profile stared back at them.

"Minor nobility, of the lesser-known branch of the Dweller family. An only son and a self-made man. About five years ago, he quietly began to liquidate his assets and invest all of his money into Blackwolf Imports and Exports."

"Blackwolf?" Richard grimaced.

"Not really an imaginative guy." Kaldar tapped the picture. "You were right, by the way. Height, weight, skin and eye color. Everything is consistent. If it wasn't for the nose and the chin, he could be part of the family."

"What family?" Charlotte asked.

"Our family," Richard said. "I'll explain in a minute."

"Then we have Earl Maedoc."

Kaldar tapped the second picture. On it, an older man

glowered, his features harsh, his stare direct. His gray hair was shorn close to his scalp, and his hooded eyes looked unfriendly.

"Veteran of the Adrianglian Army, decorated, praised, respected. He oversees recruiting efforts. He also supplies new muscle to the slavers."

"Being in charge of the recruiting allows him to weed out those unsuitable to military service," George said. "Those with a penchant for sadism, for example. He steers them toward the slavers."

"Lady Ermine."

Kaldar touched the next image. A woman in her late twenties. Delicate bone structure, coils of caramel hair, narrow eyes but a rare, highly prized color: a translucent light green.

"Another investor. Lady Ermine also takes a special interest in female slaves. She selects several each season and trains them to increase their value."

"How do you know this?" Richard asked.

"The Mirror has a list in her file, which she had forgotten in her room at one of the state functions. It details purchases of personal items, including slinky garments and various inappropriate but entertaining things for seven women with different garment sizes and detailed prescriptions for Midwife's Bane . . ."

Those bastards.

". . . which is apparently . . ."

"Used as a means of birth control." Charlotte ground out, furious. "If the dose is large enough, it can cause damage to the lining of the uterus, rendering a woman infertile." They were robbing the slave women of their fertility to prevent inconvenient offspring. She was infertile, and she understood the full enormity of their loss. She would crush that Ermine woman like a maggot under her shoe.

"What she said," Kaldar said. "The names on the list had the flair of the Broken. There was a Britney, which doesn't occur here that often, but there was also a Christina, which is a completely Broken name."

Good point.

"Why?" George asked.

"Because it's derived from the word 'Christian,'" Charlotte said. "In the Broken, Jesus Christ was viewed as the son of God, and his followers are Christians. In the Weird, it was John the Nazarite, whose followers are called the Nazaratians. In the Weird, a Christina would be named Johanna."

Kaldar shrugged. "It's clear that at least some women on that list came from the Edge, if not from the Broken itself. There's no logical reason for Angelia to have made that list, and when a covert Mirror operative posing as a servant attempted to return it, Lady Ermine claimed she had never seen it before. The Mirror put it into her file as an oddity. Now that we know she's connected to the slave trade, it makes much more sense."

Richard was staring at an image of an urbane, groomed blond man with sharp features and an overly elaborate haircut. There was a focused, predatory edge to his glare. "What about him?"

"Baron Oleg Rene." Kaldar crossed his arms. His face had gained an unexpected vicious edge. "You wouldn't believe who he's related to. You see the family resemblance?"

"Spider." Richard spat the word like it was poison.

"A distant cousin. How about that?"

The two men glared at that picture, the hate on their faces so similar, they looked like twins.

"The same Spider who killed Sophie's mother?" Charlotte asked.

Kaldar nodded. "Rene is Spider's younger half sister's son, the Adrianglian branch of the family. Because of this inconvenient connection, he's been blacklisted from military service, the Department of the Interior, and the Diplomatic Corps."

"What does he do?" George asked.

"Arts, sports, and entertainment," Kaldar said. "He travels around the country working as a glorified event planner.

Organizes festivals, tourneys, and so on. The Department of the Interior has no issue with it as long as somebody else provides his security. He's very good at it, apparently."

"So he can move around the country pretty much at random," Richard said.

Kaldar nodded. "I'm thinking they use him as a buyer/scout/trouble fixer."

He turned to the last photograph. On it a man in his middle forties looked at the world with hazel eyes. He was handsome, with a masculine beauty that was just a shade too rugged to be perfect, and that slight roughness only added to his appeal. His expression was dignified but free of pretense. An engaging smile played on his lips and in his eyes, proclaiming loudly that this man was worthy of loyalty because he was good and would do the right thing. Its power was so pronounced, Charlotte felt compelled to smile back.

"Viscount Robert Brennan," Kaldar said. "The main head of this twisted hydra."

He sat down. "How do you want to go about it?"

"We need a confession," Richard said. "Or at the very least, an admission of guilt."

"Brennan is a tough nut to crack." Kaldar's face turned grim. "It's not just that he's a cousin of the king. He's also popular. Blueblood ladies think he's darling, and men think he's a man's man. He's athletic, charming, funny, and they all love him. You'll be fighting against the tide of public opinion."

"Then we'll need to turn it against him," Richard said.

"How the hell are you going to do that?"

"Why can't we simply remove him from the equation?" George asked.

"Because if we kill him, the organization wouldn't die," Richard told him. "Think of a monarchy. One king dies, another takes his place, but the institution survives."

"Richard is right." Charlotte rose.

The two men and a boy immediately stood up.

"Why did you get up?" she asked George.

"You're a woman," George answered.

"Yes, but what is the reason?"

"I don't know."

"You rose because hundreds of years ago, when a woman entered a room full of men, she wasn't exactly safe. Especially if she was beautiful or had holdings. Our magic is just as deadly, but physically, an average male is stronger than an average woman, so when a woman entered the room, men who knew her stood up to indicate that they would shield her from danger. The three of you just declared yourself my protectors."

They looked at her.

"A modern woman is hardly in danger of a direct assault," Charlotte said. "So why do men still get up?"

George frowned.

Charlotte smiled at Kaldar. "You know, don't you?"

"We get up because women like it." Kaldar clapped George on the shoulder. "You don't want to look like an unmannered bumpkin in front of a girl. And if you get up and she notices you, she might sit by you."

"Exactly. There is no law that says men should rise, but you still do because women enjoy this show of attention. It's so ingrained in your nature that when we first met, Richard refused to sit down until I did, even though he was half-dead at the time."

Richard cleared his throat. "That's a wild exaggeration. I was a quarter-dead, at most."

Kaldar swiveled toward him and peered at his brother's face. "That's two jokes in less than an hour. You feeling all right?" he asked quietly. "Feverish, eh?"

"I'm fine. Get out of my face."

Kaldar looked at her, then back at Richard, then at her again.

Charlotte sat down. The three men sat.

"The monarchy survives because the bluebloods like it," she said. "Most Adrianglians like it. It's an idea that appeals to them on some level. The king has less power than the collective Assembly or the Council, for example, so he can be overthrown. But we like to pretend we're still a warrior nation under a single strong leader, and we idealize the throne and those who sit on it."

"Or stand close," Richard added.

"The bluebloods don't fear laws," she continued. "Some of us still think they don't apply to us. We fear only public judgment. The public has judged the royal family to be paragons of virtue. We can't fight that, or we'd have to rub the blueblood noses in the fact that their long bloodlines don't bestow them with nobility of spirit the moment they pop out of their mothers."

Richard nodded. "The bookkeeper on the island is a prime example—she was so committed to Brennan, her eyes practically glistened at the thought of him. In her mind, he could never do anything base."

Their minds ran on parallel tracks. "We can't fight the system," Charlotte agreed. "But we can tarnish one individual. To crush the slaver ring, we have to get Brennan to admit to an act so base, so at odds with the standard of blueblood behavior, that society will have no choice but to judge him as defective. He will be viewed as a freak, unworthy of his pedigree. Anything he engaged in would become unclean. The bluebloods will destroy him just to escape the taint."

"I like the way you think," Kaldar said.

Richard nodded. "I agree. The public disdain and disgust must be so severe that it would cause a cry of outrage. The slave owners must recognize that being discovered would make them instant social pariahs. That's the only way the institution of slavery can be rooted out."

Richard rose and walked to the board. "Brennan built this organization. He made it efficient, resilient, and profitable. We don't know why. He doesn't need the money, and if it ever became public, he'd lose everything. Something must've compelled him to create it. He cares a great deal about it. When we fought the Hand, we suffered setback after setback, but we didn't break until the end."

A muscle jerked in Kaldar's face. "Erian."

The half brother Richard had mentioned. "I don't understand," Charlotte said.

"Our youngest brother betrayed the family to the Hand," Kaldar said.

"What happened to him?"

"He disappeared," Richard said.

"Richard let him go," Kaldar told her. "He saw Erian walking away, and he let him go. We'll all regret this one day, mark my words."

"Back to Brennan. We make him think he's being betrayed," Richard said. "Make him think there is a coup and one of the others is trying to take over. It will drive him over the edge."

"You'll need at least two people for that," Kaldar said. "A single person stirring up trouble is too easy to trace. You need at least two people pretending to act independently. And you're right out, my dear brother, because your mug has by now reached Brennan's desk."

"I can do it," Charlotte said. "They don't know me. I don't even have to pretend to be anyone but myself."

"Okay, that's one," Kaldar said. "But I can't help you and neither can Audrey. The Mirror would have our asses, and, besides, we're on call. The Grand Thane Callis is marrying Marchesa Imelle de Lon in a month. Why couldn't that old geezer find himself an Adrianglian woman to marry, I'll never know. There is a realm full of old ladies waiting for him, but no, that old goat had to go to Louisiana to get himself a wife."

The Grand Thane never concerned himself with playing by the rules. Roughly eighty years ago, when Rogan Brennan sat on the throne, his sister Solina Brennan married Jarl Ulrich Hakonssen of Vinland in the north. After Rogan, the crown passed to his son Olred, which made Jarl Ulrich Grand Thane, a title traditionally held by the king's oldest uncle. As Grand Thane, he had defended the realm, leading the Adrianglian Army and Fleet to victories in the Ten Year's War. Olred managed to get himself killed before he produced an heir. Because of Jarl Ulrich's foreign birth, Solina couldn't assume the throne, and their daughter Gallena became the monarch of Adrianglia. Now Gallena's son sat on the throne. The Grand Thane was father to the previous queen and grandfather to the current king and Brennan, but he had kept the title that made him famous. Charlotte had seen him twice from afar: he was a massive, battle-scarred bear of a man, famous for his magic, physical might in battle, and roaring voice. Lady Solina had died almost fifteen years ago, and now he finally chose to remarry. She imagined he didn't want to spend the twilight of his life alone.

"Anyone who is anyone in both Louisiana and Adrianglia will be at that wedding," Kaldar continued. "The entire Mirror is on full alert."

"That would be an excellent place to expose Brennan," Charlotte thought out loud.

"It is, but I can't be the one to do it. I tried to hint at it to Erwin, who is in charge of operations for my unit, and he shut me down, fast. You're still short a player," Kaldar said. "You need that overlap of influence. That's the way that con works. You must work completely independently from two different angles toward a common goal."

"Perhaps I—" George said.

"No," all three of them answered in unison.

"You have your future to think about," Charlotte told him. "If we fail, Brennan will make it his mission to ruin you in the most gruesome way possible."

"Not only that," Richard added, "but you are well-known and well connected. If you fall, you will drag your sister, your brother-in-law, and your brother down with you. You can help, George. But you must do it covertly."

"We're out of luck," Kaldar said.

"Not if I become Casside," Richard said.

What?

"Come again?" Kaldar asked.

"I've met him," Richard said. "He wouldn't be difficult to impersonate. You said yourself, there is a strong resemblance between us."

"You're good with prosthetics, I'll give you that." Kaldar crossed his arms. "But this isn't some meeting in the middle of the night in a dimly lit tavern. You don't look enough like him to pass, and if you glue shit to your face, it will be clearly visible in the bright lights of all those ballrooms."

"Not if it's under my skin," Richard said.

She realized what he was saying. "Facial surgery?"

He nodded.

Charlotte stared at the picture, comparing the two faces. Richard's chin was too sharp, his nose bridge too low, his features too defined, and the eyebrows too high . . . No, too much, too many differences. It would never work.

"You're insane. Who's going to do this?" Kaldar demanded.

"Dekart," Richard said.

Kaldar frowned.

"Who is Dekart?" she asked.

"He is a defector from Louisiana," Kaldar answered. "They were going to exile him for some creative surgeries, and he turned tail and ran across the border into the waiting arms of the Department of the Interior. What makes you think he'll go for it?"

"I have access to the Camarine and Sandine combined finances," Richard said. "Dekart needs money."

"Ridiculous," she told him. "You're going to trust your face to some defector?"

"Charlotte is right. The man is an artist with a scalpel, but you'll still die on the operating table," Kaldar said.

"Not necessarily." Richard looked at her.

No. Not in a million years. "Forget it."

"Charlotte . . ."

"I said forget it!" She got up off her chair. "I would have to continuously heal you while the surgeon cut at your face. Look at your chin and look at his. It means cutting the living bone, Richard, and reshaping it. I will have to regrow it beyond its natural shape. Do you have any idea how difficult that is? I've assisted in reconstructive surgeries before.

I know exactly what's involved. What you're proposing is suicide. There is no guarantee I can keep you alive. Best-case scenario, you would be disfigured. Worst case—dead. It's too dangerous."

He simply looked at her.

"It's too dangerous, Richard. I won't do it. One slip of the blade, one overlooked infection, and you'll be gone."

"Charlotte," he said quietly. "You don't have to assist. I can hire a healer."

"First, then you will die for sure. Second, no healer is going to do this for you. It's suicide."

"What other way is there?"

"I don't know, but this isn't the way."

"I'm willing to take the risk," Richard said.

"I'm not!"

"I ask that you respect my commitment," he said.

The words lashed at her. She had said the same thing to him when he tried to dissuade her from going with him. They had agreed that they would keep their relationship from interfering with the mission. If they hadn't made love and he was simply a man she knew, she would caution against the operation, but she wouldn't become borderline hysterical trying to prevent it.

But they had made love. And she was in love with him, whether he felt the same about her or not.

The words tore out of her before Charlotte could catch them, but she had summoned her poise, and when they came out, she said them calmly, with a touch of distance. "What if I lose you?"

"You won't. You're the best healer of your generation."

RICHARD lay prone on the table under the harsh sterile light of the surgeon's lamp. From this position, he had an excellent view of Dekart, a short, lean man, dressed in surgeon's robes. His face had a look of complete concentration as he reviewed his instruments. On the table in front of him, an imager presented Casside's face, enlarged to twice its normal size. The imager captured one's likeness completely, and Dekart was very good.

Charlotte stood next to the surgeon. Her face was glacially cold, her iced-over beauty almost sharp enough to cut. He was on the receiving end of the coldest stare he had ever seen.

Dekart's daughter-assistant tightened the last leather belt, pulling Richard's left arm tight against the surface of the table. The buckle clicked, locking. He was strapped in.

"Suicide," Charlotte said.

Richard smiled at her.

Ever since he pointed out that she was thinking with her emotions, Charlotte had shut them down. She had argued for three days with cold, flawless logic, trying to overwhelm him with facts. She explained the operation in detail as they sat by the fire. She found an anatomy volume on the shelf and detailed how easily a scalpel could cause damage. She threatened him with the lingering, chronic pain that came with reshaped bones and nerve damage. And when they made love, she took his breath away. She was trying to give him a reason to back off.

She had no idea she only made it worse. He wanted to keep her away from using the darker side of her magic at any cost. He had come up with a plan that would call for him to bear almost all of the danger. She wouldn't have any cause to kill anyone. It hinged on his having Casside's face, and so he had listened to everything she said and acknowledged the full validity of her arguments, but he refused to budge.

Dekart began drawing lines on Richard's face, holding the ink stick in gloved hands. "How proficient are you in healing, my lady?" His voice was soft and quiet. A slight Louisiana accent tinted his words.

"I'm the Healer," she said in a brisk tone.

"I understand you are a healer," he said.

"Not 'a.' 'The,'" she said.

Dekart glanced at her. "You will forgive me if I don't

believe you. The Healer worked miracles until she retired. Still, you must have some ability, since my patient places such confidence in you. Such procedures are . . . quite gruesome. I ask that you restrain yourself from healing until I ask, or you will prematurely heal the changes I will make."

Charlotte fixed Richard with a deadly gaze. "If you die, I'm coming after you. Don't expect a peaceful afterlife."

It must be excruciating for her, he realized. If their roles were reversed, and she lay on the table, while he was forced to watch her face being cut open and mop up the blood, could he do it?

"Dekart, give us a minute."

The surgeon gave a one-shouldered shrug, and he and his assistant stepped out.

"Did you have a moment of clarity?" she asked. "Should I undo the belts?"

"I'm sorry for making you do this. It must be difficult for you." He couldn't let her realize why he was doing it. If he did die, she would never forgive herself.

Her narrow eyebrows rose. "Have a care, my lord Mar. First you ignore my advice, now you insult me. I assure you that watching living flesh sliced by a surgeon is nothing new to me. Contrary to your expectations, you are not that special."

She was furious with him. "If I could trade places with you, I'd . . ."

Her eyes sparked with anger. He'd clearly said the wrong thing.

She reached over and slapped him.

"If you could trade places with me, I'd die on the operating table. You deposited the responsibility for your survival on my shoulders against my will. Don't offer me empty platitudes." She turned away from him and walked out of his field of vision. "He's ready."

The door swung open. A moment later, Dekart loomed over him. "Please don't damage the patient. If you feel the need to injure him, kindly do it on other parts of his body."

"I'll heal it before you start," came the icy reply.

A cold needle punctured his arm.

"I will count to ten," Dekart said. "I want you to repeat the numbers after I say them. Ten."

"Ten."

The room grew fuzzy. "Nine."

"Nine."

"Eight." Dekart's voice sounded as if coming over a great distance.

"Eight," Richard whispered.

"Seven."

The light blinked out. Everything went dark.

"LOOK at me."

A voice called him. Richard swam toward it through the endless colorless water. He wasn't sure whose voice it was, but it had awakened him, and now he moved. A small part of him wondered why he wasn't drowning and where the surface was, but those questions were too faint to need his attention.

Below him, darkness gaped. It was reaching for him, its long tendrils twisted, ready to coil and pull him under. He knew it wasn't death. Death was nowhere near. It was something else. As he swam, he felt its coldness, spreading through the waters underneath. It smelled like blood, he realized.

He wasn't afraid of it. Far from it, it felt familiar, as if it were a part of him.

"Richard?"

Charlotte . . . He spun around in the water looking for her. *Where are you, love?* The water stretched out on all sides of him, a transparent eternity.

"Come back to me, Richard."

I'm trying. I'm trying, my sweetheart. I'm looking for you.

"Come back to me."

He felt warmth on his skin and turned toward it. A luminescent golden glow suffused the crystalline depth. He swam into it.

The darkness chased him. The icy restraints of its tentacles wound about his legs. It pulled, but the light anchored him, refusing to let him go.

"Come back to me, Richard."

I love you, he wanted to tell her. Don't let me go.

"Come back."

He pushed away. The darkness broke. The torn shreds of its tentacles burned into his skin, long black marks. He knew they would be there forever. He kicked his legs and swam into the light.

His eyes opened, and he saw Charlotte leaning over him, her eyes luminescent. She had saved him. He wanted to tell her, but pain claimed his mouth, pooling in his jawbone.

She took his hand and kissed his fingers. He realized that the restraints were gone.

Dekart leaned against the cart with instruments. He looked ill.

Richard fought through the pain. "How did it go?"

"My finest work," the surgeon said. He pushed from the cart and bowed to Charlotte. "It was an honor."

"For me as well," she told him.

Dekart turned on his foot and left the room.

Charlotte bent over him. He saw tears in her eyes and opened his mouth. She put her fingertips on his lips.

"Be quiet," she whispered, and kissed him. He tasted tears and desperation on her lips. She held on to him for a long moment and let go, pulling on her composure like a mask. He almost wished she hadn't.

"Would you like a mirror?" Charlotte asked.

"Yes."

She nodded at the hand he was gripping. "You have to let me go."

"No."

She smiled back at him and sat in a chair. Ten minutes later, he finally decided she wouldn't dissolve into nothing and released her hand. She brought a mirror. A strange man looked back at him. He could still see the old shadows of himself. His eyes were the same. Possibly his eyebrows, and even his forehead. The rest belonged to Casside.

"It's not me," he said.

"That's what you wanted," Charlotte reminded him.

"Does it bother you?"

"Your new face?"

He nodded.

She sighed. "It bothers me that you risked your life for it. But I don't care whose face you're wearing, Richard."

He realized he loved her, painfully, intensely, with the desperation of a dying man eager for every last moment of life.

TWELVE

WARM lips touched her mouth.

Charlotte opened her eyes. She had fallen asleep on the couch next to the fire pit. The marathon healing session had taken its toll. Fatigue blanketed her body. She had the absurd notion that it covered her like a blanket, draining her life force with each breath she took.

Richard was looking at her. She reached over and touched his new face, probing for any sign of infection. He was clean.

"Does it hurt?"

"No."

Dekart was truly an artist with the knife. What they had accomplished together was nothing short of a miracle. Richard's face matched Casside's with uncanny precision, but where the other noble's eyes were guarded, Richard's intelligence shone through, giving the blueblood's features a dangerous air. Casside himself looked morose and melancholy, his expression pessimistic. Illuminated by Richard's intellect and will, that same face became fierce—not just handsome, but masculine and strong, the face of a warrior and a leader. It was a pity Casside had done so little with the gifts nature had given him.

"You must try to look less like yourself," she told him, caressing Richard's cheek with her fingertips. He was still hers, no matter whose face he wore.

He caught her fingers and kissed them. "When the time comes, I will. Do you feel up to walking?"

"Depends on how far."

"To the back door. I have someone I would like you to meet."

"I think I can do that."

Charlotte pushed off the couch and followed him to the back, past the table filled with precisely organized stacks of paper and crystals. Days of peering over the documents had paid off. They knew the Five, as they had come to call the slaver bluebloods, better than they knew themselves, and they had formed the plan. Richard's face was the first part of it. Her part involved befriending Lady Ermine. She would do it with pleasure, Charlotte reflected. She would become her best friend and confidante; all for that moment when their scheme came to its conclusion, and she could snuff her out like the flame of a foul candle.

"Once I become Casside, I can't watch over you." Richard paused at the back door and took an orange from the fruit dish on the kitchen counter.

"I'm hardly helpless," she told him.

"Yes, but you can't use your magic in public, or you'll risk an arrest. And you don't have a fighter's reflexes."

Charlotte didn't argue with him. He was right. She could easily kill on a massive scale, but an average fighter would cut her down. Her reaction time wasn't honed enough. Her trek through the island had demonstrated that.

"A bodyguard would be a welcome addition," he said.

"I can't be a part of blueblood society with a bodyguard," she told him. "It isn't customary and more importantly, the presence of a trained fighter among them would set the Five on edge, including Brennan."

"Not this one." Richard opened the door.

Sophie stood on the lawn. She wore loose blue pants and a white shirt. Her dark hair was pulled back from her face into a neat ponytail. A sword in a sheath hung from her hip.

"No," Charlotte said.

Richard threw the orange at Sophie. The girl moved, too fast, her strike a blur. The four pieces of the fruit fell onto the grass. Sophie flicked the juice off her blade.

"No," Charlotte repeated.

"Just as a precaution," he said. "It's typical for you to have a companion. Why not her?"

"Because we're playing a dangerous game, and I don't want her to get hurt."

Sophie didn't flinch. Her face remained placid, but hurt pulsed in her eyes. She was used to being rejected, Charlotte realized.

"Why don't the two of you discuss this?" Richard said, and stepped into the house.

Oh great.

The child on the lawn looked at her with an almost canine expectation, like Sophie was some half-starved puppy and Charlotte held a steak in her hand. Charlotte stepped down onto the grass, fighting the slow burn of her aching muscles. "Shall we walk?"

RICHARD watched Charlotte and Sophie walk away into the forest. The dog with no name trotted after them.

The faint sound of steps came from behind him. He recognized that walk.

Kaldar came to stand next to him, his face thoughtful. "Very pretty, both of them. The two women you care about most." There was a slight hint of disapproval in his tone.

"I suppose you came by to inform me I'm making yet another grave mistake."

"No." Kaldar grimaced. "Yes."

Richard sighed and motioned to him with his hand.

"I checked on her," he said. "Do you know who the first ten are?"

"The first ten blueblood families who arrived in Adrianglia." The cream of the crop.

"They took Charlotte from her family when she was seven and brought her to Ganer College, where she met Lady Augustine al Ran, a direct descendant of the Ran family, who just happen to be one of the first ten. The Lady adopted her."

"Mhm."

"Richard, you're not listening. She formally adopted her.

Charlotte's full name is Charlotte de Ney al-te Ran. If the king hosts a dinner, she can sit at the first table, right next to the royal family."

Richard turned to him.

"They didn't publicize the adoption, probably to give Charlotte a fair chance at a normal life. It isn't even on her marriage license—she signed it as de Ney. I don't think that moron she married ever knew. But it is in her Mirror file. Do you have any idea how many men would kill for a chance to marry into a first-ten family?"

He had a pretty good idea. "Your point?"

"Princesses don't marry swineherds in the real world," Kaldar said. "When people hear her name, they stand up. You're an Edger, a swamp rat."

"I remember," Richard said. "But thank you for reminding me."

Kaldar ground his teeth. "Let me remind you of something else: when Marissa left, you drank for two months straight, then tried to drown yourself."

"For the last bloody time, I didn't try to drown myself. I was drunk and out of wine, and I walked out onto the pier because I remembered I had left a bottle in the boat." And then he'd slipped and discovered that swimming while drunk was a lot more complicated than it seemed. He'd made it to shore and passed out on the bank from exhaustion, where Kaldar had found him. For some reason, everyone in the family insisted it was a suicide attempt, and nothing he said could convince them otherwise.

"You're the only brother I've got," Kaldar said. "If you follow through with this plan of yours, she will enter society without you. I'm not faulting your plan—you can't keep her locked up, and she would have to dip her toe into those waters sooner or later. The reality is, she's unattached, beautiful, and has the kind of name that will turn every head. The moment she's announced, they will start circling around her like sharks. These are people who have never in their lives had to worry about where their next meal was coming from. They can rattle off ten generations worth of ancestors at the drop of a hat. They're a different breed. Someone young, handsome, with the right pedigree and the right amount of money might catch her eye."

"You are really worried about me."

A muscle jerked in Kaldar's face. "When Marissa left, you were still young. A part of you knew you still had your whole life to live. You're older now, and you've lost your head over her. You don't fall for women often, but when you do, it's all or nothing."

"Since when did you become an expert on my love life?"

Kaldar waved his arm around. "It's obvious. You watch her. You try to make her laugh. If she leaves you, it might break you, and I might not be here to hold your head above the water. I just want you to consider the possibility now, so it doesn't shock you when it comes."

"If I need help swimming, I'll let you know."

Kaldar opened his mouth as if to say something else and snapped it shut.

"Is there more?" Richard asked. "Out with it."

"If you marry her, you would become a member of the al Ran family. Lady Augustine al Ran, the woman who adopted her, must grant her approval." Kaldar pulled a small clear imager cube out of his pocket and handed it to him. "Watch this before you do anything else."

He walked away.

"Kaldar!"

His brother turned and looked at him. Kaldar was genuinely worried for him. His brother wore his jokes and humor as armor. That he'd dropped it for his sake spoke volumes. When Declan had first approached him with his proposition to hunt down the slavers, Richard never considered what might happen to Kaldar if he failed. Seeing families torn apart had taught him to pay better attention to those who mattered most to him. His brother had a wife who loved him and the support of what remained of their family, but if something happened to him, Kaldar wouldn't take it well. At the very least, he could give Kaldar the satisfaction of knowing he did everything he could to save Richard from himself.

"We'll watch it together."

Kaldar grimaced, turned on his heel, and joined him. They walked to the house side by side. Richard had considered the possibility that Charlotte might leave him, stolen away by the glamour of blueblood society. Her adoption into the first ten made it even more likely.

The cube was cold in his hand. He entered the house and approached the imager. It sat to the left of the couches, a tall, round table about a foot and a half in diameter, with ornate metalwork decorating its single leg. A brown-and-gold carapace of polished metal guarded the top of the table. He touched it, and it split down the middle, the two halves of the carapace sliding down the table's sides, revealing a delicate surface inlaid with strange designs. A pale blue glow shimmered along the surface, bathing the designs in its gentle radiance. At the center, three metal prongs rose in the semblance of an inverted bird leg armed with wicked talons.

He looked at the cube. Something told him he really didn't want to know what was on it. The Mirror was the realm's magpie: it gathered bits of information, some precious, some useless, and dragged them to its archives, like a foolish bird dragged baubles that caught its eye to its nest. There was no telling what he would see.

The talons waited.

He would rather know. Richard dropped the cube into the claws. The prongs closed about it. A dim blue light ignited within the cube, and an image of Charlotte formed above it. She was sitting on a balcony, somewhere high above. She looked younger, softer somehow. Her hair was gathered into a roll like a crown on her head, and her dress, a pale green, spilled on the floor. She truly did look like a princess.

A man stood next to her. He was slender, his hair a light brown. He wore a light jacket, fitted with crisp precision to his frame, matching pants, soft boots. The clothes announced money and a good tailor.

"You look very nice, Elvei," Charlotte said.

"Thank you. You look divine, as usual."

Elvei. Her ex-husband. Richard peered at the man's face,

assessing him as one fighter would assess another. Unless the man was an incredibly gifted flasher, Richard was reasonably sure he could take him. He could find no resemblance between himself and Elvei. They looked nothing alike. Perhaps that was part of the attraction. A selfish part of him said it didn't matter why she liked him, but still, he wanted her to be with him because of who he was, not because of how he compared to the man she'd chosen before.

Elvei sat in a chair near the bench. "I hope you don't mind if I pry."

"I can't say that I will until you ask me the question."

"Then I will just come out and ask it plainly. Why is it necessary for Lady Augustine al Ran to approve our union?"

Charlotte leaned back. "I've told you the story of how I came to be at the College. I was taken from my family when I was very young. Over the years, I've come to think of Lady Augustine as my mentor. Her opinion is very important to me. Why is this troubling to you?"

Elvei smiled. "It appears today is my day to be blunt. I commend you for your devotion to your mentor, but the extent of the Lady al Ran's inquiries into my background has been exceptionally . . . comprehensive. She requested the files on the first seven generations of my ancestors."

"Do you have something to hide?" Charlotte asked.

"Of course not."

"Then don't trouble yourself." She smiled and reached out to caress his face. The muscles in Richard's arms tightened.

"You worry too much, Elvei."

"Charlotte, you are of age and have been for quite some time. You don't really need her permission to marry."

"Elvei, I would never consider a long-term relationship, let alone marriage, with any man who hadn't met with Lady Augustine's approval. She's like a mother to me, and her view is vital."

"And if she disapproved of me?"

"I would break our engagement. I'm afraid that's the price you have to pay for being with me."

"Then I will gladly pay it."

Charlotte smiled. The image melted.

"There you have it," Kaldar said. "If you want a life with Charlotte, you'll have to battle Lady Augustine, and that's not a war you can win. When she asks about your background, what will you tell her?"

"That I'm a Mire rat." Richard grinned. "That my father was a Mire rat, his father before him, and on and on, all the way to the beginning of our family when the ancient Legionnaires first settling the continent got trapped in the Mire and mixed with the natives."

"Yeah, you should mention Vernard while you're at it." Kaldar shook his head.

"Yes, how could I forget. Dear Lady, my granduncle-in-law was an exile, one of my uncles was a changeling, and a few of my cousins aren't even human. I have a tiny slice of land and very little money, and the only reason I'm allowed in Adrianglia at all is because my cousin Cerise married a changeling, who promised the Mirror ten years of service in exchange for asylum and citizenship for the Mar family. Did I miss anything?"

"You should have Charlotte there when you tell her that, or the noble lady might suffer an apoplexy. You're not taking this seriously, are you?"

"That's rich, coming form a man who never took anything seriously."

"I take the safety of my wife and my family very seriously. What has gotten into you? Is any of this penetrating that thick skull of yours?"

"I'm not worried about the bluebloods stealing Charlotte away. She has seen them before, and she chose me instead. We also have bigger problems than Lady Augustine." Richard crossed the room to the bookcase and pulled a heavy, embossed volume from the top of the shelf. He'd moved it there so Charlotte wouldn't find it.

"Like what?"

"Charlotte can kill with her magic."

Kaldar stared at him. "She's a fallen healer. Richard, they'll kill her if they find out."

"That's part of the problem."

"What's the other part?"

The book felt heavy, like a chunk of solid rock. Richard flipped through the pages, turning the thick paper sheets to a particular article, and offered the book to his brother. He had read it so many times, he had committed the words to memory. He kept hoping it would say something different. It didn't.

The act of draining another's magic to fuel oneself is colloquially known as life-force drain, a term which originated from the first-person accounts of the rare few who had experienced it. They describe this phenomenon as draining or stealing the target's life. In reality, the user and the target form a magic feedback loop, and it is the target's magic energy, not some mysterious life force, that is being drained. However, since a human body is unable to sustain life without this magic energy, when a target's magic is depleted, the target dies, so the term isn't as inaccurate as it may seem at first glance.

In the event of life-force drain, the user attracts the magic of the target, pulling it to himself and absorbing this energy. The user quickly becomes overwhelmed with the influx of incoming magic, and his body begins to radiate it out in whatever form feels most natural to the user. The user then invariably sends out more magic than he takes in, which in turn, causes him to absorb more magic in a greater volume, which he again must disperse. This essential cycle of absorbing and dispersing is ever expanding; the longer it continues, the harder it is to stop. Consider a snowball rolling down the hill: the longer it rolls, the bigger it grows. The longer the duration of the feedback loop, the greater the amount of magic that passes through the user, until eventually the user becomes a mindless conduit for the flow of magical energy.

There are known instances of interrupted feedback loops, where the user had begun the draw of energy but engaged in it for only a few brief moments. These users report feelings of euphoria and extreme pleasure associated with the absorption of magic. No doubt, this contributes to the difficulty of feedback-loop interruption. In plain terms: stealing magic produces pleasure and is self-rewarding, so much so that many users do not want to stop, and, after a few minutes, they find they cannot.

For the purposes of this study, eleven confirmed instances of interrupted feedback loop were examined, and in nine out of eleven cases, the users reattempted the feedback loop at a later date. All nine lost their humanity and had to be destroyed, as they presented an imminent threat to others. It is this author's opinion that surviving one interrupted loop is possible; however, interrupting such a loop for a second time is beyond the limits of human will.

Kaldar looked up from the page. "What does that mean?"

"How much did George tell you?"

"I know that you were injured, ran into the Edge, she healed you, then the slavers came, killed the boys' grandmother, set the house on fire, and threw you in the cage. Charlotte saved you."

"When she found us, she initiated a feedback loop. It was her first time killing, and she didn't think she had enough power. She can kill without it, but every time she does, her magic pushes her toward making it again."

"And if she does?"

"She will pull magic to her from her enemies and send it out as a plague, then she will drain more magic and send that out, and on and on, until everyone around her is dead. She would become a plaguebringer. She would never stop."

"So she would become an unstoppable crazed mass murder."

"Yes."

"Does she know?"

"She knows. She asked me to kill her if she succumbs

to it. I tried to talk her out of fighting the slavers, but she refuses to walk away."

Kaldar sank into the couch. His face was completely serious, something that almost never happened.

"Congratulations," he said, his voice dry. "You finally managed to find a woman as tragically noble as yourself. I didn't think one existed."

"I'm not tragic."

Kaldar held up his hand. "Spare me. Some children are born wearing a silk shirt; you were born wrapped in melancholy. When they slapped you to make you cry, you just sighed heavily and a single tear rolled from your eye." He dragged his finger from the corner of his left eye to his cheek. "Your first words were probably 'woe is me.'"

"My first words were 'Kaldar, shut up!' because you talked too much. Still do."

"You have grimly acknowledged the sadness of your situation since you were a kid. You don't even notice it anymore."

Richard leaned forward. "Would it be better if I turned everything into a constant joke?"

"Well, someone has to make you laugh; otherwise, you'd collapse under the burden of being you. People can share in the joke. Nobody can share in your anguish."

"I've been the butt of your jokes all my life, and let me tell you, it's not quite as fun."

They stared at each other. If Richard had a wet wig in his hands, he would've thrown it against the wall and kicked his brother in the chest. Sadly, they were too old to brawl.

"That's why the face," Kaldar said. "You did it for her, so you can be on the inside, working against the Five instead of her. Is she worth it?"

"Is Audrey worth it?" Richard asked.

"Leave my wife out of it."

"You gave yourself up to the Hand for her. Was it worth it?"

"Yes. And I'd do it again." Kaldar sighed. His shoulders slumped in defeat. "What do you need from me?"

"I'll need your help," Richard said.

"You have it. We're family."

Richard went to the wine cabinet, got a bottle of green wine and two glasses, and brought it over. He poured the wine. Kaldar swallowed some and smiled. "Tastes like home. Where did you find the berries? I thought they only grew in the Mire?"

"Aunt Pete grew them somehow in a greenhouse behind her home." He let the wine roll down his throat. The delicious light taste refreshed him, whispering of swamp and home.

Brennan, Lady Augustine, blueblood society, all of it, he could handle. They were just people. But he had no idea how to protect Charlotte from herself. He couldn't lose her. He tensed at the thought, his muscles locked, as if he were fighting for his life. Fear gripped him. He was so rarely afraid, and here he sat, terrified.

Suggesting that she sit this one out would only have the opposite effect. She would just fight harder.

He went over the plan in his head. They would lay a two-part trap for Brennan, and he would take care of the first half of the plan. With luck, Brennan would take his bait, and Charlotte's involvement might not even be necessary. If he failed to entice Brennan, the plan didn't call for her to use much of her power, only for the use of her name and position. She would be in minimal danger.

If they succeeded by some crazy stroke of luck, he would do everything in his power to make her happy.

"You really didn't try to kill yourself?" Kaldar asked.

Damn it. "Killing yourself requires desperation. I wasn't desperate. You know why I drank? I drank because I was angry. I swore to love her and defend her. I gave her a house, I provided for her, and I treated her well. Even if she didn't love me, it should've been enough. Had she left me for a man, I would understand. I would be angry, but I wouldn't want to keep her with me against her will if she chose another man. She left me because her life wasn't nice enough. That's how low I ranked, somewhere down below the 'nice house' and 'no mud in the yard.' I drank because I was pissed off and didn't want to do something stupid."

"Don't hold back. Tell me how you really feel."

"I deserved better than a fucking note!"

"Maybe she was afraid she couldn't leave with you there," Kaldar said.

"What the hell does that mean?" Richard spread his arms. "Are you implying I'd hurt her?"

"No, I'm implying that Marissa was never much for confrontations. Although I don't know, you're a scary bastard when you get going." Kaldar winked at him.

Richard pointed at him.

"Oh gods, the finger of doom. Deliver me!"

He would not pummel his brother. It wouldn't be right. Richard forced himself to sit down in the chair. "Are you quite finished?"

"Yes. Well, no, I could go on, but I'll spare you." Kaldar poured more wine. "It will work out. It always does."

Richard raised his glass. "I'll drink to that."

SOPHIE pulled a cloth from the pocket of her tunic and carefully cleaned the blade. She and Charlotte strolled down the path into the woods, the wolf-dog trotting in front of them like some monster from a child's fairy tale.

"Do you have to do this every time you take your sword out?" Charlotte asked.

"If I draw blood," the girl answered quietly. "And the orange juice is acidic. It will corrode the blade."

"Why not make a stainless-steel sword?"

"Stainless steel doesn't bend. A sword must be flexible, or it will break."

Much like people. "Did Richard talk you into becoming my bodyguard?"

"I asked him. He said that the opportunity exists, but the final decision is yours, and he had 'neither the capability nor the inclination to compel you to do anything against your will.' He's very formal sometimes."

He would say something like that, wouldn't he? "The people we're up against will not hesitate to kill you even though you're a child."

"I won't hesitate either," Sophie said with quiet determination. "And I'm faster and better skilled."

"You're still a child."

Sophie took a step. Her hand blurred again: strike, strike, strike—was it three? Four?—and she sheathed her sword.

The woods stood silent. Nothing moved.

Sophie sighed, reached out, and pushed a four-inch-wide sapling with her finger. The tree slid aside, breaking into four pieces as it fell.

"It's not as dramatic when it doesn't fall by itself," Sophie said. "I'm faster than Richard. It takes him a third of a second longer to stretch his flash onto the blade. Do you know what that means?"

"No." Somehow she knew the answer wouldn't be good.

"It means I can kill him," Sophie said.

Dawn Mother. She chose her words carefully. "Do you want to kill Richard?"

Sophie shook her head. "When Spider fused my mother, William killed her. He is my brother-in-law, and it was a mercy killing. My father died with her. He's alive, technically. He eats and breathes and talks. But he is . . . absent. He tries to take care of the family because it's his duty, but if the rest of us disappeared tomorrow, he would walk off the nearest cliff." Sophie turned to her. "It's not fair. I didn't die. I'm still here, but he doesn't care."

She'd said it so flatly, her aspect so neutral. She was barely fifteen years old and already she was masking her pain. Charlotte fought an urge to reach out and hug her. It probably wouldn't be welcomed.

"He must care. A parent doesn't just abandon a child."

"My father did. He loved my mother so much, and now she is gone, and the world stopped for him. He stopped training me. He stopped talking to me after dinner. He stopped talking to everyone unless it's absolutely necessary, so I suppose I shouldn't expect special treatment just because I'm his daughter."

So much damage. A low pain squeezed Charlotte's chest. It felt like her heart had turned over.

"Richard is the only father I have now. He takes care of me. But I'm faster, and he would hesitate to cut me down. He loves me very much. So I know I can kill him."

"That's a cold thing to say."

Sophie glanced at her, surprised. "You think so?"

"Yes."

"It's just a fact." She shrugged. "I can't help it."

Anything Charlotte said to that would sound like a criticism. The coldness was likely a barrier Sophie had built, and the fact that it was there meant fragility. Charlotte stayed silent. Perhaps later, if they had a chance to forge more trust, she could return to it.

"You're planning to expose Brennan at the Grand Thane's wedding," Sophie said.

"How do you know this?" *Did Richard actually tell her?*

Sophie raised her head. Light filtering through the trees dappled her face. "Hawk."

Charlotte looked up as well. A bird of prey soared above the treetops, circling around them.

"It's dead," Sophie said. "George is guiding it. He is very powerful."

The realization washed over Charlotte in a cold gush of embarrassment. "Is George spying on Richard and me?"

"Always," Sophie said. "All those perfect manners are a sham. He spies on everyone and everything. Declan hasn't been able to conduct a single business meeting in the past year without George's knowing all the details. He does let go when you make love. He is a prude."

" 'Prude' is a coarse word. He has a sense of tact," Charlotte corrected before she caught herself.

"A sense of tact," Sophie repeated, tasting the words. "Thank you. The other one is somewhere around here, too."

"The other one?"

Sophie surveyed the woods. "I can smell you, Jack!"

"No, you can't," a distant voice answered.

The dog barked and shot through the bushes to the side.

"I told you." Sophie smiled. "Spider will attend the wedding of Grand Thane. He's a peer of the Dukedom of Louisiana. His rank demands it."

"You can't kill Spider," Charlotte told her.

"I just want to see him. He took my mother and my father away from me." Sophie's dark eyes looked bottomless. "I want to see his face. I want to brand it in my head." She tapped her skull. "So I'll never forget it. Because we will meet again, and when we do, I want to be absolutely certain that I kill the right man."

She was frightening.

"Please let me do this, Lady de Ney. Please." Her words were a fierce, savage whisper. Sophie dropped on one knee. "You have lost someone. You know how it feels. I'm running in circles, like a mouse on a wheel. I just want a way to get off. Please."

Charlotte's memory conjured the nightmare of her house burning. She had felt so helpless standing there, on that lawn, watching Éléonore's remains smolder as the ash rained on Tulip's hair. She chose to do something about it because she possessed the means to do it. When Spider tore this child's parents from her, she must've felt helpless, too. She banished Sophie, gave up the person she was, and became Lark, who cut trees into pieces faster than the eye could follow.

She and Richard, they were exactly alike. Ice over fire, a cool exterior hiding uncontrollable passion and emotion beneath. If Charlotte shut Sophie out now, she would be inflicting another wound. The very fury that fueled the child's transformation might tear her apart.

Charlotte sighed. "How proficient are you in etiquette?"

Sophie stood up. "I took lessons."

"Same instructor as Rose?"

"How did you know?"

Charlotte reached over and brushed a twig off Sophie's

tunic. "The gown you wore when I saw you the first time. It's a decade too old for you. We have a lot of work to do, my dear. If you really want to come with me, you must be flawless."

SOPHIE drank from a tiny cup, holding it with effortless grace. Charlotte sat across from her. In the three days she had spent with her, Sophie had soaked up information like a sponge. She was a natural mimic in the best possible sense of the word—she imitated not only the action but the air, the atmosphere Charlotte projected, and the change in her demeanor was immediate.

The door swung open, and Jack strode into the cabin. Moving in complete silence, he approached the table and dropped a crystal in the middle of it.

"This is everything."

"Thank you," Charlotte told him.

He surveyed Sophie sitting in a simple pale peach gown and crouched by her, his eyes big in his handsome face. George had the elegance, there was no question. But Jack was wildfire. There was something about the child, about the way he held himself, the raw potential for unpredictability, perhaps, or the air of danger he emitted, that would give Jack an allure all of his own in a few years.

"I have an idea," he said.

Sophie tilted her head, looking at him with her dark velvet eyes.

"Ditch the dress and come hunting with me."

"You're such a child," she told him.

"You're turning into an old lady."

Sophie smiled and stabbed a dagger into the table. She moved so fast, she was a blur, but somehow Jack had moved his hand, and the dagger pierced wood instead of flesh.

Charlotte sipped from her cup. "One more, and both of you will be down with dysentery for a week."

Jack moved backward and sprawled in a chair, exasperated.

Charlotte slid the crystal into the thin metal claw of an imager. A light filtered through the crystal, forming the image of a young girl in a vivid blue gown.

"Next."

Another young blueblood flower, another blue satin.

"Next."

More young girls. Cornflower blue. Royal blue. Sky-blue.

"Boring people doing boring things wearing boring clothes," Jack said.

"Blue is in season." Charlotte surveyed Sophie. "What shade of bright blue looks good on you?"

"I don't know, my lady," Sophie answered.

"None," Jack said.

Sophie arched her eyebrows at him. "When I want your opinion, I will cut it out of you."

"In this case, he's right. You would be surprised, but men do usually have an excellent eye when it comes to female clothes. Look at your wrist. You too, Jack."

Both of them turned their right arms, displaying their wrist. She did the same. "See how the veins in my wrist and Jack's look really blue? We have a cool undertone to our skin. Veins in your wrist have a slight green tint because of the warm undertones of your beautiful golden bronze skin. Cool colors such as blue, purple, or turquoise won't look good on you."

"I could wear white," Sophie offered. "Lady Renda says white is always in season."

"White is for cowards," Charlotte said. "And Lady Renda is a dinosaur."

Sophie choked on her tea. Jack chortled.

"When people say white, they often mean a really icy white, which has cool undertones. Pure black isn't a good idea either. Jack, because of his cooler skin tone, would look very well in black; you wouldn't. Richard's skin tone is similar to yours. He wears black, and although he's a very handsome man, it doesn't resonate with his skin; it just makes him look menacing. True white is a neutral color—everyone looks well in it, but there is no daring in it, no sense of style. Wear it, and you might just as well announce that you're playing it safe. We don't play it safe. We make a statement." Charlotte passed her hand over the crystal to reactivate it. "Color wheel, stage twelve."

A complex color wheel ignited in the air above the reader. In the center, twelve bright colors formed the inner core: first, the primary shades of red, orange, yellow, green, blue, and violet. Between them were six transitional shades. Past the center, the color wheel split, with each of the twelve inner colors fracturing into four shades. Just outside the center, the color shades turned dark, nearly black. Hair-thin lines sectioned off the wheel into individual colors, each new tone a shade lighter than the previous one, until at the outer rim of the wheel, the colors became nearly white.

"This is your secret weapon. Remember that first blue gown?" Charlotte nodded at the wheel. "Find the color segment."

Sophie stared at it for a second. "Number twenty-six."

"Very good. It's a saturated derivate of cobalt blue." Charlotte touched the gears. The color wheel slid higher, and the row of pictures she had viewed ignited below it.

"They are all within the same segment," Sophie said. "The color varies slightly, but they are playing it safe."

"Exactly. These are the unmarried young women who are supposed to be on the cusp of fashion, which is why they are all wearing what they consider to be the cutting-edge trend. The older the woman, the more vivid the color, but none of them are deviating from the blues—they're like goats in a herd all following the leading goat. Women who are either attached or are not looking to impress their awareness of fashion onto others will wear whatever color they please. This is the daughter of Duchess Ramone." Charlotte pointed at the next-to-last picture of a tall, slender young girl. "I've met her before. See, she's wearing green."

"Shocking!" Jack called out from his chair.

"She is young and 'in the market,' so to speak, but she has enough status and daring to do whatever she wants. She also knows that vivid blue isn't her color either. Still, if you look at the dress closely, there are notes of blue in it. The idea is not to spit in the eye of the current trend but subtly twist it to make it your own."

"This is ridiculous," Jack said.

"Fashion is utterly ridiculous," Charlotte told him. "And ninety-nine percent of the fashion is who is wearing it. Some no name wears an ugly hat, and people say it's an ugly hat. If Duchess Ramone wears an ugly hat, people say, 'What an interesting new trend.'"

"So it's about money?" Sophie asked.

"No. It's about poise. You must be supremely confident in what you're wearing and comfortable in your own skin. Being a blueblood isn't just knowing the rules. It's knowing the precisely correct thing to do in every situation, then doing it with unshakable entitlement."

Sophie frowned, puzzled.

Charlotte smiled at her. "It's not very difficult. Have no fear, we'll practice. But back to the color wheel. Forget white and black. We must show off your skin, your neck, and that face. This is where the impact should be." Charlotte picked up a drawing pad. "Segment 28, row 17."

A beautiful warm gray, reminiscent at once of the pearly inside of an oyster shell and the soft glow of polished aluminum, ignited above the imager.

Sophie leaned forward, her eyes wide. "It's the color of my sword."

Charlotte smiled and began to sketch. They would have to add some pale blue accents to nod at the trend, but nothing major.

"But where will we get the dress?" Sophie asked.

"Dresses. We each need a set of at least six outfits, all tied together with similar design elements. We'll take a page out of Richard's playbook, contact the best dressmaker we can find, and throw an obscene amount of money at her." Charlotte continued to sketch. The dressmaker would likely balk—the silhouette that emerged on the paper was slightly uncommon for a young girl, but it suited Sophie perfectly. "If she digs her heels in, we'll find another. I'm not without means, and when it comes to dresses, money makes a most convincing argument."

"You don't need to spend money on me," Sophie said. "My sister is married to William Sandine. I can get bucketloads of money."

"I don't have to—I want to." Charlotte grinned and turned to Jack. "Would you like to help?"

The expression on his face underwent a lightning change, from surprise, to fear, to a bored, distant expression. "I suppose," he said, and yawned. "If I'm bored."

"That's his nonchalant expression," Sophie said. "He puts it on when he doesn't know how to respond."

"Are you on good terms with the Duchess of the Southern Provinces?" Charlotte asked. Declan's mother was precisely the kind of heavy hitter who would make a decisive difference in their entrance to society.

"I'm adored," Jack said.

Sophie snorted.

Jack glanced at her, indignant. "That's what she always says." He slipped into a perfect imitation of a highborn blueblood accent. " 'Oh, Jack. I adore you, you silly boy.' "

Charlotte lost it and laughed. "Do you think your adorableness can arrange for the two of us to have tea with Her Grace?"

"Piece of cake," Jack said.

RICHARD opened his eyes. Charlotte had come up the stairs and paused, studying him lying in bed. Darkness had fallen, and the gentle lights of the lanterns played on her face. She was beautiful. Looking at her opened a gaping hole inside him born from the knowledge he soon would have to let go.

They hadn't made love since the operation on his face. He wanted her so badly, it burned, more than a want, a need akin to an addiction. He was addicted to Charlotte, to her scent, her taste, the soft touch of her skin against his. To watching her gasp in surprise when he brought her to a climax. He needed her the way he needed air, and anticipation of their separation set his teeth on edge.

In this moment, he regretted everything: every word he had said to her seemed wrong, every gesture coarse and stupid. She deserved . . . someone better than him, but he was deeply selfish and would do everything in his power to keep her.

"Where is Sophie?"

"She left," Charlotte said. "Supposedly to say good-bye to her sister. Unfortunately, Jack had let it slip that Cerise and William are already out on assignment. She's giving us privacy. I suspect all of the undead mice, squirrels, and birds watching your Lair are gone, too."

He slipped into formal blueblood affectation. "Dear gods, are they expecting us to have intimate relations?"

"It appears so. Do the children know something I don't?" she asked.

She'd changed the subject. "Kaldar sent a message through George," Richard said. "Brennan left for the Southern Coast. Supposedly he's visiting a sick friend."

"He went to tour the island," she said.

"Yes."

"And now with him out of the way, you want to make the switch and become Casside?"

"If you're ready to begin our scheme." And once they began, they couldn't be seen together. No hint of their alliance could exist.

"I'm ready," she told him. "Choosing a dressmaker presented a dilemma, but I found one who is talented, poor, and hungry to make her mark. The dress orders are in, and I've piled money on her with promises of more. The first two gowns will be ready in record time. Jack is arranging a tea with Declan's mother. I plan to come clean and ask for her assistance. My introduction will be much smoother if she lays the groundwork. I think I could convince her to help us. With or without Her Grace's backing, I should make an appearance at the capital within two days at the celebration of Spring's End."

"Will Sophie be ready?"

"Yes and no." Charlotte shook her head. "The basics are there, and she is very smart. Being a maiden of escort isn't exactly complex. I did it when I was her age—you walk three steps behind your sponsor and don't talk unless spoken to. While she doesn't know everything yet, she'll do fine."

The anxiety ate at him. "Sounds like you have things in hand."

"Yes."

"Should we go through the plan again?" They had gone over it a dozen times, but the moment he left, events would spiral out of his control.

"You will travel to the capital and replace Casside. You're planning on kidnapping him on the way to his weekly card game, which he will attend. The attack on the island likely made Brennan furious, and the four bluebloods under him will strive to maintain the status quo out of sheer self-preservation. You will kidnap Casside, remove his retainers from the house, and your family will detain them until we're done." She invited him to continue.

"In two days, you will make an appearance at the Spring's End Ball," Richard said. "You will make an impression on Angelia Ermine. You will befriend her. It's likely that she is sleeping with Brennan."

"You said that before," Charlotte said. "What makes you so sure?"

"Do you remember that speech Brennan had written while in Academy about leadership as the true purpose of the monarchy?"

She nodded. They had read it to each other out loud.

"He wants the throne. He thinks he's destined to rule, but he will never acquire the crown," Richard said. "He's too far removed from the line of succession. It's killing him inside. The slaver ring is his kingdom, and Casside, Angelia, Rene, and Maedoc are his thanes. He would demand absolute loyalty from them. Angelia is young, unattached, and attractive. He would want the satisfaction of owning her completely."

"Angelia is scum. I'll have to strain not to kill her." Charlotte shook her head. "While I'm working on her, you will stage an attempt on Brennan's life, making him think that Maedoc is trying to kill him."

It was a difficult plan, one that demanded that both of them surrender their best weapons. He would have to use his sword without the benefit of the flash technique, but she wouldn't be able to use her magic either. That fact filled him with relief. Still, killing Brennan would have been so much easier with it.

Suddenly Charlotte stepped toward him and embraced him. Her lips touched his. He kissed her deeply and tasted desperation. "Are you afraid?"

"I'm terrified," she said.

He held her to him. "I wish I knew what to say," he murmured. "I wish I had the right words."

"Tell me what will happen if we win," she asked.

"If we win, I will find you," he told her. "And if it's in my power, we will never be apart again. If you will have me."

"And if I won't?"

He raised his eyebrows. "I'll probably beg. Or do one of those stupid dramatic things men do to win women over. If we still lived in the time of knights, I'd just unhorse anyone who stood in my way."

"I'll hold you to it," she whispered, and kissed him back.

HER Grace, Lady Jane Olivia Camarine, Duchess of the Southern Provinces, was flawless, Charlotte reflected. She looked to be in her late forties although likely older since her son, the Earl of Camarine, was past thirty. Her tunic and trousers, a gorgeous emerald green and cream, were tailored with a deceptive simplicity that masked her thickening waist while playing up the duchess's curves. Her hair, artfully layered on her head in twin plaits, elongated her round face. She wore a single piece of jewelry, a wedding ring crafted from spider-silk-thin tendrils of gold. It was both extremely expensive and superbly tasteful. She stood on the terrace, next to a picnic table, bathed in morning light.

"Look at the way she stands," Charlotte murmured, as she and Sophie followed Jack to the table. "Chin tilted upward to make the neck appear thinner; light on the left, so it will play up the draping lines on her tunic. Long vertical lines, like those, make you appear thinner. You must always be aware of the light and know your best angles."

"Your Grace," Jack said. "May I present Charlotte de Ney and Lark."

"Sophie Mar," Charlotte murmured under her breath.

"And Sophie Mar," he intoned.

Charlotte curtsied. Next to her, Sophie sank down gracefully.

"What a pleasure to meet you both." The duchess smiled warmly. "Children, do you actually want to be here?"

"No," Jack and Sophie chorused.

The duchess grinned. "Broderick fixed the fountain in the pool." She pointed with her thumb over her shoulder in a distinctly unblueblood gesture. "Flee while you can!"

The two teenagers took off down the wide white stairs toward the pool gleaming in the middle of the lawn. At the last step, as if by some signal, they broke into a run, flying across the grass. Jack spilled out of his clothes. Sophie grasped the hem of her gown. *Dear Dawn Mother, please let there be something under it.* The gown flew off, revealing a small bikini. The two teenagers leaped in unison and vanished into the water.

"They planned this, didn't they?"

"I'd imagine so," Her Grace said. "Shall we?"

They sat at a table.

"I remember you. You were only fifteen at the time, but I recall you escorting Augustine al Ran."

"I'm flattered," Charlotte said.

"So is it Charlotte de Ney?"

There was no point in hiding. "Charlotte de Ney al-te Ran, Your Grace."

"I thought so. Jack mentioned that you've been living in the Edge for the past three years. Have you been to see your mother since your return?"

"No, Your Grace."

"The boys have given me a summary of your plan. Is it true? A Brennan is dealing in slaves?"

"Yes, Your Grace."

The duchess looked at the two teenagers splashing in the pool. "I knew his parents. They were nice people. Capable, morally upright, conscious of their responsibilities. I wonder if they know. I doubt it. As a parent, you always worry and wonder if you went wrong somewhere, if something you said or did caused your child to stray from the path."

"With all due respect, he did more than stray," Charlotte said. "You wouldn't believe the horrors I've seen."

A shadow passed over the duchess's face. "Perhaps I would. I will help you, my dear. We have a duty to bring him down."

"Thank you, Your Grace."

An outraged howl came from the pool, followed by Sophie's laugh.

The duchess sighed. "Sophie doesn't trust many people. I've tried to forge a bond, but she very politely keeps me at arm's length. If Sophie chose, she could live with her sister, but she selected not to do it. She holds herself apart, but she seems to respond to you. It's a precious connection. Please safeguard it."

THIRTEEN

GEORGE stood next to the Duchess of Southern Provinces, or Lady Olivia, as she preferred to be called, and surveyed the glittering gathering of the Adrianglian elite. Not all of them were blueblood, but all were rich or powerful or both. Lady Olivia wore a green bracelet on her left wrist, which signaled that she wished to maintain her privacy, and they were left to their own devices.

Around them, the vast terrace of the Evergreen castle stretched into the night, bordered by tall, pale columns, each supporting a tasteful cascade of flowers growing from marble planters. Dense trees surrounded the terrace on the north and south. To the west, the entrance to the castle's first floor gaped open, illuminated with golden light. There, the new arrivals paused at the entrance to be announced and recognized before drifting on to mingle. To the right, the trees had been cleared, and the ground dropped to the shimmering waters of the Evergreen Lake. Above burned the sunset, a garish spectacle of red and gold so vivid, it almost hurt.

Standing there, watching people flutter by, George felt a peculiar sense of detachment, as if he were in a dream. The end of spring was an ancient celebration, born in a more violent time, when starvation decimated the population, war was frequent, and human life cheap. The people who'd begun it wore simple clothes and carried savage weapons. They gave thanks to their gods for surviving to summer. Now their descendants floated on, dressed in fine gowns and tailored jackets, aware but unwilling to acknowledge the tradition of blood that gave the festival its roots. But they were still just as brutal as their ancestors. If a threat were to appear, the entire gathering would spark with bursts of lightning as their magic sliced it to pieces.

The George Camarine side of him reminded him of the commonly known facts about each familiar face, while the Mirror agent side served up their secrets. Here came Lady Olla in a beautiful gown of sea-foam green, a white flower in her red hair. She had a penchant for collecting crystal figurines of dragons and a severe addiction to sumah. He knew the names of her suppliers and where they could be found. Lord Ronkor, a former logistics officer and now a transportation supervisor in the Department of the Interior, broad-shouldered, confident, exuded an air of masculine swagger as he took wide strides across the floor. Lord Ronkor enjoyed being spanked by young women and was notoriously quick in bed, according to the prostitutes he frequented. His wife hadn't noticed—she was carrying on a decade-long affair with her best friend's sister. Yes, hello, how are you? How's your cousin, the one working in Kamen Port Authority? Is he still taking bribes? What a delightful scamp.

A small hand rested on his shoulder. "You look distant, my dear."

He bowed his head slightly. "Apologies, Your Grace."

The woman next to him frowned with her eyes. Her face remained perfectly pleasant. Her Grace Olivia Camarine wore a gown of deep regal purple. The theme of the festival was nature and rebirth, a celebration of spring, and the hue of her dress precisely matched the clusters of widow's tear flowers spilling from the planters. Her dark hair was put away into a tasteful arrangement. In her late fifties, she looked twenty years younger, and despite her age and a life that was more than trying, she remained beautiful. She was Declan's mother, and she had stepped into the role of George's grandmother as soon as Jack and he arrived in the Edge. That role had been officially chiseled into stone when Declan and Rose formally adopted him and Jack.

"Don't let them trouble you," she said.

"They don't." He felt a rush of gratitude. Many of the

people gathered here would never let him forget that he came from the Edge. Very few of them dared to recall that Her Grace's mother was an Edge rat just like him. She was above reproach by virtue of her position and success, but he was still a fair target. "I know their secrets."

She raised her eyebrows. "Gloating?"

"Only a little."

"See that it doesn't go to your head."

He bent toward her and smiled. "Too late."

"George, you are a terrible scoundrel."

"Lady Virai wouldn't have me otherwise."

"That is, sadly, true."

The fact that his direct supervisor and the woman in charge of the Mirror was Her Grace's best friend occasionally made his life complicated, but he'd learned to deal with it.

Lady Olivia's dark eyes sparked. "Shall we start our little game?"

"As you wish."

Her Grace slipped the bracelet off and slid it onto her right wrist. Immediately, the current of the crowd changed. Small eddies formed as the nearest lords and ladies found graceful ways to disengage from their conversations in favor of greeting the Duchess of the Southern Provinces.

Lady Olivia hid her amusement in a placid half smile. He hadn't been present when she met Charlotte, but since then he'd had plenty of chances to observe the two of them. Lady Olivia had liked Charlotte instantly. It was very clear that they were two birds of a feather—neither was born into a blueblood line and both had attained the pinnacle of social achievement. They were astute, adept, and intelligent, and listening to them he had felt slightly out of his depth.

People approached. He uttered pleasantries, making them sound as if he meant them. About ten minutes later, with the crowd at its peak, Lady Olivia turned to him.

"George, have you seen her yet?"

"No, my lady." He could see the question form on the faces around them.

"She did say she intended to attend?"

"Yes, my lady. You made it very clear to her that she would suffer your wrath otherwise."

Lady Olivia heaved a martyred sigh. "I'm really not that frightening."

Nobody laughed. History was a required subject for anyone hoping to achieve any significant position in Adrianglia, and every person within earshot knew about the massacre that ended the Ten Day War between the Dukedom of Louisiana and Adrianglia and who was responsible for it.

"Do check on her for me," Her Grace prompted.

George bowed his head. A falcon shot upward from its post on the nearest column and streaked away, in the direction of front gate. He concentrated, looking through the bird's eyes at the string of phaetons. There, latest model, delicate ornamentation, Sophie's face in the window.

He left the bird soaring. "Your Grace, they are about to arrive. Ten minutes at most."

"Delightful. Thank you, my boy."

He slid back into his affectation of boredom, surveying the faces, noting the minute details, as people pulled on polite masks, frantically trying to figure out who was the subject of their conversation. A tall, dark-haired man paused on the periphery of the gathering. Lord Casside. A member of the Five. It didn't seem like his type of affair. He must've gotten a personal invitation from someone he couldn't ignore . . .

George caught himself. Not Casside. Richard.

He had watched through the eyes of a bat when, two nights ago, Richard's people grabbed Casside off the dark street. He'd left a club where he'd fenced with his usual partner, turned the corner on the dark street, heading to his phaeton, and three men jumped him. They sealed his mouth, brought him down, thrust a bag over his head, and yanked him into the dark archway. A moment later, Richard strode out onto the street, dressed in exactly the same clothes, walking at exactly the same speed. He walked over to the phaeton, got in, and rode off. George knew this, but when he looked at the lean man across the terrace, his mind didn't say Richard. It said, "Casside," and insisted on it.

It had to be some sort of subtle magic, George decided. One of those secret talents the Edgers hid from everyone.

Richard glanced in their direction, looking bored.

CHARLOTTE paused before the entrance to the terrace. Through the doors she could see the gathering: the people, the clothes, the jewels . . . An electric zing of excitement dashed through her. She had done this dozens of times, but that preappearance rush never got old.

Sophie stepped forward and passed a small card with their names and titles to the crier. The man took it, and the child moved back to her place next to Charlotte. She looked a shade paler than when they had exited the phaeton. Poor kid.

Charlotte wrapped her arm around Sophie's shoulders. "It will be fine," she murmured. "Breathe and hold your head high. Remember—poise. You belong here. It's your right to be here."

Sophie swallowed.

"Baroness Charlotte de Ney al-te Ran and Sophie al-te Mua," the crier announced.

"HERE she is," Lady Olivia exclaimed.

Every head at their side of the terrace turned to the entrance. Charlotte stepped through, and George blinked. She wore a shimmering gown of delicate blue. It hugged her body. It *really* hugged her body, showcasing every curve before it flared into a flowing skirt that fell to the floor, and he felt vaguely embarrassed for looking. The top of the dress featured strips of brown fabric that narrowed on the side and spread across the blue skirt, imitating thin, twisted, apple branches. White blossoms, accented with silver, bloomed on the branches. The silhouette was simple, yet the color, the cut, and the pattern combined into an elegant, refined whole, and Charlotte, with her pale blond hair and gray eyes, floated in it, like the queen of spring.

He could almost hear a barely audible collective gasp from a dozen women who realized they had just been upstaged.

George chanced a glance at Richard. The man stood very still, his gaze fixed on Charlotte as she walked across the floor, and despite his new face, in that moment Richard looked nothing like Casside. A mix of emotions reflected on his face, desperation, passion, longing. It lasted for half a moment and looked like torture, then Richard slipped back into Casside, the way one put on a shirt in the morning. He must miss her.

George glanced back at Charlotte and forgot to breathe. Three steps behind her, to the left, Sophie walked across the terrace.

The world took a step back.

She wore a flowing gown of a pale gray with a touch of blue, draped at the top, caught by a sash, then floating in a weightless long skirt. He'd seen that precise color when she unsheathed her sword. The dress shimmered as she walked, slick and fluid, as if the metal of her blade had come to life and streamed over her like liquid, shifting with every movement.

He saw the graceful lines of her neck.

He saw her dark hair and a single pale blue flower in it.

He saw her face.

She was beautiful.

He realized he was standing there like an idiot, with his mouth hanging open, and clamped it shut.

A moment later, Charlotte joined them. Her Grace hugged her, gently. "My dear, I had almost given up hope."

"I wouldn't disappoint you if it is at all in my power." Charlotte smiled.

"And you've brought Sophie." Her Grace opened her arms, and Sophie hugged her. "How can you hide this beautiful flower in that country house of yours?"

"The country is where the flowers bloom the best," Charlotte replied.

"Oh please." Lady Olivia made a dismissive gesture that could've done a premier dancer proud. "It's about time for the child to see the wider world."

"Excuse me, Lord Camarine?"

A singsong female voice tugged on him. George turned. Lady Angelia Ermine stood next to him, wearing a fishtail gown of light powder blue. Her caramel golden hair cascaded in a tumble of locks on her left side, drawing attention to her delicate shoulders and long neck. She was quite attractive, George reflected in a detached way. She also profited from the sale of slave women and robbed them of their future children.

Her escort, a well-groomed, elegant blond man in a tailored russet doublet smiled at him with a sardonic spark in his eyes—Baron Rene, Spider's cousin. He seemed perfectly at ease and enjoying himself. Two of the Five for the price of one.

George smiled. "May I help you, my lady?"

"Do you happen to know Lady de Ney?"

"I've only met her casually. I understand she has a very rare talent. Her Grace holds her in the highest regard. Some sort of family favor."

"Her dress is divine," Baron Rene volunteered. He was looking at Charlotte with a distinctly male appreciation.

"It's probably one of her own designs," George said, keeping his voice light. "Would you like an introduction?"

"I suppose we can spare a moment or two." Angelia shrugged.

She was clearly dying to be introduced. George stepped to the side, waited until Her Grace leaned over to Sophie, and caught Charlotte's gaze. "My lady, Lady Angelia Ermine and Baron Rene."

Charlotte smiled. "A pleasure."

Baron Rene bowed, bringing Charlotte's fingers to his lips. As he bent, George caught sight of Richard's face. His expression was so perfectly placid, so even, it was slightly alarming.

Baron Rene straightened. Charlotte and Angelia touched

the back of their hands to each other. As their skin connected, a tiny tendril of black shot from Charlotte's hand to Angelia's. If he wasn't looking closely, he would've missed it.

The two bluebloods said a few more words about the festival and weather and disengaged.

The center of the terrace rumbled. That's right, he realized, it was almost dark.

The tiles in the middle slid aside. Magic surged in a translucent wall, forming a tall column. Inside it something sparked. Flames burst, roaring upward at the sky, perfectly contained by magic—a perfect imitation of an ancient bonfire.

The bluebloods applauded. He clapped with them, watching Charlotte and Sophie out of the corner of his eye. The ground was prepared. It was up to Charlotte to set her trap.

TIRED, Charlotte descended the staircase from the front entrance where their rented phaeton waited, the driver holding the door open. Sophie walked next to her. They conquered the last few steps, got inside, and sank onto the soft cushions of the seats. The driver shut the door, and, a moment later, they were off.

Charlotte pulled her shoes off and thrust her feet onto the opposite seat. Across from her, Sophie groaned and did the same. They wiggled their toes at each other.

"Ow, ow, ow." Sophie bent forward and massaged her toes. "Why do the heels have to be so high?"

"First, because they elongate your calves and make your legs look leaner. Second, because you couldn't possibly do any work in shoes like this, so if you own them, you must live a life of leisure." Charlotte leaned back. "All in all, it went very well. We owe Lady Olivia a favor."

"What did you give Angelia?" Sophie asked.

Charlotte grinned. "You saw that?"

"I was looking very carefully."

"She was already infected with Dock Rot, a very strong, virulent form of herpes. I just coaxed it into an outbreak."

Sophie's eyes went wide. "Is that one of the sexual diseases?"

Charlotte nodded. "Oh yes. They call it Dock Rot because it's often found among port prostitutes. It's curable, but the regimen is long and expensive, and it's quite easily preventable through the use of the male sleeve and vaccination."

"So why wasn't she vaccinated?"

"Probably because it didn't occur to her that she might catch it. The question is how did a blueblood flower such as Angelia end up with a dock-prostitute rash?"

Sophie grinned. "That's an interesting question."

"Isn't it?" Charlotte rubbed her hands together. "I think we're going to contact Lady Olivia and make sure Angelia gets an invitation to a tea. Mmmmm, about two days should do."

"You're scary," Sophie told her.

You have no idea, sweetheart. You have no idea. "Yes, but I'm on your side." Charlotte reached over and squeezed Sophie's hand. "You did so well today. It will get easier, I promise."

"It was . . . exciting."

"I'm so glad." Charlotte grinned. "Did you notice George?"

Sophie leaned against the back of the seat. "I know! He is so perfect, it's sickening." Her eyes grew wide. "That woman next to me, the one with the green rose in her hair? She leaned over to the other lady, and she said, 'I bet I could teach him a thing or two.' And the other woman said, 'He's just a boy,' and the green rose woman said, 'That's the best time in a man's life: they're easy to steer, and they can go and go and go.' Can you believe that? She must be thirty! It's disgusting."

Sophie stuck her tongue out and made a retching noise.

Charlotte smiled. "I don't think George is in any danger. He does the distant, I'm-above-it-all impression quite well, and the duchess would fry anyone who looked at him the wrong way."

Sophie's dark eyes turned serious. "Is that how it's supposed to be?"

"Is it how what's supposed to be?"

"Are we supposed to be obsessed with sex?"

She'd asked it quietly, and Charlotte sensed the answer was very important. "It depends on the woman. We're not all cut from the same cloth. Some women mature faster, some slower; some actively seek out sexual pleasure, and some don't value it as much. Why do you ask?"

"I don't want to do it."

Charlotte tilted her head, trying to get a better look at Sophie's face. "Which part?"

"I don't want to have sex," Sophie said. "Maybe later. But not now. I have friends. They kiss each other. The boys are . . . you know. Hands."

"Mhm." Charlotte nodded.

"I don't like to be touched. One of them tried, and I told him I didn't like it. He acted as if there was something wrong with me."

Charlotte paused. There was so much she wanted to explain, but the little bond of trust they had between them was so fragile. She had to find the right words.

"There is nothing wrong with you. Your body belongs to you alone. Touching it is a privilege, and it's up to you to grant it. Some boys—and men—don't handle rejection well, and they will try to shame you or pressure you into letting them do what they want because they feel entitled. They're not worth your time. Also, there is nothing wrong with not enjoying sexual touching or kissing. For some girls, their sexual awakening comes early, for some, later. I was almost seventeen before I became aware of men sexually, and even then, it was because of a particular boy I liked rather than men in general."

Sophie looked out the window.

Charlotte couldn't tell if she had said the right thing or the wrong thing. This is what parenting must be like. The duchess was right. Never knowing if you had done harm or good was awful.

"I'm sorry," Sophie said. "It's just that I don't have any-body else to ask. My sister is gone a lot with William. My aunts always want to know who is it and what's his name. And I can't ask Richard."

"Oh gods, no, don't ask Richard."

"He would be scandalized." Sophie pressed her lips together, as if trying to hold something back.

"If he gets an idea that someone tried to touch you against your will, he'd kill them." Charlotte cleared her throat and tried to produce a reasonable imitation of Richard's raspy voice. "I'm going to decapitate that ruffian. Please don't hold dinner. No need to trouble yourself on my account."

Sophie squeezed her lips tighter, but the laughter burst out anyway. "He would say that! 'I shall bring you his head. You may use his skull as a vase. No use in wasting a perfectly good cranium.'"

Charlotte giggled. "We're so morbid."

They giggled again. Sophie tried to hold it in and snorted. "Oh no, I'm so unladylike."

That only made them laugh harder.

Finally, they stopped.

"You can ask me anything," Charlotte said. "I don't mind."

"What happens next?" Sophie asked.

"Tomorrow, Richard is going to the club for his weekly card game. It's possible that Brennan will be there." Charlotte's heart skipped a beat. There was no danger, she reassured herself. Richard had fooled everyone, except for the old house servant, whom he had replaced. The real Casside and his servant were now safely tucked away in one of Declan's dungeons. The chance that Brennan would realize that Richard was an impostor was very slight.

Very, very slight.

"So what then?" Sophie asked.

"Then we will make Brennan think he's being betrayed."

RICHARD sat at a pentagonal table and reviewed his cards. He had the winning hand. He surveyed the faces of the four other men at the table. Much like the Broken's poker, the

Weird's council was a game of strategy and bluffing. He'd
learned to count cards when he was barely old enough to
understand the game. It required a good memory and paying attention. Child's play.

To his right, Lord Korban frowned slightly, trying to hide
his tells. Next to him, Robert Brennan smiled at Richard from
above his cards. The man was unconcerned and completely
at ease, as if relaxing at home. He didn't look like the man
whose island slave operation had turned to ash a week and
a half ago.

Lorameh, a veteran of the air force, sat next to Brennan.
As a human being, Lorameh was thoroughly unremarkable:
pale blond hair gathered into a ponytail at the nape of his
neck, light eyes, neither handsome nor unattractive. He'd
known Brennan for a long time, and the two of them treated
each other with easy familiarity.

At Lorameh's side, Maedoc, his severe gaze fixed on the
cards, completed the circle. Where Brennan was carefree,
Maedoc reviewed his cards with a deadly serious air, as if
the fate of the realm rode on his winning hand.

If Richard called a challenge, Lorameh would fold, Korban would panic and go in, then change his mind and fold
at the first opportunity. Maedoc would stubbornly hold,
because although his hand was mediocre, he viewed surrender as the weakest of the options. Brennan . . . His hand
was weak, but Brennan was an enigma.

"Challenge," Richard said.

"Accepted." Korban slid a coin toward the stack of gold
in the center of the table.

"Withdraw." Lorameh tossed his cards down. "Too rich
for my taste."

"Accepted," Brennan said, adding his own doubloon. The
corner of his mouth curved.

"Accepted," Maedoc growled.

"Living dangerously, Robert," Lorameh said.

"Danger adds spice to a mundane existence," Brennan
said.

"You just took a voyage to the Southeast Coast, while I

slave away at my desk," Lorameh said. "Of the two of us, my existence is much more mundane."

"I was visiting a friend," Brennan said.

"A friend with soft curves and beautiful blue eyes perhaps?" Lorameh asked.

"A lord never tells. Your play, Casside."

"Challenge," Richard said again, and slid a gold coin into the center of the table. There had been a very slight note of command in Brennan's voice. Brennan had also counted the cards. He knew exactly what sort of hand Richard had. Where was he going with this plan?

"Withdraw!" Korban dropped his cards.

"Accepted." Brennan added more money.

Maedoc hesitated.

"Our brave soldier is thinking of surrendering," Brennan said.

A light laughter rolled around the table. Richard allowed himself a sparse smile to not stand out.

Maedoc's face turned redder. He slid another coin to the stack. "Accepted."

What was going on? Richard sorted through the available responses. Casside would keep playing. He was driven by money, and the hoard of gold on the table was substantial. "Challenge."

"Another challenge, Casside?" Brennan looked directly at him. "You should make it a big one."

His tone was mild, but his stare left no doubt—it was an order.

"Very well." Richard slid the entirety of his coins into the center of the table.

Lorameh whistled quietly. Korban turned a shade paler.

"Accepted," Brennan said. He pushed a tower of coins to the center with a careless sweep of his hand and turned to Maedoc.

Punishment, Richard realized. Maedoc was being punished for the failure of the slavers on the island. He oversaw the slaver muscle. The breach in security was Maedoc's fault, and now Brennan was publicly humiliating him.

The big man looked back at Brennan, his teeth clenched.

"Are you with us or against us, Maedoc?" Brennan asked.

The muscles on Maedoc's jaws bulged. He stared at the coins. Of the Five, he was the least wealthy. Both Brennan and Casside had means, but for the other three bluebloods, the lack of funds was a real danger.

The strain on Maedoc's face was clearly visible. Richard felt no sympathy for him. The memory of rain-drenched holes filled with children, of the boy with his lips sewn shut, and barely human slaves was too fresh.

"Well?" Brennan tapped the table.

"With you." Maedoc shoved the gold forward.

"Your move," Brennan looked at Richard.

"Triple Royal Charge." Richard dropped a king, three knights, and an archer on the table.

Maedoc's face turned purple. "Double charge," he croaked, and let the cards fall. Two knights, a squire, a page, and a blacksmith.

"Two pages, two squires, and a carpenter." Brennan spread the cards on the table. "You win, Casside."

"That's the lousiest hand," Korban said.

"Luck of the draw." Brennan grinned.

He rose and slid the money toward Richard. "Take it before we change our minds."

Maedoc looked ripe for apoplexy. Richard hid a smile. It said volumes about his own morality, but anything that hurt the Five brought him joy.

Lorameh had an odd look on his face—he wasn't sure what had just happened, but he didn't like it.

"I think I shall take my winnings home." Richard swept the coins into a bag.

"I'll join you." Brennan rose.

They walked out of the club into the night. It had rained. Dampness hung in the air, and rainwater pooled in the uneven cobbles under their feet. The club occupied one of the restored buildings of Carver Castle, and the narrow street curved, snaking its way through the tangle of buildings that had once housed servants, knights, and soldiers. Here and there, magic lanterns cascaded from the walls, their pale lights diluting the darkness rather than banishing it.

"You played rather aggressively tonight," Brennan said.

What would Casside say? "I dislike losing money."

Brennan grimaced. "We have *all* just lost a great deal of money."

"How fast can the enterprise be rebuilt?" Richard asked.

"The efforts are under way now. Six months." Brennan's face jerked. An ugly scowl distorted his features, as if the fury inside him struggled to tear through the paper-thin mask of his easygoing demeanor. The man had a temper. Richard filed it away for future reference. "It was the Hunter. Three hundred men and a yearlong hunt, yet they can't kill one man."

The irony was too rich. It was time to carefully push Brennan in the right direction. "One wonders why."

Brennan pivoted on one foot toward him. "What are you implying?"

"I find it odd that these three hundred men can find a set of twins of particular age and coloring but can't find the Hunter."

The passageway widened, circling the main keep. A few moments and they would pass through the arched gate and reach the main courtyard and their phaetons.

Something moved in the darkness by the arch.

Brennan halted. Richard put his hand on his rapier. Casside was a skilled fencer—like many bluebloods, he had a proper martial education. The slender sword wasn't Richard's preferred weapon, and being divorced from his magic hindered him. Casside couldn't stretch his flash onto his sword. It was a lost art, known by a select few. And now that he was Casside, Richard would have to make do without it.

People moved within the arch, ink black silhouettes in darkness.

Brennan raised his head. "What have we here?"

Arrows whistled through the air. Brennan's magic sparked,

bursting from him in a brilliant white flash shield, disintegrating the missiles.

A bright blue flash shot from behind them, threatening to cut Brennan in half. Richard shoved him out of the way. The flash scorched the cobbles between them.

Richard dashed into the darkness in the direction of the flash, his rapier bare, counting under his breath. One, two, three, four. Another bolt of blue lightning tore at him. The flasher needed four seconds to recharge. The most accomplished magic users could do it instantly, but most needed time to refocus their magic.

Richard dodged, and the magic scoured the cobbles. The flasher gave himself away. He saw them now, three people waiting in the alcove to the left—the magic user and two fighters.

Richard charged. *One.*

The fighter on the left, a lean, agile woman, struck at him, spinning, her twin wide swords slicing like a razor-sharp tornado. He dodged left, right, left again. *Two.* The bigger sword grazed his chest, cutting through the doublet. Steel burned his skin.

Three.

The woman pressed her advantage.

Four. He dodged right, avoiding the flash by a mere second, lunged, and smiled as the tip of his rapier burst his opponent's heart. The woman fell.

One. The large man behind her leaped, taking her place, chopping at him with a vicious short axe. *Two. Three.* Richard backed away. *Four.* His instincts screamed, and he dived left, half a second before another flash bolt cut a gash in the stone wall behind him.

The axe fighter smashed into him, knocking him off-balance. Too close for a lunge. Richard veered left, grabbed the axe fighter's right arm, yanking him forward, and smashed the heavy hilt of the rapier into his left eye. The man howled in pain. *Three.* Richard spun him around and shoved him forward. The flash tore into the axe fighter. The stench of smoking human meat filled the air.

Richard sprinted, putting all of his speed in the run. Time slowed down, stretching like viscous honey.

He saw the magic user, a short, overweight woman. Slowly, as if underwater, she opened her mouth, raising her arms. The first brilliant blue spark of the flash formed between her fingers, biting at her skin with roots of lightning.

He thrust.

The blade passed under the growing tangle of magic, under the woman's left breast and into her lung. He'd missed the heart by a hair.

Richard threw himself left. The magic tore from her in a wide beam. She tried to scream, but the words gurgled in her throat. He dropped the rapier, grabbed her from the side, and snapped her neck with a quick jerk.

It cost him half a second to recover his sword. Richard dashed back. When he'd sent Garett, his cousin, to hire the thugs to kill Brennan, he warned him to hire enough to make a serious statement but not so many that Brennan would be overwhelmed. As satisfying as it would feel, Brennan couldn't die. But Richard had never counted on a flasher or a skilled swordsmen. There was a slight chance that they could actually succeed, and their scheme would fall apart before it had even begun.

He rounded the bend. Brennan bent over a prone man, breathing hard, his face an ugly, feral mask. A thick drip of bright red blood spilled from his scalp onto his face. Three bodies sprawled on the cobbles. None of them moved.

Brennan clutched a man by his shirt and stabbed him.

The man cried out.

"Who?" Brennan demand, his voice a ragged growl. "Who?"

"I don't know," the man groaned.

Brennan twisted the dagger in the wound. "Who?"

"Kordon said . . ." The man's voice was fading. "He said . . . it was . . ."

"What?" Brennan yanked him higher.

"Eagle," the man whispered. His eyes rolled back in his skull. His body convulsed once, and he sagged in Brennan's grip. The king's cousin stared at the limp body, his eyes bulging. He looked deranged. Then the anger vanished, and Brennan pulled his composure back on like a mask.

"Robert!" Richard sank force into his whisper. "We must leave. There will be questions."

Brennan let go of the corpse, dusted his hands, and strode into the arched tunnel, his pace brisk. "Did you bring a phaeton?"

"Yes."

"We'll ride in it, then. Can your servants be trusted?"

Richard hid a smile. He had replaced all of the staff in the house with his family. There wasn't a single person in that house whose name wasn't Mar. "Implicitly."

"Good."

The arch ended, opening into a well-lit courtyard filled with phaetons and horses. Richard stopped, pulled a hand-kerchief from his clothes, and thrust it at Brennan. "Blood."

"Thank you." Brennan pressed the cloth over the blood. They crossed the space quickly. Richard opened the door of the phaeton, and Brennan ducked inside on the wide bench. Richard climbed in after him and let his fingers fly over the controls. The ornate panel buzzed, the gears began turning, and the phaeton whirred to life. He drove out of the court-yard, maintaining average speed.

Seven lives were lost. They belonged to professional kill-ers. He felt no guilt but a vague dissatisfaction. Some part of him must've secretly hoped Brennan would die.

Brennan wiped the blood off his scalp. "Well! That was more fun than I've had in a while. How about you?"

Richard sorted through Casside's possible responses. "You have a strange idea of fun."

"You always were a cautious man, Casside." Brennan gave his shoulder a friendly punch. "Come on. You must've felt alive there for a few minutes."

"I was keenly aware that I was alive. I wanted to stay that way, too."

"And you did. All that fencing paid off. Don't fret, Cas-

side. You weren't the target. They went straight for me."
Brennan grinned that infectious smile that made him
famous. "A shame they didn't provide more of a challenge."

If Richard didn't have irrefutable evidence that Brennan
was responsible for hundreds of broken lives, he could've
imagined that he might have liked this man.

In ten minutes, Richard parked in front of Casside's mansion and ushered Brennan inside. Orena, his second cousin,
met them in a foyer, saw Brennan bleeding, and made big
eyes. "Alcohol, salve, rags," Richard told her. "Quickly."

Brennan winked at the woman. "Is he always so
demanding?"

Orena bowed her head and escaped.

"Your people are very serious, Casside."

"They've known my family for a long time. They don't
take their duties lightly." Richard led Brennan into the study.
Orena reappeared with medical supplies, followed by Aunt
Pete.

"They are both trained surgeons," Richard assured
Brennan.

Brennan leaned back, offering the gash on his forehead
to Orena. "Do you think you can make me pretty again?"

"Yes, my lord."

In ten minutes, the gash on Brennan's head was washed,
disinfected, and sewn up. His own wound required only
dressing and some butterfly bandages. The women departed,
taking bloody rags with them.

Richard slumped in a chair. "I abhor violence."

Brennan looked at him. "Don't we all, my friend? Don't
we all."

Richard nodded. Casside had never sought military service, a fact Brennan likely knew. He reached for a pitcher
filled with red tea and made his hand tremble as he poured
it into the glass. The glass spout of the pitcher knocked
against the rim of the glass.

Brennan rose. "Let me do that." He took the pitcher from
him and filled two glasses.

"Thank you." Richard gulped his drink.

"It really took the wind out of your sails?" Brennan watched him carefully.

"Not at all," Richard said, making an obvious effort to keep the glass steady. "I just want to know who and why. What in the world is the 'eagle'?"

Brennan drank from his glass and studied it. "Good tea. The eagle is on Maedoc's family crest. His father was known as the White Eagle. Maedoc, in his own time, was called the Dark Eagle. His son, provided he chooses a military career like the four generations before him, will be some sort of eagle as well. Beautiful tradition, isn't it? There is a subtle elegance in the old blueblood lines."

"Maedoc?" Richard raised his eyebrows. "I suppose he knew exactly where you would be. I'm sure losing the money hit him hard, but murder? Why?"

"A bid for power, perhaps." Brennan turned the glass right, then left, studying the play of light in the raspberry red tea. "He might have grown tired of my leadership. The attack on the island destabilized our little enterprise. It would be an excellent time to make a bid for the new head wolf, and he means to take my place."

Beautiful. Richard leaned forward. Brennan had taken the bait, hook, line, and sinker. "Maedoc can't run this operation. He knows it. Not only that, but the three of us wouldn't stand for it."

Brennan furrowed his eyebrows. "Please. Rene hates Adrianglia for holding him back. He doesn't care who's in charge as long as he's permitted to profit from thrusting a stick into our realm's gear. Angelia is a twisted creature; she will follow whoever hands her the biggest diamond and whispers sweet nothings in her ears while pouring coin into her purse. And you, well, you seek the money. You're for sale, my friend. That's how I got you in the first place. I'm too old for illusions—friendship and loyalty are fine qualities, but the voice of ethics grows weak in the face of riches."

The plan hinged on throwing suspicion on the retired general. Both Rene and Angelia were too weak for Brennan to ever see them as a true threat. Of all of them, only Maedoc could pose a serious challenge to Brennan's rule of the slaver trade, and Brennan *had* to view the threat as significant or it wouldn't topple him off-balance.

"Maedoc was in charge of the security of the island," Richard thought out loud.

Brennan gave him a sharp glance. Icy and calculating, that stare gripped Richard and for a second he felt the same calm that descended on him when he faced a fighter with a naked blade glaring at him from across three feet of open ground.

Inside Richard's head, an alarm wailed. *Careful. Careful, now. Don't be too obvious.*

"Do you know how the island was sacked?"

Yes or no? What was the right answer? "Not the particulars."

"The bandits pretended to be slaves and commandeered our ship. Drayton, that moron, must've let them right on board. They sent all the right signals and were permitted to enter the harbor and dock in plain view of the fort. Witnesses say that a crew of slaves began to disembark. They slaughtered the slavers meeting them and spread through the island, hitting precise targets. One group attacked the fort, the next hit the barracks, the third opened the slave pens. Beautiful, isn't it? Daring. Imaginative. Risky."

Brennan paused, offering him an opportunity to make a contribution. It was a trap. It had to be a trap. He was watching him too closely. He needed a neutral answer. "It's difficult to admire them knowing how much money we stand to lose."

"Divorce yourself from finances for a moment. Think of the brazen elegance of it. This raid is everything Maedoc is not. Oh, he's hailed as a brilliant tactician, but I've studied his military record. Maedoc is a bull, my friend. He sees the target and plows toward it. Deception and sleight of hand are quite beyond him. If he wanted to replace me, he would've attacked me directly. Not only that, but why would he identify himself as the Eagle? Why not simply make up a name? In fact, why give a name at all? Those were contract killers; their bargains are simple: money for a life, their quarry or their own."

Brennan didn't buy Maedoc's treason. Richard's disappointment was so sharp he could taste it. He buried it, in the same deep place he buried his guilt and memories. Nothing could show on his face. He had hoped to spare Charlotte from getting involved, but Brennan was too logical and too cautious. She would have to implement her part of the plan. Damn it.

Brennan took a deep gulp of the tea. "No, this matter is a lot more complicated. The mind that conceived the raid is likely the same mind that would cash in on the ripples it would cause. That person would seek to utilize my weakness to his or her advantage. We know that this person is deceitful and sly. This person would have considered the possibility of failure and would take precautions to point the finger at someone other than themselves. Therefore, the culprit can't be Maedoc. It's simply too obvious, even for him. No, it's one of you—Rene, Angelia, or perhaps even you, my friend."

Richard sat the glass down. "What are you implying?"

Brennan grinned, another charming smile. "Oh, relax, Casside. You're at the very bottom of my suspect list. I don't believe platitudes or assurances of loyalty, but I do believe that tremor in your hand. You simply don't have the guts for it. You wouldn't have put your own life in danger."

"I'm inclined to take that as an insult." Richard stood up from his chair.

Brennan sighed. "Oh, do sit down. You're brave enough. I'm not impugning your courage. You can't help the simple biological reaction of your body. The point is, we have a traitor in our midst. I intend to find them out."

He smiled.

"This is so much fun, Casside. And here I was planning to be bored."

"I will take boredom instead of this, thank you. Are you tired? You're welcome to stay the night."

Brennan waved his hand. "No. I need night, wind, life. A woman. Perhaps I'll pay Angelia a visit although she really is too much trouble. She enjoys being coaxed, and I'm not inclined to bother. Do you ever go slumming?"

"No."

"You should." Brennan's face took on a dreamy quality. "It's good for the body and occasionally the soul. There is a wonderful place down in the Lower Quarter. They call it the Palace of Delights. Ask for Miranda."

"Let my people take you home. Head wounds sometimes have hidden consequences. Robert, don't gamble with your health. We don't know how many of them there are. Perhaps there is another group . . ."

"Fine, fine." Brennan waved his hand. "Ruin all my fun."

Richard rose. "I'll tell them to have the phaeton ready."

"Casside?"

"Yes."

"I won't forget what you've done for me today," Brennan said.

"What would you have me do?" Richard asked.

"Act normal. Nothing out of the ordinary. I'll call on you when I'm ready. This promises to be a brilliant game, and I intend to enjoy every moment of it."

FOURTEEN

CHARLOTTE sat across from Angelia Ermine and watched the other woman attempt to ignore the burning itching under her lacy Sud-style tunic. They sat on a verandah of Lady Olivia's city house, at a delicate table carved out of a solid piece of crystal. The table bore a dozen desserts and three different teas, which the six other women present at the gathering seemed to be enjoying. What Angelia would've enjoyed most of all would be a good scratch, possibly with some fine-grade sandpaper. Unfortunately for her, Her Grace was telling a charming story from her past, and the half dozen other attendees hung on her every word. Excusing herself wasn't an option.

"And then I told him that if he was going to stoop to that level of rudeness, I would be forced to retaliate . . ." Her Grace appeared completely engrossed in her anecdote, except for the occasional brief glance in Charlotte's direction.

The itching must've reached torturous levels, because Angelia gave up on maintaining an attentive facade and locked her teeth. Sweat broke out on her forehead. Her disease had reached its peak, and Charlotte had been quietly spurring it on. Any other woman would've sent her apologies and stayed home, but Angelia was too much of a social climber. She was a minor blueblood, her bloodline undistinguished, her achievements mediocre, and a tea with the Duchess of the Southern Provinces was a lure she couldn't ignore.

Charlotte sipped tea from her cup. The refined taste, tinted with a drop of lemon and a hint of mint, was uniquely refreshing. She'd have to beg Lady Olivia for the recipe.

"And then I slapped him," Her Grace announced.

The women around the table gasped, some genuinely surprised, some, like Charlotte, out of a sense of duty.

"Excuse me," Angelia squeezed out. She jumped to her feet and ran from the table.

A shocked silence claimed the gathering.

"Well," Lady Olivia said.

"With your permission, Your Grace, I should check on her," Charlotte folded her napkin.

"Yes, of course, my dear."

Charlotte stood up and headed toward the washroom. Behind her, Lady Olivia inquired, "Where was I?"

"You slapped him," Sophie helpfully suggested.

"Ah yes . . ."

Charlotte left the verandah, crossed the sunroom, and stopped by the washroom. Hysterical sobs echoed through the door. Perfect.

Charlotte slid a key from the inside of her sleeve, unlocked the door, and stepped inside. Angelia froze. She stood before the mirror, her tunic thrown carelessly to the floor. Bright red blisters covered her body, some as big as a thumbnail, surrounded by smaller ulcers, like some sickening constellations. Some had broken open, weeping pus.

"Oh my goodness," Charlotte murmured, and shut the door behind herself.

Emotions cascaded across Angelia's face: shock, indignant outrage, fury, shame, contemplation . . . She hovered between them, trying to choose the right one, the one most to her advantage. It lasted only a few seconds, but Charlotte saw it clearly. Angelia Ermine's sweet and often vacant face hid a strategist's mind. Charlotte would have to be exceptionally careful.

Angelia clamped her hands to her face and cried. Appropriate emotion, sure to gain sympathy. Charlotte squeezed the key in her fist. Angelia had stripped motherhood from dozens of women. If only she could kill her. Oh, if only.

"Shhh, shhh." Charlotte forced soothing calm into her voice. "It's all right."

Angelia bent over the sink, weeping like a hysterical dove. "Oh, Lady al-te Ran. Look at me."

Very dramatic. "Do you know what illness this is?" Charlotte asked.

The woman sobbed. "Look, it's on my neck now. Everyone will see."

Nice misdirect, my dear. It won't work. "You're wearing lace with raw silk fibers. Raw silk tends to aggravate Dock Rot."

Angelia choked on her tears.

That's right, I know exactly why you're bearing these sores. She was sleeping with Brennan, who was by all indications possessive. Likely he was her only current lover, but she wasn't his only entertainment. Brennan had visited a professional and brought back this disease as a present for Angelia.

"It's all right." Charlotte feigned hesitation. "Look, this is your secret. I have my own secret, too. I will help you with yours if you promise to keep mine to yourself. Will you do that, Angelia?"

The woman nodded.

Charlotte reached over and touched her, fighting revulsion. Helping Angelia turned her stomach. Charlotte let her magic seep into the afflicted body. She found the disease and forced it into dormancy, spurring the skin cells into regeneration. The blisters burst, dried, and healed, turning into faint red stains.

"Oh my gods," Angelia whispered, for a moment forgetting about putting on a show.

Charlotte looked at the two of them in mirror, standing close to each other. "Feel better?"

"You're a healer!"

"And you can't tell anyone, Angelia. No one. Healers are not safe outside of their colleges. We're forbidden to do harm, and we're easy targets. Do I have your promise?"

"Of course. Anything."

Charlotte picked up Angelia's tunic. "Here, put this on."

The younger woman slipped into the tunic. Charlotte straightened her hair. "As beautiful as ever."

Angelia sniffed. It was an adorable sniff. It would've worked even better if she weren't a monster.

"After today, you must call on me. Healing you completely will take a much longer session, and we don't have time. Chin up."

"What will we tell them?"

"We'll tell them you had an attack of food allergies. It will be fine. The duchess knows about me, and she trusts my judgment." Charlotte opened the door and held it. "Do you know who's responsible for exposing you to this atrocity?"

"Yes." Angelia's face turned grim.

"I don't know who he is, and it isn't my place to ask, but you should know that this disease is easily preventable. He didn't use a sleeve, probably letting you shoulder the burden for preventing a pregnancy, but potions and pills do not prevent the spread of diseases."

"It was very selfish of him," Angelia said. If her voice had substance, it would've cut. "But then, that's what men are—selfish pigs."

"Well, I'm outraged on your behalf. Not only is he being unfaithful, but he is forcing you to suffer the consequences of his infidelity. I hope you let him have a taste of his own medicine."

The younger woman turned to her, her face puzzled. "What exactly do you propose?"

Charlotte shrugged, scorn dripping from her. "He is cheating on you. Perhaps you should show some interest in a mutual acquaintance he considers beneath him. Someone masculine."

"Someone who may threaten his ego," the other woman said.

"Indeed."

"I know just the man." Angelia smiled.

"What a beautiful smile."

"You know, Charlotte, I believe we will get on quite well."

"I surely hope so. Come now, before we are missed."

＊ ＊ ＊

CHARLOTTE stood on the balcony of her house. The sun had set, but the sky was still lit with the wake of its passing. The house faced a park, and the evening wind rustled in the branches. Tiny insects, luminescent with green and orange, chased each other through the leaves.

Two days had passed since she healed Angelia in the bathroom, followed by another three-hour session at her house. The poisoned tree should've borne fruit by now, and it was time for an update.

Somewhere out there, Richard waited, just as she did. Charlotte hugged herself.

She missed him. She missed the easy intimacy and the feeling of being held, not just physically, but emotionally. When they were together, she didn't have to face things alone. She hadn't realized until now how much she needed that closeness. In the worst time of her life, she had leaned on him, sometimes without realizing and sometimes consciously, and now he was gone. It felt like something had been ripped out of her.

Is that what love felt like? She had barely met him, but she felt like she knew him, intimately knew him better than she had known anyone in a long, long time.

She wondered if he missed her.

A bluebird landed on the rail of the balcony and held unnaturally still.

"Hello, George."

"Good evening." George's voice emanated from a point somewhat higher than the bird's head.

"I still don't understand how you do this."

"It's a technique I learned in the Mire. One of Richard's relatives is an accomplished necromancer, and Richard took me to see him."

"Is he ready?" she asked.

"Yes, I'm in contact with Richard as well." George paused. "He says hello."

She wished they could meet, but meetings could be

observed, and communication via magic devices could be intercepted. This was the only safe way.

"I attended Lord Caraway's lunch," George reported. "Lady A spent the entire time hanging on M's arm and his every word."

"Good." Angelia was paying attention to Maedoc. Brennan would notice it, especially now that Richard had put the idea of Maedoc's betrayal into his mind. With luck, he might view Angelia's sudden interest in the retired general as a sign of her switching loyalty.

"Richard says that you are brilliant."

"Please tell him thank you for me. How did the attack go?"

"Richard says that the attack went as planned, but B didn't take the bait."

Damn it. "He didn't buy M's betrayal?"

George paused. "No. Richard says that he underestimated B. B judged the attack as too obvious. He's likely making inquiries into the rest of the players."

Brennan didn't trust anyone, even an ally who stood next to him in a sword fight. This was bad news. "Are we going to Step 2?"

"Yes. He sends his sincere apologies. He hoped to keep you from being involved."

It was up to her to execute Step 2. In the planning stage, Richard had hoped that the attack alone would be enough to make Brennan suspect Maedoc. In the event it failed to do so, she had to provide a confirmation of Maedoc's guilt to Brennan. Since Richard and she acted independently, Brennan had no reason to suspect a conspiracy.

Before they started the game, Richard had his brother plant a file in the records of the Military Archive. The image of Richard's face was now tied to the fabricated identity of a veteran of the Adrianglian Army, who had served a number of years under Maedoc. The Five knew what the Hunter looked like, and now it was up to her to connect the dots between the Hunter and Maedoc, and present it to Brennan.

"No apologies necessary. I need some things. I didn't have to infect A. She already carried Dock Rot. B isn't faithful to her, just as Richard anticipated. I need to track down the prostitute he's sleeping with."

"Her name is Miranda," George said. "She works out of the Palace of Delights on Griffon Avenue in the Lower Quarter."

Sometimes Richard was frighteningly thorough. "Tell him thank you."

"He says he misses you."

"I miss him, too."

"Please be careful."

"You, too," she murmured.

The bird spread its wings and shot into the air.

She missed Richard. If she closed her eyes, she could picture him, his eyes, his muscular body, the smile on his lips . . . Her memory conjured the feel of his skin against hers and even his scent. She missed him so much, it almost hurt. The sooner they destroyed Brennan, the faster they could be together. Assuming he still wanted her.

She'd sensed a certain distance between them before they left, as if he was consciously building a barrier between himself and her. Something had changed between them. She wasn't sure what, but it troubled her.

Charlotte stepped inside. Sophie sat on the couch, her legs tucked under her, a book spread in front of her. The wolfripper hound sprawled on the floor next to her.

"I need your help," Charlotte said. "We're going to visit a dangerous part of town."

Sophie uncoiled from the couch. "I'll get my sword. Can we bring the dog?"

"Of course."

Half an hour later, wrapped in a hooded cloak, Charlotte dropped two gold doubloons on the counter of the Palace of Delights. "Miranda."

The proprietress, an older woman in a crushed silk gown, didn't even blink. "Second floor, blue door."

The blue door opened into a comfortable room with a canopy bed, all in various shades of red. The sheets were black silk. A thick red rug hid the floor. The furnishings were rich but slightly vulgar.

A moment, and a woman walked through the door. She was slender, blond, and doe-eyed. She saw Sophie.

"I don't do kids."

"Let's talk."

"Who about?"

"Brennan."

"I don't know any Brennan."

Charlotte opened her wallet and dropped a coin on the desk. Miranda's eyes widened. That's right, a gold doubloon. Charlotte added another to the first, making it clink. Another doubloon. Another. Five now. Five doubloons was probably more than Miranda made in a month.

"I could just take the money," Miranda said.

"I'd cut off your hand before you touched it," Sophie said. Her eyes were glacially cold. Miranda looked at her and took a small step back.

Six doubloons.

"Once I stop dropping coins, my offer to pay for your information is withdrawn," Charlotte said. "Better make up your mind."

Seven.

She held the eighth doubloon between her fingers for a long moment. Miranda sucked in a breath. The coin clinked against the others on the table.

Charlotte sighed.

"Fine!" Miranda shrugged. "I'll tell you. Money first."

Charlotte let her sweep the gold off the table.

"He comes, he fucks, he leaves. If you're looking for state secrets, he doesn't share."

"Tell me about his habits. What does he like?"

Miranda sat on the bed. "Nothing too twisted. He likes to feel he owns you. Sometimes he makes me crawl to him and beg him to fuck me. I don't care—as long as he's paying. He's got this thing about all women being secretly whores. Sometimes he makes me dress up in a nice prim outfit, formal gown, flowers in the hair, the whole thing, and suck him. He gets off on the perversity of it, I guess."

"Do you know that you have Dock Rot?"

Miranda grimaced. "I know. Damn soldiers. I already took my medicine."

AFTER the perfumed air of the Palace of Delights, the cold night breeze felt refreshing. Charlotte and Sophie walked down the street. Charlotte walked fast. Regrettably, the closest place where they had been able to leave their phaeton was a brisk five-minute walk away, and the neighborhood wasn't exactly safe. They left the dog tied to the vehicle just in case.

"Making her crawl to him is sick," Sophie said.

"Brennan likes to debase women. He also likes to feel powerful."

"Why did we need to know that?"

"Because he's investigating Richard, which means he hasn't bought our story completely. Angelia's ignoring him in favor of Maedoc. He'll look for ways to punish Angelia and possibly replace her. There may come a time that I will have to distract him."

Sophie mulled it over. "Just like that?"

"Brennan is power-hungry, and I'm his type: tall and blond."

They turned into the phaeton lot. Two men blocked their way. The taller of the two flashed a knife. "Money. Now."

Nice tactic. The Palace had to have maintained security because mugged patrons were bad for business. So someone there either noticed that they left early and surmised they were looking for information rather than pleasure, or Miranda had raised an alarm. Likely the first option—the proprietress had given them a sharp look when they left, and Miranda was paid too well to blab. Now they were being scared off, just in case they had any thoughts of coming back.

"Money, you cow!" The man raised his knife.

"May I?" Sophie asked. "Please?"

"Leave, or she will kill you," Charlotte said.

"Suit yourself, whore." The man lunged and gasped as his arm slid off his body and fell to the pavement. His mouth gaped open in the horrified beginning of a scream. He never got to make one. Sophie swept past him, and he crumpled to the floor. The other thug backed away, his hands in the air, and fled into the night.

Sophie pulled a cloth from her tunic and cleaned the blood off her blade.

Charlotte looked at the body on the ground. He was damaged beyond her skill. A child had just ended the man's life and seemed completely untroubled by it.

"Come." Charlotte headed toward their vehicle. "Do you enjoy killing, Sophie?"

"I enjoy the shadows," Sophie said.

"The shadows?"

At the phaeton, the wolfripper hound licked her hand. Charlotte let it into the back, and they got into the vehicle. Sophie started the phaeton, and they rolled off into the night.

"I walk the path of the lightning blade. A warrior poised between light and darkness. It's difficult to explain."

"I would appreciate it if you tried anyway."

Sophie frowned, her profile, lit by the golden glow of the instruments panel, etched against the night outside. "The death isn't important. The only thing that matters is the moment of decision. My path is a line. My opponent's path is another line. In the instant we meet, we're forever altered. We may both walk away, or my line or his line may end, but for a brief time we exist in the same space on the verge of action, and that space is full of possibilities. It's the moment in which I truly live. It's short. It's always so very short."

An old memory flashed before Charlotte. She was sixteen, attending a dance during a summit with another college, and as she stood there, chatting with her friends, she saw an older boy looking at her from across the floor. She saw admiration in his eyes. In that brief instant, when their gazes met, an array of possibilities flashed before her: he could come over, he could talk to her, there could be the start of something . . . It was a sweet kind of thrill, slightly frightening, but exciting. But Sophie found it in battle and was addicted to it. *How could you even begin to fix something like that?*

"What's the next step?" Sophie asked.

"The next step is to prepare for the Grand Thane's wedding. We need to pack and leave in three days. It will take us at least a day to get there, and we need to make sure we don't arrive too early or too late. You will love Pierre de Rivière. I saw it first when I was your age, and it is a beautiful castle. We'll attend the wedding, where I'll catch Brennan's attention, and find some way to connect Hunter and Maedoc." She wasn't quite sure how she would go about it.

Thinking about the wedding made her feel uneasy. Anxiety took her heart into a cold fist and squeezed. What if something happened to her or to Richard? This was no game. If they stumbled, Brennan would kill them.

She didn't want to do it, Charlotte realized. She was afraid. She wanted to run away with Richard back to the cabin in the woods and pretend none of this had ever happened. The anticipation of what she was about to do pressed on her like a crushing weight. She wanted to escape.

"That's where Spider will be," Sophie said. "At the wedding."

"That's where you won't kill him."

"What if I could?" Sophie asked.

"Tell me, what does Spider do?"

"He's an agent of the Hand and the head of a Hand's crew," Sophie said.

"People under his command are enhanced to monstrous levels. I find it very unlikely that he would travel alone. Look at me, Sophie."

The girl turned her face to Charlotte.

"Promise me that you won't kill him. I placed so much trust in you. Tell me you won't betray it."

"I won't," Sophie said. "You've been very kind to me. You don't have to worry, Lady Charlotte. I keep my promises."

FIFTEEN

THE long-distance phaeton shot out of the woods. It was time to wake Sophie. Charlotte touched the girl's hand, and she awoke instantly, fully alert.

"Look out the window," Charlotte said.

Sophie leaned toward the wide panel of glass in the phaeton. A vast river stretched before them, its placid waters golden and pearl, reflecting the glory of the setting sun. A flat bridge spanned the endless width of the river, and in the middle of the bridge, thrusting straight out of the water, a castle rose.

Sophie took a sharp breath.

The castle of Pierre de Rivière towered before them like a massive stately mountain of buildings crafted with cream stone. Couched in green trees growing from planters, its walls and countless terraces and balconies all but glowed in the sun. Thin, ornate spires stretched to the sky. Giant windows looked out onto the world from among the textured parapets and ornamental wall carvings so delicate, so light, that the entire enormous structure seemed to float upon the waters of the river.

"It's so beautiful," Sophie whispered.

"I hoped you would like it. It's one of the wonders of the continent."

The phaeton entered the bridge. The wolfripper dog raised his shaggy head in alarm.

"It's fine," Charlotte told him.

She'd suggested leaving the hound at the Camarine estate, but Sophie had hugged him and looked at her as if

she'd suggested cutting off an arm. Faced with two pairs of
sad puppy eyes, Charlotte had capitulated. She had insisted
on a leash, a bath, and a haircut, all of which had failed to
turn him into a pampered pet. He still looked like he chased
wolves through the woods. They would have to make an
effort to walk him, and he would make things less convenient, but it couldn't be helped.

A high, forlorn cry rolled through the sky, as if the clouds
had sung.

"Look!" Charlotte pointed at a bright green spark dropping from the sky.

The spark plummeted, growing, becoming an enormous
scaled shape armed with massive wings. The wyvern circled the castle, the sun reflecting from the cabin on its back.
Another joined it, then another . . . One by one, they landed
on the castle grounds.

"The elite of both realms will be there." Charlotte smiled.
"Are you excited?"

Sophie nodded.

"I'm so glad. Enjoy it," Charlotte told her. "It's magic."

They had work to do, but for now she would just sit here
and watch the world of wonder blossom in the child's eyes,
and for a few brief moments, she could be fifteen again,
riding in a phaeton to her first ball.

The bridge brought them beneath the portcullis to the
main thoroughfare that circled the castle. The phaeton
veered right, along a side route, and finally came to a stop
in the courtyard before a grand stairway. A familiar man
stood on the bottom step, speaking to a noble in a dark doublet. Brennan, Charlotte realized.

Their driver opened the door, and Charlotte stepped out.

"Charlotte!" Angelia called.

Oh Dawn Mother. "Angelia!"

Angelia Ermine swept into her view. "I'm so glad you
could make it."

At the stairway, Brennan turned. His gaze snagged on
them. He smiled at the man he was speaking too and strode
toward them.

Anxiety pierced Charlotte. She pretended to listen to Angelia. She wore a silk tunic and trousers, both in a beautiful shade of green. The clothes were formfitting and only a hint suggestive, which made them rather prim by the standards of society. She hadn't counted on meeting Brennan right off the phaeton, but the possibility existed, and she had dressed precisely for that occasion.

"Angelia," Brennan said.

The other woman spun, surprised. "Robert . . ."

"My dear, I'm most put out." Brennan took Angelia's hand and kissed her fingers. "You've been denying me the pleasure of your company. One would almost think you were displeased with me."

Angelia blinked. "Of course not."

"Who is your friend?"

Angelia produced a charming smile. "Charlotte de Ney al-te Ran."

Brennan blinked. The name had the desired effect.

"Charlotte, Lord Robert Brennan."

Charlotte curtsied. "Your Highness."

"Oh no, please. No titles." Brennan waved his hand. "My memory may be betraying me, but I'm almost positive I haven't encountered you before. I would have remembered our meeting."

"May I tell him?" Angelia asked. "May I?"

"As you wish."

"Charlotte comes to us from the Ganer College of Medicinal Arts. She has spent quite a long time there."

"They don't let us out much." Charlotte smiled. "It's almost like a convent."

Interest sparked in Brennan's eyes. She was right—the idea of seducing a woman shut off in a convent appealed to him.

"How peculiar," Brennan said. "I don't believe I've ever met a College escapee."

"Then I'm flattered to be the first, my lord."

"Are you a healer?" Brennan asked.

"Only a physician, my lord." Lucky for her, Ganer College

was home to both magic healers and their mundane counterparts. Given that Brennan had gone to visit the Island of Na, he must've heard of Silver Death killing people on the island with strange magic. She didn't want to advertise her talents. He could connect the dots.

"She's a healer," Angelia blurted out. "An excellent one."

Charlotte heaved a small sigh. "Forgive me, my lord. We don't usually identify ourselves outside of the College."

"Perfectly understandable. I imagine you would be inundated with requests otherwise." Brennan glanced at Angelia. "I had no idea you kept such exotic company. I do hope you haven't been ill, my lady?"

Angelia's composure crumbled. "Lady Charlotte is a friend," she squeezed through her teeth. "But now that you mention it, yes, I have been ill. I've caught a most unpleasant disease from a most surprising source. I can't wait to tell you all about it."

"I would love to hear it, but we're being rude to your friend."

"Oh no, not at all," Charlotte said. "I'm tired from my journey, and I need to do all those small secret female things women do to make themselves presentable before the dinner. Please excuse me."

"Thank you for your understanding," Brennan said. "The loss is entirely ours."

Charlotte curtsied and watched them walk away. Angelia's spine was rigid like a spear—she was fuming. She was about to reveal to Brennan that he had infected her with Dock Rot, and that conversation couldn't possibly go well.

"How did it go?" Sophie murmured at her elbow.

"It went well. Now we must lay our trap."

An hour later, Charlotte paced in her dressing room. Her dress waited on the bed. She wore a long black robe. Her undergarments had been very carefully chosen—she wore the tiniest of black lace panties, a bra that was a collection of translucent lace and black straps, and black stockings held up by thin ribbons simulating leather. She'd had the ensemble custom-made, modeled after some of the sexy garments she had seen advertised in the flyers from the Broken. The outfit wasn't just seductive, it was erotic, explicit, and raunchy. A woman of her status had no business wearing these kinds of undergarments unless she was aiming to provide very specific entertainment to her lover. Her spike-heeled shoes raised her to dangerous heights. Her hair had been arranged into an elegant wave appropriate to a formal function. Her makeup was perfect, and she was as ready as she could be.

This was a prime opportunity—Brennan still remembered her—and capturing his attention later would be significantly harder. Being unmarried, he would be inundated with women. She had to make an unforgettable impression immediately.

Sophie sat on the bed and watched her pace. "What if he isn't interested?"

"He will be. Men like Brennan think that every woman is secretly wanton. He loves the juxtaposition of the prim and proper with the dirty and seductive. He loves to corrupt. It makes him feel powerful."

"How can you walk in those shoes?"

"Practice. Lots of practice."

"What if he—"

The door swung open, and Jack stuck his head into the crack. "He's coming!"

Thank you, gods.

The door clicked shut.

"Quick!" Charlotte tossed the robe aside and moved into position in plain view of the door. Sophie grabbed the gown and held it up as if to put it on her.

GEORGE leaned against the column and watched out of the corner of his eye as Brennan walked up the stairs. The Guest Keep resembled the Broken's hotels in its architecture: a stairway led from the bottom floor to a long landing connecting to a hallway, then another stairway at the opposite end of the landing led to the next higher floor. Each of the visiting bluebloods had been assigned a set of rooms, and the roster of the rooms had been posted at each intersection of stairs and hallways. From his vantage point on the fourth-floor landing, George had an excellent view of the lower stairway and the roster.

Brennan was a third of the way up the stairs.

Kaldar, dressed in the gray-and-blue uniform of the castle staff, walked out of the hallway. He casually stepped to the roster, slid it off the wall, hung a new one in its place, and walked away.

Cutting it close. Kaldar liked to live dangerously.

Brennan conquered the stairs and paused before the roster. The original list put Brennan and the rest of the royal relatives on the fifth floor. This roster placed him on the third.

George pondered Brennan's back. He was a large man, strong, athletic. Thick, muscular neck. Jack could snap it, but he would have trouble.

This man was responsible for Sophie's torment. He turned slavers from random raiders to an organized force. His hands were stained with Mémère's blood. He made it possible for John Drayton to sink so low, he drowned.

A small, furious voice chanted inside George, *"Kill him, kill him, kill him . . ."* But there would be no killing, not now. No, first there would be public humiliation. Then there would be shame, then anguish, then punishment.

Brennan turned to the right, heading down the hallway toward Charlotte's room. George concentrated, sending his voice to an undead mouse riding in Jack's pocket. *"He's coming."*

Brennan disappeared into the hallway. Kaldar strode to the roster, swiped it off the wall, and placed the original in its spot.

THE door swung open.

Charlotte took a deep breath.

Brennan stepped into the suite and stopped. His eyes widened. He gaped at her, his mouth hanging slightly open.

Sophie froze, her face suitably shocked.

Charlotte met Brennan's gaze. She knew her poise was perfect, but inside she was trembling. She made no attempt to cover up. She simply stood there, as if she were wearing the most conservative of gowns, her expression even.

Brennan's gaze roamed over her body, pausing on her breasts, her stomach, and finally on the triangle between her legs, barely obscured by translucent black lace. She had his complete attention. A woman of noble name, who was proper in all outward appearances and who had just come out of seclusion, secretly wearing an outfit that would embarrass a professional. He had to take the bait. It was made to order specifically for him.

A long moment passed.

Charlotte raised her eyebrows, and said, her voice perfectly even, "I believe you're in the wrong room, my lord."

Brennan blinked as if waking up. A lifetime of experience in etiquette kicked in. "Of course. My apologies, my lady."

He shut the door.

"Knowing the precisely correct thing to do in every situation, then doing it with unshakable entitlement," Sophie whispered.

Charlotte's knees trembled. She collapsed into a chair.

GEORGE watched as Brennan emerged onto the landing and marched to the roster. His face wore a look of intense concentration. He stopped before the roster and stared at it for a long moment.

His room number and Charlotte's differed by exactly one digit. Hers read 322 and his 522. It had taken a great deal of manipulation on Kaldar's part to arrange this. Any significant difference between the numbers, and Brennan would've smelled a rat.

The man shook his head and started up the stairs. George stepped away from the column, back out of Brennan's view, and walked away quickly, staying close to the wall. He turned the corner just as Brennan stepped onto the fourth-floor landing.

DINNER was served on one of the massive terraces and consisted of light appetizers.

"I'm hungry," Sophie murmured.

"It's expected that after the ball we'll have a late dinner in our rooms," Charlotte murmured, and adjusted the strap on Sophie's left shoulder. This dress, a beautiful variation of blue-gray with a metallic sheen, was a collaboration between her and the dressmaker. Two thin shoulder straps held up a modest linear bodice that hugged Sophie's slender figure. Thin leaves of pale and darker blue overlapped on the bodice, built from the left side and spreading in a fan to the right. Two gathered lengths of fabric draped over Sophie's hips, tight enough to accentuate the modest flare of her hips but loose enough to still be appropriate. Past the draped fabric, a wide skirt built from layers of chiffon streamed down to the floor.

It was a refreshing dress, youthful and light, and its style matched Charlotte's own gown. She'd chosen a blue-green chiffon. Two leaves of silvery fabric served as her sleeves. The pattern continued along her sides, the leaves stretching to hug her, underscoring her waist and the curve of her hips. Tiny silvery dots, each slightly less shiny than the leaves, traced a delicate pattern over her chest and stomach, until finally her skirt flared into layers and layers of weightless chiffon.

Sophie looked beautiful. She herself looked elegant and every inch a blueblood, which is exactly what Charlotte was trying to project. The music was getting louder. Soon the dancing would start. She wasn't expected to dance but once or twice, but Sophie would enjoy it. And likely cause a stir. Charlotte had asked her to demonstrate a couple of dances, and her footwork was exquisite.

She felt the pressure of someone's gaze, scanned the gathering, and ran into Richard's face. He stood across the terrace, in the shadow of a column, and he was looking at her with shock and longing, as if he were thunderstruck. It hurt. It hurt so much to stand there across from him and know that she couldn't walk over there, she couldn't touch him or go away with him. Charlotte looked away.

No matter what happened around her, deep inside she always remembered that either of them, or both of them, might not survive this. They were in constant danger, and a happy outcome wasn't guaranteed. That knowledge pressed on her like an ever-present, crushing burden. She awoke with it, and she went to bed with it. It haunted her through the day. Occasionally, she would get distracted and forget, but inevitably she would remember, and when she did, the fear and anxiety hit her like a punch to the stomach. Her throat closed up, her eyes watered, and her chest hurt. For a few moments, she would hover on the verge of tears and have to talk herself off the cliff.

She missed Richard. She worried about him more than she worried about herself.

She wasn't made for this, she realized. Some might revel in danger and intrigue, but she just wanted everything to be done. She wanted it to be over. The stress and the pressure chipped at her, and she felt herself cracking under their chisel. The harder the pressure ground, the more she wanted to escape. Last night, she'd dreamed about walking up to Brennan, killing him, and throwing herself from the balcony. In the morning she had been horrified—not by the suicidal fantasy, but because for a brief moment before she returned to reality, she felt relief.

She couldn't shatter. Too many people depended on her, Sophie, Richard, Tulip . . . Speaking of Sophie, where had she gone?

Charlotte turned and saw a group of young people, all on the cusp of adulthood, surrounding a blueblood in a dark green doublet. He was tall, blond, and strikingly beautiful. He was telling some sort of story, and his face wore the comfortable expression of a practiced speaker. His audience hung on his every word.

Charlotte drifted closer, analyzing his gestures. Not just blood, old blood. Not Adrianglian, definitely a Louisianan bend—he'd raised his hand in an elegant gesture, palm up, index finger almost parallel to the floor, three others bent slightly—a clear tell. Louisianan court etiquette dictated that when the Emperor was present, the nobles carried a token, a small silver coin engraved with his likeness, worn on a chain wound around the fingers. The gesture was designed to display the coin and was so ingrained in the manners of the older families, they made it unconsciously when they presented a point during an argument or acknowledged someone's else's point.

She'd drifted close enough to hear him.

". . . After all, as Ferrah states, excelling in the service of the multitude is the highest calling. The ego can attain its pinnacle only when laboring for the greater good of the majority."

There were nods and sounds of agreement. He really had them entranced.

"But doesn't Ferrah also say that compromising one's ethics is the ultimate betrayal of self," Sophie's voice sounded from the back. The group of young people parted, and Charlotte saw her. "And since he defines ethics as the ultimate expression of individuality, his arguments are contradictory and suspect."

The blueblood looked at her with genuine interest. "The contradiction is present at first glance, yet it disappears if one assumes the moral code of the individual is aligned with the goals of the multitude."

"But does not the multitude consist of individuals with wildly conflicting moral codes?"

"It does." The blueblood smiled, clearly enjoying the argument. "But the attitudes of the multitude are aimed at self-preservation; therefore, we have the emergence of common laws: don't murder, don't commit adultery, don't steal. It is that commonality that prompted Ferrah to embark on the examination of multitude and self."

Sophie frowned. "I was under the impression that Ferrah embarked on the examination of multitude and self because he desired his sister sexually and was upset that society wouldn't permit him to marry her?"

The young people gasped. The noble laughed. "Whose treasure are you, child?"

"Mine," Charlotte said.

The noble turned to her and executed a flawless bow. "My lady, my highest compliments. It is rare to see a well-read child in this day and age. May I have the pleasure of your name?"

"Charlotte de Ney al-te Ran."

The noble straightened. "An ancient name, my lady. I'm Sebastian Lafayette, *Comte de Belidor*. And this is?"

"Sophie."

The noble smiled at Sophie. "We must speak more, Sophie."

Sophie curtsied with perfect grace. "You honor me, my lord."

"I hope she didn't upset you, Lord Belidor," Charlotte said.

The noble turned to her. "Sebastian, please. On the contrary. I often become frustrated at the lack of mettle among the younger generation. It seems that we had . . . not a better education, per se, but perhaps more incentive to use it. They learn, but they hardly think."

Behind Sebastian, Sophie mouthed something silently.

A woman in the dark blue uniform of the castle staff approached them and bowed, holding a small card out to Charlotte. "Lady de Ney al-te Ran."

"Excuse me," Charlotte smiled at Sebastian and took the card. "Thank you."

On the card beautiful calligraphy letters said, *"His Highness Lord Robert Brennan cordially requests the pleasure of your company for the Rioga Dance."*

Charlotte blinked. The Rioga Dance was an old tradition. The floor was cleared, and a single pair—one of whom was of royal blood but never the reigning monarch—danced alone. It was the official start of the ball, and a privilege most women here would kill for, quite literally.

"It's seems I'm to dance the Rioga," she said.

"Congratulations." Sebastian bowed his head. "What an honor."

Before he straightened, Sophie mouthed something again. *What was she trying to say?*

"Give way to the Grand Thane!" the crier barked.

Charlotte curtsied. As one, the nobles around her bowed.

A procession spilled out of the doors, led by the Grand Thane, a huge bear of a man, his mane of hair completely silver. The Marchesa of Louisiana, his future bride, who walked next to him, seemed tiny in comparison. She was only five years younger, but she moved with the grace of a much younger woman. Her dress, a shimmering gown of pale cream sparked with tiny lights, as if studded with stars.

Behind them, the immediate members of both families strode side by side. Charlotte glimpsed Brennan directly behind the Grand Thane. He looked positively splendid in a formfitting jacket, its red tone so dark, it was almost black. *You terrible bloody bastard.*

The procession swept through the gathering. The Grand Thane led the Marchesa to a pair of thronelike chairs. She sat.

The women in the audience rose, Charlotte with them. The Grand Thane took his seat, and the men rose as well.

Brennan stepped forward.

"It's time, my lady," the woman who had delivered her invitation said.

Sophie was smiling. There was something deeply disturbing about her smile.

In the circle, Brennan nodded to Charlotte.

"My lady, it's time," the woman prompted again.

Sophie's lips moved again.

Spider.

Sebastian was Spider. *Dawn Mother. I am leaving Sophie standing next to Spider.*

The opening notes of the Rioga floated on the breeze. Charlotte had no time to stop. All she could do was step forward.

RICHARD pretended to be bored. Next to him, Rene chattered about something with Lorameh and Lady Karin, Rene's cousin. Soon the dancing would start.

He hadn't spoken to Charlotte for nine days. Nine days of no contact. George's birds didn't really count. Nine days of brooding and sleeping alone, just him and his thoughts, and his thoughts had turned pretty dark. He wanted to see her. He wanted to tell her he loved her and hear that she loved him in return. The moment his mouth didn't have to make small talk, thoughts of her intruded into his mind. He imagined a life with her. He imagined a life without her. Perhaps he was going crazy.

Brennan walked out into the open expanse of the terrace.

Richard had to fight from grinding his teeth. Being in Brennan's presence was becoming harder and harder, both because he hated the man and because Brennan's good fortune brought his own shortcomings into focus. The man who had been given literally every advantage in life, while he himself was given none, used all his resources and talents to profit from the misery of others. He couldn't wait to bring Brennan down.

"I guess Robert is the sacrificial lamb on the Rioga's altar," Rene quipped.

"I wonder who his partner is," Lorameh said.

"Angelia?" Lady Karin suggested.

"She wishes." Lorameh laughed.

The music began.

"I do hope he won't be stood up," Rene said with mock concern.

The crowd parted, and Charlotte walked out.

The world came to a screeching halt. Her dress flared about her with every step, the diaphanous layers of blue-green fabric thin like gossamer, suggesting the contours of her body, then obscuring them. She didn't walk, she glided.

"Divine. Who is she?" Lorameh asked from somewhere far.

"Lady de Ney al-te Ran," Rene said. "Exquisite, no? And such a name."

"Oh no," Lady Karin said. "She mustn't have expected to be asked to dance. Her heels are too high."

His memory told him that Charlotte couldn't be as tall as Brennan during the Rioga: he was a man and of royal blood. It would be a critical social blunder. Most people watching her knew it. She had to know it as well.

Without breaking her stride, Charlotte stepped out of her shoes. She didn't slow down; she didn't give any indication of what she had done. She simply kept gliding forward, leaving two high-heeled shoes behind her. Sophie scooped them up and melted into the crowd.

Lady Karin gasped. Someone to the left clapped, then someone to the right, and Charlotte curtsied before Brennan to the sound of appreciative applause.

Brennan bowed, offering her his hand. She placed her hand onto his palm.

Sharp pain stabbed Richard between his ribs on the left side. Suddenly, the air grew viscous. He struggled to breathe.

Brennan rose to his full height and rested his arm around Charlotte's, touching her back.

He was touching her.

The music broke into a fast rhythm, and the two of them spun into the dance, Charlotte's dress streaming around Brennan like water currents around a rock.

His hands were on her. His fingers were touching her skin. She was touching him. Her hand rested in his. She was smiling. She looked like she was enjoying it. She looked at Brennan, and her face glowed with admiration.

A wave of ice rolled over Richard's skin and evaporated, burned off by all-consuming anger. He was watching Charlotte and Brennan turn and turn on the dance floor, helpless to do anything about it.

"They look so beautiful together," Lady Karin said.

"You've got to hate the man," Rene said. "Royal blood, rich, smart, good fighter. You'd think fate would disfigure him just out of the sense of fairness, but no, the bastard is handsome, and the moment a sophisticated, enchanting woman enters society, he snatches her up before any of us even trade two words with her."

That's right. Brennan was handsome, rich, with royal pedigree. And who was Richard? A penniless swamp rat with a sword and a stolen face.

In his mind, Richard stepped out onto the dance floor. He held his own sword in his hand, not Casside's weak rapier. He cut in between them, spun in a burst of magic and steel, and Brennan's head rolled off his shoulders onto the floor.

Charlotte gasped. He walked over to her . . .

The music ended, and he heard his own heartbeat, too loud, like the toll of some giant bell. Brennan was bowing. Charlotte curtsied. Brennan straightened. The emotion on his face was unmistakable: it was the primal need of a man who had found a woman he had to have.

People applauded. It sounded like a storm to Richard's ears. She never said she loved him. She gave him her body in the cabin, perhaps in a moment of weakness, but she never promised anything to him. And if she had, promises were often broken.

Brennan led Charlotte over to the Grand Thane and the Marchesa. She curtsied again, a deep, graceful bow. The Marchesa said something. Charlotte replied. Brennan grinned, displaying even teeth.

The crowd turned into a smudge of faces, the voices blended into a loud hum, and Brennan's face and those gleaming teeth came into sharp focus.

Richard pictured driving the blade of his sword into Brennan's eye. Everything within him wanted Brennan's blood. He stood poised on the edge of his blade, fighting to keep his balance.

"Casside, are you unwell?" Lorameh asked, looking at him very carefully. "You haven't said a word."

Answer, you fool. Say something.

He forced his lips to move. "I have a headache. I think I shall retire."

"It's the flowers," Lorameh said. "That much perfume and pollen mixing together, it's a wonder the lot of us haven't collapsed from breathing it in. Let's get a drink, my friend."

Richard willed himself to move, but his feet remained rooted to the floor.

"Come now," Lorameh said. "You'll feel better after some fresher air and a bit of wine."

Staying here, watching the two of them, would do nothing except put him at risk of jeopardizing everything. Richard turned, snapping the chain of jealousy and pain that anchored him in place, and followed Lorameh into the castle, where drinks had been set out.

CHARLOTTE wiggled her toes in the ceramic footbath. Dancing barefoot across the ancient stone wasn't the most pleasant of experiences. She'd stepped twice on some sharp pebble, and the dirt of the stones, although they had been cleaned, was now permanently embedded in her feet. She'd soaped them, scrubbed, and even tried a pumice stone, but the dirt remained. Finally, she had resorted to soaking.

It went so much better than expected. She had made an impression on Brennan and coincidentally a favorable impression upon the Marchesa. Brennan was feeling distinctly possessive. He held on to her a few moments too long after the dance and seemed unwilling to step away from her side. She finally excused herself to the washroom. He waited nearby, but she'd bet that a lone royal cousin wouldn't remain unattended for too long, and she proved right. A group of Louisianan ladies surrounded him, and she quietly made her escape.

She found Sophie at Spider-Sebastian's table, attentively listening as he debated some point of Louisianan politics with some older man and his entourage. While they made their good nights and said thank-yous for the stream of compliments received, Charlotte composed a devastating chewing-out in her head, which she delivered the moment they stepped into their quarters and shut the door. Sophie listened to every word and at the end hugged her, said, "Thank you, you're the best," and disappeared into her room.

Charlotte stood by the door, staring at it for a little while, not sure what to do, and went to take a shower. And now she was soaking her feet.

Charlotte slumped back in her chair. The room was quiet and dark around her. The glass doors to the balcony were open, and the night wind sifted through the gauzy white drapes. A big, pale moon lit the sky and the stone rail of the balcony. Beyond it, the river stretched, reflecting the moonlight.

How did she even end up here? Eight weeks ago she was just plain Charlotte living her life quietly in the Edge. Now she was attending a royal wedding, her name out in the open. She thought of Lady Augustine. Her surrogate mother wouldn't have approved of airing out the name. The moment her adoption was made public, she'd become a target for the enterprising social climbers. But then the name was the least of her worries. She'd broken her oath. Lady Augustine would be horrified to know how far her star pupil had fallen.

A rope dropped from above, stretching to the balcony.

Charlotte blinked.

The rope was still there.

Feet in dark boots slid into her view, followed by long, lean legs, followed by narrow hips, a muscular chest clothed in dark fabric. Richard.

Her heart pounded in her chest. She tried to get up and splashed water all over the plush white rug. Damn it. And now she was swearing in her head. Wonderful.

Charlotte stepped out of the bath and ran to the balcony on her toes.

He landed on the rail.

"What are you doing?" she hissed in a loud whisper.

"I had to see you."

"What? Get on that rope. You're going to ruin everything."

"Brennan isn't everything."

His face was sharpened, almost contorted, by desperation.

"What is it?" she whispered. "Did something bad happen? Are you hurt?"

He jumped off the rail, pulled her inside the room, and clamped her to him. His mouth found hers, hot, possessive, and demanding. He kissed her as if this was the last time he would see her.

For a moment she almost melted, but alarm won out. "Richard, you're scaring me."

"Let's go away," he whispered. "Let's just leave, you and me."

"What? Why?"

"Because I don't want to lose you. I love you, Charlotte. Come with me."

She studied his face. "Are you jealous of Brennan?"

"Yes."

Oh, for the love of . . . "Richard!"

"I know that I can't give you a title or riches or—"

She put her hand on his mouth. "Shut up. I have a title and riches. You don't get to abort the plan because you didn't like that I danced with him."

"You liked it," he said through her hand.

"No, I didn't."

"You looked like you were enjoying it."

"I was supposed to look like I enjoyed it, you moron. It's called 'acting.'"

He looked at her, clearly at a loss for words.

"If you can go under the knife risking death, I can dance with Brennan and parade in front of him in my underwear."

"What?"

She shouldn't have said that.

"Charlotte?"

"I let him see me half-undressed. I'll model it for you

later if you wish. Now you need to get out!" She pushed him onto the balcony. "Get out, get out, get out. And take your rope with you. You're too old for this. I'm too old for this." She shut the glass doors.

He stood for a long moment, then jumped, caught the rope, and pulled himself up.

Charlotte fell backward onto the bed. Idiot. Moron. He scaled the wall for her like some sort of robber-prince from an adventure novel. Climbed a rope in a fit of jealousy. *Really, who climbs a rope?*

A knock sounded through her door. Now what? She walked over, pulling her thin robe tighter around herself, and checked the glass window in the door. Brennan.

"This is highly improper," she said through the door.

"I'm a highly improper man."

"Who shall remain in the hallway."

"Charlotte, I just wish to talk."

"One moment."

Charlotte walked over to a communicator and dialed the castle staff. The gears spun and a man's face appeared above the copper half sphere. "At your service, my lady."

"Robert Brennan is at my door. He wishes to have a conversation. I require an escort."

The man turned away for a moment and faced her again. "The escort has been dispatched. They will be at your door in twenty seconds."

"Thank you."

She walked over to the door and peered through the glass. Moments crawled by. She counted to twenty in her head. At eighteen, a man and a woman in castle uniform rounded the corner and came to a halt by her door.

Charlotte unlocked it.

Brennan sighed. "Chaperones? Are we children?"

"We are adults, which is exactly why I require witnesses."

He grinned. "Do I scare you, Charlotte?"

"Your Highness, I've seen things that would turn most people's hair white overnight. I don't fear you. I'm simply being prudent."

He tilted his head. "You undo your hair at night."

"Of course." Wearing her hair down wasn't one of the best hairstyles for her. She looked much better with an updo, but her scalp did have to rest at some point.

"Why did you leave?"

"My ward had enough excitement for the evening."

"The little girl? Who is she to you?"

"She's the daughter of a friend. Her mother is dead, and her father is unfit to care for her."

Brennan shook his head. "This would be so much better without an audience."

"And that's precisely why we have one."

"I'd like to continue our acquaintance," he said.

"Are you fond of tea in the morning?"

"I could be."

"In that case, I could give a morning tea tomorrow at ten."

"In that case, I would definitely attend. Who else will be there?"

"My ward and I. If you're planning to attend, perhaps I will invite a couple of other people to maintain propriety."

"You seem to be very concerned with propriety."

You seem to be very concerned with making a profit on selling children into slavery. "There are times when I can be inappropriate."

A small, hungry light sparked in Brennan's eyes. "How inappropriate?"

"If you bide your time, perhaps I'll show you."

He grinned. "You're going to make it into a game, aren't you?"

"If you choose to look at it that way."

"I love games." He leaned forward, picked up her hand, and kissed her fingers. "I never lose."

She leaned toward him and said, pronouncing the words very clearly, "Go to bed, Your Highness."

He smiled, a self-satisfied, happy baring of teeth, and headed down the hallway.

"Thank you," she said to the escort.

"Of course, my lady," they chorused.

Charlotte shut the door, locked it, turned, and ran into Richard.

"I told you to leave."

He stared at the door with that familiar predatory focus. "I'm going to kill him."

"No, you won't. You will climb your rope and leave."

He wasn't listening to her. He wasn't even looking at her. He simply moved to the door, and she knew that she had to stop him now, or he would chase after Brennan and fight him, and their entire scheme would crumble.

Charlotte grasped the back of his head and pulled him down toward her. Kissing him was like drinking spiced wine—the heat of him dashed through her, burning through her body. Immediately, she wanted him.

He wrapped his arms around her, pulling her close. His tongue touched hers, and she shivered. When she opened her eyes, he was looking at her, and this time he did see her.

"You have to leave," she whispered.

"No."

"Yes. You must go. What if he goes to find Casside, and you're gone?"

His eyes turned dark.

"Look at me, Richard. You cannot kill Brennan until we expose him. You can't do it, or it was all for nothing." She kissed him again, trying to pull him away from the destructive anger. "You have nothing to worry about."

He blinked, like a man waking up from a deep sleep, focusing on her.

"You have nothing to worry about," she repeated. "I love you, Richard. Go."

"What?"

"I said I love you, you fool."

"When this is over—"

"Yes," she told him.

He stared at her.

"The answer is yes, Richard. Yes, I will go with you and live with you in your Lair, because I love you. Now you must leave. Get out of here!"

She pushed him out to the balcony, shut the doors, and made sure to lock them.

Richard looked at her from behind the glass. He had the strangest look on his face, a kind of stunned amazement.

"*Go!*" she mouthed at him.

"*I love you, too,*" he mouthed, then jumped and climbed back up his rope.

She crossed the room, fell on her bed, and put a pillow over her face. She felt hot and giddy. He loved her. It made everything worth it.

What if he stopped being there? What if something happened, and he was gone?

The anxiety shot her in the heart. *Here it is again. Hello there.*

Please, she prayed silently. *Please, please, please, let it be all right. Please, let it all work out.*

Please.

SIXTEEN

CHARLOTTE sat in a chaise on her balcony, sipping bloodred tea from her cup and subtly watching Brennan seethe in his chair, directly across the coffee table. To the right Sophie sat quietly reading a book. To the left, on the divan, the Duchess of the Southern Provinces lounged, drinking her tea in tiny swallows and carrying on a conversation.

He must've expected that Sophie and whoever she had invited wouldn't be much of an obstacle. He could bully most people out of the way by the simple fact of his birth. But Lady Olivia provided an impenetrable barrier. She was older, well regarded, and her influence and power surpassed his. His Highness was forced to behave, and he didn't like it. The small talk was clearly grating on him. He was desperately bored.

Almost bored enough to pick up the album she had placed on the coffee table within his reach. A foot long by a foot wide, bound in luxurious brown leather and embossed with a silver serpent biting his own tail, a symbol of the Ganer College, the album held approximately eighty pages of heavyweight paper interweaved with glassine tissue. It beckoned to be picked up.

Just a little more, Charlotte thought. A little longer.

Lady Olivia launched into a discussion of the agricultural properties of oranges.

Brennan hid a yawn, leaned forward . . . and picked up the album.

Lady Olivia glanced at Charlotte and took a moment to snack on cookies.

"What an exquisite book," Brennan said, obviously relieved at the opportunity to jump-start the conversation. "Are these members of your family?"

"No, my lord." Charlotte sipped her tea. "They are my greatest triumphs as a healer. The truth is, we are a vain lot."

Brennan turned the page and winced. "Dear gods, this child is horribly burned."

"An unfortunate accident," Charlotte said. "She was trapped in a barn during a brush fire that had overtaken the village. If you turn the page, you will see that she was considerably better after I was done. Burns are difficult to heal completely, but we had a modest success with her."

Brennan turned the page. "This is uncanny."

"You give yourself too little credit, my dear," the duchess murmured.

She had to keep him looking through the book. "I believe there is a worse case a little further."

Brennan flipped a page. Another. Another. His hand froze.

Bull's-eye.

"This man." Brennan turned the album, holding it with one hand so she could see it. A picture of Richard looked back at her. He looked a few years younger. His hair was longer, but the image bore an unmistakable resemblance to the poster of Hunter.

Brennan's quiet voice held the steel overtone of command. "Tell me about this man."

Lady Olivia raised her eyebrows. Charlotte leaned forward, looking at the image. "This isn't one of the worst cases."

"Please. Indulge me."

"Very well. He was a soldier, one of those extremely dangerous, covert types. You know, the sort who are released into the woods with nothing but a knife and a length of rope and retrieved a week later, after they have single-handedly demolished an enemy legion. He'd been very badly wounded. His liver and kidney had been sliced through with a spear, and by the time he was brought to me, he was delirious. He kept recounting his proudest moments in life—being chosen for his unit, his son's being born, and Lord Maedoc presenting him with the Shield of Valor."

"Are you certain?" Brennan's face had gone completely flat.

"Yes. Fever does strange things to the mind. He went on and on about his son's eyes and Lord Maedoc's demeanor. I believe he got to spend some time with Lord Maedoc after the ceremony, and it was the highlight of his service. His healing took approximately sixteen hours. I was exhausted and had to rest. When I came to check on him the next day, some soldiers had collected him and left."

"Maedoc?" Brennan repeated. "Was that their commanding officer?"

"Yes. I was upset that the College released him—he was in no shape to travel, really—and so I made the staff get the release order so I could check the seal on it. Is this important?"

"Not at all." Brennan shut the album and turned to Lady Olivia. "You were telling us about oranges, Your Grace?"

RICHARD studied himself in the mirror. The man who looked back at him was nothing like him. Stolen face, stolen clothes, another man's sword. They were tools, he told himself. Tools of his trade. She loved him anyway. She loved *him*.

Someone knocked on the door in a rapid staccato. Kolin, his second cousin, glanced at him. Richard nodded. Kolin swung the door open.

Brennan strode in, almost knocking Kolin over. His face shone with grim determination. Behind him Rene paused at the doorway, his face bloodless.

"Get your sword and come with me," Brennan said.

"Did something happen?"

"Casside, get your sword."

Richard belted his rapier on. Brennan spun on his foot and marched out. Richard followed him, striding side by side with Rene down the hallway. They climbed the ladder, crossed another hallway, and stepped into a metal-and-glass lift. Brennan punched a code into the panel, and the small cabin slid upward. Stone flashed by, then daylight streamed in. They were rising straight up the side of the castle.

"Hunter belongs to Maedoc," Brennan said. "He's his creature."

"Are you sure?" Rene asked.

Brennan turned to him, his face skewed by fury, and Rene took a step back.

"It was quite clever of him. Use the Hunter to destabilize the slave trade, make me appear weak, foster the discontent as all of us lost money. I thought he was too limited for a plan like this, but he fooled us all."

"What are you going to do?" Rene asked, a note of anxiety in his voice.

"Not just me. All of us."

The cabin stopped. The gears in the wall turned, the doors opened, and they stepped out onto a narrow balcony, overshadowed by a spire. Far below, the river glistened. They were at the very top of the castle.

At the other end of the balcony, Maedoc and Angelia stood by the stone rail. Angelia's face was bloodless. Fear shivered in her eyes like a small animal trapped in a corner.

"What was so important?" Maedoc asked.

She pointed at them.

Maedoc turned. "Brennan? What's going on?"

"We have a traitor," Brennan said, closing the distance between them. "The one who's behind Hunter and the attack on the island."

"Who?" Maedoc frowned.

Brennan jerked a dagger from his sheath and thrust it in Maedoc's right side.

Angelia choked on a scream.

Brennan pulled the dagger down through the flesh with a sharp jerk, his face inches from Maedoc's shocked eyes, and pulled the blade out. The initial thrust probably punctured the lung, Richard decided. The rip lacerated Maedoc's liver.

"What are you doing?" Rene squeezed out. "Robert, what are you . . ."

Maedoc sank against the rail, struggling to stay upright. Brennan stepped over to Rene and thrust the bloody dagger into his hand. "Your turn."

"What?"

"Your turn, you spineless shit. We're in this together. Do it or join him."

Rene stared at Maedoc. The big man raised his left hand, his right clutching the rail. "Don't . . ."

"I will not suffer traitors in my house! Do it!" Brennan barked.

Rene stabbed Maedoc in the stomach. Blood spurted, drenching the dagger's handle.

The soldier cried out.

Rene dropped the dagger and stumbled away. Brennan picked it up and turned to Angelia. "You're next, my lovely."

"No." She backed way. "No."

"Yes." Brennan's voice vibrated with fury. "I'll help you."

He grabbed her hand with his bloody fingers, slapped the dagger into it, and locked her fingers around it with his hand, moving behind her, pushing her toward Maedoc.

"No," she moaned.

Bile rose in Richard's throat. Finally, the mask had ripped open. Brennan was flying his true colors. To kill a man in a fair fight was one thing, but this—this was a sickening, perverse butchery.

"Come on," Brennan said in her ear, holding her from behind in a half embrace. "For once, you'll be the one who gets to stick it in. It's not hard."

Brennan forced her forward, raised her hand with his, and stabbed Maedoc in the chest. Blood gushed. Maedoc groaned.

Angelia whimpered.

"Oh no, there is a little bit of blood," Brennan said. "But you can handle it, can't you? You think all that money that poured into your accounts isn't bloody? You think those shiny stones in your ears aren't soaked in it?"

She tore away from him.

Brennan turned to Richard and held out the dagger. "Casside. Join us, my friend."

Richard strode forward, took the dagger, and thrust, between the ribs and up, piercing the heart. Maedoc gasped and sagged to the stone. The light went out of his eyes. The torture was over.

Brennan stared at the prone body. "Look, the three of you. Look very well. You all did this with me. Now we're bound by blood."

Angelia hid her face in her hands and wept.

"Take his legs."

Richard picked up Maedoc's legs. Brennan slid his hands under Maedoc's arms. They heaved and threw the body over the balcony into the river below. Brennan picked up the dagger, wiped it on a handkerchief, and hurled it into the water. The blade caught the sunlight, sparking as it flew, and vanished far below.

Rene hugged Angelia and drew her toward the lift. Richard followed them. Brennan remained at the rail, his back to them, his arms crossed.

"He is crazy," Angelia sobbed in the lift. "He's gone crazy."

"It will be all right," Rene told her.

It wouldn't be all right. The house of cards Brennan had built was tumbling down, and Richard was waiting for the right moment to set it on fire. And as the lift slid down, he thought of a perfect way to do just that.

Five minutes later, Richard walked into his quarters. "George! I know you're here."

A mouse scuttled out from under a bookshelf.

"Find my brother," Richard said. "We have things to arrange."

GEORGE stood in the shadows, leaning on the column, and watched the dining hall fill with people. The ridiculously pretentious book he'd read on Pierre de Rivière claimed that the Grand Dining Hall was a room of "almost painful elegance." It wasn't. It was a room of opulent old wealth.

The pale walls rose fifty feet high, reaching a glass ceiling so clear, it was invisible except for the three enormous chandeliers suspended from it. Each twelve-foot-wide chandelier was woven of hair-thin metal-and-glass strands in a perfect imitation of a cloud backlit by sunlight. Thousands of crystals suspended by thin wires cascaded from the chandelier, like rainbow-hued raindrops. The wires were invisible from the floor, and looking up gave one an illusion of standing under a spring shower.

The floor was seamless cream marble shot through with veins of silver and gold. Beautiful ornate vines cast out of bronze climbed the walls, bearing crystal- and gemstone-studded flowers. The same vine pattern decorated the chairs and the tables, shrouded in silk cloth. The book claimed that no two chairs in the dining hall were alike. Looking at the detail of the tiny leaves and buds, George believed it. The plates were silver, and the silverware had a gold tint. The room itself was enormous, and a full floor-to-ceiling mirror to his right reflected the space, making it appear even larger.

This space wasn't just old, it was timeless. It would never go out of style by virtue of the wealth concentrated within it. It was a room built by old rich men and women to entertain other rich men and women, none of whom had ever tasted poverty. Just one of those flowers or plates would feed an Edge family for a week. The amount of food they would throw away after the bluebloods were done picking at their plates could sustain a small Edge town for a day.

He had known crushing poverty. He remembered it keenly, and this display of lavish luxury made him nauseous.

Torn shreds of conversation floated about.

". . . found the body . . ."

". . . water. Stabbed a dozen times . . ."

"Gods, how horrible . . ."

". . . the wedding might be postponed . . ."

He caught sight of Charlotte and Sophie. Sophie was walking their dog on a beautiful leash with silver metalwork.

The leash looked like it should belong to a fluffy ten-pound puppy with delicate paws and manicured claws. Seeing a large, muscular dog on its end was disconcerting.

Charlotte and Sophie took their seats next to a blond blueblood. He turned, displaying a familiar profile. Spider. Also known as the Count of Belidor. Sophie murmured something. He leaned over with an almost paternal expression on his face and said something. She nodded.

It must've hurt her to sit close to him. George had tried to talk to her about it last night, as much of a conversation as one could manage when one communicated by means of a dead squirrel and voice projection. She said it was so painful, it was almost sweet. He thought about it for a while, but he still couldn't figure out what she'd meant.

He saw Jack drift in through the doors. He moved quietly, sliding between groups of people, and nobody paid him any mind, as if he were invisible. A moment later he stopped next to him. "Hey, Ugly."

"Hey, Stupid."

"Can you smell it on me?"

George gave him a look. "No."

They had spent the last three hours in the room behind the mirror. It was a narrow space used mostly by staff and currently empty. The two of them and Kaldar had pulled apart the thin wooden panels until the back of the mirror was exposed, stripped the protective paint layer, then sprayed a silver solvent on the back of the mirror, turning the reflective surface into simple glass.

Kaldar had raided the Mirror's stash of gadgets, and they attached four barrier generators on the back of the now-transparent glass, stretching a spell across its back surface. As long as the room remained undisturbed, nobody would be able to tell that the mirror had been tampered with. Immediately after they finished the job, Jack began obsessing that he had a chemical smell. Normally, George tolerated his brother's quirks, but at the moment they had bigger things to worry about.

"Do you think it will work?" Jack asked.

"If this doesn't work, I'll kill him myself."

George didn't need to specify—"him" meant Brennan. Brennan was the root of the evil that had damaged their lives. Too many people had suffered, too many had died. He couldn't be allowed to exist.

"Agreed," Jack said. "We'll do it together."

Across the hall, Richard stepped inside. He saw Rene and Angelia standing together in the corner and walked in the opposite direction, taking position against a column, much like George's.

The Grand Thane walked into the lobby, the Marchesa on his arm. The conversation died. The older man led his bride-to-be to the center of the room, to their table, and sat. Brennan followed him among the other bluebloods, taking the seat at a table nearby. His face wore a solemn expression.

Jack bared his teeth, quick like a knife cut, and hid them again.

"Come on." George pushed away from the column, and they walked to their seats at their assigned table next to the Duchess of the Southern Provinces.

"Boys," she greeted them with a smile.

"My lady." They both bowed.

"Please sit down."

They sat.

"How is it going?" Lady Olivia asked quietly.

"Well so far," George answered. The most difficult thing about Brennan was that he made an unpredictable opponent. The murder of Maedoc had proven that. What they were about to do was calculated to unbalance him, make him spin out of his orbit, and once he did, he would become a human wrecking ball, destroying everything in his path.

A tall man in the uniform of the Castle Guard strode into the room and onto the raised platform at the front. "My lords and ladies, may I have a moment of your time."

Quiet fell onto the gathering.

"My name is Celire Lakita. I'm in charge of the security for the Pierre de Rivière. This morning, a murder occurred on these premises."

Nobody gasped. Everybody had already heard the news.

"I want to assure you that your safety isn't in question." Celire paused. "We know that the murder took place on the Upper Northern Balcony. We know that four assailants were involved. We know why it occurred. We know who is responsible."

George focused on Brennan. The big man sat absolutely still, his face a cold mask.

"I will now speak to the killers directly." Celire looked at the gathering. "We know who you are. Rest assured that this matter will be resolved by the day's end. Attempting to escape is futile—you will note increased security presence in the hallways. You have until this evening to make things easier on yourself and retain some small measure of dignity. If you don't cooperate, your fellow conspirators will. The measure of my mercy is small and dwindling by the minute. To the rest of you, please enjoy your meal."

He stepped down.

The hall buzzed with a dozen simultaneously started conversations. It was a carefully crafted speech. Kaldar and Richard had spent forty-five minutes writing it. Once Kaldar flashed his Mirror credentials and dangled the possible arrest of Maedoc's murderers in front of Celire, the head of castle security proved more than willing to play his part in laying the trap. Now, Brennan had to react.

Do it, George willed silently, staring at Brennan's back. *Do it. You know you want to talk to them.*

Brennan flicked open a pen.

"Pen," Jack murmured.

"I see it."

Brennan wrote something on a piece of paper and flagged down a waiter. The waiter weaved his way to the table where Rene and Angelia sat together. The waiter dropped off the note. Rene looked at it. His face turned pale. He passed the note to Angelia.

Five minutes later, he sent one of his own. The second note arrived at Richard's table. He folded his napkin, rose, and walked out.

Three minutes later Angelia rose. Rene carefully escorted her to the door. Brennan was the last to leave.

He had to take them to the side room. It was the only private room quickly accessible from the Grand Dining Hall. Security blocked the hallway on the left, and the hallway on the right opened into staff areas and kitchens filled with people.

The mirror shivered. Someone had opened the side room's door, and the draft had disturbed the delicate web of the spell.

"Yes," Jack hissed.

The spell tore like a film of oil being swept from the water's surface. The mirror vanished, revealing a perfectly transparent sheet of glass and Brennan behind it. Rage distorted his face. Angelia flattened herself against the wall. Rene bristled. Richard remained impassive, like a dark shadow. He was looking straight at the dining room. No alarm registered on his face. The spell must've worked as intended—from inside the side room, the glass still appeared to be mirrored.

"They know nothing," Brennan snarled, his voice slightly muffled but clearly recognizable as it issued from the grates hidden among the ornaments on the wall. "They have nothing, they know nothing, they are lying."

The Grand Thane raised his hand. The noise in the dining hall died, as if cut off by a sword.

"Wake up!" Rene snapped. "They know. We should deal."

Brennan hammered a punch into Rene's jaw. The blond man staggered back.

"Now you listen to me, all of you." Brennan barked. "There will be no deals. Don't speak to anyone, don't say anything, don't even break wind without clearing it with me first. If you do, I will crush you. Don't think for a second that you will get out of this unscathed, while I'll go down. I'm a royal peer of the realm. You're nothing. You're trash."

He spun to Angelia. "You're a whore who can't keep her legs together. You"—he turned to Rene—"are a fop and a weakling." He faced Richard. "You're a greedy coward. I can replace every one of you, and there will be a dozen fighting to take your places. *I* made you what you are. *I* took the fractured bandits and scum and molded them into a military force. Not a single slave was sold on this coast in the last five years without my getting a cut. I command three hundred slavers. I own the seaboard. I am the real power."

The Grand Thane rose. His eyes bulged. His face turned purple with rage. George felt an overpowering urge to be very quiet and small.

"You want to open your mouths? Try it. You won't live to see the sunset. Do you hear me?"

The Grand Thane started toward the glass.

Brennan spun, his eyes deranged. "You will be lucky if I kill you. I may just strip you of everything you are. I'll have you sold to the vilest degenerate I can find. You'll end your days drowning in the basest of perversities, kept on a chain for his amusement—"

The Grand Thane grabbed the nearest chair, almost as an afterthought, and smashed it into the glass. Shards rained down, scattering across the floor. Suddenly, the two rooms became one. Brennan saw everyone in the dining hall looking at him and froze.

"You vain, pathetic brat," the Grand Thane roared.

Brennan reached for his sword. "Don't put your hands on me, old man!"

"These hands will end you, boy!"

Rene put his hand on the hilt of his sword.

A hair-thin streak of pure white flash pulsed from the left, and hit Rene's hand. Blood poured. Rene screamed.

At the far table, Lorameh stood calmly, white lightning dancing on his fingers. There was something familiar about his face. The recognition hit George like a punch. "Erwin!"

The man had been his supervisor for two years. How the hell did he not recognize him? He wasn't even wearing much of a disguise.

"Of course, it's Erwin," Jack said. "He smells the same. Did you just now figure it out?"

Magic sparked in Brennan's eyes. A shield of white cloaked him.

The Grand Thane planted his feet.

Richard backed out of the room into the hallway.

White streaks of lightning clutched at the Grand Thane's hair. An enormous magical pressure built around him, winding about the old man like a cocoon streaked with radiant veins of power. Shit.

People at the front tables scrambled away.

"We have to go!" Jack jumped up.

"No need," Lady Olivia said.

A whip of white lightning shot from Brennan at the Grand Thane's chest and bounced off. He'd actually tried to kill his own grandfather.

"I began you," the Grand Thane thundered. "I will end you, whelp!"

He opened his arms, his palms up. A brilliant ball of coiled magic spun between them.

"Stay close to me, children," Lady Olivia said.

Kaldar popped up between the tables and dashed over to them.

A wall of white sheathed Brennan.

The pressurized cocoon of magic tore. A torrent of power ripped out of the Grand Thane. The flash explosion smashed into Brennan.

Kaldar landed between Jack and George. George braced for the blast wave. His flash shield was strong, but he wasn't sure it would hold.

A sphere of white unfolded from Lady Olivia, encasing the table. Around them, tables flew back, as if slapped by a giant's hand. The duchess sipped from her cup.

The sphere melted.

The walls of the side room had disappeared. A colossal hole gaped in the side of the castle. Angelia lay on the floor. Rene was crouched against a sidewall. Brennan stood, unharmed. He'd shielded himself and Rene, who'd hidden directly behind him.

Brennan unsheathed his blade. "Is that it, old man? That's all?"

No more magic. It must've taken all of Brennan's power to shield himself.

The Grand Thane had no sword.

Brennan struck, a fast overhand blow. His sword gleamed in the sun and clanged against Richard's blade. It wasn't Casside's rapier but Richard's own sword.

Richard's jacket was gone. He wore a loose white shirt. Tiny red dots marked Richard's face and hands. Blood, George realized. Richard's flash screen was weak. He had managed to block enough of the Grand Thane's explosion to survive the blast, but it had cost him, and now he was bleeding from every pore. They called it flash punch, a sure sign that his magic was expended—and so was Brennan's. Without their magic, if they fought now, it would be down to sword against sword.

Brennan's eyes bulged. "Casside, what the hell are you doing? Have you lost your mind?"

"I'm not Casside." Richard glanced at the Grand Thane, a question obvious on his face. The old noble pondered him for a moment.

Let him do this, George willed. *He needs this.*

"You have my permission," the Grand Thane rumbled.

Richard stepped between the old man and Brennan.

To the left, Charlotte jumped to her feet and stood utterly still.

Brennan stepped back, raising his sword. It was a plain, functional sword of a simple but brutal design that had served Brennans for centuries, carving their path to the throne. It had a thirty-five-and-a-half-inch double-edged blade, sharp and polished to a satin smoothness; a ten-inch hilt with a seven-and-a-half-inch grip, wrapped in plain leather cord that allowed Brennan to wield the sword one- or two-handed; a round pommel and cross-guard. George had held a sword like that before, made by the same smith—Declan had it in his armory. The balance of the blade was at five and a half inches, and it weighed about two and a half pounds, a combination that made the sword nimble despite its size. Holding it in his hand had made him feel indestructible.

Richard's sword was single-edged and curved ever so slightly. It was razor-sharp, weighed only a pound, with a twenty-five-and-a-half-inch blade, and a four-inch grip. Brennan's sword was ten inches longer, a pound heavier, but also slower, a powerful butcher blade to Richard's sleek scalpel.

Brennan slashed to the right, aiming for Richard's right side, just below the ribs. Richard moved to parry, but instead of following through, Brennan reversed the strike and lashed at Richard's left. Richard brought his sword across, point down, meeting Brennan's blade just in time. Brennan was testing for speed, George realized.

"If you're not Casside, then who are you?"

"You call me Hunter."

Brennan struck again, the sword dancing in his hand. Right slash, left slash, right slash, left. The swords rang from each other. Richard moved back under the onslaught, his movements short, economical. Brennan drove him across the room. Blades flashed, Richard moved a touch too slow, and the point of Brennan's sword grazed his shoulder. Blood swelled across the white sleeve. Damn it.

"No!" Jack growled.

"It's just a paper cut. He's fine." First blood was to Brennan. Not a good sign. George's pulse rose. Richard couldn't lose. He simply couldn't lose this fight.

The two men circled each other like two predators stalking. Richard, a lean wolf, and Brennan, a pampered tiger.

"Why?" Brennan asked.

"You profit from the sale of human beings."

"A true believer, then." Brennan bared his teeth. "And who are you to judge me?"

"Just a man," Richard said.

Brennan grasped the sword in both hands and struck, bringing it in a circular motion across Richard's chest. Richard moved back, and the sword whistled past his shirt.

Brennan reversed the swing and struck diagonally down. Richard parried, deflecting the blow with the flat of his blade. Steel rang. Richard staggered back. Brennan was bigger and at least thirty pounds heavier, all of it solid muscle. George knew Richard had ungodly stamina, but the flash punch had clearly taken its toll.

Brennan swung again, a high, horizontal cut. Richard parried in a clamor of steel. They crossed swords again and again, blocking with the flats of their blades. Brennan grunted and hammered at Richard, blow after blow, sinking his enormous strength into it. Richard was backing away, staggered by the hits. George clenched his fists. *Get out of there. He's going to pin you against the wall. Get out.*

"He's just beating on him," Jack squeezed through his teeth. "He isn't using any technique at all."

"He decided Richard was too damaged to survive a long fight. He wants to end it fast."

Brennan was familiar with all the techniques of proper swordplay—and knew all the tricks as well. Members of his family received expert instruction in the martial arts from early childhood. George hadn't been allowed to start practicing until he was nine. At his age, Brennan had already been learning swordplay for six years. He was banking on his raw power now. This wasn't a duel; this was a fight to the death, fast and brutal. Only one would walk away, and Richard looked desperate.

Brennan cut Richard's right shoulder. Another graze. *Damn it.* George hid a growl. He wanted to run out there on the floor and finish this.

Jack tensed next to him, gathering himself like a cat before a pounce.

"Don't you dare," the duchess said. Hearing her voice was like getting a bucket of ice water dumped on him. George recoiled.

"This isn't your fight. You must stay out of it."

Brennan slammed his shoulder into Richard, shoving him back. Richard crashed into the wall.

Get out, get out, get out . . .

Brennan thrust. Richard knocked his blade aside and spun left, breaking free.

Brennan pulled a dagger from the sheath on his belt. The brute assault had failed. He was going for the smarter plan now. Brennan cut from the right. Richard deflected the blade, and Brennan slashed his hand with the dagger, flinging blood into the air.

Argh!

Richard spun and thrust. Brennan knocked the blade aside and carved at the inside of Richard's forearm. The sword hand was vital. One cut in the right place, and Richard would lose mobility, strength, or his sword altogether. Brennan was taking him apart piece by piece. Richard looked like he was on his last breath. He was slowing down. His shirt was crimson with blood.

Another cut. Damn it all to hell.

Brennan sensed weakness, like a shark senses blood in the water. He slashed in a wide, horizontal cut, left to right. Richard leaned back with sudden speed. The sword sliced empty air. Richard clamped his left hand on Brennan's sword wrist. Brennan lunged with the dagger, striving to drive it into Richard's throat. Richard ducked under the blow and rammed the pommel of his sword under Brennan's chin. Blood spilled from Brennan's mouth. He jerked back, and Richard sliced across the inside of his left biceps. Brennan dropped the dagger and stumbled back. "Who are you?" he gasped.

"I'm an Edger, a nobody. You preyed on my people, so I took it all away from you. I killed your crews, I destroyed your island, I misled you into thinking Maedoc was a traitor. The pieces of your kingdom are crashing down around you because I made it happen."

Brennan growled, spitting blood. "I'll kill you, you piece of Edge shit."

"You'll never rule," Richard snarled back. "You're unfit."

Brennan lunged into a furious melee. His sword shone, slicing in wide arcs: left, right, left. Richard deflected.

Brennan head-butted him. Richard scoured Brennan's side. They clashed again, bloodied, focused only on each other. The ringing of steel on steel was like a heartbeat.

Brennan made another slash at Richard's neck. All his blows were above the chest, George realized. Enemy fixation. He had heard about it but had never seen it. In this moment, Brennan hated Richard so much that he was unable to look away from his face. All his cuts were designed to chop Richard's head off.

Richard spun out of the way and hammered a kick into Brennan's side. The bigger man took a step back. The point of his sword drooped. Tired! He was tired. The blade was slow to come up.

Brennan exhaled, blood bubbling on his lips, and charged. Richard let him come and slashed at Brennan's stomach in a lightning cut.

Brennan stumbled, clamping his arm to his stomach, trying to hold his guts inside. Richard paced back and forth, stalking him like a lean, hungry wolf hounding a lame bear. The bigger man tried to straighten. Richard dropped down, almost to his knees, and sliced across Brennan's legs, left-right, his sword blurring.

Brennan staggered. The fabric of his pants split, showing crisscrossing cuts. Blood swelled. He growled and sank to his knees. Richard hammered a knee to his face. Brennan toppled over. Richard flicked the blood off his sword with a sharp jerk and looked at Charlotte.

She still stood at the table, so pale, she looked bloodless. Slowly, Richard raised his sword in a kind of salute.

The Grand Thane boomed. "Someone, take out this garbage."

Celire appeared, backed by half a dozen guards. They swarmed Brennan. Three swords pointed at Richard.

"Not him," the Great Thane said. "He can go."

Richard bowed his head. The guards parted, and he strode toward them.

"A disgrace." Erwin said. George turned. The spy was standing at their table. He looked a lot less like Lorameh and very much like Erwin. Some sort of magic had to be at work here. He would have to get to the bottom of it.

"Erwin?" Kaldar peered at him. "You're Lorameh?"

"Yes, I am. What part of *back off* was unclear to you? I have sat on Brennan for ten months, building my case so I can bring him in quietly, without scandal and embarrassment to the realm." Erwin raised his arm, indicating the wrecked dining hall. "This is exactly what I was trying to avoid."

Richard reached them. "Where is Charlotte?"

George glanced at Charlotte's table. It was empty. Charlotte was gone. So was Sophie—and so was Spider.

"She was just here," he said.

"Jack!" Richard barked.

"I'm on it." Jack dashed through the dining hall, crouched at the table, inhaled and pointed to the doorway. "Right hallway."

Richard sprinted across the hall.

"MY lord!" Sophie called out.

Spider stopped and turned. He was midway through the gardens, and as he spun on his foot to face her, the gorgeous flowerbeds framed him. He seemed an elegant painting, drenched in sunlight. She let the dog off the leash.

"What are you doing here, Sophie?"

"I was scared when the screaming started," she said. "I ran out and saw you walking away."

He raised his hand, inviting her to walk next to him. She caught up, and, together, they strolled down the winding path. The dog ran sideways to investigate some flowers.

"I see you brought your dog. Have you finally settled on a name?"

"Yes. I think we should call him Callis."

"After the Grand Thane?" Spider smiled.

"They have the same type of rough dignity. Where are you going?"

The stiff blade of her short sword, the only weapon that could be hidden in her dress, was warm against her thigh.

Roses bloomed on both sides of the path, pink, dark red, and cream, their velvet petals sending a refined perfume into the air.

"I came here to disrupt this wedding," he said.

"But why? Don't you like the Marchesa?"

"I do. I'm very fond of her, in fact. She is a beautiful example of the best noble blood has to offer. But I'm a patriot, my dear. And sometimes the needs of my country conflict with my personal likes."

"I understand," she said. "Duty." He wasn't a monster by choice, oh no. He was a patriot. The only difference between a common psychotic sadistic murderer and Spider was he had Louisiana's mandate to be one.

"Yes." Spider nodded. "The Marchesa has great land holdings. It wasn't in our best interests to let those lands fall under Adrianglian influence. I was planning something quite spectacular. But a true professional knows when he is beaten. They have created such a glorious chaos on their own, I can't possibly contribute anything else to it. It's time for me to walk off the stage."

He stopped. They stood in the very center of the garden, where the path formed a ring.

"I very much enjoyed your company. You're very intelligent," Spider said. "You have the ability to reason and keep an open mind. If you develop ambition, it will carry you far. I wish you the best of luck, my dear. I will keep an eye on you if I can. I'm interested to see how far you will go."

"How does one develop ambition?"

He tilted his head. "Have you ever wanted something? Something you know you can't have? Something that is your heart's desire?"

"Of course."

"Convince yourself that you should have it. Realize that it is yours by the right of your might or intelligence or simple desire. Reach for it and take it. Do you understand?"

Oh, she understood. She understood quite well.

"Farewell." He turned away. He was about to walk out

of the garden. She might never get another opportunity like this.

"Lord Sebastian?"

"Yes?"

She sank her hand into the hidden fold of her skirt. "Would you like to know what my heart's desire is?"

Spider turned to her, a light smile on his lips. "Very well. What is it, sweetheart?"

She thrust her knife into his chest, stretching the flash across the blade in a tiny fraction of a second.

Spider gasped.

She clamped him to her and tore the blade through his innards, mincing soft organ tissue. Blood poured from Spider's lips, his face stunned with disbelief.

"It's to watch you die, you piece of shit," she said. "You fused my mother."

He lunged forward, impaling himself deeper on the blade. His hand clamped her throat, squeezing it in a steel grasp. Her air vanished. Don't panic. Whatever you do, don't panic.

"Sophie Mar, I take it." His voice was a ragged, inhuman growl. His eyes bored into her. The world was fading into darkness. "Well played, my little one. Well played."

She freed the sword with a sharp tug. The air in her lungs boiled.

"You have no idea how much I loathe your family."

Out of the corner of her eye she saw a black blur dart across the grass. Callis rammed Spider and clamped his teeth on his right forearm, adding his hundred pounds to Sophie's weight. Spider groaned. His fingers opened, releasing her throat. She fell and landed into a crouch, gasping for air. She needed to move, but her body refused to do anything but breathe, wasting precious seconds.

Callis snarled, pulling at Spider, trying to yank him off his feet. With his left hand, Spider jerked a blade from the sheath at his waist and bashed the dog over the head. Callis growled. Spider sank his blade into the dark fur of Callis's back, and it came out crimson.

No! You don't get to kill my dog! Her legs finally obeyed. She sprang up, sword raised, and slashed across his ribs. Why in the world wasn't he dead? What if he couldn't die?

He kicked Callis aside. The dog dropped to the ground with a vicious snarl and tried to lunge.

"No! Mine," she told him.

Spider laughed. "Let's see what you're capable off." He struck. He was fast, so fast; he might have been almost as fast as Richard.

She parried and slashed at his shoulder, cutting a gash in his doublet. Blood swelled. Not deep enough. Her sword was too short. He sliced at her in a vicious, horizontal cut. She had no way to dodge to the side, so she bent back. Pain seared her just under the collarbone. The tip of his blade had cut across the exposed top of her chest. Blood poured onto her gown. As he finished the strike, she grasped his wrist with her left hand and sliced across his chest. The flash-sharpened blade cut through his ribs.

Spider snarled. He was still standing.

"Not good enough, Sophie Mar."

"Good enough for you. You don't get to take anything else from me."

He laughed.

"Die." She cut him again. "Die, die, die!"

He stumbled back and kept laughing.

She slashed at him again and again, becoming a whirlwind, her blade an extension of her, bound to her by her magic. She cut him again and again, oblivious to the wounds she took.

Finally, he fell to his knees.

She stopped. Her breath was coming in ragged gasps. Callis whined at her feet.

"Not bad," Spider said, his mouth dripping blood. "Look behind me. What will you do now, my dear?"

Sophie raised her head.

Monsters were climbing over the brick wall into the garden.

* * *

CHARLOTTE ran down the stairs. She'd lost track of things for a moment, watching Richard win, and when she turned around, both Sophie and Spider were gone.

The hallway ended in an arched entrance, flooded with sunlight. She dashed through it. A large garden spread before her. In the middle of it, Sophie stood in a gown scarlet with blood, holding a small sword. The big dog stood shivering next to her. Sophie's gaze was fixed on the far wall. Charlotte looked up.

People were climbing over the wall, dropping into the flowers one by one. Some were human, some were a grotesque collection of animal parts grafted onto human bodies. Their magic splashed her like a wave of sewage. The Hand. They must be Spider's people. Sophie stood alone against two dozen trained killers, and she was holding an oversized knife.

Charlotte ran. The time slowed to a crawl. She saw everything with crystalline clarity—the monsters in the flowers; Sophie's pale face as she turned to glance at her; the desperation of knowing she was outmatched in the child's eyes . . .

The magic tore out of Charlotte, the dark currents streaming like black dragons to find their victims. They stung the first agent, biting his muscular body. He snarled, an inhuman sound, and kept coming. The regeneration, Charlotte realized. His enhanced body was healing the damage she inflicted with her diseases as fast as she could hurt him. She would have to give it more power.

She snapped some of her inner chains. The magic shot out of her, its black streams luminescent with red sparks, carrying death. The magic sped toward the Hand's agent, brushing against the wolfripper in passing. The dog howled, spun, and fled past her to the safety of the castle. The darkness stung the agent again. He went down on his knees. A bloody red lesion split open the skin on his back. Charlotte struggled to keep the wound open, feeling his body fighting her. He healed with unnatural speed. How was this possible?

Sophie dashed through the garden to her. "I'm sorry. I'm so sorry. I didn't mean to. It just happened. Spider was walking away . . ."

Charlotte thrust herself between the child and the monsters. "Stay near me."

She gave the magic more of herself and pushed. Her dark current snapped and struck, biting deep into the approaching fighters. They still kept coming. There had to be fifty of them in the gardens. They were circling them, closing in a ring. In moments, the two of them would be surrounded.

This was a death stand. If Charlotte didn't start feeding on them to fuel her own magic, the Hand would rip her and Sophie apart. But even if she then managed to kill them all, it would destroy who she was and she'd take Sophie's life without even thinking about it.

Sophie held her knife, her face bloodless and terrified.

She had to save Sophie. Her years of making quick decisions in a crisis paid off. Fear vanished. Her head was suddenly clear. There was only one way out, Charlotte realized. It was impossible for both of them to get out of this alive, but if she bought Sophie enough time to escape . . . It was just possible the child could survive. It was their only chance.

You will turn into the plaguebringer, a tiny voice warned her.

True—once she went down this road, nothing would prevent that—but the Hand were too many, and they healed too fast. They would overwhelm her before she could move on to the castle and cause damage to innocent people. It was suicide, but it was the best possible option.

The first agent Charlotte had downed, rose, shaking off his injuries like they were mere scratches. Charlotte whipped her magic, and the dark currents clenched the revolting hybrid of human and beast. An exhilarating influx of life force flooded into her. She siphoned off his life and turned it into power.

The dark serpents of her magic smashed into the second agent, draining her dry and dumping her desiccated corpse into the flowers. They stung another and another, stealing more life, feeding it back into her.

Charlotte squeezed Sophie's shoulder. "Run!"

"I won't leave you!"

"If you stay, I'll kill you. I'll clear the way. Run, sweetheart. Keep Richard away from me. Run!"

Sophie ran. She flew along the path back to the castle like she had wings.

Charlotte opened the floodgates. Her power surged forward, biting deep into the monsters in Sophie's path. She stole their life force and vomited it back as an all-devouring plague. The Hand's agents shuddered and fell.

Sophie dashed through the gap between the bodies.

Her magic reaped its grisly harvest. The enhanced agents fought to reach her and fell, cut down, and she fed on their lives, reveling in their taste.

Sophie shot up the stairs and through the arched doors.

Enough. She could pull it back now. Charlotte strained, reeling the magic back. The darkness buckled inside her, fighting to stay unleashed. So strong, so overpowering. Her hold on her power slipped a little, then a little more. It was if she were caught in the current of a violent river that pushed her back, and no matter how hard she tried, she couldn't force her way against the flow.

She had become an abomination. The magic streamed out of her like a black storm, and she was powerless to stop it. As if in a dream, bodies were falling around her, slowly and softly, like wilted flowers. The dark river inside her rose, the furious current creeping higher and higher.

Oh, Richard . . . It had all gone wrong. It had gone so, so wrong. She was crying, the tears rolling down her cheeks. *I'm so sorry, love. I'm so, so sorry. You were all I wanted. You were all I hoped for. I'm sorry.*

She shouldn't have pushed him away last night. She should've invited him in, to love and be loved one last time.

The current inside her swelled, and she drowned.

* * *

RICHARD ran through the hallways, the walls a smudged blur. Ahead, Sophie dashed through the arched entrance, her face wet with tears.

"She's gone!"

"What?"

"Charlotte's gone, she's gone!"

He pulled away from her, but she grabbed onto his clothes, dragging him away from the arch. "No, Richard, no! No, you'll die. No! Don't go! She said for you not to go!"

He hugged her to him, kissed her hair, and pushed free.

"Richard," she screamed.

He burst into the sunlight.

Charlotte stood in the middle of the garden. Her magic raged, striking down the Hand's agents, the black streams boiling, twisting, like a terrifying storm. The Hand's freaks tried to run, but the magic bit them again and again. Some crawled, other lay unmoving, little more than desiccated husks, and some were decomposing.

Charlotte turned, and he saw her eyes. They were solid black.

The flowers by her feet withered. The blight ran from her, spreading through the garden. Roses died, rotting at the root. The last of the Hand's monsters swayed and fell.

She had become what she always feared. She had turned into a living death.

He had to get to her. He had to reach her.

The flowers by the stone steps on which he stood withered. He stepped on to their dried corpses and walked across the garden.

The darkness streamed to him. It cloaked him. He felt its deadly cold sting.

"I love you, Charlotte."

Ten feet separated him from her.

His body buckled. It felt like he was being turned inside out.

Eight feet. The bones of his legs melted into agony.

"I love you. Don't leave me."

Three steps.

His heart was beating too fast, each contraction slicing him as if someone were stabbing shards of glass straight into his aorta.

He dropped his sword—his fingers couldn't hold it—and closed his arms around her. "My love, my light . . . Don't leave me."

SHE *stood submerged within the black current of the magic river. The red pockets of magical essence washed over her one by one, glowing weakly, and she absorbed them in a cascade of euphoria.*

No thoughts. No worries. Just freedom and bliss.

Another wash of red splashed against her. She tasted it and recoiled. It tasted too familiar. She hadn't taken it. It was freely given, but everything in her rebelled against consuming it. How could this be?

She forced herself to sample the essence, letting it permeate her. It streamed along her, coursing through her, so unbelievably delicious. Wrong. It was wrong. Her magic shrank from it.

She strained, trying to identify it. There had to be a reason. Richard!

He was Richard.

She heard a voice from a great distance. It cloaked her, separating her for a brief second from the darkness.

My love, my light . . . Don't leave me.

She was killing him. She was draining his life, drop by precious drop.

No! No, she didn't want it. Take it back! Take it all back!

She tried to reverse the flow and send life back into him, but the current gripped her, smothering her, trying to banish reason. She felt herself drowning and fought against it with everything she had.

No! I am the Healer. You're part of me. You are part of me. You will obey me.

Pain flooded her, the current hammering against her body. Hundreds of pinpoint needles pierced her, burning her. The agony overwhelmed her, and she melted into blinding pain.

If she gave up now, Richard would die.

Charlotte ripped through the pain. A golden glow coated her. The current of the dark river shrank from it.

You will obey.

The pain was excruciating. She screamed, although she had no voice. The glow shot from her, igniting the river into a radiant gold. Her magic boiled.

The darkness fell apart. She saw Richard's prone body in the dead grass and dropped to her knees next to him.

Don't die. Please, don't die.

She pushed, but no magic came. There was nothing left of it, neither light nor darkness.

Richard was barely breathing.

She strained, trying to pull on that roiling gold. The magic buckled inside her, threatening to rip her apart, but would not obey. Pain exploded inside her in excruciating bursts of agony. Charlotte tasted blood in her mouth.

Tiny specks of blood formed on her skin, coming out of her pores. Finally her voice obeyed, and she screamed, the pain streaming out of her. It felt like she was dying. She almost wanted to die just to end the agony, but she had to save him.

Obey me. Work. *You will work.*

Something broke inside her.

Her magic burst out of her, the gold so potent, it lifted him above the ground. Her power bound them into one. Everything she had taken, every life she had stolen, all of it went into Richard. She drenched him in the healing gold, again and again, hoping against hope that he would live.

Come back to me. Come back to me, love.

It felt like her body was melting. She had to hold on. She had to heal him.

"Come back to me. I love you so much."

He opened his eyes.

She didn't believe it. It was a trick.

He raised his hand. His fingers touched her lips. "I love you, too." He pushed from the ground and sat up.

She collapsed on his chest and surrendered to the pain.

RICHARD sat by the heavy wooden doors. Behind them, the healers of Ganer College worked on Charlotte. He'd thought she had fallen asleep from exhaustion. It took him five precious hours to realize she couldn't wake up. He'd loaded her into a phaeton and drove at a breakneck speed to Ganer College. He walked through the gates, carrying her, and people came and took her away from him. He followed them through the labyrinth of hallways and stairs to this corridor and this room, where they shut the doors in his face, and he'd been sitting here for hours, not knowing whether she would live or die. A man had brought him a platter of food at some point, but he felt no need to eat. He got up a few times to relieve himself in the bathroom two doors down.

He was so monumentally angry.

The two of them had done so much, they had sacrificed so much, and after all of that, now she would die. He wanted to rage and punch the walls at the unfairness of it, but instead he had to sit still. He tried picturing going home without her and couldn't.

If she died . . . What was the point?

"There is often no point. Seeking some sort of justification in the flow of life is useless," a woman said.

He looked up. An elegant, older woman stood before him, tall and very thin, with dark hair and intense penetrating gaze.

"Will she live?"

"Yes. She's resting now."

Relief flooded him.

"My name is Lady Augustine al Ran. Walk with me, Richard. There are some things we must discuss."

He rose and followed her down the hallway. "Are you reading my mind?"

"No, I'm reading your emotions. You're drowning in bitterness. I'm a sensate, and over the years, I've become very good at connecting the dots."

They reached another set of doors. He held them open for her. She strode through. He went after her and found himself in a long, stone breezeway about fifty feet off the ground. A roof sheltered it from the elements, but the large, arched windows had no glass, and the breeze blew through them. The sun was out, its light bright and golden. When he'd brought Charlotte in, night was falling.

"What time is it?" he asked.

"It's late morning," she said. "For you it is tomorrow. You've spent the last fourteen hours waiting."

"Has it been that long?"

"Yes."

His anger was melting into the wind, carrying off his bitterness. He felt . . . calm.

"What are you doing to me?"

"I need you to have a clear head," she said, stopping at one of the windows. "You have some decisions to make, and I don't want your emotions to interfere with them. I know about you, Richard. She wrote to me before leaving for the wedding. She told me all about you. She loves you, which explains why she has done the impossible for your sake. I wasn't there, but her body and her mind bear the scars. Tell me what happened."

He told her everything. The slavers, Charlotte, the dark magic, Sophie, all of it.

"I had surmised as much," she said, looking at the gardens far below. "Charlotte was always very strong."

"Will there be repercussions?"

She raised her narrow eyebrows. "Officially? No. She is too valuable as a healer, and the idea that a feedback loop can be broken would only give fools the pretext to experiment with it. No, there will be no sanctions, but there are consequences. When Charlotte broke the feedback loop to heal you, she did it at a terrible cost. She experienced discordance. It's a very rare phenomenon, where the magic user becomes so absorbed in channeling her magic that she loses motor skills. Charlotte must relearn basic things, Richard. She must learn again how to walk, how to hold a spoon or a pencil, how to turn the page of a book."

His heart sank. "But she can learn?"

"Oh yes. There is nothing physically wrong with her body. We've repaired the damage and made her as healthy as she could be. But it will take a lot of patience and practice. She will be bedridden for weeks."

She was alive. She was healthy, and she had survived. That was all that mattered. "When can I take her home?"

Lady Augustine turned to him. "That may not be a good idea. I don't think you understand. Charlotte will need to be carried to the bathroom. She will need to be bathed. She will need to be spoon-fed and will be bedridden for weeks until she is able to begin rehabilitation, which will likely take months. Do you have any children? You will have to take care of her as if she were a child. Think of what it will do to any romantic feelings you may have for her. You will never be able to see her in the same light again. Walk away, Richard. Leave her here with us. This is what we do. We care for the sick, and we're very good at it."

"Did she say she wanted me to take her home?"

"She did."

"Then I'll take her home."

The older woman stared at him. "You must know that I won't consent to your marriage."

"I don't care," Richard told her. "I don't care about your family, your title, or your bloodline. I'll be with her in any way she will have me."

He turned and marched back the way they had come. He pounded his way through the hallway and walked through the doors. Charlotte was awake. She lay in bed, her hair fanning across the pillows like a golden veil, her silver eyes alert and aware. He knelt by the bed.

"I can't hold you," she told him.

He kissed her lips gently. "I don't care."

"I care. You don't have to, if it's too much . . ."

He heard tears in her voice.

"I won't leave you," he told her. "I will never leave you. We'll do this together. Come home with me. Please."

He hugged her to him. "Say yes, Charlotte."

"Yes," she told him.

EPILOGUE

THREE MONTHS LATER

THE evening sky had just begun to darken. Strings of colorful, round lanterns hung from the trees, glowing gently with yellow, green, blue, and red. Tiny golden fireflies floated in the air. The September air was warm and pleasant. Charlotte rocked back slightly in her chair. Before her a vast lake spread, calm and shiny like the surface of a coin. If she leaned forward, she would just be able to make out Kaldar and Audrey's house across the water to the left.

The lake splashed against the wooden pier. Jack lay on his back on the boards, looking at the sky, his hands behind his head. George skipped a small pebble across the pond next to him. Sophie sat on the edge, her feet in the water. Two weeks after the house was built, she asked if she could come and stay with them for a few days. She never left.

Charlotte smiled. She would've loved to get up off her chair, walk down the winding path from the deck, and soak her feet in the green water too, but she knew her limits. She would have to wait.

In an hour or so, Richard would get a phaeton, and they would go over to Declan and Rose's house. The Lord and Lady Camarine were expecting. George and Jack would become uncles. Now there was an interesting thought.

At her feet, Callis raised his shaggy black head. The wolfripper dog let out one quiet woof. Someone was coming.

Light, unhurried steps made her turn. Lady Augustine walked up the porch.

They hadn't spoken to each other for a quarter of the year. Charlotte gripped her cane, planted her feet down, and stood. "Hello, Mother."

Lady Augustine's eyebrows crept up. "You're standing."

Charlotte took a step forward. "And walking. With much difficulty." She had the best caretakers in the world, but her progress was still painfully slow.

They looked at each other. Her legs trembled, and Charlotte lowered herself back into her chair.

Lady Augustine sat next to her. "That is an enormous dog."

"Yes. He used to be a slaver dog, but he mellowed out." Charlotte rubbed Callis's shaggy side with her toes. "Are you done being angry?"

"You almost threw away your life. I don't think I'll ever stop being angry." Lady Augustine sighed.

"Then why did you come?"

"Because even though I was never very familiar with the Camarines, I received an invitation to celebrate the pregnancy, and the rules of propriety dictate that I attend."

Charlotte smiled. "Richard."

"I would suppose so. It was quite elegantly done. I will admit that while he's not of noble birth, he does understand our mind-set."

"And exploits it, quite ruthlessly."

"I see he built you a house." Lady Augustine glanced at the house behind them. "By what means did he pay for it?"

"I do believe it's extremely crass for you to inquire." Charlotte couldn't help but grin.

"I'm inquiring not as Lady al Ran, but as your adoptive mother. Mothers are permitted to be crass."

"His family built it. I offered to pay for it, but he declined. They got together and raised it in about two weeks. I watched it go up. It was fascinating. Did you know that Lord Sandine is a changeling?"

"I heard something about it, but I thought it was simply a rumor. What kind?"

"A wolf. I saw three people struggling with a beam, and he took it away from them and carried it by himself."

"Lord Sandine helped build your house?"

Charlotte nodded. "He's married to Richard's cousin."

"Would you like to?"

"To what?"

"To marry." Lady Augustine pronounced the word with a crisp exactness.

Charlotte shrugged. "Perhaps. I have a man who loves me. I have a daughter, who lives with us in this great house he built for us. We're happy. Marriage is only a formality. You should meet your granddaughter, Mother. She is beautiful, and she needs you and me both."

Lady Augustine glanced toward the pier. Her face took on an odd expression, as if she were staring over a great distance. "Dear gods," she whispered. "She's so damaged, darling."

"She is. She doesn't trust easily, but she loves me and I love her. We can help her together."

Richard walked up on the porch. "My lady, Charlotte. The phaeton is ready. Would you care to accompany us, Lady al Ran?"

"I believe I would." The Lady rose. "But first I'm going down to the pier to meet Sophie. Excuse me."

"Good luck!" Charlotte said after her. She stood up. Richard hugged her, supporting most of her weight as she leaned against his strong body.

"Mad?" he asked.

"No. I meant to write her, but my penmanship is still horrid. It looks like chicken scratches in the dirt."

"I love you," he told her.

She kissed him. The touch of his lips woke a lingering need inside her. "I love you, too," she whispered. "Do you think you could show me tonight how much you love me?"

He laughed quietly, a satisfied male chuckle. "I think that could be arranged."

She leaned her head against his chest. They stood

together, wrapped in each other's warmth. Tomorrow would be a new day, new worries, new problems, new concerns. But tonight was peaceful and sweet.

"Can we do this again tomorrow?" she murmured. "Can you and I come out here and sit on the deck, drink wine, and watch the water?"

"It's a date." He kissed her.

She smiled.

ABOUT THE AUTHORS

Ilona Andrews is the pseudonym for a husband-and-wife writing team. Ilona is a native-born Russian, and Andrew is a former communications sergeant in the U.S. Army. Contrary to popular belief, Andrew was never an intelligence officer with a license to kill, and Ilona was never the mysterious Russian spy who seduced him. They met in college, in English Composition 101, where Ilona got a better grade. (Andrew is still sore about that.) Together, Andrew and Ilona are the coauthors of the *New York Times* bestselling Kate Daniels urban fantasy series and the romantic urban fantasy novels of the Edge. They currently reside in Austin, Texas, with their two children and numerous pets. For sample chapters, news, and more, visit www.ilona-andrews.com.

The Edge lies between worlds, on the border between the Broken, where people shop at Wal-Mart and magic is a fairy tale—and the Weird, where blueblood aristocrats rule, changelings roam, and the strength of your magic can change your destiny . . .

FROM *NEW YORK TIMES* BESTSELLING AUTHOR
ILONA ANDREWS

FATE'S
EDGE

A Novel of the Edge

Born into a family of con men, Audrey Callahan left behind her life in the Edge, and she's determined to stay on the straight and narrow. But when her brother gets into hot water, she takes on one last heist and finds herself matching wits with a jack-of-all-trades . . .

Kaldar Mar—a gambler, lawyer, thief, and spy—expects his latest assignment tracking down a stolen item to be a piece of cake, until Audrey shows up. But when the missing object falls into the hands of a lethal criminal, Kaldar realizes that in order to finish the job, he's going to need Audrey's help . . .

facebook.com/Ilona.Andrews
facebook.com/AceRocBooks
facebook.com/ProjectParanormalBooks
penguin.com

M1134T0712